The Snipe Hunters'
Deadly Catch at Muskrat Creek

StoryTel Press

StoryTel Press

StoryTel Press
A division of StoryTel Foundation, a 501(c)(3) organization
10506 Burt Circle
Omaha, NE 68114
www.storytel.org

© 2022 Michael Boucher

All rights reserved.

Illustrations © 2022 StoryTel Foundation
All rights reserved.

ISBN: 978-0-9995087-5-6

Printed in the United States

First printing, October 2022

PUBLISHER Don Carney
EDITOR Phil Halpin
THEOLOGICAL AND EDITORIAL CONSULTANTS
Reverend Patrick Bruen, Deacon, Archdiocese of Detroit
Fr. Clifford Henning, Holy Family Catholic Church, Novi, MI.
Chad Daniels, Family Technical Advisor.
Brandon Harvey
Jennifer Tutwiler

The Snipe Hunters'
Deadly Catch at Muskrat Creek

by

Michael Boucher

Illustrations by

Robin Ward

StoryTel Press

In gratitude for the lives and love of:

My greatest generation parents:
Myles & Kathryn Boucher

My beloved wife:
Catherine Chavdarian Boucher (1953-2019)

Chad & Juliette Boucher Daniels, Faith Boucher Chaaban;
Grandchildren: Michael, Charlotte, Logan.

Publisher's Note

A snipe is a wading bird characterized by a long bill, eyes high on the head, camouflaging plumage, and erratic flight patterns. Difficulties involved in hunting snipes gave rise to the term "sniper," meaning a hunter highly skilled in marksmanship and camouflaging.

Being sent on a "snipe hunt" is a lighthearted practical joke associated with summer camps in the mid-20th century. Much like sending someone on a "wild goose chase," the prank involves describing in creative detail an imaginary variation of the real snipe and convincing the hunter to wait for it until he figures out the joke.

We hope you enjoy The Snipe Hunters' Deadly Catch at Muskrat Creek.

Table of Contents

PART ONE	11
In the Beginning Was the River	13
Released into a Forest	17
Room 216	27
AWOL	35
The Search	47
The Quonset Hut	53
The Main Post	65
Under the Willow Tree	77
Judas Iscariot at Bosco Hall	83
The Bad Breath Bandit	107
Time to Hug a Cactus	131
Scoutmaster Bailey's Discovery	143
A Grasshopper Strikes	169
Fireside Chat	189
Back to Havenwood?	203
PART TWO	215
A New Season	217
A Season of Second Chances	235
PART THREE	257
To the Shores of Muskrat Creek	259
A Snipe Hunt Like No Other	277
The Silver Beaver	305
EPILOGUE	317

AKE SUPERIOR
CANADA
MICHIGAN UPPER PENINSULA
LAKE MICHIGAN
LAKE HURON
GRAYLING
72
AU SABLE RIVER
OSCODA
131
55
CADILLAC
I-75
127
CATALPA FALLS
BAY CITY
MICHIGAN
HAVENWOOD STATE HOSPITAL
I-69
GRAND RAPIDS
I-94
CANAD
I-94
DETROIT
DEARBORN
I-94
LAKE ER
INDIANA
N
W
E
S
OHIO
50 miles

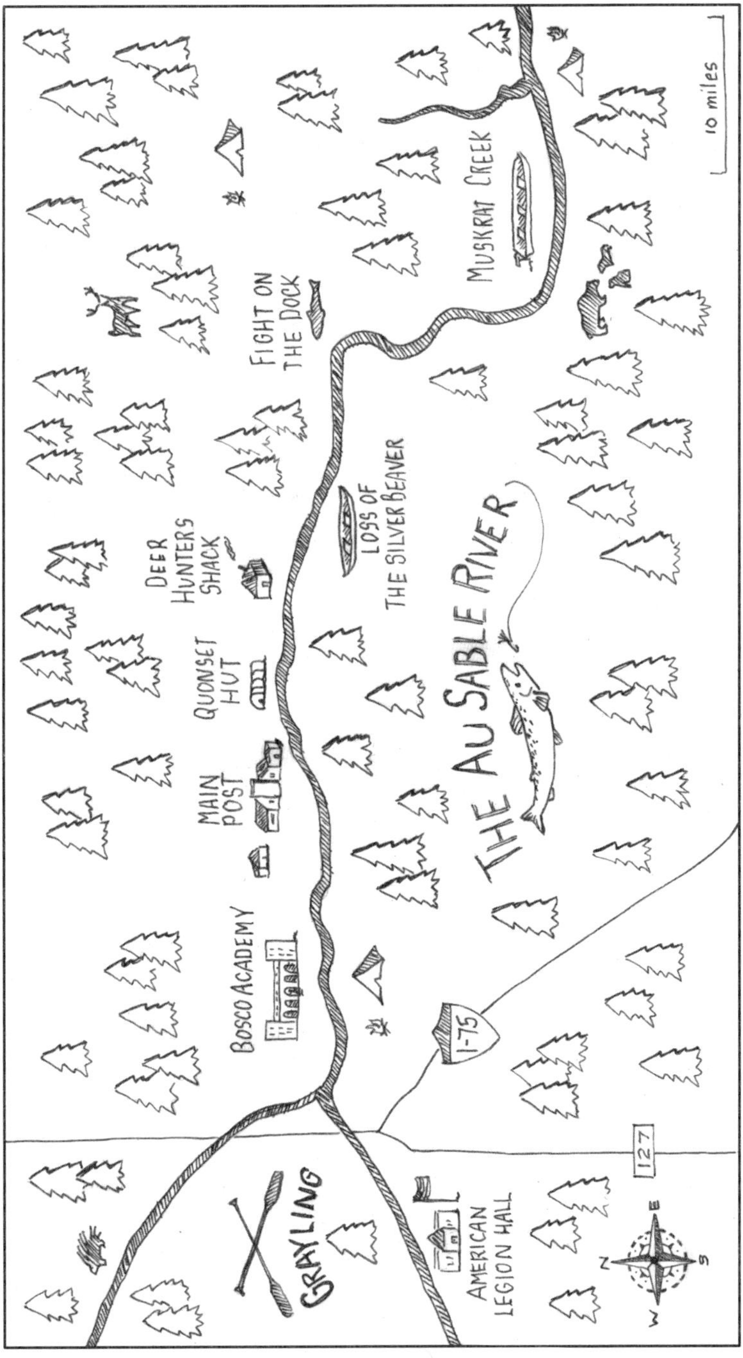
GRAYLING
AMERICAN LEGION HALL
127
I-75
BOSCO ACADEMY
MAIN POST
QUONSET HUT
DEER HUNTERS SHACK
LOSS OF THE SILVER BEAVER
THE AU SABLE RIVER
FIGHT ON THE DOCK
MUSKRAT CREEK
10 miles
N
E
S
W

PART ONE

The Snipe Hunters' Deadly Catch at Muskrat Creek

Chapter One

In the Beginning Was the River

Saturday, September 29, 1979, 5 pm, Au Sable River

The three pistol shots to the head were seared into his memory. For Kenny, though, reliving the "event" always meant being transfixed by the pool of blood. He did not even attack the shooter and flee into the dark until the blood started to drip off the porch. Nightmares and daytime flashbacks filled him with rage, guilt, and bare-naked terror. Foreign stuff to fellow teenagers, so Kenny chose silence. Coping meant planning his revenge. His mind sometimes drifted away like dandelion fluff in a slight breeze. Even now, when in the middle of a forest hundreds of miles and three years away from that death scene, his mind took flight.

"Bang!" The wooden paddle smacked the metal thwart. Kenny's head snapped up and out of the land of reverie.

"Hey, Kenny, this canoe is not up in the sky. Leave the clouds alone. You can play with them later."

Joe, at the bow of the canoe beside the river, chided him back to reality. Caught gazing into space once again, Kenny quickly recovered.

Shaking it off with a smile, Kenny returned to a topic that had intrigued him back at the Quonset hut, where they'd found the canoe. He adjusted his hat to block the sun.

"So, Joe, you're telling me you went three days and four

nights with nothing to eat on this thing called 'solo'?"

"No, Kenny, the program is called Au Sable Adventure. Solo is just part of the twenty-eight-day program. You are alone in the forest with access to water and a poncho, but no food, tent, or sleeping bag. Ya get the clothes on your back, a knife, some fishing line, one hook, and one match."

"One match?"

"Yup. One 'Ohio Blue Tip'. I wrapped mine in a piece of aluminum foil just in case."

"But, Joe, what if it rains or …?"

"Hey, enough with the jaw-boning, we gotta get launched. If Doc Hollis has his way, you'll see soon enough. I'll tell you this though. All those Westerns you see with cowboys sleeping around a campfire, that's all Hollywood. In this forest, those boys would be too darn cold for sleep, that's for sure."

Soaring aloft in the grey Michigan sky, a peregrine falcon barely noticed the two young men lashing gear to a canoe. It was late September. Overnight, chilly winds had arrived from the north. Only brief shimmers of sun snuck through the towering trees of the Au Sable River Forest to provide a little warmth.

Joe stepped to the stern of the canoe.

"Now look, Kenny, you are strong, so you sit up front. Paddle hard when I tell you. You do what I say. We ain't gonna get wet today. I got our gear and weight trimmed out, like Doc Hollis teaches. When we hit the rapids or the deep parts, you listen up and we'll be fine and dry."

"Hey, I don't know where we're going. I don't know what we're going for, but okay, 'Captain'. What's next?"

"Sit in the bow. Ready the paddle on the left side. Wait till I launch this baby."

Joe splashed into the water at the back of the canoe. He aimed the bow into the river. With a hearty push, he lifted himself by expertly balancing his weight on the gunnels.

In the Beginning Was the River

Depositing his fit frame squarely on the seat, he gripped his paddle and pushed hard off the bottom toward the main current.

"Paddle hard, left side till I tell you to stop. Dig that blade in, Kenny boy. See that black sky up ahead? It tells me some more Canadian wet stuff is coming our way. Those chilly winds are brooming those storm clouds straight at us."

Within two minutes, he had steered the canoe into the middle of the river. Now came his favorite task: alternately steering and paddling right as Kenny dutifully powered it on the left.

With as little conversation as possible, they paddled for three hours as the sky turned an ominous, inky black. The temperature dropped. And dropped again. The sun completely disappeared shortly after launch time. Then rain began, first as a steady drizzle. Ahead, Joe saw streaky black clouds reaching down to the forest's treetops. The boys were warmed solely by the effort of paddling.

"OK, Kenny, we might need our ponchos today. If so, keep your knees dry, best you can."

Less than fifteen minutes later, Joe bellowed over the noise of the rain on the gurgling water, "Now put it in fourth gear. Paddle hard. Go!"

They powered their paddles in unison for five hundred yards. Just as they rounded a huge bend in the river, Joe hollered loudly, "Paddle up!"

Joe expertly guided the canoe under the protection of a huge willow tree with thick branches hanging out over the river. Some twenty yards downriver was a Forest Service sign high up on a large white pine. It read, "Brown Trout Bend." Securing the canoe to some logs, Joe motioned for Kenny to relax. The rain pounding on the trees coupled with the running water made conversation impossible. So did his heavy breathing.

Kenny, now marooned in the bow, pulled his wool watch hat

over his ears against the cold. He silently evaluated his predicament. "Yesterday I was bussed from the state hospital to Bosco Hall. I got my room and had dinner with some high school kids living in my new dorm. At five o'clock in the morning, Joe wakes me up. He asks my help. He says we can make money. But he never explains this trip. Now I'm cold. We are … God only knows where in this deep forest. And this Joe, who I know now for a whole half a day, is in charge of this canoe." Kenny slumped back on the seat. In utter disbelief, he addressed the welcoming willow. "And this Captain Joe thinks I've canoed before."

Pounding rain drummed away all other thoughts. Kenny's mind again fixed on the disaster that took him away from his home in Catalpa Falls for three years. "I wonder. I just wonder, why my social worker thinks this high school in the woods, the new kids at Bosco Hall, and the priest with a kind attitude can make my life any better?"

Chapter Two

Released into a Forest

Friday, September 28, 1979, 4:45 pm, Bosco Academy
One day earlier

"There it is. 'Bout 50 yards up on the hill. That's your new home, Bosco Preparatory Academy for Boys, and that's John Bosco Hall. It houses 200 students, grades nine through twelve."

Kenny merely glanced at the aide. Saying nothing, he politely nodded in his direction from across the aisle in the Ford utility van.

Michael, the patient aide from the psychiatric hospital, had said little on the three-hour trip from the Havenwood State Hospital in Tuscola County, Michigan. He'd been reading a paperback. Kenny was more than happy to stare out the window and take in the September landscape of mid-Michigan's rolling farms and patches of forest. He enjoyed a few glimpses of Saginaw Bay. A south-bound, Lake Huron steamer and a couple of sailboats had caused him to dream about being a sailor one day. North of Bay City, that's all he thought about: sailing, not his new destination; certainly not his past.

The driver stopped the van in a long, circular drive with a bus station-style hut. It was sheltered by two huge oak trees. To the right of the walkway were well-lacquered pine benches. The American flag was slapping against the metal flagpole due to a cool and quickening breeze.

The Snipe Hunters' Deadly Catch at Muskrat Creek

Released into a Forest

Apart from the diesel engine, all was quiet. Michael walked up the tree-lined walkway to the hall alone. The driver turned the engine off and removed Kenny's trunk from the side of the van. The driver set the trunk at Kenny's feet.

"Here ya go, son. Good things happen here. Best of luck to ya."

Looking up at the residence hall, Kenny saw Michael, now accompanied by two men. One was dressed in a brown robe with a knotted, white rope around his waist. The other man was younger, dressed in blue jeans, and pulling something flat that looked like a wagon. Soaking up the sun, he wearily wondered if there'd be those questions again. Questions he never answered.

The brown-robed, tall man approached him with an outstretched hand, "Howdy, son. I'm Father George. How was your trip up I-75?"

Kenny shook the priest's hand but said nothing as he shouldered his backpack. The man in the blue jeans lifted his trunk onto the dolly. He turned toward Kenny as he slid it forward toward the handle.

"Welcome to John Bosco Hall, Kenneth. I'm Brother Edmund, the dorm director. We have a room ready for you. You'll meet your roommate later. He's off campus now. But your suitemates are around."

Kenny limply shook Brother Edmund's hand and said nothing while looking up at John Bosco Hall. Instead, he tended to the straps on his backpack. Brother Edmund, looking a bit puzzled, turned toward Michael.

Michael grabbed a clipboard with a thick manila envelope, turned to walk toward the hall and he reached up high to briefly put his hand around the tall brother's shoulder, a former athlete who played center on his basketball team.

"Hello once again, Brother Ed, I'm Michael. Remember when I transferred Clayton to ya two years ago?"

"I surely do," replied Brother Ed as he walked now shoulder

The Snipe Hunters' Deadly Catch at Muskrat Creek

to shoulder with Michael, about fifteen yards ahead of Kenny.

"You still got that great French roast coffee for your visitors, Padre?" he inquired.

Brother Ed laughed, "Sure do. The pot's been on since you left, but the bread and rolls came out of the oven this morning. Come on in. Invite the driver too. You have another three hours in front of you, don't you?"

"Closer to four now with nightfall and once we're off I-75 and hit those farm roads in the Thumb."

Michael then motioned for the driver to follow him up the walkway.

Michael counseled as they walked, "Well, don't let this one bother you none. He don't talk much; leastwise to adults. He probably talks most to me. And at that, he don't talk much or often. Only 'cause I play ball with him. Say, Brother Edmund, you still playing some round ball with the boys?"

Brother Edmund stopped and faced Michael, "Oh, yeah, and I organized a volleyball tournament for the guys. We get to go up against some local groups this year for the first time."

Michael advised, "Well, Kenny will probably like the competition. You'll have to really coach him up on sharing, being a teammate; but the record says he was on a baseball team before he was hospitalized. But just know, his talking muscles don't get much of a workout. And I actually don't think he means to be rude or offensive. And he don't say much meaningful to me, neither. Lord only knows if he talks to his therapist. I doubt it. But he'll chat with his own kind, sure enough."

Brother Ed guided Michael through the entrance and toward the staff cafeteria.

Looking sideways as he turned down the hall, Brother Ed observed Kenny walking beside Father George as he pulled the dolly with his baggage. They crossed under the canopied archway and the large wooden crucifix over the entryway.

Released into a Forest

Kenny ignored most of Father George's questions. He quickly turned down the volume whenever an adult entered his personal space. Then he simply endured the usual questions. Ignoring adults or shaking his head yes or no had been his habit now for three years. While admiring the arborvitae trees, Kenny enjoyed the scent of pine on the walkway to John Bosco Hall.

His new home ... maybe. His musings once again included that curious thought. It came at night just before sleep. It started two months ago. "I used to hate the police for catching me. Now I'm not so sure."

John Bosco was pleasant enough to enter. There was a long, imposing desk with a clean white counter. At the right end of the desk, on a raised platform allowing for a great field of vision, sat a senior resident advisor. Under a sign titled "R. A. On Duty" was the name, Bernard.

Father George, a ruddy complected fireplug of a man, who betrayed his Boston background with almost every quip, entered first. Kenny was slightly behind him.

Bernard immediately got up, put the phone system on hold, and took charge of the dolly.

"Where to, Father?" Bernard inquired.

Smiling, Father George replied, "Room 216. And please ring up Marie. Tell her we have guests."

Bernard ushered Kenny onto the elevator. "You'll like Father George. He's strict on rules; still tough, he wrestled his way through college, but he plays ball and hockey with us. He keeps us laughing with his Irish jokes, too." Bernard spotted a patch sewn onto Kenny's backpack when they exited the elevator. "So, you play some three on three B-ball, eh?" Bernard observed.

"Some," replied Kenny.

As he wheeled the dolly down the hall, Bernard continued, "Yeah, I do too. Well, at least last year. Just to help out my floormates with the Gus Macher Tournament. We didn't do so well. But I had fun. How about you? I liked the banquet the best."

Kenny looked Bernard in the eye for the first time. "Food's good."

Bernard looked up at Father George searching his face for an answer. Then he pulled the dolly up to Room 216. "Well, you probably had a long trip. Here's your room. Food here is good, too. Some guys grouse about dorm cooking. But in my home, we never had three choices for dessert. How about you?" Bernard stood by the dolly and smiled at Kenny.

Kenny said nothing. He stared straight ahead, stepped by Bernard, and entered the room. Without looking up, he unshouldered his backpack and turned to get his trunk off the dolly.

Bernard, realizing he was not going to get an answer, took one end of the trunk. Kenny took the other and slid it off onto the floor. With that, Bernard stepped back into the corridor with the dolly.

Speaking to Father George, Bernard commented with a hint of relief in his voice, "Well, I got desk duty to get to."

"Bernard, where are Joe and Saltz?" asked Father George as he stepped into the hallway.

Bernard shrugged his shoulders. "It's free time. So, I'm guessing at the gym. Saltz is likely out on the trampoline, though."

Father George turned and regarded the blond-haired, blue-eyed Kenny with a sidelong glance, "Your roommate, Fred, is off campus on a community service project. You'll meet him later. You have two hours before supper. Settle in. Unpack. The empty half of the closet is yours." Pointing to his left he said, "This is your desk. We'll send someone up for you if we don't see your suitemates accompany you to dinner."

Father George walked the length of the first-floor hall and descended to the basement level. When Bernard resumed his

Released into a Forest

perch at the desk, he silently concluded, "Looks like Dubay's got one tired boy or a psych case."

After the door was shut, Kenny sat down at his desk. Ignoring his trunk, he grabbed his sketch pad and began to draw. He heard some jazz music and later some students talking about French lessons. But mostly he sat engrossed in his sketches. He took no particular interest in the room, the posters of his roommate, or the portion of his surroundings that comprised his new home. He did not even observe the grounds from his second-story window.

As Father George entered the small staff cafeteria, Marie, the Polish cook was busy cutting up pastries and freshly made bread. The three men were discussing the Big Ten football season with gusto.

Michael, raising his mug of coffee, exclaimed, "I tell you, Padre, toasted pumpernickel with caraway mounded up with sharp cheddar cheese from Pinconning is the only way to prepare for hours of winding Michigan roads in the dark."

Marie smiled as she took quiet pleasure in another satisfied customer. "I tell him, Father: 'Take some of Marie's homemade Polish kielbasa for the road. You're gonna be happy all the way to Havenwood! Am I right?'"

Holding his right hand high as if to testify, Father George commented with dramatic flair, "I've never seen a person leave Marie's kitchen hungry."

While packing up his sandwiches for the road, the driver nodded in silent agreement and winked at Marie.

Father George grabbed a mug of coffee, took a piece of whole-wheat, French bread, and sat at the far end of the table. Dipping a bit of the bread in his mug, he looked Michael in the eye. "We gotta talk in private. How about I walk you to the van when you're done?"

Michael simply winked at Father George as he drank another slug of French Roast.

Father George gave Michael a nod of understanding and immediately changed the mood of the conversation. 'So, did you hear the one when Pat and Mike walked into the pub carrying a wild goose …"

For the next forty minutes, the talk was of Michigan State's unexpected football victory over arch-rival, Michigan, last year. The inevitable revenge match was coming up in a few weeks.

The driver had warmed up the van in response to the chilly September air as Michael and Father George stood at the side of the van on the circular drive.

"Father George, this Kenny … ahh … has been through a lot. It's in the record our social worker sent to your Dean of Students. He accepted him on probationary status. I do understand that. It may not work out. But you remember it worked once with Clayton."

Father George agreed, "Yes, Michael, that was a great success."

Michael continued, "We're hopeful that the John Bosco magic works again. Don't expect him to speak to adults. He'll mind you here in the dorm but he's slow to respond. He can be non-compliant in the classroom though. He observes everything. But he trusts no one and nothing. He has night terrors even with medication."

"Academics?" inquired Father George.

Michael replied, "Good in math, but he loves art and weight lifting."

"Yes. I did note his muscles on the way up the walk."

Michael continued, "All he did for months after he came to us was draw, paint, and weight lift. Some outdoor running when the weather was good. The social worker and psychologist said we needed to be happy with that due to the trauma experienced. The confidential stuff is in the records. I say be sure you have a good supply of those artist sketch pads."

Father George breathed heavily and took the manila folder

Released into a Forest

from Michael.

Michael confided, "About two years ago during the second semester, an Asian therapist got assigned to the ward. Kenny started to progress and get out of his room more often. We found out the therapist made him a deal. He'd teach him the martial arts if Kenny agreed to participate more in the social program. Now, according to that therapist, Kenny is good enough to test for a black belt."

Michael held the folder briefly and looked intently at the priest. "A couple more things stand out. He made no use of group therapy. Lately, he's shown some moderate classroom progress. But personal talk, he still won't do."

Pausing, Michael hushed his voice as if whispering a secret. "One time he shocked the staff and spoke without being asked to speak for the first time in almost three years."

"What was that about?" asked Father George.

"He wanted us to send one of his paintings to the social worker he saw before the critical incident. He absolutely begged us to be sure it got to him intact and safe. We bought extra insurance and shipped it off to Catalpa Youth Services in Catalpa Falls, Michigan. Actually, that's where he comes from, Catalpa Falls, Huron County, not Tuscola County, where the hospital is located."

"What was the painting about?"

"I dunno. He kept it private. But I know the social worker was good." Michael reported.

"How's that?"

"His name was Michael. That's why!" he joked.

Approaching the van Father George gestured toward a 1976 election sticker, "Michael, are you still supporting Jimmy Carter, that peanut farmer from Plains, Georgia?"

"Nope. That's my dad's sticker. He's still for Carter, but not for his policies or his peanuts. It's because of my dad's service in World War II." Michael nodded.

"The Navy, right, Michael?" Father George queried.

"Yup, submarines in the Pacific. Carter is the only U.S. President to have served in the all-volunteer submarine service like he did," Michael reported with pride.

Smiling broadly Father George quipped, "Well, tell your dad I do like peanuts at Tiger ballgames."

They shook hands and Michael entered the van. Father George began to saunter up the long walk while breathing in the brisk night air. He always enjoyed the sweet aroma of the arborvitae. "So, math, martial arts, and weight lifting with sketch pads at the ready... Hmmm." Then he reflected upon all the unanswered questions as he strolled along the walkway.

Chapter Three

Room 216

Friday, September 28, 1979, 6:15 pm, John Bosco Hall

"Who the Sam Hill are you?" Joe Duvalle bellowed as he entered Room 216 through the bathroom door. Kenny was on the floor in shorts and an undershirt, doing push-ups.

"My name's Kenny Dee. They call me Kenny. I'm the new student in 216. Are you Fred?" Kenny asked, with sweat on his brow. Rising off the floor revealing a compact, muscular frame, he stood facing the much taller and heavier Joe Duvalle.

"Nope. Joe, your suitemate. We share a bathroom. This here is Saltz. Gary Saltz, a runner for our cross-country team. You call him Saltz. What are you doing working out here?" he asked.

Kenny replied, "I got here two hours ago and I got bored. So, I did some cals ..."

"Some cals ...? Saltz said with puzzlement.

Kenny, noting his bewilderment, "You know, calisthenics? Like your gym teacher makes you do in P.E. ..."

"Oh. Yeah. Ah, well, I do 'em in the gym or on the field, not in my room." Noting Kenny's bulging muscles Joe said, "I guess you like doing them anywhere, huh?"

Kenny explained, "When I get bored, I exercise. I been bored a lot lately."

"Bored, eh?" Joe broke out laughing. "Wow, Saltz, can you see this kid in Latin class? When old Mrs. Schultz looks in the back of the class and sees Mr. Muscles here doing one-handed push-ups, she'll invent a new Latin phrase ... right after her heart attack."

Joe described his devoted old spinster Latin teacher, imitating her mannerisms. All three boys laughed with ease.

"Hey, you need help?" Saltz motioned toward the untouched trunk. Looking at his watch, "We only got about fifteen minutes till dinner," he warned.

Kenny hesitated while looking both boys in the eye and then replied, "Ah ... sure, I guess that'll be okay. Ahh ... But don't touch my art supplies."

Turning to Joe, in a louder voice Saltz said, "Hey, I guess that means you get the moldy socks, sweatshirts, and gym shorts, eh, Joe."

"Hey, you get the moldy stuff today, not me," quipped Joe. He joined Saltz and hoisted one end of the trunk on the bed.

For the next fifteen minutes, the three boys worked as a team against the clock to complete the unpacking. Kenny got settled into Room 216. When the trunk was closed, a sense of acceptance and belonging descended upon Kenny. He'd had a sense of camaraderie only one time before. Yet, just as those welcome feelings began to emerge, the pain in his past bubbled to the surface.

Minutes passed, and banter about sports helped re-orient his thoughts to the here and now. Yet he had to confess that he felt comfortable with these helpful guys, his first experience with suitemates.

They headed down the corridor for dinner. Joe spoke first. "We can get the R.A. to store that trunk for you. He's tough on rules, loves silence after ten, but he's a nice guy who helps new guys, even when they make mistakes. Just don't make 'em twice, eh Saltz?"

Saltz abruptly halted the walk down the hall with his tall muscular frame, pointing to a plaque on the wall he read in a loud voice.

"The principal trap that the devil sets for young people is idleness."

"That's the dorm's namesake, St. John Bosco, and you gotta know Brother Edmund will quickly convince you: your idle days are over. But don't worry, I think you'll actually like one part of my favorite John Bosco quote. He's famous for them."

"Run, jump, shout, but do not sin."

"Yeah, well I've certainly done all of that. What's an R.A.?" Kenny wondered aloud, now gaining more comfort with his suitemates.

Saltz stepped forward and gestured toward the wall. "Resident Advisor. Well, among other things, he is the guy who enforces rules and dorm policies like the one on this poster. He read it aloud in an exaggerated stage voice.

PROFANITY IS THE EFFORT OF A FEEBLE MIND TO EXPRESS ITSELF FORCEFULLY.

"Profanity is the effort of a feeble mind to express itself forcefully."

Joe joined in. "Yeah, apart from accidentally banging your thumb with a hammer, you don't wanna be heard swearing around here. There's no fines. They just embarrass you for polluting the airwaves, showing a bad example, and being a lame brain."

Brother Ed will say something like, "Is that the best you can do today? You think your Mom would be proud of you? Time to ask your guardian angel for some guidance."

"This must be your first time in a dorm, eh?" Joe guessed.

Joe then began to parrot the student handbook with an exaggerated sense of importance. This was the first time he got to orient a new resident, "The R.A. is in charge of the forty guys on the second floor. He enforces the rules, the curfew, the lights out, the quiet hours, and conducts the periodic room inspections. He also is there to help you with your studies. You know, help make you a success as a student."

Saltz continued, "Yeah, like what your dad is paying all that tuition for."

Abruptly, Kenny stopped walking, turned to face Saltz. "You don't talk about my dad."

There was a pause as all three boys stood, frozen mid-stride in the hall. Kenny's face had suddenly turned red. His eyes were fixed as if riveted onto Saltz's face. An icy aura enveloped the boys in the hallway.

Saltz began to stammer, "Ah, yeah…sure I didn't mean nothing. I just …"

Kenny, staring straight into Saltz's eyes, vehemently projected the next word as if firing a salvo at Fort McHenry. "Ever!"

Standing slightly behind and to one side of Kenny, Joe caught Saltz's eye. He wordlessly motioned with his hand, mimicking a pirate slitting his throat: "Cut it."

Room 216

Joe broke the silence. Gently tapping Kenny on the shoulder, he loudly declared, "Hey, you gotta get cracking or they'll be closing the cafeteria door in your face."

The three boys walked in awkward silence to the end of the corridor. The physical activity helped to dispel the icy aura. The atmosphere gradually warmed. Saltz felt his stomach muscles starting to relax.

Without comment, Joe pointed up to a poster on the wall at the end of the hall. It read: "Success is there for those who prepare."

Saltz counseled, "That's the resident assistant's favorite. That and the 'Five P's.'"

"And he'll be telling you soon. You can bet on that," Joe added.

The walk along the hall had released some of Kenny's tension. His more trusting demeanor returned as they approached the end of the hall.

Saltz resumed his explanations, "Resident assistants help out with problems of dorm living and conflicts with other students. Joe knows about that."

"And he also can help out with faculty problems, eh, Saltz?" retorted Joe as he glanced over at him.

They started down the stairwell. Saltz explained, "Usually they are seniors with great GPAs, excellent community service, and conduct records. Mark Dubay is a smart cookie who turns nineteen this month. But he is a long way from a brown nose. If you mess up, he'll give you a chance to clean up before the write-up. But you are dead in your tracks if you mess with alcohol, nicotine, or try to cheat on academics. He's a straight arrow there. He makes no apologies because he warns everybody. You'll see."

Stopping on the bottom step, he paused for dramatic effect and assumed a deeper voice while raising his finger like a teacher. He looked Kenny in the eye: "If you are fool enough to play, I'll see that you pay."

"Did I get it right, Joe?" Saltz inquired with a smirk.

"Perfect, Mr. R.A. of the day, Dubay."

Saltz smiled, "Now let's get to the cafeteria on time."

A young, uniformed, female clerk from the food service company stood at a podium adjacent to the door.

Joe and Saltz flashed their identification cards to the clerk at the door.

"Where's yours?" She demanded of Kenny.

Joe then turned to explain about Kenny, but the clerk cut him short.

"OK, so you don't have ID. Who is your R.A.? If he vouches for you, I'll let you in. Otherwise, I can't let you in."

Kenny's suitemates protested. The clerk was adamant.

"Look, no one gets into Bosco without an ID."

"Yeah, but he just …" Joe began, but his voice trailed off. He spotted Mark Dubay walking over from his table.

Mark Dubay introduced himself and then reached for his ever-present clipboard. He gave Kenny his identification.

The clerk finally smiled and waved them in.

Mark tugged Kenny by the arm to one side and explained, "I did not want to leave the card by your door. I figured you'd get hungry and show up. It's my fault. I should have sat in the lounge outside here until you showed up. I could have prevented the hassle. Sorry. Hope your first day here goes better for you now."

Tall, older, and athletic looking, Mark advised Kenny: "Keep this ID with you. Park it in your wallet or, if you want, I'll get you a fancy, colored 'John Bosco' lanyard. Just keep it handy on campus and off. 'We can't help you if we can't claim you,' is my motto. Got it? You ask Joe about the claiming part sometime."

"Yup, okay," replied Kenny, putting the badge in his pocket.

"Now, go enjoy your dinner with your suitemates. Your roomy is off campus till Monday. I know you've had a long day with a trip in from the Thumb. I'll do the rules meeting tonight

Room 216

before lights out or in the morning, your choice."

"Is that the 'Pay to Play' discussion?" Kenny gamely inquired.

Mark burst out laughing, "So you've gotten clued in by some of my best, reformed rule breakers, eh? Yeah, you best believe that's part of it." Looking Kenny in the eye, Mark spoke with feigned seriousness while nodding in the direction of Joe and Saltz. "Hey, one last thing you gotta know, new guy. My RA contract requires me to alert the administration of any and all situations, building issues, or events that could impair the health and welfare of any resident. That's my job. You keep hanging around these characters and I'm gonna be making out a report."

Laughing, Joe nudged Saltz. "See, Saltz, he never forgets."

Mark whacked him on the shoulder and motioned toward the line. "Food is getting cold. Don't forget Marie's desserts."

Kenny joined up with Joe and Saltz. He met several other Bosco residents during the dinner. Sports and talk about funny or tough teachers comprised most of the discussion until dessert. Later, he returned to the table with Marie's apricot cobbler laden with whipped cream.

A red-headed senior from the first floor interrupted the banter and addressed Kenny directly.

"So, Joe here thinks you could win the push-up contest on Spring Field Day already."

Kenny shrugged his shoulders and deflected attention to Joe. There were other guys joshing each other about feats of strength or speed on the athletic field. But no one seemed mean-spirited at all. Kenny felt that comfortable, relaxed feeling again as he had with his first baseball team.

Amidst the din of the joshing and jive talk, Kenny silently noted to himself "Seems like these Bosco Boys are gonna be okay."

Then, talk turned to the weather forecast for Saturday and the rest of the weekend. The radio broadcast a storm front

The Snipe Hunters' Deadly Catch at Muskrat Creek

coming out of Canada. One boy remarked, "Here comes Alberta, maple leaves and all."

"Yup, the temperature is dropping," Gregory said in reply.

Joe sat straight up in his chair. He put his hands behind his head. He stretched and loudly exclaimed, "Nuts! That's terrible."

Gregory teased Joe, "Hey, Joe, you did not sign up for the flag football game anyway, why the 'Gloomy Gus' face? And we'll be set up for table tennis anyway. Otherwise, we plan to hit the fields ten minutes after breakfast clean-up. If we get chased off the field early, the team with the highest score wins."

Joe was still displeased. He seemed to be worried. Even Kenny could tell he was still brooding when he joined the group to return to his room.

Mark, carrying his clipboard with a pink message note, met the threesome as they reached the top stairs on the second floor.

"Hey, Joe, Saltz, you both know David Cowdrey, the guy who won Doctor Hollis's kayak contest from Room 220?"

"Yeah sure," They both intoned together as if in a chorus.

"Well, I just got a message from the clinic in town. He's out for up to a week with some kind of infection. It might be contagious, so he can't come back here."

"Yikes, that's bad for him, but worse for us. He was our quarterback for next Saturday's playoff game," Saltz lamented.

Joe said nothing but stared down at the floor. He was still silent as he entered his room. Joe looked intently at his roommate when the door was shut. "Hey, Saltz, can you hit the library, lounge, or gym till nine-thirty? I need to be alone."

Puzzled, Saltz grabbed his book bag and left. "Sure. Yeah. Catch you later."

Kenny entered his room. He grabbed his sketchpad and stretched out on his bed. The last sounds he heard on his first day at Bosco filtered into his room from Joe's radio. "High winds, freezing rain, a Canadian cold front ..."

Chapter Four
AWOL

Saturday, September 29, 1979, 4:30 am, John Bosco Hall

Kenny, alone in Room 216, had none of the usual dreams that had plagued his sleep for the last three years. In truth, the long journey was less exhausting than the social interaction with new people. The wool blanket on top of the sheet created a warm, cozy cocoon in which his body and soul found comfort. Seconds after he slipped his black wool watch cap on his head, he fell into a deep sleep.

The calm, dark room's only sound was the slow rhythmic breathing of Kenny. Suddenly, strong hands gripped his muscular shoulders.

"Get up. Wake up! Kenny, wake up! It's Joe."

Kenny, startled out of his deep slumber, thrashed out in fear. He swung his right hand up and across the bed, catching Joe in the chest. Then his whole body was up, out of the bed. His bare feet were planted firmly on the cold, tile floor. He stuck out his left leg, assumed a defensive crouch, and cocked back his right arm, fist clenched. His left arm was raised in front of his chest. His fist was closed.

Joe was knocked to the end of the bed with Kenny's first reflexive punch. He was staring up in awe of the fury of Kenny's catlike response. Joe turned a flashlight on. The beam of light highlighted Kenny's face. There was a fixed stare in his eyes.

"Hey, Mr. Kung Fu, it is only me, Joe, your suitemate. You see?" Joe, swinging the beam of the light around the room, tried to assure him, "Everything is alright."

Kenny did not release from his defensive stance.

"You seem like you want to knock me into the middle of next week. Remember me, your friend from next door? Settle down. We don't want to wake anyone up. Saltz's still sleeping"

Kenny took a deep breath. He relaxed his defensive pose. Expertly grabbing the flashlight in Joe's hand, he focused the beam directly in Joe's eyes. Kenny spat out his words with whispered intensity, "Don't you ever do that! You don't ever do that to me. You understand me now. Don't ever do that to me again!"

Joe remained frozen in his position at the end of the bed. Holding both arms up as if to block a blow, he urgently cautioned Kenny in a calming voice, "Relax, I'd only dream of pinching your toe if I had armor on and made a good Act of Contrition."

"'Trition. What's that?" Kenny demanded.

"You know. Saying you are sorry for your sins … Ya got some, don't ya?" Joe injected some humor into the tense moment.

Returning the flashlight, Kenny glowered at him, "What the heck do you want from me at five o'clock in the morning? And what's with the flashlight? We don't eat breakfast this early. Hell, even I know that."

Smiling, Joe teased, "Hey, watch that language. You want Dubay down here showing the new boy that poster about profanity and feeble minds?" Joe slowly lifted his hand to his lips and cautioned silence with the "Shhh …" gesture. Then he tiptoed to the door. He slid the throw rug up to it. It blocked any light from bleeding into the hallway. Joe checked to be sure the door to the bathroom remained shut. Then he turned on the reading lamp.

AWOL

Gently Joe turned the desk chair around to face Kenny. "Hush up a little, will ya? Just listen, please!" Joe's manner was one of impatience, but his voice had an odd, plaintive tone. He looked directly into Kenny's eyes. "I need your help. I mean I really need your help. And I need it in a big hurry, too. Those muscles of yours could be useful to me ... to you, too. You remember what Mark Dubay said about David Cowdrey being sick?"

"Yeah. What's that got to do with me?" Kenny demanded. He was still irritated.

"Me and David. We had weekend passes to visit our foster family in town. We were going canoeing on the Au Sable. We had an off-campus pass until Sunday night. But he can't come because he's sick. You canoe?" he abruptly demanded.

Kenny, suddenly interested, lied, "Some." He'd only been in a rowboat and observed canoeists. The field trips from the state hospital often went to parks. He did field trips to please his therapist and get merit points. It was one way to qualify for more art supplies.

"Well, I need a guy with some muscles. And I need someone who knows how to be quiet around grown-ups. You look like that type of guy so far. I got a special project. A project I need to keep under wraps for a little while. Bernard said you were really quiet around authority yesterday. So, you know how to have a quiet voice?" Joe questioned. "Mind your own business, no one else's?"

Smirking, Kenny reflected aloud, "I think that's half the reason they sent me here. So, I could learn to talk more. I know my therapist kept harping on that idea: socialize more, draw less. What are you and Cowdrey up to? It sounds like ... illegal or underhanded ... something fishy."

"Never mind that. We gotta get going or it won't matter none at all. 'Time is of the essence,' as Mr. Garson always says."

There was silence in the room. An air of suspicion filled the space between Kenny and Joe like an early morning fog.

"Look, you gotta just trust me. Got it? Trust me. I need your muscles, some canoeing, and a quiet voice. I promise you we'll have some fun, and probably make more money than your pockets have seen in a while. How's two hundred dollars for art supplies sound?" Joe looked Kenny in the eye and waited. "I got a pass till Sunday night at eight."

Kenny interrupted, "Yeah, well I don't."

"Don't sweat it. I'll cover for you," Joe assured him. "You like challenges, don't you? Well, I got one for you." Joe rested the persuasive part of his argument.

There was a long pause from the edge of the bed as Joe looked at Kenny and waited. Outside John Bosco Hall, it was dark and cloudy. A hint of dawn was on the horizon. In minutes, the birds would start to chatter. And it was far chillier than last night.

Kenny thought back to the previous three years of being in the hospital after the incident. There were few kids there. Then he recalled the sense of accomplishment when he completed a double play for his baseball team. The team pizza parties were great, no matter who won. It was there he had that feeling; that way of being connected. What was it? His therapist used the term … a sense of belonging. Belonging to something …

Joe opened his hands up as if praying. He faced Kenny, "Well …"

Kenny's mind was still in Catalpa Falls on the playing field, and then in the barn with Uncle Bobby's pony. That pony was supposed to be his. No, actually it was his, at least for a while. It was for some time. Those were the two places he felt the best. He had that feeling, on the field and in the barn. He mused to himself, "I never did have that feeling at home. Least not since dad died back in the second grade."

"Come on now, Socrates, quit staring off into space. This ain't no marriage proposal. We'll be back here Sunday night," Joe teased. "In fifteen minutes, it won't matter. We gotta go, while it's still dark. We gotta get outta here fast. Or forget it. And I mean forget it for good, too!" he said, anxiously looking at his watch.

Joe stood up to search for light through the second-floor window. "A lotta easy money will be gone too, for no good reason."

Looking Joe in the eye, Kenny took a deep breath. As he exhaled, the fog of suspicion dissipated. Inside he was laughing about being teased for being lost in thought. "Okay. What's up?"

"You are. Off the bed too. And that's good. You'll be glad, really," Joe said. Smiling, he stood up. "Now, grab your backpack. Get dressed. Keep that hat on and bring your jacket. Put it in your backpack. I'll be back here in five minutes. Wear your sneakers. A sweatshirt would be good. Remember, be quiet. Saltz is sleeping."

Joe returned in outdoor clothes, wearing a backpack, and carrying a plastic bag with handles. Inside it was a brown grocery bag. He thrust it up to Kenny's chest. "This is yours. Put it in your backpack. Keep it dry." Quietly opening the door, he admonished Kenny in a whisper. "Follow me. No talking. No noise. Lock your door quietly. If there's any talking to do, I'll do it. We gotta be quick."

Joe turned to face the door. Kenny followed behind him. He felt rushed, but excited to be in on this adventure. It seemed like Joe was trusting him with a special mission. He obviously wanted to be his friend. Kenny sensed a special feeling about being selected for this task. But just what was the big secret?

When Joe turned his back, Kenny quietly taped a note to the room number sign as the door locked.

They quickly descended the stairs. Joe gently pushed the bar to open the door onto the first-floor corridor. He eased the door back without the latch making any noise. Turning right, he crossed the foyer with Kenny in tow. He eased open the door to the basement. Walking quietly down two flights, Joe held up his arm as he peeked around the corner. Joe stood still.

A light filled the small staff kitchen that Marie used to host adult guests. The aroma of fresh-brewed coffee filled the air. Chester, the night watchman, was reading the sports page. The small clock radio's volume was barely audible from the distance. A forecast was ending, "… and there could even be snow in the western counties of the Upper Peninsula."

Joe leaned back and whispered, "Plan B."

Abruptly Joe turned left and scampered down the short hall to a door labeled Utility Room. They snuck across a garage partially filled with tall trash containers. Joe inched his way to a service door that opened onto the side of the building. Looking Kenny in the eye he whispered, "Now, say a prayer." He reached up to the ledge on the very top of the door. He gently moved his hand along the top while standing on his tippy toes. "Ah … Good old Chester, the predictable."

Taking the key he had located, Joe opened and exited the door. He wordlessly pulled Kenny outside. He blocked the door with his backpack. Then he stepped back inside, replaced the key, and exited the building. He eased the door noiselessly back to its closed position.

Standing under the dim security light, Joe tightened his backpack. Then he gripped the straps and did the same to Kenny's backpack.

"Now, 'Mr. Kung Fu', you get to use those leg muscles. Follow me. Keep up." Joe rapped Kenny on the left shoulder with his right hand, turned around, and took off on a dead run into the darkness, slowly blending into a new dawn.

The grass was wet. The gray sky was just starting to show some light. The wind was blowing in from the northwest. It was much, much chillier than yesterday. A damp fog was rising up in response to an overnight visitor, cold Canadian air.

Joe ran with deliberate speed. It was one hundred yards to the short end of the playing field. He entered a path there that ran parallel to a stream. The path was well-traveled, but the terrain was uneven and rocky in parts, with roots and fallen branches. The thick woods bordered the Au Sable River State Forest. Wet bracken ferns dampened Kenny's jeans from the knee to the ankle. The light fog dampened the atmosphere. Low, gray clouds all but announced moisture was coming their way.

They ascended a hill. The going got tougher. Joe did not ease the pace with the more difficult terrain. Kenny's breathing became labored. He was determined to keep up with his friend. Kenny was sweating profusely when they crested the hill. He wiped his forehead without breaking stride. He shoved his wool hat into his belt.

Descending the hill demanded Kenny's full attention. He could not observe the surrounding forest in the dim light of the new dawn. He had to focus on where to place his feet. Roots, rocks, branches rapidly lurched into his view. A fall would hurt more than his knees. His eyes were riveted to Joe's sneakers. Where Joe placed his foot, that's where he aimed his foot. Just like his cross-country coach had warned him, downhill was worse than uphill. Just like his last race three years ago, his lungs began to ache before his legs.

The pain came, but Kenny would not submit. If the sneakers in front of him were moving, so were his—in the same spot, at the same pace, for the same length of time. His right side began to ache. He wiped his brow again to keep his eyes clear. He could hear the water of the stream, the singing of birds welcoming the morning. The steady, unrelenting plop of Joe's sneakers preceded him. They plopped. He plopped. The forest echoed with "plops." Joe plopped. Kenny plopped. Onward they plopped. The sweat came. The pain stayed. Legs ached. Lungs screamed for relief. But onward came the plops.

Without warning, Joe turned left. He departed the path, leaving the gurgling stream to continue toward the mighty Au Sable River. He slackened the pace for about ten yards. They

The Snipe Hunters' Deadly Catch at Muskrat Creek

traversed a clearing less than a hundred yards long and about thirty yards wide. Joe brought the pace down to a steady lope in the clearing. He stopped and turned his reddened face to Kenny. "So, you are in shape!" Joe chortled as he sucked in some air. He leaned on a tree.

"What's the big hurry, anyway?" Kenny begged as he held his aching side. "Can we take a seat?"

"Nope. The sitting part is coming soon enough. But you can walk now. C'mon, this way."

Joe traipsed off toward the deep forest while unshouldering his backpack and stopped about eighty yards from the forest's beginning. The tall trees were in a neat row as if lined up for inspection. He leaned his back up on a tree, pulled out a canteen, and drank one swig of water.

Joe replaced the top and flipped the canteen to Kenny. "Take a swig of water. One swig only. We got many miles to go."

Kenny gulped a swig in between breaths. He flipped the canteen back to Joe. He looked skyward for the first time in this early light of fresh dawn. He noticed the clouds had darkened since they'd left John Bosco Hall.

Waving his hand toward the neat and orderly forest, Joe began the march at a steady pace. Kenny noted row upon row of pine trees neatly spaced. All rows had the same spacing as if Mom Nature had her own green regiment on parade.

"Doc Hollis says the C.C.C. did all this after some forest fires decades ago," Joe said. "See how tall they are now? Smell the pine scent. After a rain on a hot day, it is so beautiful. The scent of pine is better than you get at Christmas with a newly cut tree in your living room."

"Who is Doc Hollis? What is a C.C.C.?" Kenny wondered aloud.

"Doc Hollis is a great guy. You'll see. Likes kids and has a neat cabin up river. Bosco Boys get to go there for field trips. He sponsors competition events. He's a retired doctor on Bosco's Board of Directors, a friend of Father George and all the rest. But Doctor Hollis and his retired neighbor, Paul Beaupré take us on expeditions and campouts. We get to go on fishing and canoe trips."

"So, the C thing is?" Kenny asked.

"Oh, that's Civilian Conservation Corps. I don't think they are around anymore. They were working decades ago when Doctor Hollis was young," Joe reported.

They silently continued for over an hour through the forest as the cold wind began to bite into their wet clothes. Kenny welcomed the trees since they blocked the full force of the cold wind.

Joe stopped at a ridge that overlooked a small bend of the Au Sable River. Looking down, he pointed out a doe with two fawns near a clearing on the riverbank. Then he took his backpack off and motioned for Kenny to do the same. "Shucks, the radio was right. That darn Canadian storm is real. It's coming our way. We can't afford to get chilled. Take your sweatshirt off. Then get that sweaty T-shirt off of you. Do not put it in your pack. Just wait."

Joe flipped his weather-worn but rather elaborate woodsman-like backpack over. Using some quick knots, he tied the shirt using the leather loops that seemed to adorn the outside of his pack. He stood up and took possession of Kenny's pack. "Well, got an urban bunny special on sale, eh? It's nice for books, but is this thing waterproof?"

"Dunno. I haven't been caught out in the rain. But I got two black trash bags still in the outside pocket; big ones," Kenny reported.

"Good thinking for an urban bunny, Mr. Kung Fu," Joe teased as he looked for loops to anchor the already spread-out T-shirt. Seeing none, he reached to the ground, grabbed two pebbles, inserted them inside the pack, and pushed them so

AWOL

that they protruded out of the fabric of the pack. Then he used the nylon strips and tied slip knots to anchor them to the pack. The shirt was now expertly tied to the pack.

Joe gave the backpack to Kenny and instructed, "Now take the entire contents of your pack, especially that package I gave you this morning, place it in the black trash bag, and put it back in your pack. We can't afford to get that stuff wet. You got a way to tie the end securely?"

"Yeah." Kenny swung into action and completed the task.

Joe removed a hunting knife from its leather holster on his belt. Unscrewing a metal top on its handle he held it out before him and scanned the horizon.

Noticing the needle on the compass, Kenny interrupted Joe's gaze. "So, Daniel Boone, we lost already?"

Ignoring the taunt, Joe replied, "Hollis says 'Two things in life will never lie to you, your compass and your hunting dog.' You can count on them when nothing else will come through for you!'"

Joe replaced the knife compass. "The radio was right. The storm is coming right out of the northwest. It looks like it is right on time. Wind certainly is getting colder by the minute. We gotta get cracking. We gotta make it to the Quonset hut by at least one. Noon would be better."

With the plop of Joe's tennis shoes, Kenny knew better than to ask the burning question echoing about in his mind: "What is a Quonset hut, and why by one?" He fell in behind Joe as they resumed their march through the forest.

Breezes, colder breezes than when they started, caused Kenny to put his wool black watch hat back on. He took pleasure in knowing that his shirt was slowly drying on his back. Drying, just like Joe's. He reasoned that the wind will probably dry them before the few rays of sun creeping through the clouds. He glanced at his watch while thinking about the one o'clock deadline. It was fifteen minutes past ten. At that instant, his stomach growled. Pushing his legs forward, he calculated that Marie's tasty dessert was over sixteen hours ago. Hunger consumed him as he thrust his legs onward to match Joe's pace.

Chapter Five

The Search

Saturday, September 29, 1979, 10:15 AM, John Bosco Hall

Senior Resident Assistant Mark was worried as he approached the academy director's office. His insides were churning. He tried to keep his men out of trouble and reported conduct violations only when necessary. But he knew he had to make a report to Father George, even though he wished he could investigate; perhaps he could even avoid a disciplinary report on the new resident.

He clutched a small piece of paper in his hand as one word bounced around his skull: "But ..." Still, averting a headache is better than facing one.

He turned the corner to knock on the door. Brother Edmund almost collided with him while holding a sheaf of papers in his hand.

"Oh, Mark. How did the Advanced Placement tests go for you?"

"Not done. I still got one this afternoon over at Grayling High School. Say, Brother Ed, I got a problem. I can't locate the new kid, Kenny. I went to see him before breakfast for the orientation talk. Last night it was late so we didn't connect. He's not there. I guessed he went to breakfast with his suitemates, but I checked with them; Saltz, at least. He said he has not seen him since last night."

The Snipe Hunters' Deadly Catch at Muskrat Creek

Brother Ed quickly reversed his walk down the hall. He returned to his desk, grabbed a clipboard from the wall, and asked, "What about his roomie?"

Mark reported, "Fred's our language specialist and living with the host family in town to help the new foreign exchange student. So, the new kid Kenny got an empty room for his first night. Plus, Saltz says he has not seen Joe Duvalle since late last night. Saltz said Joe was acting a bit strange too. Joe asked him to get lost for a few hours before curfew. He was polite, but still."

"So where's Joe now?" Brother Edmund inquired.

Mark shrugged his shoulders. "Not in the room when Saltz got up before seven-thirty and no one saw him at breakfast either."

Brother Edmund grabbed another clipboard from the opposite wall. He searched through a red folder titled Second Floor. Fingering a form, he advised, "Duvalle had permission for a weekend visit with his foster parents. David Cowdrey was to go, too. They are both fostered by the Pagnucco family. He's not due back until eight o'clock Sunday night. So, I assume the foster parents picked them up late yesterday or early today, did you pre-check him out or have Stuart Vincent sub in for you?"

"Nope," Mark said. "David Cowdrey is in isolation at the infirmary in town. He's got that infection they are still investigating. The county won't get the report back til Wednesday. I doubt that the foster parents would take Joe alone. The plan was for them to go canoeing, fishing with the Pagnucco kids on the Au Sable."

Shifting his stance anxiously, Mark hated giving this feedback on his own guys.

Brother Edmund picked up the phone and called the other resident assistants and the assistant dorm director to the office. When all the men were assembled, he directed them to conduct a search of John Bosco Hall, the gym, the grounds, and the library. "Report in person or by phone within fifteen minutes.

The Search

Ask their basketball buddies. I'll call Father George at the rectory."

In a worried voice, he mused aloud with only Mark present. "I sure hope I don't have to call the state psychiatric hospital. I don't want to report that their second probationary student is AWOL from John Bosco twenty-four hours after placement."

As he dialed Father George, he looked up at Mark, "It is strange, isn't it? Roomie out, new kid in, and one suitemate approved for a weekend pass with foster parents."

As Mark approached the door, Brother Edmund stopped him, "Send Saltz to me."

Mark exited the office thinking, "Strange? Well, Brother Ed, if you want strange you should read this note from Room 216."

Over an hour later, the staff at Bosco had conducted their fruitless search of the grounds. Saltz had been interviewed by Brother Edmund. All staff members were assembled in the director's office.

Father George entered the office to address the staff. "In light of the information you have brought to my attention, I am forced to conclude that we have two residents, one who just got here, who are missing. They are to be considered absent without leave at this point. Do any of you have anything to add or anything that we should know?"

Brother Edmund spoke first. "Well, there is another possibility. Joe Duvalle had an approved weekend pass to accompany David Cowdrey on his visit with their foster family, the Pagnuccos. Suppose he took Kenny with him instead of David. Remember Cowdrey is sick and in the clinic. It would not be appropriate or approved, of course. But these are kids and they were planning a follow-up canoe trip. We know they loved fishing at Rainbow Bend with Hollis and Paul Beaupré. That was about a week ago."

Father George interrupted, "Yes, you are right. They wrote about it in literature class with Mr. Garson at Grayling High

School. Getting Duvalle to finish a writing assignment was quite remarkable in Garson's view."

"So, they were staying with the Pagnuccos or at Hollis'?" Father George inquired.

Brother Edmund leaned in a little closer and reported, "Neither. They were planning to camp with the Pagnucco family at the primitive campsite at Rainbow Bend on the Au Sable. At least until the weather reports started coming in. At noon on Friday, Gino Pagnucco called to say that they were cutting the trip short and staying in town."

"Where is that, Brother Ed?" Father George asked.

"That's Grayling for Gino and Josephine Pagnucco, Father. We called them without success. But we know the clinic staff told them about Cowdrey and the contagion precaution."

"How is David Cowdrey?"

"Actually Cowdrey is feeling fine as of an hour ago," Brother Ed replied. "He just has the rash now. He's awfully frustrated about the canceled trip and the weather."

"Bet no one has heard him complain about missing school," one of the assistants chimed in from the back of the room.

Mark addressed Father George. "I just called Gino Pagnucco's home. There's no answer. So, I called Gino's brother, too. Angelo Pagnucco owns an Italian restaurant that they take our students to periodically."

Puzzled, Father George wondered aloud, "Angelo's Restaurant. Seems I've heard of that ...?"

Brother Edmund interjected, "You will recall, last October Angelo hosted our entire staff for a sumptuous dinner when Pope John Paul II was elected. Since John Paul was the first Non-Italian Pope in four hundred and fifty-five years, Angelo had a smorgasbord of spaghetti, Polish kielbasa, and lots of sauerkraut under a banner with the Polish Eagle that read: "All is forgiven."

Chuckling, Father George reminisced, "Yes, yes, I do recall I

The Search

was at the hospital with a parishioner and you brought me goodies, including a cannoli."

Mark continued, "Angelo said he thought the trip was canceled due to the incoming storm. In any event, Angelo has not had any contact with Gino since Thursday night."

Turning his puzzled gaze on Brother Edmund, Father George questioned, "Doctor Hollis?"

"He was not listed on the weekend pass form, so we have not contacted him. We could ask him if he's heard from Joe. He certainly knows Joe and David very well. He knows a number of the guys on second floor. Doctor Hollis and Paul Beaupré fund and run the Au Sable Adventure Program in the summer. It is pretty popular with our guys." Brother Edmund then glanced up at the Crawford County map on the wall. "His cabin is upstream of McMaster's Bridge on the Au Sable River. Not far from the Rainbow Bend campsite."

"Well, okay. I'll call Sheriff Jalonick and start the process for filing a missing person's report. Can you get in contact with Doctor Hollis, just in case? I certainly would like to avoid alerting the folks at the hospital. Telling them that we lost the second resident that they placed with us is not something I want to do. Whew ... that's just ..."

Father George's voice trailed off as he ran his hand through a white shock of hair while staring up at the ceiling tiles. "Lord, have mercy," he sighed. "Brother Edmund," Father George continued in a curious tone, "What about Chester, our night watchman? Did he see or hear anything unusual? He'd have to see a car or hear a door."

"He's home by nine o'clock in the morning. We called him after ten. He had nothing to report. That's what his daily log revealed: some maintenance items and lights that needed replacing. That's Chester; he's very thorough and ex-military as well." Brother Edmund began to document the timeline of the contacts and the staff's response to the missing boys on a yellow, legal pad. With his free hand, he rang up Doctor Hollis' phone.

Father George thanked the staff. Before dismissing them, he spoke gravely. "Listen, as you go through the day please keep an eye out for the missing boys from second floor. Instruct the RAs to rotate search duties by twos, including the grounds, on the hour, every hour. If they think of anyone who should be interviewed, send them to my office. One of us will be here in the office all day."

Tapping Bernard on the shoulder, he continued, "Bernard, I'll need you and Mitchell on the switchboard six to midnight. Call that young deacon at St. Mary's. He has a military background. Long hours won't faze that guy."

Mark, as senior resident assistant, remained in the office awaiting any further instructions. When Hollis' phone went repeatedly unanswered, he abruptly interrupted Father George and Brother Ed. "Hollis frequently visits with his Canadian neighbor, Paul Beaupré. Paul chooses not to have a phone hooked up. They often play cribbage and have dinner together. They could be there for hours. If you'd like, I could drive up there when I'm done with my advanced placement exam at Grayling High School. I could check in on them directly and call you back. After five years here at Bosco, and being involved with their adventure programs, I know them pretty well."

Brother Edmund observed, "Evidently." He looked into the worried face of Father George for guidance.

Mark turned toward the door, "I could go there when my exam is done at four o'clock this afternoon."

Father George silently nodded agreement to Brother Edmund, who then opened a cabinet door, reached up, and unhooked a set of keys. He threw them underhand across the office to Mark.

"Good thinking. And for God's sake and ours be safe, eh?"

Chapter Six

The Quonset Hut

Saturday, September 29, 1979, 1:07 pm, Beaver Pond

Joe halted on the top of a hill overlooking a beaver pond. It was past one o'clock. It was cold. Though they had put their jackets on some miles back, they were still cold. Joe heard Kenny's stomach growl as they stood under the shelter of an expansive balsam fir tree looking down into the valley with the beaver pond.

"Hey, I thought I told you to eat some more of Marie's desserts, Kenny boy?"

"That was last night and what, about twenty-five miles ago? Man, am I hungry and cold! When are we done with this marching stuff? I gotta eat," Kenny demanded.

"See that pond in the little valley? We cross over those logs. Climb up that hill and ..." he broke off his sentence while looking at the compass on the end of his knife. "... then we should be looking at the hut. If not, Kenny boy, this will be one of the coldest nights you've spent in the woods."

He paused to observe the grimace on Kenny's face. Joe let out a hearty laugh. He pulled on Kenny's arm to lead him downslope, down into the valley. The bramble bushes pulled at his jeans, but soon they were crossing the open field toward the beaver's dam.

Joe spoke loudly as they continued, "We find the hut. We eat.

And then … remember I promised you that there would be a sitting part to this job? Well, it starts after we eat. These are all good things, Kenny."

"Yeah, well, I ain't seen a street light or a McDonalds in quite a while, Joe," taunted Kenny.

"We are late enough as it is. The radio said the storm is due any minute now. The wind is colder. Those clouds have taken away 'Mr. Sun'. Been awhile since we got our backs warmed, eh?"

Joe stepped up on the back end of a huge beaver dam. "To stay dry, Kenny Boy, follow my steps. It's time to be agile or wet. But we save time." Delicate balance was required. Both boys were agile enough to cross without mishap.

Together they ascended the small hill and both looked eagerly into the next valley. Kenny saw it first. It was metal. It stood out against the backdrop of the thickening green forest about twenty-five yards beyond it. From the top of their small hill, they were looking at the north end of the building.

Kenny remarked, "It looks like someone stuck a silver dollar halfway in the ground and left it. Is this hut made out of aluminum foil or what?"

Joe started to explain as they descended the hill on an angle. "Just about, it is corrugated metal or something like that. The Army used them during World War II. They were on bases all over the world, in the Pacific even. There's a National Guard Army base in this county. When they decommission stuff, stop using equipment, they put it up for sale. Doc Hollis got one for hunting with his group of friends."

A clap of thunder, no longer in the distance, filled their ears. A light sprinkle of rain began falling throughout the valley. They were already cold enough, without getting wet. They were about a hundred and fifty yards from the hut. "Let's go, Kenny."

They started to jog as best they could. Thick bushes had replaced the harvested trees in the valley and tugged at their

The Quonset Hut

legs. The valley led up to the beginning of a section of the Au Sable River Forest. Both boys were breathing heavily as they came within twenty yards of the hut. "Keep going to the end of the building. I'll be right with you," said Joe.

Joe veered off to the west side of the hut. Kenny noticed a small, renovated wooden shed about thirty yards away. There were two wooden steps made out of pine logs that had been halved. A metallic gray stovepipe came out of the shed roof.

Kenny walked slowly around the nearest end of the Quonset hut looking it over. It was easy to see that the wooden part had been added on to the original metal part. The metal had rusted in the harsh elements of this northern forest. Kenny headed toward the sturdy wooden porch. The ceiling provided protection from the elements. A sign read, "The Outpost. Welcome, friend. Be at ease."

Kenny sat on the top step of the entrance to the hut, looking thoughtlessly at the padlocked outer door. A utility shed was almost hidden in a clump of trees. On the side of the utility shed was a large lean-to that housed a lot of cut wood. Four rows of cut wood in fact. The custom-made, wooden door was padlocked.

Kenny finally got a chance to sit down out of the light rain. He placed his backpack in the shelter of the porch.

Joe smiled as he approached and dangled some keys on a ring in front of him. "We are in business, Kenny boy! I got the keys to the kingdom here ... well at least to the Quonset hut! That's something we need!"

"What's in the shed?"

"Never mind," said Joe as he handled the rusty padlock on the Quonset hut. "First we eat. Then we can talk. Hey, your favorite part is next, the sitting part."

"Ah, right now, eating tops all other parts of this jaunt of yours, Joe."

Opening the door with a heavy shove of his shoulder, Joe

The Snipe Hunters' Deadly Catch at Muskrat Creek

bellowed, "Grab your pack. Get in here. No need in getting any wetter. We are cold. We are hungry. And we need a rest. Agreed?"

Kenny happily scurried in to observe his first Quonset hut ever. He was curious about the "sitting part" of the journey. Now though, he wondered anxiously about one thing: food.

Taking a seat on a well-lacquered, almost shiny, knotty pine picnic bench Joe motioned to Kenny. "Get that bag I gave you out of your pack. Take a seat. It's time to see what Marie's got for us today."

Opening the pack, Kenny pulled the sack Joe gave him back in Room 216. Marie had neatly wrapped sandwiches, apples, and a bag of peanuts. One long, paper bag contained a brown-colored loaf of bread, cut in half. There were four breakfast biscuits that had been made into peanut butter sandwiches with honey. Kenny devoured the biscuits. He had just grabbed a carrot when Joe asked him if he wanted some water.

"Yeah, sure."

Joe walked the length of the hut, exited the far end, and walked out under a long porch. At the end of the porch was a hand pump. Kenny could see his arm swinging up and down. When the squeaking stopped, Joe reappeared with a bucket and two blue metallic cups with handles. Kenny drank in gulps of water.

"Dig in," said Joe. "There's more where that came from. I'll even show you how to do it yourself."

"Can't be too hard," Kenny observed. "You did it."

Joe looked him right in the eye, searching for a challenge.

Kenny winked and continued, "But I ain't never used a hand pump."

"How'd you get all this tasty food?" Kenny asked as he tore off a piece of freshly baked pumpernickel bread. "What are those little seeds in this bread? I never had them before."

"Marie. Marie loves anything to do with food and making

The Quonset Hut

people happy. She's from Poland. Father George said she was a "D.P.", whatever that is. She came here after World War II. And for your information, you are eating a lunch prepared for Dave Cowdrey. That's the guy you replaced on this little adventure." Joe finished his sandwich, gulped some more water, and continued. "Marie makes goodies whenever we have outings or field trips. Marie's lunch sacks always come back empty, believe me."

Pointing to Kenny's brown bread, Joe continued, "That bread you are eating ... is baked fresh. Bosco used to get factory bread delivered until Marie arrived. Wholesome Bread, I think. She told Brother Ed she could make real bread like back in Poland. Ain't no one in Bosco ever looked for the Wholesome Bread truck since. Marie's cobblers are heaven. And she'll watch for the look on your face when you taste 'em. That lady is what every kid wants for a Grandma. But she lost her whole family in the war, so we are her grandkids, I guess."

Kenny was finishing his pumpernickel and swallowing some water. "So, you don't know what's in the brown bread?"

"Caraway seeds," Joe informed him. Then he retrieved an apple, closed up his sack, which was identical to Kenny's, and stood up. "Save some munchies, Kenny boy, 'cause that's all we got. We may not be eating regular anytime soon. Finish up in a couple. Meet me out by the utility shed."

Joe tightened up his sack and placed it carefully in his pack. Grabbing the ring of keys, he walked out and turned right. Kenny watched Joe exit and grunted. Mumbling only to the walls of the Quonset hut, he stood up. "Jeez, lunch is over? I just got comfortable."

Once Joe left, Kenny started thinking, "What's next? Why did I have to replace Dave Cow ... whatever? If he was sick, why didn't they just cancel the foster parent visit? Exactly where are these foster parent people? What is a 'foster' parent anyway?" Carefully replacing Marie's goodies, he reclosed his pack then

57

looked out at the windblown rain. He once again thought to himself, "Darn, this hut is nice. I'm dry, warm, and not hungry. So, of course, Joe wants me outside."

Joe had the long utility shed opened up when he walked into the light rain. "See, Kenny boy, I promised you a 'sit down' job and here it is."

Kenny followed Joe's outstretched arm pointing into the interior of the shed. There were four canoes hanging from large J hooks installed on the beams of the ceiling. Two were aluminum and two were wooden.

"Remember I told you I'd need to use those muscles of yours, Mr. Kung Fu?" Joe reminded him with a hearty tone in his voice.

"Canoeing in the rain?" Kenny looked up at the sky and motioned with his hands. "What's the point?"

"C'mon, Kenny, get on the other end of this Silver Beaver."

Kenny noticed the name stenciled in on the side of an aluminum canoe. Joe unlocked the chains and they jointly lowered the canoe to the ground. "Now behind you, grab two of those Army packs off the rack. Bring 'em both to me."

Kenny turned around. On the opposite wall was a large set of four shelves with an orderly array of tools. On the third shelf, in a neat row, were over a dozen olive drab-colored packs with "U.S. Army" stamped on the top flap. Below, in the middle of the pack, stenciled in red, were the words, "Au Sable Adventure." On the right side, in brown, were two crossed paddles with animals painted on the broad ends. On the left side was the image of a Boy Scout in uniform reading a compass, while holding a hiking stick in the other hand. It reminded him of a Cub Scout trip, but he quickly stopped that thought when his emotions welled up.

Lifting the heavy packs off the rack, Kenny asked, "Wow, what all is in here? What's 'Au Sable Adventure' anyway?"

"It's loads of fun and lots of exercise. If you're still here in the

The Quonset Hut

summer, you'll find out for yourself!" Joe advised. He opened both packs and inspected the contents. "Super. They are all set, as usual."

"OK, Kenny. Open your pack. Reach in the very back and pull out the first item your hand touches," Joe instructed Kenny as he did the same.

Kenny pulled out and opened up a neatly folded rain poncho with a visor on the hood. "How'd you know where that was in there?" he demanded of Joe.

"A place for everything, and everything in its place, Kenny Boy. You got a lot to learn."

Pausing momentarily, Joe advanced to the front of the canoe. "Let's start with your place. See this seat? That's your place. You provide the power. I'll be guiding us. We're going upriver, Kenny Boy. That's against the current. We'll need those muscles. We'll both be working hard for a while. It won't be a long trip, just a hard one. The trip back will be nice though. You'll like that a lot."

"Uh, Joe?" Kenny looked him in the eye and, with an exaggerated, inquisitive tone, said, "What are we doing, and why are we doing it in the rain?"

"Portaging is what we're doing. I'll talk on the trail. We don't have time on our side with this storm, Kenny."

"What the heck is portaging?" The novice wondered aloud.

"French for carrying; you'll know soon enough," Joe said ominously.

As he approached the canoe Kenny felt a tingling sensation run down his spine as his first ever outdoor adventure began.

Grabbing the front end of the canoe where a loop of rope formed a handle, Joe motioned for Kenny to do the same at the back end. They carried the canoe out of the utility shed.

Returning from a quick trip to the shed, Joe dropped packs and paddles at Kenny's feet. "Now I'm going to close the place up. Put on your poncho."

The Snipe Hunters' Deadly Catch at Muskrat Creek

Pointing to the metal bar that anchored the front seat, Joe continued, "Then strap your 'Au Sable Adventure' pack here. Do mine back there. Stand it up to the rear of my seat. Use this small bar here and strap it upright and tight. I can't have any movement. A canoe is no place for objects on the move, except your paddle, Kenny."

Joe turned to head back to the Quonset hut and then stopped. Looking Kenny in the eye, he posed a question with a sincere tone in his voice. "You can handle those straps and buckles, right?"

"Yeah, sure," Kenny lied. He'd never worked with military or camping packs before. Doubt began to plague his mind now. "Should I have lied about my canoeing background?" He was glad Joe was out of sight as he feverishly began to fiddle with the straps after unbuckling them. The light rain made things slippery as Kenny fumbled around in his first effort to stand the "Adventure Pack" upright.

A few minutes later, Joe walked back to secure the utility shed. He noticed Kenny's feverish efforts. Kenny thought he heard a slight sneer from Joe as he passed by.

Joe returned, wearing a broad-brimmed tan hat with a chin strap. He flipped Kenny an identical hat. "We only get these on 'Au Sable Adventure'. But I know where they are kept. Besides, today we'll need them to keep warm. Keep the rain out of our face, too. Medium's all we got. Make it work."

Without comment, Joe knelt down and expertly re-strapped the pack in the front. Upon inspecting the one in the rear he mumbled aloud, "That'll do."

"OK, Kenny. We are ready to find the Au Sable. Everything we'll ever need and more is in the canoe."

Sliding the paddles under the gunwales, he hitched them to leather loops on the sides so that they would not slide on the journey.

Pointing to the forest, Joe announced, "See that path, and the

The Quonset Hut

opening in the woods about fifteen yards away? We'll head that way. I'll lead and be on this side. You are on the opposite side. Use the rope loop to carry it. We got about a hundred yards to water once we hit the opening in the forest. Keep it steady. Don't trip. The path is full of rocks and roots."

As he hoisted the front end of the canoe, Joe turned around to face Kenny, "Let me know if you need a break, eh?"

Kenny nodded in agreement as he adjusted the chin strap on his hat. In the secret recess of his mind, he vowed to himself that he would never take a break. He would not let his friend down on this trail. A trail to ... Gripping the wooden handle in the middle of the rope, Kenny decided to get some answers when they entered the path in the forest.

The light rain was cold and steady. Crossing the field to the forest's edge went without difficulty and without a word. Both Kenny and Joe toted their load, looking down to place their feet away from rocks and roots. The hats kept the rain out of their faces. Ponchos protected them from getting wet, except for their ankles. As soon as Kenny put his poncho on, he was happy that little rivulets of rain stopped running down the back of his neck.

The path into the forest was visible from ten yards away. Kenny decided right then to pursue an answer. "OK, 'Daniel Boone,' you don't have your compass out, so you know where we are going. But I don't."

Kenny opened up the topic quite directly two yards into the forest and while on flat land. "So far you got me tired, hungry, wet, and cold. I'm probably in trouble with Brother Ed. Dubay, the resident assistant, was supposed to see me at breakfast. These folks are supposed to actually help me. But they don't even know where I am. For that matter, neither do I. And I still don't know why I'm toting a canoe through this wet forest!"

Joe responded with a laugh, "So, I take it you don't read mystery novels much, eh?"

The Snipe Hunters' Deadly Catch at Muskrat Creek

The Quonset Hut

"None with me in them," Kenny volleyed back at Joe.

He had to turn to the side so Kenny could hear him at the end of the seventeen-foot canoe. At the back of the canoe, Kenny hollered forward to be sure he was heard above the din of the wind blowing and the rain pelting their ponchos.

"OK, OK," Joe said. The tone of his voice seemed like he was conceding to Kenny's demand for more information.

When they reached the top of a ridge, Joe looked down the slope and explained, "That's the mighty Au Sable. The river of sand ranges up to four feet deep. The tannins make it tobacco-colored in many parts. We're going to be canoeing right up that patch of river you are looking at, going that-a-way, against the current." He nodded toward the back of the canoe. "Our put-in is only about fifty yards down this slope. Just think. Half a football field and the sitting part starts, Kenny Boy."

"Not before the talking part, Joe," Kenny cautioned. "I did not come to Bosco to play 'Dick Tracy!'" He decided to hint about quitting his end of the toting. It was obvious that Joe needed him. He certainly could not drag a seventeen-foot canoe through the forest by himself. And what could Joe do, go upriver without him paddling on the other end?

"Let's get down to the water and then we'll chat, OK?" Joe turned to him before starting down the path laden with brown pine needles and cluttered with pine cones. "The path leads down this slope and opens out to a little beach. You need to adjust your end as I descend. Watch for the low branches that'll slap you right across your face. Just like your mamma did for swearing, Kenny Boy."

Looking back to the stern of the canoe, Joe began his descent. "Don't lose your grip. I can't have you dropping your end."

Kenny simply hoisted his end of the canoe up, rested it on his left shoulder. Joe smiled as he congratulated himself for picking a strong canoe mate for this venture.

The Snipe Hunters' Deadly Catch at Muskrat Creek

The descent to the river was steady, with only two slaps from the pine branches. Once again, Kenny saw it was wise to copy everything Joe did in the woods. He had donned his poncho and hat exactly as Joe did back at the hut. He observed there was no easy way to halt progress on a downhill trek while holding one end of a seventeen-foot canoe with forward momentum.

Kenny was coaching himself, "Just take it in stride. Be ready for the next step forward and hope there is no branch or root sticking up waiting for your next step." His vision was limited to the three feet in front of him.

About twenty yards down the trail, Joe simply hollered, "Log!"

Kenny stepped briskly over a fallen log, creating a roller coaster motion for the canoe on the trail.

Finally, the forest cleared, the ground leveled, and Joe stopped. Panting, he motioned to put the canoe near, but not in, the fast-flowing water. The canoe was nestled in the reeds and surrounded by bracken ferns. Joe leaned back against a tree and put his leg up on a fallen log. He looked directly at a sweaty Kenny who was standing out of breath with his hands on his hips as if to say, "Well?"

Their eyes met. Kenny was anxious to get some answers about this journey. Joe leaned forward as if to speak. Kenny peered into Joe's eyes while breathing in the aromatic scent of the cedar trees.

Just then both boys were startled by a darting blue blur between them and the river. Kenny and Joe froze and looked out on the Au Sable. A kingfisher expertly speared a minnow right out of the flowing waters.

Chapter Seven

The Main Post

Saturday, September 29, 1979, 1:51 PM, Just Outside of Grayling, MI

Mark's eyes started to register the presence of a large doe with two fawns on the road. Yet, Bosco's Jeep Cherokee continued to hurtle toward them. Mark was mouthing Monsieur LaTour's mnemonic device, "Doctor and Mrs. Vander ..."

"Yikes!" Mark slammed the brakes and swerved the vehicle onto the shoulder of the road. A family of deer scampered off into the forest. Mark exhaled, loosened his grip on the steering wheel, and screamed aloud at the wall of forest before him, "What is wrong with me today?"

Panting like a runner, Mark resumed driving below the speed limit. "Man, I gotta get focused here." He thought to himself, "I'm going to kill some deer over tricky irregular French verbs."

"Yikes!" Mark exclaimed aloud. Panic swept over him. His stomach was on fire. He realized his body was bound for the AP test, but his mind was elsewhere. "I can't recall a thing. I gotta stop thinking about Kenny for the next couple hours or I'm sunk. Bosco's first missing person report, and it has to be my guy. Why me?" He unconsciously thrust his hand into his pocket and fingered the note from Room 216. "Jeez, just how am I ...? How can I keep my guy out of trouble now?"

The Snipe Hunters' Deadly Catch at Muskrat Creek

Mark drove into the parking lot of Grayling High School, unconsciously grinding his teeth. To survive the test, he had to force his mind, like a chess piece, off the Bosco square, and onto the French square.

He rushed into the library building and scurried past fellow students to a quiet study carrel.

He opened his notebook. The vocabulary word "trust" leaped into view. His mind went right back to Bosco. "Am I violating the trust that Father George and Brother Ed have placed in me? I gotta find a way." The image of Beaupré's cabin sprang into his mind's eye. Mark seized upon it and stapled a note to his brain's clipboard. "Ah ... that's enough. I can't handle this solo. I need some advice."

Hours later, Mark turned in his test with his final thought in French, "C'est fini."

Mark deliberately outpaced his classmates down the hallway and headed towards the parking lot. "Hey, I gotta go. Bonne chance. Adieu!" Even Grace, the charming Belgian redhead, barely got a nod from Mark. During previous study sessions with Grace, he silently applauded the guy who created the exchange student program. He exited the building and marched off to the parking lot.

His retreat with haste took him to a familiar forest road. Cold winds and thickening rain pelted the Jeep Cherokee. Driving through the tall, sentinel-like pines on the Au Sable River Road, he listened to his favorite Grieg tune, "In the Hall of the Mountain King" on the vehicle's eight-track player. With the Jeep Cherokee snaking its way into the ancient forest, Mark was reliving his first taste of Au Sable River magic and its delicious woods teeming with life and adventure now, as it was five years ago.

The Jeep Cherokee came to rest in the gravel parking area of Doctor Eugene Hollis's cabin. It was one of two cabins connected by the "Partridge Path" and bottomless friendship

The Main Post

with Paul Beaupré, known collectively as the "Main Post." Mark thrust himself out of the seat to approach Doc Hollis's cabin. Drenched in the cold rain, he immediately jumped back to retrieve a windbreaker and hat.

It was almost five o'clock now. If anyone was home, they'd be in the living room facing the river and tending a fire in the fieldstone fireplace. There was no smoke, no sign of life.

Mark chose to jog down the well-traveled "Partridge Path" to Beaupré's cabin. Mark was the very reason they adorned the path with the well-lacquered wooden sign. He caught the scent of burning oak at the halfway mark.

He ascended the four steps to Beaupré's back porch in two bounds. The aroma from the fireplace and the scent of popcorn invaded his nostrils. The gastric juices in his stomach immediately responded with a "Help Wanted" message.

Mark knocked hard, though he knew the door was unlocked. Looking over the back of the chairs he was able to spot Paul Beaupré's ebony black head of hair contrasted with Doc Hollis' short-cropped gray, still in the U.S. Navy style decades after his service. Their easy chairs, facing the fireplace, allowed a view of the river.

"Why look who's here!" Paul exclaimed with joy in his voice. He was a large, strong lumberjack of a man. Walking toward the door he said, "Come on in! You know this place is always open to you, Marko."

Hollis commanded, "Jeez, get on in here, Mark, before Beaupré scarfs down all the popcorn."

Mark opened the door. He instinctively reached for the note as he entered the room. Paul and Hollis approached, and then another man entered the room from the kitchen. Mark shoved the note back in his pocket.

Hollis, still sporting the frame and fitness of his college lineman days, reached out his hand and shook hard. Then he put a vice-like grip on Mark's shoulders and turned him toward Paul.

The Main Post

"Now look at that, Paul, a finer Bosco Boy you'll never find."

"Good to see you, young man." Paul shook his hand and slapped Mark on the shoulder as Hollis released his grip.

"You hungry, Mark?" Paul asked. "I'll be glad to make a fresh batch of popcorn for you!"

Mark began, "Well, yeah, I'm hungry but you don't need to make ..."

"Nonsense. Sit down. Warm up. I'll put another log on. You know the way to the ginger ale and root beer. Just help yourself there, Marko." Beaupré motioned to the small room off the kitchen.

"You paddle up here or drive?" Hollis asked. "We didn't hear a car,"

"No. I'm not ... uh. Well, I drove. I got Bosco's Jeep Cherokee actually. I gotta talk. Uh ..." Mark took a step for the ginger ale but stopped short. He looked over at a taller, slightly thinner version of Paul Beaupré standing in the way.

Hollis explained, "Oh. I almost forgot. We keep getting foreigners in this forest when I'm not looking. This is Jean Luc. You'll soon see he's an older, but smarter edition of the Beaupré clan from Quebec. His sons are running a hockey clinic in the Detroit-Windsor area so he gets to sneak in a visit with us."

Glancing at his lifelong friend, Paul Beaupré, Hollis raised his voice a little. "You remember, when Paul came along, they broke the mold. They stopped that production line forevermore; out of respect for mankind."

Smiling Mark stepped toward Jean Luc and extended his hand.

"Brother, Jean Luc," Paul began rather formally. "This is Mark, a senior resident assistant at Bosco Hall, known as Marko here at the Main Post. He's been coming around for about five years. You'd be proud to have him on one of your hockey teams, sans doute."

Jean Luc, a slightly smaller version of his brother graying

only at the temples, stepped forward with both hands outstretched. He held a ginger ale in one hand and a root beer in the other. "It's always a pleasure to meet another friend at the Main Post. Which one, mon ami?"

"Oh, I'll take the ginger," replied Mark. "Thanks. Ah, merci beaucoups, I mean."

"But, of course, de rien, my dear Marko. I note a slight Belgian accent there."

"Certainment. I'm a Michigander by birth actually. I just studied with a Belgian this summer." Mark was clumsily groping around now that he had a chance to practice his French.

"Ya, see, Marko, ya can't judge all Canadians by Paul, the class-less Beaupré here," Hollis announced, gesturing toward Jean Luc, as if teaching a lesson. "Look at that. Same brood even. Yet this here 'J. L.' has got more class and savior-faire in his little finger than—"

Paul Beaupré interrupted, "Hey Hollis, put a cork in yourself. Let's hear what brought Marko to the Main Post on a cold, rainy Saturday night. I'm betting he didn't come all the way from Bosco to hear your blathering."

All eyes in the room focused on Mark, as Paul pulled an extra chair into the circle facing the warm fire. He motioned Mark in its direction. "Here, relax. How was the drive on that two-track road?" Paul inquired.

"Well, fair. I took it in slow motion. It'll surely be worse with more rain," Mark reasoned as he plopped into the chair and took some warmth from the fire. "This is nice. I'm all wet."

"Well, son, what do you have cooking today?" Hollis asked as he pulled his chair a little closer.

"Well, I have one of those … under-your-hat discussions to have. You know? It is a vest-pocket kind of issue. Just between …" Mark's voice trailed off as he looked in the direction of Jean Luc.

The Main Post

"Oh. I see," Hollis assured him. "A man-to-man chat is what you are after?"

"Well, yes, eventually, but first I got to know in a hurry if you've seen Joe Duvalle with a new student named Kenny today? Then I gotta use your phone and call back to Bosco. You see we have students missing at Bosco for the first time ever. We just don't know where they are."

"OK, Marko. Slow down," Doctor Hollis, sensing his anxiety, reassured him. "You drove all the way out here to ask me that? Why didn't you call?"

"We did. I mean Father George and Brother Ed called in the morning when we searched Bosco. We found no trace of them. So, then we called here. We know Joe likes coming here and canoeing."

Paul interjected, "Remember, Hollis, you came over for breakfast. We started playing cribbage, waiting for my brother to drive up from Detroit."

Looking back at Mark, Paul explained, "When Jean Luc arrived, we all had lunch." He concluded by reminding Doctor Hollis, "You've been here ever since."

Looking at Mark, Hollis responded, "Ah ... yes. I forgot. And the rains came. Plus, Beaupré here rejects the modern convenience of a phone. But he relies on me to be his darn secretary when he gets calls."

Paul Beaupré retorted, "Yeah and where do you go when it is time to hide from that bothersome world out there, dear doctor?"

Motioning with his hand toward the fireplace, Beaupré pointed to an overstuffed leather chair. "As I noted this morning, after an omelet and toast, of course, right there, safe from the disturbances of the world. I believe those are your exact words. We all know you like to wrap yourself up in pine trees and watch the waters of the Au Sable flow by."

Deflecting the well-placed arrow, Hollis turned his attention to Mark. "Oh, don't confuse this young man with such details. How can we help you, Marko? We have had no Bosco visitors today. That I can confirm for you."

Leaning toward Mark, he gestured with his right hand and continued, "Slowly now, what's up with this Kenny guy?"

"Well, we really don't know. I actually do know some, hmmm ..." Mark stammered and hesitated before continuing.

"Or at least they ... Father George, I mean. Brother Ed does not know. I actually think that. I mean there's evidence to suggest that ..." Mark, clutching the note, just wanted to confess it all.

"Hold on there, Marko, my boy. Get a grip. You are getting me confused. From my end of the canoe, you seem confused there yourself, son. Sounds like you know something that the Bosco people don't know," Hollis observed.

Looking in the direction of Jean Luc, Mark stifled his original impulse. He released his grip on the note. He breathed in deeply like his speech teacher taught him. He reasoned a news reporter's approach ought to work.

"Well, this much we do know. Joe Duvalle did not show up for breakfast. That's also true for the new kid, Kenny Dee. He failed to show for his breakfast meeting with me. He just got to Bosco yesterday. Kenny was supposed to have the rules discussion and orientation with me at breakfast. But he never showed up."

"That's strange. You said it was his first night at Bosco. He can't know the lay of the land," Paul Beaupré reasoned.

"He's missing along with Joe," Mark said. "We don't really know if they are together. We've searched and searched. Brother Ed has the whole Bosco campus on lock-down. We got search teams by twos going out on the hour. When I left the staff meeting, Father George was calling Sheriff Jalonick for a missing person's report."

Pausing in his story, Mark realized they did not know about

his afternoon. "Uh, I got the Jeep Cherokee to come here after … Ya see I had a French test today. I drove here from school after the exam finished at four."

Feeling positively sick to his stomach, and trying to avoid total disclosure, he continued, "See, Joe and David Cowdrey had a weekend pass to go canoeing with his foster family, the Pagnuccos. As far as we know, the Pagnuccos thought it was canceled. They did not show up at the office. They did not follow the check-out procedures like they've done before."

"What did they do?" Hollis asked.

"Don't know for sure. Brother Ed phoned them a lot. We can't actually reach them. But we talked with Angelo Pagnucco, Gino's brother. At least his brother Angelo thinks the whole weekend, the pass and all, was canceled because of Cowdrey. Or it may be off because of the weather system coming in. It sure ain't canoeing weather today."

"No argument there," Paul agreed.

"Oh yeah, the car radio came on with warnings for all the northern counties even before I left Detroit. They labeled it an early season Alberta Clipper. Even snow is possible in the Upper Peninsula," Jean Luc observed, standing slightly behind Paul with his foot on an ottoman.

"A gift to my Yankee cousins, eh?" Jean Luc chuckled.

"So, David Cowdrey. What's up with him?" Hollis inquired.

"Sick," Mark replied. "That's why we think the Pagnuccos assumed the trip was off and never bothered to call and cancel. You need two for a canoe."

"Sick? He was here last weekend and healthy as a horse. Dave and Joe can paddle all day and not get tired," Hollis asserted. Then Hollis continued, "Cowdrey and Joe were trout fishing last weekend up river from Brown Trout Bend. But you're the R.A., so you know that. We had great weather all last week. Just look at what our Canadian visitors brought along with them, eh? Seems like November out there now."

Pausing, Hollis stepped to the window and peered out. "Now I know Joe and David wanted to go back and fish that stretch of the river again. I did tell them I was not free this weekend. But I offered them the use of the Quonset hut if Bosco gave them a pass. So, Joe is missing only? Where's Dave Cowdrey?" he demanded.

"We know where Cowdrey is," Mark replied. "He's not in the dorm either. He's been at the clinic for most of the week. He showed up with an infection. The clinic quarantined him till the blood tests come back from the county. He's fine now, with no fever. But he can't come into the dorm till they get the test results. But, hey, it is almost five-thirty. Can I call Bosco?" He stood up and placed the can of ginger ale on the table.

"Yes. Yes, of course. You know where the key is. Help yourself. Hurry back here." Hollis stood up facing Mark. "Don't forget to put a dime in the jar, there, Marko."

Paul escorted him to the door. He handed him an oversized poncho against the wind and rain. Walking beside him, he asked Mark, "When do you want to have that vest-pocket discussion? I understand you got something else you need help with there, Marko?"

"Yes. Yes. But, heck, not till I get done with the Bosco call. Like I said, Father George has RAs on extra duty hours. They are patrolling the campus in pairs. We've got a volunteer manning the desk overnight. Sheriff Jalonick has been called. It is just crazy at Bosco Hall."

He stopped long enough to put his poncho on. "This is all so new. This missing person thing is a first for Bosco. The new kid, Kenny, no one really knows. Heck, we only have a two-year-old photo of him from his transfer files. I just don't know what to do."

Opening the door onto the expansive porch, Mark turned back to face Hollis and Beaupré. "I'll be right back. I'll call Bosco. Let them know. I really don't know what to do. I've never

The Main Post

had a man on my floor go missing."

"Quit fussing there, Marko. We'll figure it out. You just get back here," Doctor Hollis counseled.

"I'm putting a batch of popcorn on now. It'll be warm and waiting for ya," Paul Beaupré advised.

Mark was off the porch in one bound. He scurried down the Partridge Path toward Doctor Hollis' cabin.

The door slammed. The three men paused to consider Mark's plight.

Paul was first to comment as he reached for the long-handled popcorn skillet designed for the fireplace. "Well, it's hardly canoeing weather. I doubt if a new kid or any kid would go out in this."

Jean Luc added, "It will be nothing but bad for three days along the storm track, both Michigan and Ontario news said yesterday: cold in the middle to late thirties with high winds. That'll make it even colder. It'll rain here. But snow is possible north of the Straits of Mackinaw. That comes from a Detroit station early this morning. And a Saginaw radio station gave a similar update just before I reached Roscommon County."

"Um. Yeah, I see what ya mean," Hollis commented. "Don't know about the other boy, but if Joe Duvalle is missing in those woods, he can handle himself. That boy was working on an Eagle with the scouts. He's been through Au Sable Adventure twice."

"This boy Marko's pretty trustworthy, eh?" Jean Luc inquired about the young man he had just met. "He has Bosco's Jeep Cherokee and they sent him alone on this mission to find the missing boys?"

With his back to his audience, Hollis explained while opening the screen to the fireplace and adding another log. "Yup. They don't make 'em any better, especially at this age. He comes from a remarkable family. Dad's a career military intelligence officer. Two older brothers were great athletes, diligent students. They are both in the Navy now. Don't know too much about his older sisters except that they are out of the nest. He came here for Bosco Hall, the boarding school part of Bosco Academy. You know, they have some orphan and foster care placements along with the boarding school component."

"Does he have a mother?" Jean Luc inquired.

Hollis answered, "Marko's mother died of breast cancer a little over a year before he came here. Until Bosco, he'd never lived in the state apart from his infancy. Dad was at Wayne State Law School at the time of his birth. His father gets stationed all over the globe. So, after his mother's untimely death, his dad chatted with his priest and decided on Bosco. I think he was placed as an eighth-grader."

Hollis stopped and used the fireplace tools to maneuver a log into place. "Yeah, after his first bowl of popcorn, ask him about the date on that Partridge Path sign. That'll give you a picture of Marko in the making."

"There ain't no forgetting that date. That's for sure," Paul Beaupré confirmed with a chuckle rooted deep in reverie. He grabbed the huge leather mitt and placed the filled popcorn skillet over the roaring fire as Hollis slid the screen back for him.

Paul settled in on the ottoman while he enjoyed the fire working its magic on the popcorn. "Well, Marko will be back soon I bet. Cold as your cabin is. This fire has got us warm, but it isn't even 40 out there. Heck, look at that gauge over the birdbath. We won't be seeing any hummingbirds at the feeder during this storm, I'll bet."

"I'm afraid not. Not with this wind," Jean Luc confirmed.

Chapter Eight

Under the Willow Tree

Saturday, September 29, 1979, 2:34 pm, Brown Trout Bend

The rain ceased, at least for a while. When the bank of clouds passed overhead, there was a break in the rain. The sun sent some timid rays down through the skinny branches of the tree onto the boys resting in the canoe. With the willow's shelter from the wind, some warmth returned to Kenny's limbs.

Joe pulled his backpack forward and whistled at Kenny. Kenny looked back in time to see a Granny Smith apple arching toward him. He caught it shoulder high. A miss would have put it entirely past the canoe and into the Au Sable.

"Now you get food for thought and food for your tummy," Joe said. "The information you wanted hours ago will taste better now that you've had a few hundred strokes on the paddle. I promise."

Winking while biting into his own apple, he counseled Kenny, "Ya just gotta trust me a little." Munching in unison on his own Granny with Kenny, he continued, "Look, Kenny. I really don't want you frustrated. But you must understand we're operating on a need-to-know basis. So, here's the story for today."

Then he stretched out and calmly finished his apple before resuming. "Basically, you and me got a package to fish out of the river and haul back to the hut. And we gotta get it safe before this storm washes it away or wrecks it. Then we got another problem. Nighttime is a comin'. And we gotta cover some territory before dark," Joe reported as if he were a teacher giving an assignment back in the classroom.

"A package?" Kenny inquired.

"Yeah, uh … well." Hesitating like a man who opened a door into a room he did not want to enter, Joe continued, "Yup, a package of sorts." He was groping for words like a sailor fallen overboard might grope for a thrown rope.

He painfully realized that he needed to disclose more. "Last weekend, Dave and me were trout fishing with Doc Hollis up river a little ways from here. Doc had his nineteen-foot riverboat with the motor on back. It is great for going upriver. Once he got to his fishing spot, he stopped the boat. We all got out. He went downstream to fish. He told us to move upriver and tie up the riverboat just past an eddy. There was a quiet, shady spot full of reeds by a sandbank sticking out into the river from shore. But there was a huge downfall. A big spruce tree had been blown over by a storm. It was hard to get around the tree with the current against us. We had to do some bushwhacking up close to shore. When we broke free of the bushes and weeds to tie up the riverboat, we made a …" Joe's voice trailed off. The sailor was back groping again. "A, uh … a discovery."

"So, you guys don't ever get wet? Ya just walk on water like St. Peter was supposed to?" Kenny chided him as he tried to picture the story he was being told.

"We use waders, Kenny Boy. Ain't you ever been trout fishing?"

"Nope. And never been …" Kenny halted mid-sentence. He decided to leave it there. Telling Joe more about his limitations on a river, in a canoe, or with the outdoors in general, made him feel uneasy.

"Well, you are going to love 'Au Sable Adventure' in May

Under the Willow Tree

then. Wait till that Canadian Beaupré gets your 'city boy' hide in the woods," Joe chided with a warm smile. "Gonna be all kinds of fun right up till the graduation expedition, the snipe hunt."

Kenny's facial expression was broadcasting a huge question mark in bright neon lights.

He stopped and looked real serious for a moment. "Don't tell me, Kenny Boy, you ain't never got a snipe in the woods, either? What the heck kinda scout are ya?" Joe demanded with a look of disbelief on his face.

Defensively, Kenny raised his voice slightly. "Look, Joe, this is about the most time I ever spent in the woods ... a forest, I mean. I took a Cub Scout trip with my Uncle Bob once. Didn't see any snipe animals, but it was at a county park near town. I was 10. Cousins were 10, 11, and 12. We went fishing from a rowboat. I earned some merit badges."

Kenny suddenly realized that he was talking about his family. Strangely, sitting in the canoe, it felt okay. Still, he was immediately uncomfortable for some reason. He decided to stop. Yet he was proud his uncle saw him catch, clean, and prepare a fish dinner all by himself that day.

"What's a snipe? They big?" he wondered aloud.

"Well ...," Joe paused, swallowing a mischievous smile. "Don't ya bother with that. Won't see 'em now anyway. It's Autumn. When it's Springtime on 'Au Sable Adventure', you up and tell Beaupré ya wanna be first to get a snipe. He likes brave guys. He'll be proud of you."

Then Joe straightened up both legs and stretched his back. "Well, ya caught your breath? Ready to go? Radio said the heavy storm will be hitting us all day. On again, off again with those clouds coming and going. I don't wanna miss our chance for some paddling without rain."

"Maybe. What's so special about this package?" Kenny inquired. "Why we gotta get it now? Why not have that doctor get it when he had that special motorboat? Be easier than this upriver stuff with paddles." Pointing up with his hand he gestured at the ever-blackening sky. He noticed in his glance, the tobacco-colored water of the fabled Au Sable River. Even amid this tiring mystery, the magic of the Au Sable was seeping into him.

"True, if we wanted the Doc to know," Joe added with a wink. "This is something just between us guys. Gotta be that way. And now that you're here, I gotta trust ya." Pointing his finger and thumb like a pistol firing, Joe asserted, "And you gotta trust me. David Cowdrey, now sick and in the infirmary, is the only other one that knows. So that's three of us. That's all there's ever gonna be." Holding his hand aloft, he displayed 3 fingers. Joe sounded the most serious he'd been on this entire trip. Both his voice and the way he shifted his weight on the seat telegraphed that the flow of information on the package was about to be dammed up by the best beaver on the river.

"Kenny, ya like John Bosco Hall so far?" Joe demanded.

"Yup."

Joe's penetrating stare suggested that one word was not enough.

"Uh … yeah," Kenny continued. "Well, like yesterday. Yesterday I liked being with the guys. Hanging out and chatting with those guys in the cafeteria. Well, most of 'em." With a taunting tone in his voice, Kenny looked right back at Joe, eye to eye. "The mysterious ones with half-told stories get my goat a little."

Joe rolled his eyes and laughed heartily. He thought to himself, "Well, I guess I hooked into a sly one."

Joe counseled again in his serious tone, "Well, then ya gotta have a quiet voice. I noticed you being real tight-lipped around adults. And I figured you were strong enough for this venture. So here you are. Back at Bosco ya gotta be quiet about this and trust me. Ya just gotta be quiet."

Under the Willow Tree

"So, how good could this package in the Au Sable River be?" asked Kenny, continuing his quest for knowledge. "It's been there a week so it has to be pretty soggy by now."

"Me and Dave made it safe for the time being. This storm with the winds will change all that. Now there's one other thing. Like I said before, we can make some easy and quick money. We ain't stealing nothing either," Joe motioned to Kenny to grab his canoe paddle.

Kenny knew from the look on Joe's face, the talking part was over. Knowing he was about to launch on much more than a canoe trip, he gripped his paddle but did not turn around. Instead, across the distance of the seventeen-foot canoe in his bow seat, he looked again directly into Joe's eyes.

Joe, paddle at the ready, returned his gaze as if to say, "The ball's in your court."

Kenny's mind was a parade of the events since his arrival at Bosco. Thoughts streamed forth like stampeding stallions, but he could not rope even one. For a moment, wordless thoughts flowed like the Au Sable between two boys in a canoe poised for launching.

A chickadee only two feet above them commenced its hearty melody. It broke the trance.

"Ya just gotta trust me, Kenny Boy," Joe said, this time without any hint of pressure in his voice.

Kenny exhaled deeply. Joe had read his mind perfectly. The two Bosco boys were now bound together like brothers in the conspiracy.

Joe loosened the rope and raised the tip of his paddle. "Well, Davy Crockett, ya ready? The clock is ticking, and that freaking Canadian storm isn't going to wait on us."

Kenny exhaled with a hearty laugh.

It was after four o'clock when the Silver Beaver knifed into the mighty Au Sable. Cold Canadian winds were pushing dark rain clouds into the pristine forest of the Au Sable River Valley

81

The Snipe Hunters' Deadly Catch at Muskrat Creek

of Michigan. And two Bosco boys were pushing a canoe toward a rendezvous no one could have anticipated.

Chapter Nine

Judas Iscariot at Bosco Hall

Saturday, September 29, 1979, 4:35 pm, Doc Hollis's Cabin

Once Mark broke free of the path in the woods, he retrieved the spare key from the hollow of a log kept next to the chopping block. Then he dashed across the lawn, high jumped onto the porch and was quickly in the entryway of Hollis' cabin. Dripping wet, he removed his shoes and placed the poncho on the large rack.

"This is Bosco Hall, Bernard speaking. How can I help you?" Mark reached a resident assistant he had actually trained.

"It's Mark. I need to talk to Brother Ed or Father George."

"Hey, yeah. Where you been? We have been waiting to hear from you. Hang on. I gotta send Vincent to get Brother Ed." The phone was put on hold. Then Bernard came on again. "There's still no Joe Duvalle or that new kid from 216. But the sheriff's been here. The Pagnuccos actually came over when they heard from the pizza-place owner. I was on duty when they met with Father George. They ain't had any contact with Joe either. They knew about Cowdrey being in the clinic. They figured the weekend pass was canceled. Just where are you anyway? I have not seen you since the staff meeting; not even at lunch."

"I'm at Doctor Hollis' and they ain't here either," Mark reported with rising tension in his voice. Then he heard Vincent. "Here he is."

The Snipe Hunters' Deadly Catch at Muskrat Creek

"This is Brother Ed, Mark. How are you? Got any news on Joe?"

"Nope. But, sure enough, Hollis was playing cribbage next door at Beaupré's with no phone. We could've called all day. We'd never reach 'em. That's just like they want it at times, like in deer season. When the Main Post has no contact with the real world, that's what is known as a good day. That's their saying. But they have had no contact with Joe. "

"Well, thanks for your scouting and messenger services today. How'd the test go? Ca c'est bien?" Brother Ed inquired.

"I understood most everything. Thank God for Monsieur LaTour, our tutor, though. Hey, you have any news on the new kid, Kenny? What's happening?"

Brother Ed quickly added, "News? Yes. But none of it is helpful. Father George, some church volunteers, and Sheriff Jalonick searched out the bowling alley, laundry, the park, library, Jake's Bait-N-Tackle Shop, and Helen's restaurant. No one has seen them. We called Joe's favorite teacher, Mr. Garson. No contact there either, but he connected the sheriff to Scoutmaster Bailey."

Brother Ed halted there, cleared his throat, and made an aside. "That was a stroke of luck actually. We got Bailey's recent photos of Joe duplicated by Jalonick. So, Mr. Garson and Scoutmaster Bailey volunteered to visit the county campground and the State Park Campground. Actually, Sheriff Jalonick said he is not going to panic till after dark. He figures with this weather; they'll be home by dark. God knows I would be. Are you still at Doctor Hollis' cabin?"

"Yup. But it is empty and cold now. All the action is over at Beaupré's because he has his brother visiting. So, Doctor Hollis is over there, instead of at his own cabin. You know they go back and forth all the time. But Beaupré's got no phone. So, I came here. It's only ninety yards away or so."

Brother Ed paused. "You got any ideas? You're Duvalle's R. A.

Judas Iscariot at Bosco Hall

Anything we should know that we don't know now? If you got any confidences you're holding, now's the time to sing out. This is a health and safety issue that's only getting worse. After dark, it is going to get pretty tense around here."

A shot of electricity went up Mark's spine. "Well, uh ... about Joe? No. But ..."

"We're on edge here now with the campus patrols going out every hour," Brother Ed continued. "Heck, even the football game was washed out by the storm. The guys resorted to ping pong in the rec room. But if Father George and the sheriff return empty-handed, I really don't know what we'll be doing."

Unconsciously, Mark gripped the note in his pocket. His tongue lurched into motion. "But I might have something to help. Brother Ed, I have ... I mean there's this one thing ..."

Quickly, as if punched in the gut, Mark stopped. He decided he could not do it yet. Not before ... Not before, he had found a better way.

"Yeah what's up, Mark? You sound worried or confused. And that's certainly not you. You are my top-drawer R.A."

Recovering, and gaining some control, Mark launched forth. "Actually, in listening to Doctor Hollis, I had this thought. I talked with both Hollis and Beaupré about this. It seems like Joe and Cowdrey really wanted to come back and fish the river again like they did last weekend. Hollis knew he was not available because of Jean Luc."

"Who?" Brother Ed demanded.

Not handling the interruption well, Mark stumbled. "Uh, that's Beaupré's brother from Canada. Doctor Hollis said he's visiting here now. Up from Detroit where his college boys are running a hockey clinic for Detroit and Windsor high school players. They are in Detroit for about ten days running the clinic, so Jean Luc drove up to the Au Sable for a visit."

Regaining his train of thought, Mark decided to forward his guess. "So, Hollis told Joe and David that he was not available, but if they got permission and a weekend pass from Bosco, they'd be welcome to use his equipment and canoe again. They could use The Outpost, too."

"The Outpost?"

"Yeah, Brother Ed, that's what they call Hollis's Quonset hut that we use during the Au Sable Adventure Program. His buddies use it during deer season and the trout opener. You know the hut. He lets the scouts use it sometimes too."

"Yeah, I only know the Quonset hut as the hut I guess," Brother Ed mused. "What's with the Outpost thing?"

Sharing his insider knowledge, Mark continued, "Yeah, ya see, Hollis and Beaupré's cabins were built one after the other by the same carpenter, Omer. They are like brothers, so they both used the first cabin, till the second one was done. They both wanted the same top-notch builder, and at the same time. So, they flipped a coin to see who got to go first. They called both cabins the Main Post while they were a work in progress. Hollis says the name just stuck. Then along came the hut. It's more than a few miles away of course, so they dubbed that the Outpost."

"I see you know their history there, Mark."

'Well, history and today, some French, I know. But really, I'm just guessing here on Joe. But since Hollis made the canoe and the hut available to Joe and David, maybe, just maybe … Joe went anyway? Even without David? Does that sound plausible?"

Brother Ed interrupted, "What about the transfer kid, Kenny? Do you figure he's in on this? He's totally new to Bosco; new to Joe Duvalle for that matter. Seems odd they are both missing at the same time though. They are suitemates."

Mark deliberately refused to comment on this subject. "As I said, I'm only guessing; thinking out loud. We get to do that at the Main Post. I'm not good at being a detective."

"Yes. Yeah. I see. We're all new at this missing-persons stuff,"

Judas Iscariot at Bosco Hall

Brother Ed counseled. Then he resumed his inquiry. "But in this weather? In a canoe alone? How would he get to the hut? That Quonset hut is a long ways from Bosco. I remember hauling food for the guys during Au Sable Adventures. That two-track road stops about … seems like a mile away. The woods are thick. That hut, heck it's right on the edge of the state forest. It is great for hunting and fishing, but a long ways from civilization. It's hardly accessible."

"You're right, Brother Ed. We have to bushwhack around a patch of poison ivy. Hollis and Beaupré use two GI Surplus Jeeps from Camp Grayling. He's welded hitches and canoe racks for them. They use an off-road two-track access that connects to the forest road, F-97."

Brother Ed continued, "Well look, Mark, we'll be losing light here pretty soon. Father George and the sheriff are due back before dark. Can you stay there, at the cabin, to see if Joe happens to show up? I agree with the sheriff. Joe will have to have shelter before dark. This Canadian weather front has already made it awfully cold for late September. But, jeez, it'll be even colder after dark."

"Sure, I can stay. I got Bosco's Jeep Cherokee. I should be able to get down that sandy two-track road with that, even if it keeps raining. But it was slippery, with widening ruts, when I came in after the test, Brother Ed."

"Wow. I forgot your schedule. You left here about lunchtime, didn't you? I've been thinking of Joe and the new kid all day. Sorry. Heck, you must be hungry."

"Don't worry. Beaupré's making popcorn for me right now. What time do you want me to call you?"

"Let's try just after seven-thirty. Surely, Father George will be back by then. Any light left won't be making its way through the clouds and forest at that time, eh?"

"OK, Brother Ed. Remember I'll be at Beaupré's cabin and the phone is over here at Doctor Hollis'. So, don't try to call me."

The Snipe Hunters' Deadly Catch at Muskrat Creek

"OK, Mark, over and out till after 7:30 pm. Thanks."

Mark hurried back to Beaupré's. His stomach was growling. His dilemma had only gotten worse. On the one hand, he still had a chance to keep Kenny out of quite so much trouble if he were just found soon, but on the other, he still had a note in his pocket that might be relevant for the search. As he donned the poncho, he consoled himself that he had avoided lying. "Still…" He took comfort in the rain pounding on the hood of his poncho. The sound numbed his conscience.

Beaupré's cabin door had just shut when the word salvo began.

"Hey, Marko, what took you so long?"

"What the heck were you doing, reciting the Pledge of Allegiance and the Preamble of the Constitution for the good Padre?"

"Still conjugating French verbs there, Marko?

The guys were peppering him with questions as Mark stood in the entryway. He said nothing. He carefully removed the dripping wet poncho and his shoes.

Beaupré offered Mark a large wooden bowl of buttered popcorn. He motioned him back into his chair by the fireplace. On the table next to the tin salt shaker was his can of ginger ale.

"You know how hard it was to keep their mitts off your popcorn?" Beaupré nodded in the direction of Jean Luc and Doctor Hollis.

Jean Luc approached him just as he sat down. "I only do this for Yankees who don't know when to come in out of the rain." Then he handed him a fresh can of cold ginger ale.

Hollis pulled his chair a little closer. "Well, Marko, what's the latest news from Bosco Hall and Father George?"

Jean Luc interrupted the two. "Perhaps you should let the young man eat his popcorn, my good doctor."

Jean Luc turned to Mark. "You had lunch? When was the last time you ate, Monsieur Marko?"

"A little after noon, I had an apple and a pear at the dorm.

Judas Iscariot at Bosco Hall

Then I ate some peanuts on the way to the AP exam. I don't eat much on test days, actually."

Digging into the bowl while warming his feet by the fire, Mark looked up at Paul and Jean Luc. "Hey, popcorn's good. The fire is great. It's terrible out there, guys. The wind blows that rain right into your face. We must have lost twenty-five degrees since yesterday. Thanks for the poncho, Paul."

Hoisting his ginger ale can high in Jean Luc's direction, Mark enunciated as best he could. "Bien fait, mon ami! This is really great."

Jean Luc and Paul both exchanged self-satisfied glances at Doctor Hollis, who flinched at their silent jab.

Hollis erupted with an air of indignation in his voice, "So, now I have to have two country bumpkins from the frozen wastelands of the north tell me how to practice medicine?" Turning to Mark, he addressed him like a teacher. "Look Marko, have all the popcorn you want. Roast your rump by the fire all night if you like. We got all the wood you need. We got enough ginger ale for a platoon of Marines. But when you're ready to talk, I'm all ears."

Hollis put his feet up on his own ottoman and crossed his arms across his favorite Gokey shirt. Pausing long enough to get their attention, he looked pointedly at the Beaupré brothers and promptly put on his hurt face. "I, for one, thought that's what you wanted to do. I don't happen to believe Marko drove all the way out here for Beaupré's special fireplace popcorn." With a head nod at the brothers, he put more than a period at the end of his sentence.

Mark laughed. "I guess I didn't know how hungry I was till I got off the Partridge Path. Ya get warm, ya get hungry, I guess."

"Eat up young man. I see the fire could use another log," Paul slid open the wood box and brought out several well-cut logs. Opening the screen, he placed two on the roaring fire. He then placed three more at the ready to the left of the fireplace.

Mark munched on his popcorn and drank his ginger ale. Staring at the fireplace gave him some relief from his predicament with the note from Room 216. Minutes passed as the wooden bowl emptied. He decided on the direct approach when Jean Luc left for the bathroom.

"Well, guys, Bosco still has no information on the whereabouts of Joe and Kenny. They only think they are together. They know only that they both showed up missing at the same time. They know they are suitemates. Well, for a day at least. That's part of what I need to talk about. That's the confidential part. Remember that vest-pocket kind of talk you guys taught me about?"

"Of course," Paul acknowledged while Hollis simply nodded. Images of a younger maturing Mark at the chopping block years ago flashed across his mind.

Mark put the empty wooden bowl down. He stood up and drained the last of his ginger ale. Then he looked Hollis in the eye. "Well, I gotta talk. But what about Jean Luc? He's not …"

Mark glanced over at Paul Beaupré. He had an uneasy feeling in his gut.

Doctor Hollis seized the moment. He quickly diagnosed the problem. "Oh, I see now. Well, Marko. The rule of the Main Post applies. It applies at my cabin. It applies at Beaupré's cabin. It applies to all company present, short of murder, high crimes, and treason."

Rising from his chair, he tapped Mark on the shoulder. "C'mon, Mark, perhaps it's time to remind you of something important. Over here." He walked Mark across the room to a little alcove next to the landing leading up to the second story. On the wall was a solitary wooden plaque. The letters had been ornately burned into the wood. "Read this aloud. Remember it now. Remember it always. It is the code of honor amongst the men of the Main Post." Hollis spoke like a docent in a museum.

Mark read it aloud.

Judas Iscariot at Bosco Hall

> **At the Main Post**
> Welcome my friend.
> Be at ease.
> Talk if you want.
> Listen if you please.
> Unburden your heart.
> Lighten your soul.
> Share your joy
> and your woe.
> The ears at the Post
> will honor it so.
> The ears of the world
> will never know.

Mark stood motionless for a minute. He turned to Hollis with a question in his heart. A question heard without any sound.

"Read it again. Aloud, Marko!"

Mark complied and said, "So, this applies to Jean Luc, too?"

"If you want it to, we could ask him to go chop wood in the shed. Seriously, it is your choice; we want you comfortable." Taking a step back into the living room, Hollis continued, "Don't worry. He's Canadian. Be nothing new to him. He has arms of steel. His heart is as warm as a polar bear in heat. But his head's as hard as a hockey puck. Fortunately, he's half as bright as one, too. So, anything you tell him, why by morning ..." Doctor Hollis raised his hands as if asking a question. "So, I personally don't think you got much to worry about."

Pushing Hollis in the shoulder, Mark broke out in a laugh

with the description of his friend's brother. "I thought you said he's a geologist or a mining engineer, Doctor Hollis."

"They got different standards north of the border, Marko. Even you could get into a college up there."

"Give me a break, Doctor Hollis," Marko said with a laugh as he pushed him back toward the fireplace.

"Hey, I'm serious, Marko," Hollis replied. "You learn to skate real nice. Shoot a puck. Master a few Canadian phrases like, 'How 'bout a Molson, mate?' And maybe get a real shiny maple leaf on your lapel. You'll be in and probably at the head of the class, too. At least based on what I've seen from this Beaupré bunch."

Paul Beaupré came into earshot with the last sentence. "So, is he showing his poor upbringing and bad manners again, Marko?"

"Well, I'm trying to be serious about a serious thing and he's being …" Marko was groping for words as Hollis knelt down to tend to the fireplace.

"Say no more," Beaupré said. "I understand. What can I help you with, Marko? You know a favorite proverb here at the Main Post. 'Never send a boy to do a man's job.'" He flung the words of the last sentence at Doctor Hollis' back, as he was tending to the fireplace.

"Well," Mark said nervously. "It's about that vest-pocket discussion. Jean Luc's here. I just met him. You guys, I know. He's your brother and all. But I'm new to this problem and he's new to me."

Paul was quick to respond. "I see your point completely. When he comes back, we'll ask him to honor your request. It will be no problem. Jean Luc likes to tie flies. Hollis has a brand-new trout kit and a mounted vise in the guest room."

Hollis stood and faced both of them after finishing with the fireplace. "Look, I already told Mark, Jean Luc is twice as smart as his brother, so by morning he won't remember anything of note at all. Memory traces been banged up." Doctor Hollis paused for effect. "There have been too many hockey pucks to the cranium. It is a well-known syndrome north of Sault Sainte Marie, Marko, my boy. Remember, I'm a doctor."

Jean Luc closed the door to the hallway. He returned halfway to the living room. "Anyone want a mug of tea or hot chocolate? I am going to warm my innards against this wicked storm from the north."

The storm was lashing at the tree branches. Windblown rain was pelting the windows. It would be silent and calm for a while. Then a blast of wind would hurl rain against one whole side of the cabin.

"Marko, you need some more ginger ale?" Jean Luc raised his voice against the wailing of the huge tea kettle.

"Hey, thanks," Mark replied. "That'll be great."

"Brew a whole pot of tea and bring it in here when you're done, mon frère," Paul directed. "Put the kettle back on simmer too. The night is young and dry is the tongue."

Minutes later, Jean Luc had placed a ceramic teapot and mugs on the moose table in the space between their chairs and the fireplace. Mark had a fresh ginger ale. Jean Luc did not return to his chair, but to the kitchen.

Suddenly they all heard a whistle from the kitchen area. "Here, Marko!" Jean Luc underhanded a Granny Smith apple across the room to Mark. "I thought you might like some more dinner."

Hollis claimed a hot cup of tea and an apple. He resumed his position in his chair. Jean Luc took his seat.

Hollis spoke first. "Jean Luc, do you recall your first visit here some years ago? I introduced you to the Main Post, my cabin at the time, and I showed you our poem, the code among men at the Post." Hollis had a slightly elevated tone in his voice. It had the desired effect of getting Mark's attention.

"Why sure. I liked it a lot," Jean Luc responded. "It had both

The Snipe Hunters' Deadly Catch at Muskrat Creek

rhyme and reason to it. I believe it goes as follows." Jean Luc then recited the poem At the Main Post flawlessly.

Looking directly at Mark, Hollis announced with a mocking tone of admonishment. "You see, Marko. You should never underestimate our cousins to the north. Just because they spend far too much time around polar bears and not enough in the library does not mean we should question their potential. Jean Luc has been making fine progress ever since he started visiting the Au Sable river country. Am I right, Paul?"

Not allowing Paul time to respond, Hollis addressed Jean Luc directly. "You see, J. L., my young friend was admiring the poem and wondered if all the men who come here know it and abide by it." Taking a sip of his tea, Hollis commented to the room and no one in particular. "I always say, 'O ye, of little faith.'"

As Mark dug into his apple, Paul, in a low voice, averred. "Your call, Marko, is it time for some flies to get tied?"

Mark stood and looked at Hollis with a smirk on his face. He took another bite of his apple while fishing for something in his pocket. He finished swallowing. Then he pulled a slip of paper out. "No one's tying flies on my account."

He thrust the slip of paper into Paul Beaupré's lap, looked back at Doctor Hollis, and explained. "I found this note taped to the door of Room 216. I went to get the new kid for breakfast like we planned. A good time for the orientation talk is Saturday morning breakfast with no class commitments. Heck, it was to be his first breakfast at Bosco. Only no Kenny Dee was there, just this. Later I learned that Joe Duvalle never showed for breakfast either. They both went missing."

Mark walked closer to the fireplace. He turned and faced the men while warming his back. "Would you read it aloud, Paul?"

The room's only sounds were the rain being lashed against the windows from the darkening sky and the crackling fire behind Mark. Paul raised his voice and read each line slowly.

Paul concluded by observing to all. "It is written in pencil.

> Sat. 5:10 AM
>
> Mark,
> Left with Joe D.
> Sorry to miss the
> Pay-to-Play talk.
> Be back soon.
> I like Bosco.
> Help me stay.
>
> -Kenny

No spelling errors. No last names either."

"Read it again," Hollis commanded.

Afterward, Hollis addressed Mark.

"So, you have had this since breakfast, but you have told no one?"

Mark nodded in agreement.

Hollis continued, "You would have had it at the staff meeting then also? But at this point, no one at Bosco knows about this note?"

"Nope," Mark replied.

"Then you actually do know something that the Bosco folks and the sheriff don't know," Paul observed.

"Yup."

Mark stepped forward, looked at all three men, and then put his back up against the fire. "They are together. Wherever. Why ever, and however. They are together."

"Well, that would be important to know. I suppose some

have guessed that by now, though." Paul nodded to Mark. "Well, it seems logical, with Kenny being new."

"Yeah, but I didn't tell them at the staff meeting. I didn't tell Brother Ed on the phone just now. I could have. I just ... just ..." Mark's voice trailed off.

"Why not tell? Are you hiding something from the Bosco administration on behalf of Joe?" Hollis wondered aloud.

"Nope. Joe's no angel, but no, I'm not protecting him or privileged information. He has no hassles now like he had last year. I just wanted to see if I could keep the new kid out of trouble."

Paul nodded at Mark and rubbed his hands together. Mark explained some more. "I thought if I could get on top of this, get this situation in control, I could make it work for this kid, Kenny. I don't like my guys getting in trouble. I like to steer 'em right. That's my job. Bosco's made it nice for me. I wanna come through for them. I'm supposed to help keep my guys out of trouble. Steer 'em right. So, they graduate."

"Yeah, I see," Paul observed as he gulped some more tea.

Mark sighed. "It just seemed to get worse; each step of the way, each hour of the day. Cripes, I searched around. Talked to all the guys I know. But by noon, and after the staff meeting, things had really escalated. Sheriff Jalonick was called. I just froze inside when I heard about the missing person's report thing. I never thought it could be this ... bad. Man, where are those guys?" Almost wincing as he looked out the window. "Gosh, it's wicked out there now; almost dark, too."

Mark sipped his ginger ale. "I really let the staff down on this. I should have done more, and earlier. I had this darn AP test to take, too. Hard to think in French when I got a ping pong ball banging around in my skull saying, 'missing person, missing person.'"

Mark sipped again. "When they could not reach you guys, I volunteered to come here. I guessed you might be with Paul,

Judas Iscariot at Bosco Hall

Doctor. Plus, it seems logical that Joe might like to continue with his plan to canoe the Au Sable again. That's the one thing we do know he wanted to do this weekend."

"Yeah, well, take a look at that," Jean Luc pointed out the window. "Canoeing in this weather? Ain't no fish gonna bite now with the drop in temperature and all this rain. I just don't see it happening."

Mark resumed, "But I gotta assume that the new kid Kenny is with Joe, wherever that is. They covered all the places in town. Brother Ed said some folks volunteered to check the campgrounds, too. But we got nothing, nothing, and more nothing."

Sipping his ginger ale, Mark returned to his chair. "I just thought I could pull this off. Get the new kid out of trouble. Now I can't pull my own bacon out of the fire. I oughta lose my job for not telling Father George and Brother Ed about this sorry note. This ain't turning out like I thought. I was hoping, half-dreaming they'd be here frying up some trout with you guys."

Paul got up to stir the logs in the fireplace.

Jean Luc poured tea in everyone's mug. Then he pointed at Mark's ginger ale. "You ready for another one?"

Mark politely waved him off.

"Well, a cricket player would say, 'you got one sticky wicket' to grab hold of there, Marko," Jean Luc observed.

"Yup. Ya sure do," agreed Hollis. "But, if I heard you right, you did not lie. You just did not engage in full disclosure when you had the chance. Am I right, Marko?"

"Yeah, I guess. No one asked about a note, of course. I suppose a lawyer might build a defense for me. But really? I thought about it on my drive here. Our teachers will ask us to, 'walk a mile in the other man's moccasins' before making a judgment. In our theology and ethics classes, we are expected to make an argument that's the opposite of our own personal belief. That's a way to see a problem more clearly, they say."

"So, on your drive here; what did you come up with?" Paul asked.

"That I was wrong, that the Bosco staff and sheriff should have been told. Heck, I would want to know about the note if I was on the search team. I know that I was wrong for not telling them in the staff meeting; and again, just now on the phone with Brother Ed. I'm wrong."

"Yes, indeed, 'Bless me, Father, for I have sinned', eh? Isn't that the way you Catholics lead off in the confessional?" Hollis asked.

"Yup," Mark confirmed with a sigh.

"Hey, that's pretty good for a wayward Presbyterian there, Doc," Paul Beaupré chided.

"Who are you calling wayward, Beaupré?" Hollis shot back. "Why I probably have forgotten more than you know about moral issues and such."

"Well, Marko certainly has the makings of a moral dilemma on his hands. At least that's the view from my end of the canoe," Jean Luc asserted.

"I can see why you are so troubled," Paul admitted. "I would be too."

"Troubled ain't the half of it. When they find out, I might lose my job. My dad ... Well, my dad used to be proud of me for paying for my own room and board. Now Bosco has every right to fire me. I did not do my job."

"Well, I suppose one could ... " Hollis began.

Mark interrupted, "I did not uphold the standards of Bosco Hall. Here my dad's off in some far place risking his life for our country like my brothers and I flub up this assignment at Bosco Academy."

"What was your goal if you are not in on some lark with Joe Duvalle? Why are you carrying the mail for him? Protecting him? You owe him something?" Paul asked.

Judas Iscariot at Bosco Hall

"It's not him. He's made mistakes before. I've pulled his bacon out of the fire before, him and Saltz actually. It's the new kid. He's probationary. I don't and won't know his full record. Only that he comes from a hospital." Mark was unconsciously wringing his hands.

"Oh, I see," Hollis intoned. Then he and Jean Luc stood up, as if on cue, and teamed up. One held the screen back, and the other put a log on the fire. The fireplace was the only source of heat for the cabin and the night was getting progressively colder. They watched the fire in silence.

"We had one placement like that before," Mark continued. "They put Kenny on my floor on purpose. Father George met with me privately. I was to keep him on the straight and narrow. Aim him for success. I was the designated, senior RA, selected by Father George. And I lied."

"Well, now, young man, you just said you never got to give Kenny the down and distance, right? Your Bosco rules and regs talk. He didn't show for breakfast. I forget what it was. You called it something else," Jean Luc assessed.

'Yup. That's right. The guys call it my 'Pay-to-Play' talk. I let them know that I'll help them with the foolish things kids do. But if they bring drugs or alcohol on campus, I'm not going to bat for them. The fact is if they do that, I'll do everything possible to see that they get booted out."

"Good policy," Hollis confirmed.

"People do dumb things on booze and such. That's for sure," Paul confirmed.

"Dumb? You bet!" exclaimed Mark. "They hurt and kill other people driving cars. On campus they get into fights. Say stupid things. Get sick all over the place. Wreck their own chances in school and sports."

"Well, Marko, you are one seasoned piece of lumber for having lived such a relatively short time," Jean Luc commended him.

"Mr. Garson taught us about the noble Romans, soldiers, and

senators. You know, people like Cicero and that mean cat, Cataline. He showed us the values and mores in his times and all. Roman senators would choose to fall on their own sword rather than live a life of dishonor."

"I see." Jean Luc glanced at Mark and motioned for him to continue.

"Well, these boozers and druggies fall on their own sword for literally nothing. They wreck their own lives. Wreck other peoples', too."

Jean Luc had a look of interest and intrigue as if wanting to know about Mark's past. He leaned forward with a question on his lips.

Mark sat in his chair. He started to stare off into the fireplace.

"I see, Marko. I wonder—"

Paul stood up as if to tend the fire. He discreetly turned to face his brother and gave him a quick hand signal that said "Cut it!"

Then Paul faced the fire, moved the screen, and adjusted the logs.

Jean Luc looked at Mark. "So, you feel indebted to Bosco, you want to make your dad … I mean, keep your dad proud, and your original goal was to protect this Kenny. Keep him at Bosco?"

"Give me the note."

Jean Luc retrieved it from Paul's chair and handed it to Mark.

"See the last line?" Mark pointed to it.

"Yup. I see what you mean. It says, "Help me stay,"" Paul quoted.

'So, in the staff meeting, I actually had my hand right on it. It felt like it was burning or something. My hand got sweaty. I just thought I could come up with something to help out; like I did with Saltz and Duvalle last year."

"What did you do for them?" Paul asked.

"Well, after a game they got into a wrestling match with some

Judas Iscariot at Bosco Hall

town kids. They wrecked an old lady's garden, knocked down her fence, a trellis, and messed up her roses permanently. Father George got called and he took me to the scene. Identifying the only guys who played in town on that day pretty much narrowed the suspects down to my floor."

"Sounds like teenagers to me," Jean Luc said.

"Well, that old lady reminded me of my grandmother. Only ain't no one in love with flowers like that old lady. I did not think kicking Joe and Saltz off the team or restricting their privileges and passes was going to mean anything to her. Bosco paid for the trellis and fence repair of course, but ..."

"Never saw a rose grow up from a detention slip," Hollis noted.

"I saw her garage needed painting in a bad way," continued Mark. "She was a widow. I think I said that."

"You didn't," Paul observed.

"I knew our senior Scout troop was joining with the troop from the Lutheran Church in town for a community service project day. So, two weeks later, payback. The troop provided all the tools and materials and Joe and Saltz scraped and primed her garage. It took two days. They cleaned up the yard, too. The adults finished with the final coat of paint."

"Bet she was happy," Hollis concluded.

Mark laughed. "Yeah, well all the second-floor guys like to ask Joe and Saltz if they been out smelling roses lately."

"They got the message though I think," said Mark.

"Why?" Jean Luc questioned.

"About a week later, the old widow baked two huge cakes. Scoutmaster Bailey brought them over to Bosco. She said she wanted the 'ruffians' to have them. Brother Ed, in front of a full dining room, asked Joe and Saltz what should be done with the cakes. They looked at each other. Then they told Brother Ed that they wanted the other guys to have it for dessert, not them."

Mark paused and looked at Jean Luc. "That's why," Mark

asserted. "Dues paid. A lesson learned."

"'You play; you pay, eh, Marko?"

"Well, how am I gonna help Kenny and be true to Bosco? It's getting dark. I gotta call 'em back. I just don't have an answer. I sure got this all messed up. My supervisors, Brother Ed and Father George, must be told something."

"A mess, on a messy night, too, that is for sure," Jean Luc said. He stood, approached the fire, and looked out the window. The winds were lashing streams of rain against the windowpane.

"Wow, we need some more wood already. We have hungry flames tonight." He carefully deposited the last of the three logs that were adjacent to the fireplace when they'd started the 'popcorn' conference.

"Well, Marko, when do you have to call Bosco back?" Hollis asked.

"Inside fifteen minutes. I gotta call them by seven-thirty. Brother Ed figures Father George will be back with the sheriff by then. He believes Joe and Kenny will turn up somewhere around Bosco or the town, or the campgrounds, or at a friend's place. They were checking up on all that."

"So, Sheriff Jalonick thinks they'll show up someplace by dark, eh? Well, he's got the weather on his side. Exposure to this wind, rain, and sudden cold make survival an issue now. They'll have to seek shelter for the night," Paul reasoned.

Mark got up and walked to the fireplace. He put his back up against the fire and faced the three men. His bones told him his problem, the thorny question, the 'sticky wicket' in Jean Luc's mind, was best met with a warm back.

Squirming in his shoes, Mark recalled the day he pledged to fulfill his R.A. obligations and proudly signed his contract. That night he surprised his father, on a military assignment overseas, with a long-distance collect call. He happily announced that his room and board fees had dropped to zero. Now the "health and welfare of residents" clause echoed in his head along with

Judas Iscariot at Bosco Hall

visions of all the extra search efforts caused when he chose to pocket the note. His stomach tightened. He'd surely need a Philadelphia lawyer to retain his job now. Just what the heck am I gonna do?"

Jean Luc rose calmly, gathered apple cores and the popcorn bowl, and headed off to the kitchen. "I see my tea kettle is ready. Be right back, mes amis. I don't wanna miss 'Act Two.'"

"Yeah, J.L., my cup is empty and some hot tea might just warm my brain up here for Marko," Paul commented.

Hollis looked at his watch. He checked it against the U.S. Navy clock installed over the fireplace mantle. Then he walked over and flooded the porch with light. "It's dark before its time with all these clouds and rain. We could use some light on this problem, eh, Marko."

At least five minutes passed before Jean Luc returned with the steaming pot. He brought in a bowl of mixed nuts and a bowl of dried figs, dates, and apricots. He placed the tea in the middle. He set the bowls on either side. The wolf table looked rather inviting. "Ok, guys, hands off the goodies till the tea is done steeping."

Jean Luc then placed two cans of ginger ale on the table next to Mark's chair.

"What do I do? How do I handle this?" Mark asked. His eyes penetrated the sun-tanned face of Hollis. Then he glanced over at Paul.

"Well, Marko, it is not the fact you have a problem that counts, and you sure got one, but rather how you handle it," Hollis asserted. "I prefer the direct approach."

Looking at Paul to throw a life ring his way, Mark turned slightly in his direction.

"The good book says, 'The truth shall set you free.' You gotta fess up and face the music sometime, Marko. Earlier is better than later."

"So, I just tell the Bosco people that I got this note, but didn't tell them all day, because ...?"

Mark stopped and opened his hands toward them as if asking them to place an answer in the palm of his hand.

"You are not the Judas Iscariot of Bosco Hall. You just made an error in judgment," Jean Luc interjected.

Paul reasoned, "You wanted to play rescue, help that new kid. That I understand. But it's been hours, almost all day. They have not turned up. The night is upon us. It's an ugly, cold night and getting uglier; exposure to this without the right equipment ..."

"Face the umpire, Mark," Hollis addressed him rather formally. "You took your first at-bat on this problem and you struck out. It's that simple. You aren't getting to first base any time soon. This 'rescue the new kid approach' just is not working."

Paul continued. "It's understandable. You wanted the walk-off homer this morning, but now you are facing facts. You were fanned at the plate. You been sent to the dugout."

Mark looked down and felt positively sick. He felt his stomach knot as he pictured the face of Brother Ed. Just learning that Mark had the note since before eight o'clock would be devastating. Wow. Then the image of his father in his dress uniform flashed across his mind's eye. Next came a picture of his two brothers in their sparkling white Navy uniforms at the train station in Detroit. Dubays were honorable, reliable men who served—

Jean Luc abruptly disturbed his reverie. Lifting Mark's left arm, he turned his wrist and tapped on his watch. "Mark, you have five minutes to get to Hollis' phone. You must get dressed for this little jaunt, too."

"Yeah, you're right, I gotta ... I guess I'm going to have to ..." His voice trailed off as Jean Luc escorted him over to the clothes rack.

"Just what do I say? What about my dad? When he finds out?"

Paul put the poncho over Mark, he placed both hands on his

shoulders. Looking him in the eye, with Hollis standing behind him, he issued a command. "Marko, my boy, you got to focus. Concentrate on the job at hand. Do the best with what you have. You struck out on your first at-bat. Now you got a second trip to the plate. Make it count."

Reaching out, he gave Mark a piece of paper. "Here's your note back, Marko."

Mark grabbed it and crammed it into his pants pocket.

Paul nodded toward Mark's pocket. "After you get to the cabin, read the backside of that note before you call Bosco."

Hollis cautioned, "The truth, Marko, that'll make for a better second inning. Don't think about Brother Ed or your dad. You can't put a swing on a pitch that's not there yet. You gotta put your mind on what is coming at you now. You do what the rest of us do; we swing at them only when we see 'em. You got one job to do. Do it."

Stepping out onto the porch, Hollis held the door for Mark and concluded his advice, "Discipline that fine mind to do what is before you and nothing else."

Mark immediately thought of the French test. He had to physically force himself to focus then.

Mark pulled his shoes on. He stepped onto the porch while holding the door open and faced the men. "I see."

Handing Mark a large lantern-style flashlight, Jean Luc hooked his thumb in the direction of the dark sky.

"Remember your theology teacher. Think about the other guy. What if Kenny and Joe are out there, in this?"

Mark shook himself to get focused on his task. He turned the lantern on and trudged off into the rain. The wind was howling harder now than before.

The Snipe Hunters' Deadly Catch at Muskrat Creek

Chapter Ten

The Bad Breath Bandit

Saturday, September 29, 1979, 5:25 pm, Au Sable River

"Ya got a nice stroke there, Kenny. Your power is keeping us going upriver. I like how you paddle and don't chatter. Cowdrey is good, but he gives off a lotta chin music. I gotta settle him down. Some days he spooks the fish."

Joe expertly adjusted his paddle to guide the canoe in the middle of a large bend in the river with sand bars. There were low-hanging branches on both sides. "This is our last big bend. The next one will have the high rollway on the opposite bank. See that and you'll know we are there. We'll be stopping inside ten minutes, Kenny Boy."

Kenny smiled. He turned so Joe could see the side of his face still partially covered with the Au Sable Adventure hat.

"Yeah, well, okay. I like this. The Au Sable River is nicer than I imagined." Kenny projected his voice a little over the din of the gurgling river. "There's a lot of Christmas trees here, eh?"

In truth, his thoughts had retreated into the past again. Kenny's body was locked into a rhythm of paddling in the bow. His mind, lost among the leaves, had long since been captured by the yellow, burnt orange, and striking red colors of the Au Sable River forest entering the autumn season. This retreat found him back in Catalpa Falls at a river's edge picnic with his father, mother, and older cousins in the peaceful period before his father's death.

Dredging his mind up to face the present conversation was more effort than the previous hour's paddling. Kenny attempted to focus on the present. "So, what's a roll away?"

"Oh, gosh, there is a lot of lumbering history here, Kenny. You'll see soon enough. One look is worth a whole chapter. Just wait."

"Huh, I wish my American History course was like that. One look and you are done with a chapter. I might get to like that."

"Well, Kenny, there's a delightful display of history right at the end of your paddle. The lumber industry, the Indians' first contact with the French Missionaries, and the settlers of Michigan. You'd like the ninety-four miles of the amber-colored river Tahquamenon in the wilderness of the Upper Peninsula. Tahquamenon Falls is second only to Niagara Falls east of the Mississippi. We aim to canoe it next summer."

"Odd name there, Joe. How'd the river get colored amber?" Kenny asked.

"Tahquamenon comes from the Ojibwa name for amber; it shows up in a Jesuit Missionary's map from 1671. Trout rivers and streams are often surrounded by towering cedar, hemlock, and spruce forests that drain into them. Tannins in the trees leach into the water, making it amber or tobacco-colored. My Uncle Tom grew up on the banks of the Tobacco River in Midland County. Our environment is beautiful and you can have a lot of fun here."

Kenny agreed, "Canoeing here is neat."

"What were you studying before you came to Bosco?" Joe inquired.

"It was the Colonial period and the American Revolution," Kenny replied. "But I liked the book we read, 'Drums along the Mohawk.' Scenes in the book were like this forest. You know a family on the frontier, the very edge of the wilderness, but in New York. We got to see the movie on it just before I came here.

The Bad Breath Bandit

Teachers said the actors were famous back then, too. I do know that the lady, Claudette Colbert, a Frenchie, was popular at that time."

"Well, we got everything New York has, except maybe those falls at Niagara. We even got the border with our good neighbors in Canada. Yet, like I said the Upper Peninsula has the Tahquamenon Falls, though. Beautiful! Have you ever been to the U.P.?"

"Nope," Kenny replied while stroking his paddle.

"Hey, ya gotta go sometime," Joe advised. "Plus, we still got Indians. Like the Chippewa and Potawatomi Tribes with reservations right here in Michigan, Kenny Boy. They showed the French and English how to survive a Michigan winter. New York got any reservations?"

"Dunno, for sure. There were lots of Indians there during the Revolution though. That's for sure. So, are you all proud of Michigan or something, Joe?"

The canoe came in sight of a smaller bend in the river.

Joe abruptly stopped talking and sat up tall in the stern of the canoe. "Hey, Kenny Boy, we're here. School's out. Up with the paddle, I'll do the steering. Look up on those high cliffs to your left."

Kenny looked up and was puzzled as he sat back with his paddle across his knees. "Yeah, so what?"

"Well, ya asked what a rollway was. So, listen up while I steer. We're headed to that piled-up brush just past that downfall, halfway across the river. It's package time. See the spot?"

"Yup. I'm listening," Kenny replied.

"Well, picture Paul Bunyan standing on the top of that cliff. He just spent the morning chopping down an old-growth forest. One that's been here as long as that place in that Mohawk book you liked. He's cleaned off all the limbs and stacked them neatly at the edge of that cliff. Now he has to get them to a lumber mill a couple hundred miles away. So, what do ya think he's gonna do, Kenny Boy?"

Looking to his left at the high cliff, as they floated toward the opposite bank, Kenny guessed, "Push 'em off the cliff into the river?"

"Amen. Beats making Blue Babe or a team of horses the size of a regiment haul them. Plus, ya gotta feed Blue Babe and horses. The river will just push 'em along, slow but steady. All the way down stream and out to Lake Huron, eventually. Well, the lumberjacks of old just rolled them down the cliff with their high banks. Then the river floated them away. Floating logs was about the only easy thing in a lumberjack's life."

Joe halted briefly while beaching the canoe on the sandy bank.

"When you get Paul Beaupré in front of a roaring fire some time, ask him about the river runners. Best storyteller ever. He's Canadian. He knows Michigan, Ontario, and Quebec history. He knows all about the Indians. The voyageurs and French priests were actually the first to explore this country. A priest was the first European on the Mississippi." Joe paused. "Ever wonder what it would be like to be the first guy to meet a Huron or Iroquois Indian in the middle of this huge forest? Or the first guy to learn from the Indians how to build a canoe? Father Jacques Marquette explored all over this state, others too. We got a river, a college, and a city named after him. Imagine being the first European to see the Mississippi River."

"He did all that?" Kenny wondered.

"It was not easy. Hey, they had cannibals on the Mississippi back then. Beaupré read Marquette's journal to us."

Joe rested his paddle across the gunnels and quietly announced, "You can get out now."

"Well, am I right?" Kenny asked. "We don't have any cannibals on the Au Sable nowadays?"

"Nope."

"But, hey, Joe, you get me any hungrier …" Kenny warned.

The Bad Breath Bandit

Smiling, Kenny stepped on the solid ground of the riverbank. Then he pulled the canoe up on shore with the rope. He stretched his legs and looked back up the river as he bent and limbered up his back. "Wow. Look at those dark clouds following behind us, Joe."

"Yup. And the bad news is once we get our package, we'll be paddling right toward them. The good news is we'll be going downstream. Going back to the Quonset hut will be twice as fast as coming. Thank God, too, since it is going to get dark sooner tonight."

"Now, see that white handkerchief tied up there on the branch of a pine tree?" Joe pointed inland and upriver a little to a small clearing. "Look at that fallen white birch on the ground in front of the big red pine tree. Follow my finger from the ground up that pine. See, just to the left?"

Kenny saw the soggy white cloth fluttering just a little in the breeze. He nodded at Joe.

"Okay. Now we go twenty of my paces upriver from there and we get our package. Follow me."

Kenny traipsed along behind Joe at a steady pace. The wet bracken ferns soaked their pants below the calf with every step. Joe's pace slowed as he positioned himself right under the handkerchief. Then he marched upstream counting his steps.

Looking over the edge of a depression Joe began to pull apart a pile of fallen branches that had been mounded up. "Good thing I listened to Cowdrey and got this thing up and away from the river."

The top of a large, square cardboard carton encased in plastic came into view.

Kenny exhaled thinking to himself, "Finally, now we can get that thing in the canoe and get out of this weather. I'll be happy to get back to Bosco where I started." He stepped closer for a better look.

Joe pulled branches and threw them to one side. He freed up

one side of the large cardboard box. Then he pulled it up out of the gully and level with the high ground where they were standing.

It reminded Kenny of the crates and boxes he had seen off-loaded from trucks while walking with Ho Ho, his favorite therapist at Havenwood State Hospital. In block red letters Kenny could read a label even though it was upside down.

"Phillip Morris. What's that, a whole bunch of tobacco?" Kenny demanded. "What's it doing here?"

Joe, pushing the box in Kenny's direction, replied without looking up. "Dunno. Cowdrey and me found it in the river last week like I said. Heck, I don't know how it got way out here in the sticks. Lord knows there ain't no semi-trucks floating on the Au Sable. But I do know we can make some money. I can guarantee ya that!"

"You smoke?" Kenny asked as he lifted his end of the carton. They began a slow walk back to the tree and then turned toward the canoe. Joe led the way with his back to the river.

"No way! I'm out for three sports. I can't even inhale. Cowdrey jives me about it all the time. 'A real man knows how to inhale!' Heck, all I can do is cough with that stuff."

"So, Cowdrey smokes?"

"He does, but never on Bosco's campus, only in town and on visits. That's our plan. Sell this stuff to the townies. Make some easy money. We can beat the party store price and make some dough," Joe continued while holding up his end of the carton. "Tobacco and alcohol will get you booted out of Bosco. Ain't that right? I never got to hear Dubay's 'Pay to Play' talk, but I figure tobacco would be a huge violation."

"That and drugs. That's how we lost 'Boston Bob.' You are right, Kenny Boy. That's pretty good thinking for being a new boy. From my end of the canoe, you are starting to smarten up."

"I know rules from big places. You need to know that I spent three years in a hospital, Joe. Stuff like that ain't going to fly with

The Bad Breath Bandit

teachers and counselors."

Reaching the riverbank, Joe motioned for Kenny to set the cardboard box down. "I'll pull the stern of the canoe in so we can load this thing. You reach in the outside pocket of the backpack right on top and get the nylon ropes out."

A gentle but cold drizzle began to increase in intensity as Joe and Kenny positioned the box in the center of the canoe, the only place wide enough for it.

They did not hear the drone of the approaching riverboat until it rounded the bend. They both looked up at the same instant.

Joe noticed it was coming right toward their spot on the riverbank. The riverboat was long, cigar-like in shape, and bigger than Doctor Hollis'. The four men in it were dressed unlike any locals. They all wore big dark sunglasses.

Joe, observing their approach with his hands on his hips for a moment, scanned the length of the boat. He cautioned Kenny in a low voice from his end of the canoe. The clothing he saw did not spell river or forest. "Kenny, it ain't been sunny for hours. This ain't fishing weather. They ain't even got fishing gear. Those ain't outdoorsmen. Something ain't right. Stay cool."

Sweating, a chill shot up his spine as Joe reached into his backpack hoping to find something to cover the carton before they arrived.

The riverboat cut its engine about ten yards offshore. The bow of the boat knifed into the sand just behind the stern of the canoe. A large man in the bow of the boat was out of the boat and into the water before it stopped. Ignoring Joe and Kenny, he advanced straight for the bow of their canoe and took possession of the rope on the crossbar. The second man out of the boat took possession of the rope in the stern of the canoe. Standing a head taller than Kenny, he looked down at him as if waiting for Kenny to challenge him for possession of the canoe.

Joe and Kenny were tongue-tied and frozen in place as the

The Snipe Hunters' Deadly Catch at Muskrat Creek

The Bad Breath Bandit

third man stepped into the shallow water. He was large, with a poorly groomed beard, and wore a dirty olive drab Army surplus fatigue jacket like the other men. He went to the center of their canoe on the river bank. The fourth man, manning the engine in the stern, remained seated.

"Number Three," standing in between them, spoke with an accent that was hard to identify. "Seems like you boys did us a favor, finding something we lost."

Then Number Three pulled a switchblade from his jungle fatigues. He looked Joe right in the eye. He waited for Joe to look down at the knife. Then he released the switch and the blade sprang forth. He looked down at the long blade. Then he looked slowly up at Joe. He slit the nylon ropes securing the carton to the canoe. He closed the knife but held it in his hand. The motion was very deliberate and methodical. Slowly he looked back up at Joe.

He slid the knife back in his pants, and then looked directly at Joe. Patting the pocket with the knife in it he spoke to Joe. "Now, boys, I'm not needing this more today. You think, too? You agreeing with me? Yes?"

Joe stood frozen in place. He said nothing.

Number Three man hoisted the Phillip Morris box over his head as if doing a clean and jerk move in the gym. He took several steps backward, turned, and placed the carton in the center of the riverboat. The motorman moved forward and took control of the box. The very 'package' Joe and Kenny had worked so hard to locate was now in their riverboat.

Number Three returned to the same spot. He looked as if he was addressing Joe. But he gave a command in a foreign tongue. Loudly.

With one swift motion, the man at the bow reached down and took Joe's paddle.

An instant later, "Number Two," a rotund man with a scraggly beard near Kenny reached into the stern of the canoe

The Snipe Hunters' Deadly Catch at Muskrat Creek

for the paddle near Kenny. Kenny alertly grabbed it at the same time.

"Hey, that's mine," Kenny announced and held tight.

The bearded man said nothing but started to pull the paddle toward him. He almost dragged Kenny with it.

Kenny initially resisted. Then, at the height of the big man's powerful pull, Kenny deliberately let go, accelerating the backward motion of the big man. Kenny, standing right next to the large man, swiftly swung his leg around behind the big man. With a powerful upward motion of his leg, he swept the man's ankle off the ground and into the air. The big man catapulted backward with his own force. It thrust him back, minus one leg for support. He thudded onto the riverbank and partially into the water, landing squarely on his butt. His head snapped into the hard ground. The paddle was thrown into the water. It floated up to the feet of their leader, Number Three.

Grunting to regain his feet due to a sizable beer belly, "Number Two" began cursing in an unknown language. He stood up and wiped the mud off his hands. He lunged toward Kenny.

Number Three barked another order in a foreign tongue. The bearded Number Two man stopped a foot away. With foul-smelling breath, he cursed Kenny, but he did not hit him.

Number Three unzipped his Army fatigue jacket and took a step toward Joe. He opened his jacket wide by putting both hands on his hips. It revealed a large leather holster on his left hip. The silver and black pistol was holstered for one using the right hand.

"You want I should teach you boys better manners?" He tapped his holster. "My friend here teaches good lessons. It is not wise to make my friend angry. Don't you think?"

Staring straight at Joe, he seemed to expect a reply.

"Well, look, mister, we don't want no trouble. Phillip Morris is all yours. We just found it and ..." Joe was stammering with

The Bad Breath Bandit

his eyes fixed on the pistol.

"This is good. No trouble. Best you to choose no trouble. I like this. 'No trouble' is good, yes?" Then he patted his holster and addressed the holster as if it were listening. "You hear, my friend? No trouble for you today!"

Number Three nodded at Joe as if he were a teacher showing approval for an answer. With an unruly mustache, a missing front tooth, and at least three days' growth on his beard, his smile did little to comfort Joe.

Number Three addressed the two men at each end of the canoe. They took the canoe paddles and put them in the riverboat. Kenny noticed that the motorman had already strapped the carton down and resumed his seat in the stern. The straps, with quick-release buckles, were already installed on the gunnels.

The two men returned to the canoe and looked up at Number Three. A discussion erupted between the men with a lot of gesturing back and forth. Their arms pointed toward the river and back at the canoe. They pointed to Joe and Kenny. They pointed to the forest behind Joe and Kenny. They pointed at their backpacks.

Joe did not understand a word, but he could tell that the two men disagreed with Number Three. Yet Number Three seemed to be in command.

Joe, already tense and scared, felt his stomach muscles tighten. This debate, with words unknown to him, was clearly aimed directly at him, his canoe, and his new friend, Kenny.

After Number Three seemed to repeat his words with emphasis, the two men shrugged their shoulders. They ceased talking. They walked to each end of the canoe and reached into their pockets. "Number one" pulled out his switchblade first.

Number Three quickly barked another command. The two men looked at each other. They looked at Joe and Kenny. They shrugged their shoulders again. They put their knives away.

The Snipe Hunters' Deadly Catch at Muskrat Creek

Number Three spoke again, as if giving instructions. The men unstrapped their backpacks from the thwarts. As they gripped the backpacks close to their chests, there was a loud crack of thunder on the river. Everyone except the motorman sitting in the stern of the riverboat looked at the approaching storm. A steady drumbeat of rain started.

Number Three spoke rapidly. Number One and Number Two quickly threw the "Au Sable Adventure" backpacks over the canoe into the bushes further up the riverbank. Number One grasped the rope in the bow of the canoe. He waded out toward the riverboat.

Number Two, seething with only slightly dampened anger, glowered at Kenny. He gripped the rope in the stern and followed along. They tied the canoe to the stern of the riverboat. They took their seats in the riverboat. The motor came to life.

The man in the stern reversed the engine. He aligned the riverboat broadside to the riverbank about ten feet off shore. The two men held the Silver Beaver canoe alongside. The riverboat completed its maneuvering. It pointed upriver.

Number Three stepped to the side of the riverboat and then turned to look at Joe. "You make canoe riding here but," with a shrug of his shoulders, he looked at Joe as if explaining a change of plans for a tourist, "all done for canoe riding today. You go home other one way now, my friend."

Patting his now-covered holster, he winked at Joe. "That way you make my friend here happy. Best to keep him happy, yes? How you say it? 'No trouble' that way."

Number Three took his place in the riverboat. He looked Joe in the eye, though Joe could see little through his large sunglasses. He raised his hand and gestured toward the sky. "Coming is storm. Some danger for you on river. We left packs for you. Maybe good to make a camp now. Today is best for walking home, boys." Then he spoke once again to his men. The engine got louder.

The Bad Breath Bandit

The riverboat backed up a little and positioned Number Three man closer to Kenny. Looking directly at Kenny, he spoke loudly over the noise of the engine. "You, boy, getting better manners now, yes?" Patting his holster, he smiled broadly at Kenny.

The engine revved up and went forward. The riverboat angled out into the middle of the river and turned upstream with the Silver Beaver trailing along from the stern.

Kenny looked at Joe.

Joe was bewildered. The ugly python of fear gripped his body. The image of the pistol stymied all thought. Yet his mind rummaged around for answers. Joe looked back at at Kenny. He had no answers for his unspoken questions. All was silent except for the ever-increasing patter of the rain on the river. Then there was the decreasing drone of the riverboat now out of sight.

Joe relieved his tense muscles by physical activity, pacing up and down the riverbank. He stretched his arms straight up to the sky. He thrust his elbows back like he did for gym warm-ups. The blood started to flow throughout his body and mind. Thoughts started to race faster than his steps.

Kenny's body stood motionless in the cold rain. Yet all his senses were vibrating and alive. His eyes were filled with the image of the pistol and his nose with the foul odor of the bully who took his paddle. Number Three's comment about "manners" ricocheted off the insides of his skull. His whole body seized up even more when that recurring image of the blood dripping off the porch once more lurched into his consciousness.

Joe's pacing quickened, with the rain cooling him through his poncho. "Problems always have solutions." Like a schoolboy conjugating verbs in a foreign tongue, he sounded it out. "Problems have solutions."

Louder and with more vigor he sent the message to his brain.

He doggedly drove his feet into the earth. Likewise, he drove the message into his brain. "Problems have solutions. Problems have solutions."

Instructions from his Au Sable Adventure training started to echo out from the deep recesses of his mind. His mind was starting to thaw out from the fear instilled by the men in the riverboat. The first problem was tapping him on the shoulder. His brain announced, "That storm is going to hit us full force pretty soon."

Kenny wrested free of his thoughts and stepped directly in front of Joe. "Hey, Joe, what are we gonna do now?"

Fast as a coiled rattler, Joe snapped, "Shut up, Kenny. I gotta think." Joe waved him off with his hand and continued to pace.

Kenny looked lost and bewildered. He stood off to one side with the rain beating down on his hat and poncho.

After five minutes of pacing, Joe walked over to Kenny. He cuffed him on the shoulder like a coach on the sidelines. "Hey, I don't mean nothing. I just gotta think. They taught us how ... I just gotta think. There is always a way," Joe said as he paced intensely in front of Kenny.

"A way? You got a way? Yeah, sure. You had a way to make some money, too. Now 'pistol man' and the 'bad breath bandit' got our canoe."

Joe ignored him and tended to his thoughts. "I gotta do this. They taught us how."

Pacing more deliberately, and with his hand on the back of his neck, he muttered aloud, "Adapt, cope, innovate. Adapt, cope, innovate."

"What's that?" Kenny asked. "You praying or something?"

Joe waved him off and continued to pace. He tried to line up his problems and address them in order of importance, like a card player valuing the hand he'd been dealt. But the problems seemed to come at him like major-league pitches. The pitches came from the north and they came from the south. And he knew he didn't even have a bat.

Focusing on the pitches as he saw them, Joe lined them up in order of immediate importance. "Well, I got the storm, nightfall, the distance to the Quonset hut, and the loss of the canoe." He was really stuck on the last problem. "I ain't never been on the river without a canoe. There's no bushwhacking through this wilderness to the Quonset hut in the dark."

Joe kicked a stump. "Plus, there's the new boy, Kenny." His last thought was the image of the holster with the silver and black pistol. He forced his mind toward a solution. "Adapt, cope, and innovate. It's my job to get a grip on this."

Stopping mid-stride, Joe looked at, but really through, Kenny. "That's it!"

"What? What's it?"

Joe sprinted to the place on the bank where the canoe had been. He paced to the site where the center of the canoe had been located. Joe thrashed about in the bushes until he found the backpacks. He returned to the shoreline again.

"Here is yours." Joe thrust Kenny's backpack toward him. "Rule number one in the woods, Kenny. Stay dry." He winked at Kenny as warmth returned to his aching limbs.

"Yeah, well. What is the golden rule when it's getting dark and you are in a cold rainstorm that is getting worse? Plus, you are on a river with no canoe? Just what does Daniel Boone have to say now? And be sure one of your brilliant ideas includes the word dinner."

"It is time for some frontier-style bushwhacking, Kenny," Joe announced. "Put your backpack on. Take your socks off and put 'em in the pack. Roll your pants up past your knees. Put your shoes back on. Be glad your backpack is waterproof."

With a dubious look on his face Kenny complied with Joe's directions. As he hoisted his backpack on he grunted, "Dang, this thing is heavy."

"Be happy. You got useful stuff on your back now, Kenny

The Snipe Hunters' Deadly Catch at Muskrat Creek

Boy." Joe led off down to the shoreline.

Kenny got in behind Joe. They stayed on drier ground near the river's edge when the brush permitted. They splashed into the river, pushed the brush, and waded up to their knees when the forest's edge met the river. Kenny, wearing gym shoes good only for running, found the large rocks slippery. He lost his balance several times.

Joe climbed over a log and there, looking him in the eye through the rain, was a surprised doe. She froze in place.

A family of mallards became his companions. They skirted the bank of the river when the terrain allowed. Daylight was slipping away.

A lightning flash of red out on the river caught Kenny's eye. He mouthed aloud what his startled mind thought, "What the heck could that be?"

Kenny jerked to the left to see a canoe hurtling downriver with two men feverishly paddling in the rain. Kenny's heart leapt into his throat. "Rescue is at hand," his mind screamed.

Kenny hollered loudly, "Hey, guys! Over here! Help! We lost our canoe." He took his hat off. He waved it wildly to get their attention. He heard only his own voice. He frantically searched for Joe a couple yards ahead of him. He was climbing over a dead tree with his head pointed inland.

Joe stopped once he had gained his footing on the other side of the dead tree. He looked at Kenny. Then he looked out onto the river. His mouth opened wide. "Hey, over here!" He waved his arms in 'jumping jack' fashion. He screeched, "Stop. Over here. Help!"

The men in the canoe stroked their paddles in rhythm, staring straight ahead. Joe and Kenny instinctively ceased hollering at the same time. With hearts in their throats, they watched the canoe disappear downriver.

Joe felt defeated. He turned his head to one side with a look of self-disgust and stood in place for a moment as if studying a branch or a twig at his side.

Joe looked apologetically at Kenny. He put his hands on his hips. "Aw, cripes! It's my fault!" Joe looked off over the river dejectedly. Like a batter knowing he swung at a bad pitch, he shook his head while his insides winced in pain.

Kenny walked up to the dead tree and made ready to crawl over. "Ya figure with the wind and rain, and natural noise of the river they couldn't hear us?" Kenny offered.

"No. No. It's all my fault. Of course, they can't hear. They only got seconds to look up at the right spot anyway. We are just two short images against a tall wall of forest. It's getting dark anyway. But it's my fault. I'm not thinking like I've been trained. I gotta get with it here. 'You think clear in the woods or you die.' They taught us that."

Then Joe stepped toward Kenny with the dead tree between them. "Stay on that side but come to me."

Kenny stepped forward, still looking wistfully out at the river.

"Now turn around," Joe ordered. "Get your backpack in my face." Joe unzipped the outer pocket on the top flap and quickly zipped it back up. Then he slowly guided Kenny by his backpack and carefully turned him around to face him. "Here. Wear this around your neck." Joe handed him a bright yellow whistle on the end of a lanyard.

He handed him two plastic armbands. Colored in hunter orange there was no blending in with the forest now. "Slip these on and get ready to wave your arms if we see anybody else."

Joe turned around and put his backpack facing Kenny with the tree between them. "Go to the outside pocket," Joe said. "Top flap. Unzip. Leave the compass, mirror, matches, and other junk alone. Just get me my stuff. Zipper it back up."

Kenny handed him his gear. He looked at Joe with tired and sad eyes. "Man, we could have used these! We coulda' got their attention, Joe."

The Snipe Hunters' Deadly Catch at Muskrat Creek

"Yup. You're right. Now, remember. It was an aluminum canoe and from Bucky's Mountainside Canoes. Those guys looked like fishermen, but I could not tell for sure. They had poncho hoods, too. Hearing our voices was not in the cards today."

Joe stepped away from the dead tree. He shoved his yellow whistle into his chest pocket. "Ya coming my way?"

Searching his friend's eyes, Joe continued, "I got a plan, Kenny."

Kenny glared at his friend. He spoke with a vehemence born of frustration, "You? You got a plan? So, you got a ... another plan! How about we talk about this one? From my end of the canoe, which I can't sit in anymore, you ain't batting a thousand on this here plan."

Joe burst into laughter. Then the dam of tension within Kenny released as he realized how sarcastic he had been. He laughed just as hard as Joe.

Both boys were still laughing as the sun slipped behind the clouds. The twilight darkened, enhanced by the storm's clouds. The tall forest loomed over them. The last glimmers of light for this tiring day were soon to be swallowed up by an inky, dark night.

"Well, jeez, Joe. We are in the wilderness, on a river with no canoe, night is coming, and the storm is getting worse, not better. Heck, just where the Sam Hill are we?" Kenny pulled his backpack tighter by cupping his hands under the straps. He gestured toward the dimming sky. "Look, I'm supposed to be happy because Mr. Daniel Boone just handed me a whistle?" Desperation invaded Kenny's mood.

That desperation radiated directly into Joe's soul. "Hey, you are right. We gotta get out of this rain and find a spot for the night. No way can we bushwhack these woods to the Quonset hut at night. There is no path from here, that's for sure," Joe confessed.

The Bad Breath Bandit

"So, what the heck is this plan?" Kenny demanded. "I'm hungry, tired of being in the cold rain, and I really don't think there's a Holiday Inn around the bend."

"I'm sorry. I've been terrible at this. And you are right; my batting average is pretty poor. This ain't been what I had in mind. The freaky storm came. The tobacco bandits came. They got our canoe. Now I really gotta use my training. But cripes," Joe said holding his whistle. "I did not even do that right. I'm supposed to adapt to my situation and use my resources. Expect problems. The minute you hit the woods expect your plans to fall apart. 'You will encounter the unexpected. Bet on it.' So, adapt, cope, and be prepared to innovate. Beaupré and Doc Hollis drilled that into us. They would not be proud of me now."

"Yeah, well. Beaupré and Hollis ain't here now. We are. You mentioned a plan?" Kenny demanded.

"Yup. Well, on Au Sable Adventure I did two solos on this very stretch of river; this part of the forest. It's a desolate area. I saw almost no people on land both times. Well, we ain't supposed to talk to anybody on solo anyways. That's solo rules," Joe reported.

"Ahh, you were going to tell me about how …" Kenny reminded him.

"Look, on solo, you are by yourself for three complete days and four nights. I did a lot of exploring. They call it orienteering. I know there is an old logging road within a half a mile from here. Actually, it's on both sides of the river. I think that's where Mr. Pistol Man might take out our canoe."

"So, how's a logging road going to help us?" asked Kenny. "We're still in the wilderness part of the forest, right?"

"Yup. The road doesn't go anywhere, not anymore at least. But while doing land navigation and compass work, I discovered an abandoned shack up the road in a clearing. It was originally built by the railroad company. Now it's used by deer hunters. They keep it up. It ain't pretty, but it is sound. It has a solid roof. If we can get there, that's something we could use right now."

"A roof? Dang right. Lead on, Mr. Boone. I'm all set for your version of the Holiday Inn of the Au Sable River Forest," Kenny snorted with a hint of mockery.

Once they cleared the dead tree and headed downstream Joe cautioned, "Keep close. Step where I step, cause there's holes."

The shadows got longer as Kenny sought to stay close and copy Joe's steps. Joe's pace was steady and sure. It was also accompanied by a sort of droning noise. It seemed like Joe was talking to himself in a methodical way with measured pauses. Though curious, Kenny did not want to stop progress with a question. He reasoned that it must have something to do with that Au Sable Adventure training he went through. Anyway, pushing through the bushes with the patter of the rain on his poncho hood made it hard to hear his own thoughts. Joe's methodical mumbling would have to wait.

They splashed forward on the river's edge when necessary and walked the riverbank when the forest allowed until there was a distinct opening. Joe quickened his pace and advanced up the riverbank and inland. "Great. This is it! See?" he asked while pointing across the river.

Kenny turned as he ascended the riverbank and stood next to Joe. The forest had obviously been cleared and a road put down some time ago.

"So, your good friend Paul Bunyan was here, eh?" Kenny joked.

"Something like that. Not far now, Kenny Boy. Less than a half a mile, maybe a quarter up this road. It's more like a path now. But I was up it a lot on solo. See that huge blue spruce, the one blown over by a storm?"

Joe pointed to a very large tree bent halfway to the ground by a fierce storm or tornado. It was not dead. With one half of its root structure dead and pulled out of the ground and one half

The Bad Breath Bandit

still vibrant and in the ground, it was alive. It was growing but at an odd angle. It, along with the smaller trees that had fallen on it and died in the storm, created an umbrella in the forest. A tangle of vines had grown, creating protection from the rain as effective as the roof of a porch.

"Yup. I see it."

"Let's go." Joe led the way to the half-dead tree twenty yards up the path inland.

Kenny got under the tree as quickly as he could.

"Look, Joe, no rain!" Kenny held out his hand in triumph.

"Yeah, well don't get comfortable. We are on our way shortly. Take your pack off and get your lunch out. We eat here. We don't have far to go. Daylight's gone and it is awfully cloudy. No luck there."

Both boys tore into their sack lunches like two wolves surrounded by hyenas waiting to steal a spare morsel from a fresh kill.

When Joe finished, he reached into his pack and retrieved a headlamp. He demonstrated its use to Kenny. "Now get yours from the lower-left outside pocket and strap it on. We'll need some light until we get to the shed. Follow me when you're ready."

Kenny located the headlamp and copied Joe. He put his hat on and then installed the headlamp on the headband of his hat above the brim. He hoisted his backpack onto his shoulders and looked at Joe. Joe led them out from the bent tree umbrella into the darkness and cold rain.

The tunnel of light from the headlamp allowed Kenny to see the narrow way behind Joe. He was warmed by the short rest and strengthened by the food. He found walking on the path much easier than bushwhacking by the river's edge.

The path rose upwards for the length of a football field and then leveled out. Joe quickened his pace. He veered a little left. Kenny saw the shape of a roof in a clearing.

"Thank God you found it!" Kenny shouted.

Getting closer Joe exclaimed, "Man, the hunters even added a porch since I was here."

Kenny marched straight for the nearest end of the porch to finally get out of the rain. He swung his backpack off. He scurried toward the enclosed end of the porch. It blocked the windblown rain somewhat. Seasoned wood was neatly stacked on that side of the porch.

After a few minutes, Kenny realized that Joe was not in sight.

A shrieking sound at the open end of the porch brought Kenny to his feet. Tense and frightened, he faced a dark figure and movement coming at him by focusing his headlamp.

Shaking a stick with a key attached to it, Joe blew his whistle one more time. "Hey, lookie here, Kenny Boy. The Holiday Inn is open. Follow me."

Joe went around to the opposite side. He slid the key in an ancient, knotty pine door on the old storage shed. They quickly entered, deposited their packs, and took off their wet ponchos.

"Well, Daniel Boone, this is the only good news of the day. Jeez, how'd you do it?' Kenny was shivering. "It is great to be out of that cold rain."

Joe's headlamp was circling the four walls. He looked around first at the potbellied stove and then at the waist-high benches with storage underneath.

"We are in luck because deer season is upon us." Joe clutched a kerosene lantern and placed it on the knotty pine picnic table in the center of the room. He was exultant. "God Bless the deer hunters. Shut your headlamp off, Kenny, and go grab some of the dry leaves and sticks from the porch. We even got some split logs inside here."

A little kerosene helped advance the fire in the ancient potbelly stove. Twenty minutes later, Joe and Kenny were huddled near the stove, soaking up the radiant heat and mesmerized by the flickering flames. Joe and Kenny sat entranced by the stove's

The Bad Breath Bandit

magic. Heat transferred from the wood directly to their chilled bones.

Kenny's questions could wait. There was no energy for talking.

Warmth began to course through his body. The comfort signals reached his brain. His muscles relaxed. Kenny fell asleep sitting on the bench with his head in his hands and elbows on his knees.

Joe forced himself up and scouted around the shed. Returning to the bench, he nudged Kenny awake. "Hey, Kenny Boy, the Holiday Inn is short of some bedding, but this will do. Besides, we are warm and dry."

Kenny snatched the rug out of Joe's hand and poured himself onto the floor. He put his back toward the hot stove and pulled the doormat under him.

Rhythmic breathing and rain pounding down on the roof were the only sounds that accompanied Joe's murmured prayers of thanksgiving. Overwhelming fatigue gripped his body. The stove's warmth hastened the arrival of a deep sleep.

Kenny's eyes closed immediately. "Good enough."

The Snipe Hunters' Deadly Catch at Muskrat Creek

Chapter Eleven

Time to Hug a Cactus

Saturday, September 29, 1979, 7:55 pm, Paul Beaupré's Cabin

"Man, it's freezing on this porch," Jean Luc exclaimed as the three men turned to leave the porch for the warmth of the cabin. "Look at that gauge. It's thirty-four degrees. Be worse out in the wind. Isn't this the twenty-ninth of September?"

"Shut the blasted door and get some more wood," exclaimed Doc Hollis. "Better turn the heat on for bedtime, Paul. It'll be cold up in the bedrooms without the furnace."

"Sweet dreams, my friend," said Paul. "The fuel oil gets delivered on October first or within forty-eight hours following that date. Don't you have Clem delivering for you, also?"

"Sure, but I thought you were smarter than me. Well now, so you fell for that silly discounted contract thing, too. Ten percent off if you pay in the spring and take delivery on his convoluted fall schedule?"

"Heck, yes," Paul replied. "I only deal with Clem because he's the minister's brother. Lord knows, no one is setting their watch by his truck. Once he showed up with half a load."

"Some say the Good Lord only gave that boy a half a load period," Hollis retorted.

The two men scurried in to warm their backs by the fire. They grabbed handfuls of nuts and dried fruits. Standing and soaking up the heat, they gulped down their dinner with mugs of hot strong tea. Privately, they considered Mark's plight, but they did not speak of it for several minutes.

Jean Luc retrieved the last of the wood from the wood box. He stacked it carefully beside the fireplace. "That ought to do it."

"Hardly. Wood's all we got to get through the night," Paul advised his brother. He walked across the room and latched open the door leading onto the expansive porch. "C'mon. We got a backup supply on the west end of the porch. Let's get to it. No use having all the cold air in the county coming in here tonight."

The three men hauled logs and re-filled the rather large wood box adjacent to the fireplace. No one spoke of Mark. Paul closed the box. Each man placed their leather gloves, one on top of the other, next to the wood box. They'd surely be using them in the morning.

Grabbing a handful of nuts, Hollis took his seat and broke the silence. "Sure wish you Canadians would keep your weather to yourselves. I got five good months of Michigan winter coming and I hardly need a cameo appearance in September."

"Boy, ain't that right. And Mark's Bosco buddies will be in a heap of trouble out in this. Do you think they've got someplace to go?" Jean Luc wondered as he stretched out with a few Medjool dates in his hand.

Hollis stared straight into the crackling fire. "I really don't know what two kids would be up to on a venture like this and on a weekend like this. Joe's a good Scout. He's a fair student. Heck, I know he avoids study. But he's not dumb. What would he be doing? He could not have left Bosco by car. The security staff would see them. But really, whose car would they have anyway? But fishing? Canoeing? If you've got the good sense that God gave a goose, you'd be home by a fire tonight."

"Be good to be a goose tonight," Paul offered.

"Hey, don't be insulting. Canada geese know enough to fly south eventually," Jean Luc joked.

Time to Hug a Cactus

Hollis nodded at him. "You got that right, Mr. Maple Leaf."

><

Outside, Mark plunged onto Partridge Path, which connected the two cabins. Holding the lantern before him to avoid roots and fallen limbs, he was almost oblivious to the high winds bending the trees. He was formulating his first sentence to Brother Ed. His stomach muscles tightened every time he pictured Brother Ed's face. The conference at Beaupré's cabin confirmed his fears. He had to face it. He had to confess his error. He forced his body toward the phone at Hollis' cabin.

Bounding up the stairs, Mark crossed the porch. He quickly removed his wet clothes once inside. He snapped on one light then set the lantern on a table near the door. Grabbing the phone was like hugging a cactus.

He recalled his parish priest coaching up the class on the sacrament, teaching them how to make a good confession. "First, you have to conquer the worst of the seven deadly sins: pride. You have to admit you are human. You make mistakes. It is hard. Some powerful men, even presidents, have failed at it." He forgot the rest of the discussion. But the priest convinced him that paying the price for the mistake was cheaper than being prideful and denying it in the long run.

As soon as the ringing stopped, Mark barked out his words. They shot out like a runner heading toward first base. "Brother Ed, I gotta tell you about the note. I never told you about it this morning. I just—"

"Hey, Mark, stop yelling. It's Bosco Hall, but you got me, Vincent. You ain't listening. This is Vincent, not Brother Ed. Do I sound like I'm fifty?" the RA on duty hollered back at him.

"Ah. Okay. So, I mean ... Yeah. Hey sorry, Vince. So, where's Brother Ed? I gotta talk to him. I'm in a hurry."

"Sure, he's been waiting on you for over a half hour. It's dark out and you're late. But I'll get him. They are all eating pizza in the staff lounge. Marie's been cooking for all of us. You missed a big pot of hot chocolate here, Mark."

"So, Father George and Sheriff Jalonick are back?"

"Yup."

"You have any news on Joe?" asked Mark.

"Nope," said Vincent. "But part of the township has lost power. Part of Grayling was down for a while. The sheriff's emergency generator kicked in just before dark. The wind has gotten fierce around here. You're in the forest over at Doc Hollis', right?"

"Yeah."

"Ok, I'll get Brother Ed. Hang on."

While waiting, Mark noticed how cold the cabin was. Instead of the sentences composed on Partridge Path echoing in his mind, he could now hear the sound of branches buffeting the window on the west side of the cabin.

There was static on the phone. The time had come to hug the cactus. In fact it was time to squeeze tight.

"Mark, it is Brother Ed. It's good to hear from you. What's the news on your end? We've got nothing to report. The folks just got back from the search. They are cold, wet, and empty-handed." Brother Ed's voice sounded almost business-like.

"Well, no good news here. We have not seen Joe or Kenny. Brother Ed, I've just got to tell you something—"

"Well, look. I'll tell you something first," said Brother Ed. "Sheriff Jalonick said you better stay put till morning. He does not want you on the roads. There have been some washouts. There are power lines down. Many people are in the dark and there aren't enough power people out repairing the lines. Some folks have lost electricity for hours. So, can you make arrangements with Doctor Hollis?"

Wrapped up with the storm within, Mark was genuinely surprised by the news about the storm raging all around outside. "Well, I'm sure I can. I have not asked yet, of course.

Time to Hug a Cactus

But they put up whole platoons of hunters and fishermen during the season. You know what happens during the Au Sable Adventure program. So, I don't think there will be any difficulty."

"Great. Are you hearing static on your end?" Brother Ed asked.

"A little, yes. But I have to tell you about the note. I mean. You see, I know that Joe and Kenny are together. You need to know that. You see I know they are together, Brother Ed. Wherever they are, they are together." Mark forced out his words as he embraced the cactus.

Intrigued Brother Ed responded with a questioning tone. "You know this because of what, a note? How's that again, Mark?"

The static increased on the phone, but Mark took a deep breath and forced out his confession. "I found a note on the door of Room 216 before breakfast this morning. It was from Kenny to me. He was supposed to meet me for breakfast. He said ... he said he was with Joe and that he'd ..."

Lightning distracted him as he instinctively looked out the window. Then he reached for the note. Only then did he remember that Paul Beaupré said to read the backside of it before calling. "Shucks, nothing is going right," Mark thought.

After a pause, Brother Ed continued. "Well, I see. We had the meeting. I suppose you could have ... Actually, the sheriff said he figured they were together once he learned about Kenny's background. But you got it in writing? And you got it this morning? Is there anything else in that note?"

"Just that he said he'd be back soon."

The light in Hollis' cabin started to flicker on and off.

"Hey, Mark, the phone on this end is crackling with static. Can you say that again?"

"Sure. He said he'd be back soon." Mark projected his voice like a coach from the sidelines.

135

"Bring the note when you get back and we'll—"

The lone light in the cabin went out. The phone went dead.

Mark could not see the numbers on the phone. But his ears told him that it would be no use in trying to redial. The lantern's glow on the other end of the cold room was the only source of light. He shoved the note back in his pocket. He inched across the room and grabbed the lantern for his return trip.

He jumped off the porch. He scurried onto Partridge Path through intense winds cuffing tree limbs back and forth. The cold rain made him ache for the warmth of Beaupré's fireplace and a hot cup of chocolate. Newly fallen branches forced his eyes onto the floor of the forest.

Mark's progress came to an abrupt halt; he walked into a wall of green. The path was green from the floor to the ceiling of the forest! "Yikes, a downfall," He announced to himself. "Now what? I'm only half way."

A huge balsam fir had collapsed across the path from the right side. Mark headed right to find the stump and a route around it. Shivering while searching, he vowed to himself. "Man, I am not going all the way back to Hollis' and out to the road to get to Beaupré's. That'll take all night."

He winced looking over the terrain confronting him. "It's bushwhacking time. Man, I gotta bushwhack just to get back on the path."

Mark pushed the lower branches of mature trees and young saplings blocking his way until he found the stump. Hoisting himself over it, he pushed straight forward about twenty yards to distance himself from the fallen fir.

Turning left, he marched with authority back to Partridge Path, windmilling his arms left and right to forge a path until he saw an opening ahead.

Mark turned his back against the forest, held the lantern close to his chest, and pushed forward with his back. He thrust his body against the bush and broke free of the foliage and onto

Time to Hug a Cactus

the path.

Exhausted and panting heavily, he stood momentarily to regain his strength.

Mark's nostrils filled with wood smoke. A vision of Beaupré's warm fire appeared. His stomach growled. His sweat-drenched shoulders and limbs were doubly cooled by the wind blowing around, up, and through the poncho. His body ached for the warmth of the fireplace.

Twenty yards further down Partridge Path, Mark could see the chimney spewing smoke. Lights flickered up and down through two of the four back windows on the north side of the cabin. He emerged from the path trotting across the back yard and onto the dark porch.

"Just how long does it take a kid to make a call these days?"

"Did you get the call off or did you have to use smoke signals, Marko?"

"So, the good padre' had you make a good confession and perform some penance, eh?"

Mark ignored the barrage of questions as he burst through the cabin door. Removing his dripping poncho and muddy shoes, he made haste for the warmth of the fireplace.

Paul was lighting a candle holder to illuminate the kitchen. Hollis had placed a couple of candles on the side of the room opposite the fireplace. Jean Luc held a flashlight he had retrieved from an Au Sable Adventure backpack. Each backpack had the equipment necessary for two weeks alone in the forest.

Shining the light in front of Mark as he walked toward the fireplace, Jean Luc reported on the power outage. "Well, Marko, it went totally dark. So, Hollis here tells me to grab a backpack in the storage room and reach into the lower right outside back pocket at the bottom to get a flashlight. Voila! There it was. I found it in the dark while using a match."

"A place for everything and everything in its place," Hollis chanted. "Plan your work, work your plan. You country rustics could learn a lot from the U.S. Navy. That's why we rule the world's oceans."

"Well, okay, admiral, now get outside and calm the storm. I want my electricity back," Jean Luc shot back.

"Well, I would, especially for you, a wayward cousin from the frozen north. But it's above my pay grade. I only made captain."

"Sit down, Marko. Warm up," said Jean Luc. "You must be cold. We are and we've been inside. I've got a little surprise for you." He headed for the kitchen.

Paul resumed his seat next to Mark and leaned toward him. "Did you 'fess up on the note?"

Mark stared at Paul long enough for him to pause. Then Mark nodded a thank-you at him. "Confession is good for the soul. You guys were right. Brother Ed told me to bring the note back and we'd meet. Then the line went dead before we finished. So, I don't know about my job yet."

"Know now and don't forget this. You did the right thing tonight, Marko," Paul assured him.

Mark started munching on another Granny Smith. He was so relieved to be getting warm. He stood soaking up the heat radiating from the fireplace.

"So, how did it go?" Doctor Hollis asked. "Did they have any news on Kenny and Joe?"

"Yeah, yes. I mean, no. No, they have no news on Joe and Kenny. Vincent told me right away that I was late, though."

Hollis interrupted, "You were also late getting back here. Gosh, if we had a phone, we'd have called out a search party. Even thoughtful Paul here was making noises about putting on his poncho to go scouting for your stranded carcass. You know it has been over an hour there, Marko? Just to make a phone call a few yards down Partridge Path?"

Shining a flashlight on the ticking U.S. Navy clock centered on the mantle, Paul advised, "Look it is past nine o'clock."

Time to Hug a Cactus

"Well, I suppose in another hour you would figure me for coyote bait, eh? Yeah, well I invite you guys to take a walk on Partridge Path and see for yourself."

"No thanks, there Marko. I'm sitting here by the fire," Paul said. "I'll make do without power till Mom Nature lights up the lands once again in the morning."

Mark continued, "Heck, there are huge branches down. I had to bushwhack around a downed giant balsam fir. It's cold, dark, and awfully windy out there. I kept getting whacked in the face by branches. I couldn't see well, even with the lantern."

"What, our Marko not up for a little challenge?" Hollis chided him. "I wonder about this younger generation."

"Well, I suspect they need to be fed, doctor, just like previous generations." Jean Luc showed up and presented Mark with two sandwiches on a plate and a bowl of peanuts.

"Wow, my favorite, grilled cheese on pumpernickel and pickles. How'd you do it?"

"I got done about five minutes before losing power. So they are cold now. You could warm them over the fire with the popcorn pan," Jean Luc offered. "The hot chocolate is no longer hot, though."

Munching down Mark exclaimed, "Heck, no. I'm fine. This is great."

Looking over at Jean Luc's brother, Mark got a little more serious. "Hey, Mr. Beaupré, can I stay the night? They don't want me coming home tonight. The sheriff told Brother Ed there are power lines down. Many people are without electricity, and roads are washed out all over the county."

"You stay tonight or you stay any other night, the price is the same. Come time for the 'Woodchoppers' Ball' you better be here with your gloves on, my boy," Paul said with a grin.

Mark winked back as he munched on his supper.

"So, relax, fill up your gullet, and soak up some heat. This night ain't getting any warmer. Are you sleeping up or down?"

Paul asked.

"Down here. I'll tend the fire so we can all be warm. I like the bench over there, remember?"

"Bear blanket be enough, you think?" Paul asked as he walked over to the couch to retrieve it.

"Yup, it always has been."

Paul flopped the bear blanket down on the bench next to the decorative pillows with mallard ducks stitched on them.

Omer had built the bench to be multi-purpose. Mark loved it. It was a comfortable bench during the day. Raising the top revealed a storage compartment with a pillow and blankets. Both ends at the floor level were book nooks. Above the bench, a small light was installed in a recessed book nook of knotty wood paneling.

Omer's motto was "Use it up. Wear it out. Make it do or do without." Omer had promised Hollis and Paul: "There'll be no wasted space on my watch."

The fire gave Mark great comfort also. Now he knew he'd be safe from the storm and in his favorite spot at the cabin. He was enveloped by the warmth of the fire, the sight of his cozy berth for the night, and his phone call to Brother Ed. Powerful feelings of acceptance, pardon, and redemption gripped him. It was as if he had exited the confessional once again at his home church.

His reverie was interrupted by Jean Luc removing his empty dish. "Mark, I'm one tired Canadian. I'm headed upstairs. Hollis says keep logs on the fire during the night and we will get heat upstairs. Are you up for this? You must be tired yourself."

"I'm sleeping on the bench, looking right at the fireplace. Don't worry, you'll be warm. I promise."

Hollis reached the top of the stairs. "Good night to all. Marko, on your missing buddies, we'll figure something out in the morning, don't worry. This day is done."

Paul flopped some things on the bench. "Here's the overnight

Time to Hug a Cactus

kit. You know where the bathroom is. That should be everything you need. I believe your Monsieur La Tour would say it is, 'Bon nuit' time."

Mark smiled and waved at Paul from the front of the fireplace as he climbed the stairs. "Bon nuit yourself. And thanks. Thanks a lot. I feel better now about the Bosco situation."

Mark got under the bear blanket and watched the flames lick the top of the fireplace. He pictured himself shivering on the Partridge Path only moments ago. "Man, I'm warm as toast under this bear blanket. I just wonder where Kenny and Joe are sleeping tonight."

Then he remembered Paul's message on the note. Mark stepped onto the chilly hardwood floors and grabbed the note. He read it with his back to the warm fire.

"Have courage when you call Bosco. St. Paul's words to Timothy seem to apply: 'What we are aiming at is the love that springs from a pure heart, a good conscience, and sincere faith.' Confess your mistakes, Mark, but take heart, Bosco knows their own."

Mark retreated to the warmth of the heavy, bear blanket. A sense of peace about the long day entered Mark's heart. Sleep came quickly.

The Snipe Hunters' Deadly Catch at Muskrat Creek

Chapter Twelve

Scoutmaster Bailey's Discovery

Sunday, September 30, 1979, 7:24 am, Au Sable River Valley

"This is an announcement from the Emergency Broadcasting System for all residents of the Au Sable River Valley. The National Weather Service reports that the Canadian storm front bringing high winds, intense rains, and winter-like temperatures left the area as of 4:20 am. Repair crews are working to restore power. Residents are advised to be patient and avoid downed power lines."

The radio in Scoutmaster Steve Bailey's four-wheel-drive Bronco blared out what was painfully obvious to anyone living in the Lower Peninsula's thirty-three county area north of a line stretching from Huron County's Thumb on the east to Pentwater in Oceana County on the shores of Lake Michigan. Bailey, up before dawn, had packed up emergency equipment, collected two volunteers, and headed out to the area's river and forest campgrounds. He wanted to conduct an early search for the missing Bosco students.

Shortly before reaching the primitive campground, Bailey heard a holler from the rear seat. "Stop. Stop the Bronco, Bailey!"

Scoutmaster Bailey braked to a halt and turned for an explanation.

He did not get one.

The Snipe Hunters' Deadly Catch at Muskrat Creek

Scoutmaster Bailey's Discovery

Tim, the other volunteer, exited the Bronco with binoculars. Walking about ten yards back, he studied the trees to the east and across the distant South Branch of the Au Sable River. Waving his left arm, he hollered, "Come here, Bailey. See that over the horizon to the north of the old logging road?" He handed him the binoculars.

"Wow, you got good eyes. Yes. That is surely smoke of some sort. It can't be a wildfire with all this rain. And there ain't no campgrounds allowed in that stretch of forest; it's all wilderness."

Tim pulled out his compass, took a reading, and grabbed his map. "OK, Bailey, let's clock the odometer to the campground." Tim plopped back in his seat.

They emptied out of the Bronco to the scent of pancakes and sausages wafting from the picnic shelter. Three adults in Scout uniforms were gathered around the huge fireplace grill. They all knew Bailey, and the interview was short. They were the only campers and they'd had no contact with anyone else. Scoutmaster Bailey stepped back toward his Bronco.

"Bailey, I'm going to try to raise the sheriff on the radio," Tim said. "He's gotta know about that smoke on the other side of the river, even if the nearest bridge is out of service." He headed to the Bronco, balancing a full cup of coffee from the scouts.

The radio crackled to life. Tim spat out the information on the location.

Sheriff Jalonick knew the area from orienteering competitions in his youth. "There's nothing up that logging road anymore. The railroad's gone twenty years now. There's a clearing at the end of the railroad line; tracks pulled up for scrap though. The Pere Marquette folks tore down a warehouse but left a sturdy storage shed. Deer hunters, mushroom hunters, and some fishermen who bushwhack come through there. Nothing else though. Deer season starts in a couple weeks. I guess it could be some hunters out baiting."

The Snipe Hunters' Deadly Catch at Muskrat Creek

"You know how to get out there without bushwhacking?" Tim asked hopefully.

"No way. But I'm going to call Doc Hollis if his service is up. He's on our Civil Defense roster. Plus, he's on that side of the river. He's got those souped-up military jeeps. He can get close on the two-track path that borders the forest. That would cut down the bushwhacking time."

>—<

When the little clock radio went on in the kitchen at seven-thirty, Jean Luc was already preparing a cold breakfast for Mark. "Well, now we have some electricity here at the Main Post, Mark." Eyeing the electric griddle, Jean Luc began to search for some pancake mix. "It might be time to celebrate."

Mark stepped away from stoking the fire and looked outside. "There's a lot to celebrate out there. The wind is gone. The sun is out. The temperature is starting to rise."

"Were you up a lot with that fire, Mark? We were warm upstairs. Merci a toi," Jean Luc remarked with his head buried in the pantry adjacent to the kitchen.

Mark turned toward the kitchen. "Not at all. I slept well. I am so glad to be done with that day. I don't know how things will go for me at Bosco, but I appreciate the advice you guys gave me. Heck, I was even able to sleep. Thanks to that note your brother wrote."

"Well, Paul and Hollis were such good Main Post mates that I'm thinking we should surprise them with pancakes and coffee and all the fixings when they decide to greet the day. What do you think, Marko?" Jean Luc continued to grope about some cupboards. "I can't seem to find any ..."

Mark, already walking toward the door, reported, "Hey, Jean Luc, Doc Hollis has all those goodies at his place. I'll go get the goodies before they even get up. Be nice if we could treat them."

Jean Luc did not look up from preparing the coffee pot.

Scoutmaster Bailey's Discovery

"What a fine idea."

Donning the poncho and hat against the wet woods, Mark called out while exiting. "Be patient. I gotta go around that downfall."

The phone was ringing when Mark got to the porch. He raced in and across the room with the dirty boots still on. "This is Doc Hollis' cabin, Mark Dubay speaking."

"This is Sheriff Jalonick. Mark, eh? You must be that Bosco RA. I wanted you off the roads last night. Hey, did you get through the night okay? Did the jeep get stuck?" Sheriff Jalonick inquired all at once.

A twinge of guilt invaded Mark's being as he realized that the voice on the other end of the line belonged to a man who had done a lot of extra work because … "Ah, yes, sir. I mean no. No problems last night. The jeep's fine. Beaupré put me up. I've been here a lot during my Bosco days, sir. Hollis and Beaupré run the Au Sable Adventure Program, they teach us a lot of woodsmanship, and … well, they are like "Au Sable River Guides" to Bosco Academy students. So, staying here is just fine with them."

Sheriff Jalonick sighed in relief. "Well, I'm glad for you. Good to hear that some of my residents had a good night. Power's out in about half of Crawford County as of six o'clock. So, I'm happy to see you got service. Look, son, where's Doc Hollis? Is he alright?"

Regaining his composure, Mark returned to his R.A. voice. "Yeah, yes, officer, I mean. He's fine. Beaupré and Hollis go back and forth between cabins; they're neighbors, friends for decades. Hollis spent the night next door at Beaupré's when the storm hit. We're hosting Beaupré's brother, too. So, he's fine, but asleep next door," Mark reported. "I'm fixing breakfast now actually. I expect he'll be up within the hour."

"Well, look, we may have a lead on those missing Bosco Boys. At least we got something to investigate. You seem to know the lay of the land over there. Does Doc Hollis still have those military jeeps up and running?" The sheriff's heightened interest radiated through the phone.

"Sure. They use them during the deer season; sometimes the trout season too. They're kept in the pole barn they share. It was still standing when I trudged through the woods a few minutes ago," Mark eagerly reported. "Why?"

"Well, we have a lead to investigate. The nearest bridge is out. And you guys are on the right side of the river, with the right kind of equipment for this mission, that's why. I'm stretched darn thin with this storm. Can you get Hollis on the phone with me soon?"

"Certainly, sheriff," Mark said. "But please understand. I actually have to bushwhack my way to the cabin because of the storm. So, it won't be quick. The path's blocked with a downed tree. And Hollis has to walk back here for the phone. Beaupré does not have one."

"Yes, Mark, you and half the county have the same problem. I certainly understand." There was a pause while Sheriff Jalonick was rummaging through some alternatives. "Does Hollis have batteries for his Civil Defense radios?"

"He always did for Au Sable Adventure events," Mark replied.

"Have him radio me ASAP. He knows the frequency from his Civil Defense service. I wanna find those boys by noon if possible," Sheriff Jalonick directed. "Ok, son, get a hustle on as best you can. You guys can save us a lot of trouble. We have downed trees making bridges impassable. Thanks."

Mark crammed all the goodies from the pantry into a knapsack, including the waffle iron and an extra jar of thimbleberry jam from a "Yooper" patient near the Porcupine Mountains. When he stumbled into the cabin, Hollis and Beaupré were on their second cup of coffee.

Hollis led off with the first banter of the day. "How hungry

Scoutmaster Bailey's Discovery

do you want us to get there, Marko? We didn't sign up for a solo experience. That's for you young Bosco students, you know." Jean Luc jumped to his defense. "Mark, I could only hold these bearcats off for so—"

Deliberately interrupting, Mark insisted, while panting heavily from his rush through the brush. "Hey, guys, Sheriff Jalonick needs your help and your jeeps. Doctor Hollis, you gotta get on your radio and tune in the sheriff. You still got the batteries up and ready?"

"Whoa, hold on there, son. This cup of coffee has just been born. You don't want me on a radio before I—" Hollis was very comfortable in his robe, soaking up heat from the fireplace.

"No, I'm serious. Jalonick, the sheriff, says you can help in the search for Kenny and Joe. They have a lead on this side of the river. It could be hunters or somebody else, but we have to investigate. At least we are on the right side of the river. That's what he says. I was just on the phone with him. He knows you don't have a phone here, so he suggested the CB radio if it's operable." Mark was speaking excitedly and with great intensity. Slinging the pack off his back and onto the counter, he announced, "Anyway, here are the breakfast goodies as promised."

"Radios should be fine. They're boxed up with the deer season equipment. You know we keep extra batteries. You want the pole barn key?" Hollis asked while gulping his coffee.

"Sit tight, Marko. I'll get them." Paul exited the cabin with his jacket half on.

"Here's a hot chocolate for our intrepid traveler, Marko." Jean Luc ushered him into the seat across from Doc Hollis. "Tell us the story."

Reflecting on Sheriff Jalonick's comment about "your side of the river," Hollis immediately crossed the room and changed into some outdoor clothes. He refilled his coffee cup. "Nice to see the sun decided to make an appearance. And it seems your

The Snipe Hunters' Deadly Catch at Muskrat Creek

blowhard Canadian chills went back north, Jean Luc," Hollis said with a wink. He grabbed his own well-worn Au Sable Adventure hat off the shelf.

Jean Luc filled one thermos with coffee and one with hot chocolate. Ten minutes later, they had the jeeps out of the pole barn and the radio was at the ready. "This is Doc Hollis, calling Sheriff Jalonick."

The radio crackled into life. Sitting in the jeep behind Hollis and Jean Luc, Mark and Paul caught the sense of urgency in Hollis's reply. "Sure, we can run the two-track bordering the forest to the area north of the Pere Marquette site. But then we'll be bushwhacking to that shed. Be slow then. I can't risk taking the jeeps off the two-track trail, of course."

There was a pause.

Hollis continued, "Yeah, I know it. Nope, I don't need the map coordinates. I know two of the hunters who use that shack. Last year Lane Gumbler put a porch on it. I don't go there. It's too far. But I know where it is."

There was another pause while the sheriff was speaking.

Hollis concluded, "Yup, will do. I'm over and out, sheriff."

><

Unconsciously stretching out his aching limbs, Kenny's arm struck the corner of the woodstove. He came to consciousness and studied the contours of the shed. He did not recognize where he was. Then he spotted Joe sleeping nearby. It was then he recalled the fright-filled moments of losing the Silver Beaver to the tobacco bandits. The tiring trek had so thoroughly exhausted him that he had a night without his usual nightmares. There were no visions of the pool of blood during the night, so his muscles were sore, but not tight. Clutching in terror was his usual response to that scene of death.

Kenny stood up slowly and stretched. He immediately envisioned the "Bad Breath Bandit" he had pancaked into the

Scoutmaster Bailey's Discovery

riverbank. Then the image of pistol man with his phony grin flooded his mind's eye.

As Kenny headed out the door to empty his bladder, his mind started to race once again. "I suppose we can walk out of this forest with Joe playing Daniel Boone. But, heck, what are we going to do about getting the Silver Beaver back?"

The sun was warming up the forest and the high winds were gone. Back in the shed, he gazed over at Joe clutching a rug in the fetal position. When he closed the door, he noted that their ponchos, hanging over their backpacks, had dried out. Silently he crossed the room toward the stove, reflecting on the scene. "That Joe thinks of everything." With no need to stoke the fire, he decided to rouse Joe and plan their next move.

Kenny was reaching for Joe's shoulder when he spotted a set of brown wooden beads on a black string. Joe was clutching them. There was a cross on one end.

Gradually, and with minimal force, he shook Joe's shoulder twice. He thought about how Joe had startled him awake back in Room 216 but decided to gently shake to wake only. Joe leaned back and looked up.

"Hey, Daniel Boone, get up. The sun is out, it's warm, and the storm took off back to Canada. Now we gotta figure out what to do." Kenny took a step back and pointed his toe at the beads. "What's that?"

Joe stood up, scooped the beads off the floor into his pocket, and looked at Kenny quizzically. "My rosary."

"What's a rosary, Joe?" Kenny asked sincerely.

Heading for the door and some bushes close by, Joe paused as he passed by Kenny. "Wow, you really don't know, eh? Let's just say it's my favorite problem-solving tool; you pray this, you get answers." He exited the shed with a glance at his watch. "Yikes, it's late, past ten-thirty already."

When Joe returned, Kenny baited him as he entered the shed. "Well, Mr. Daniel Boone, you just get your answer beads in hand, grab that compass on the ass end of your pig sticker, and tell me how we gonna get down the river without a canoe and back to Bosco Hall. We're well overdue."

"Not so. The pass is actually till eight o'clock tonight," Joe said while standing near the stove.

His gaze quickly turned to the window. A sound caught his attention. Bushes were moving. He stepped to the side of the window and peered out. Joe motioned for Kenny to get down and be quiet.

Joe saw a hat. Then two hats were bobbing up and down in the bush. He heard some voices at the end of the clearing. Then he heard a whistle blow. He knew the sound.

"Yes!" Joe flung open the door, walked to the opposite side of the shed, and blew his whistle in return. Less than eighty yards away in the bush just before the clearing were two figures emerging from the forest.

Kenny bumped into Joe at the ready with his own whistle. "Friendlies? You know they ain't connected to those tobacco bandits on the river?" he whispered loudly.

"Nope. Not with that whistle. I don't know who, but I do know they gotta be friendly." Joe blew his whistle hard.

Mark blew long and hard on his whistle in response. He jogged across the clearing running through the bracken ferns and short maple and pine saplings to the two missing Bosco Boys. Mark embraced them like they had just washed up on shore after the sinking of a ship.

"Joe, are you alright? Kenny, you look good. You both okay?" Mark could not contain his excitement. His students were safe. Never had he been so glad for smoke from a chimney.

Kenny groped for his ID. He lifted it from his pocket, "Need this, Mr. R.A.?"

"Darn right, kiddo, you keep that handy."

"How'd you find us?"

"I got eyes like an eagle." Mark pointed to the chimney.

"Smoke. You had a fire. That shed must have a fireplace, eh?"

"A stove," Joe confirmed.

"Gee, it is great to see you alive and well. You spend the whole night in the shed or were you out in that storm? Did you walk here? Did you portage this far? I don't see a canoe. How'd you get this far without a canoe?"

"Mark, slow down with the questions. We are fine. You got any food? Who is that coming after you?" Joe's mind was spinning now.

A tall figure clothed in a khaki-colored expedition outfit sporting many pockets closed within a few feet and approached Kenny with an outstretched hand. "I'm Paul Beaupré, Doc Hollis's friend, you must be the missing Kenny Dee, eh?"

Kenny was near speechless. He was immediately reminded of an older version of his now-deceased father. He returned the firm handshake and looked him in the eye. "Yes, sir, I am."

"How'd you get through that storm? Have you been here long, son?" Paul asked.

"Ah, I just came to Bosco, sir, this weekend. I'm new. This here is Joe, my suitemate," Kenny stammered.

Joe advanced toward Paul and the two bear-hugged each other while uttering some taunts about woodsmanship back and forth.

"So, Joe, you've had another adventure on the Au Sable? This one was unplanned though; at least that's how it seems." Beaupré teased.

Laughing, Joe ignored the tease. "Boy, we are certainly happy to see you. Got any food in all those pockets?" Joe took the talk down another path.

"Gum is all I got. We got to get you back to the jeeps, then on to the Main Post. Let's go, if you don't mind. I have not had my breakfast either. Which reminds me …"

Paul reached behind his expedition jacket and snatched the radio from his belt. He brought it to life with crackling sounds

The Snipe Hunters' Deadly Catch at Muskrat Creek

foreign to the woods. "Sheriff Jalonick? Sheriff Jalonick? This is the Main Post. Paul Beaupré calling."

Finally, after two more repetitions, a reply came back. "Baker here, Deputy Baker. Can I help you? The sheriff is at an accident scene right now."

"Yes. Advise the sheriff and his search party that the Bosco Boys have been located alive and well. I repeat. The missing Bosco Boys are okay. Please call Father George or Brother Ed at Bosco Academy and cease the search. Kenny Dee and Joe Duvalle will be transported to the Main Post. Do you copy, Deputy Baker? We found Dee and Duvalle."

Joe took a step back from the radio chatter. He winked and punched Mark in the shoulder. Grabbing Kenny by the arm, he turned him in the direction of the shed.

"Hey, we gotta clear out of the shed and get our packs. Let's go. These guys are waiting on us." Joe walked quickly with Kenny falling in beside him.

Once inside, they made quick work of packing up. Joe doused the embers in the woodstove with some dirt, returned the key to its hiding spot, and took some porch wood in to replace the inside wood they had used. Before they exited the shed, Joe admonished Kenny in a low voice. "Remember our chat about the quiet voice!"

They marched back to the meeting spot in the clearing where Paul and Mark were in a jubilant mood.

Kenny addressed Mark loudly, "I suppose this means the "Pay to Play" chat will be an extended version, eh, Mr. R.A.?"

All four men in the field erupted with laughter.

"Come on, guys, I got through to Hollis on the radio. He's waiting back on the two-track with the jeeps. Let's get on the march. Lord knows, it never pays to keep him waiting," Paul cautioned.

Paul led them single file, pushing through the bush and dense undergrowth, retracing their earlier steps. There was a

Scoutmaster Bailey's Discovery

little joshing about the storm but no real discussion. It took an hour to push through the forest back to the two-track road.

When Doc Hollis heard them coming, he blew his whistle and honked the jeep's horn for good effect. When they emerged from the forest within earshot, he unleashed a volley with enough volume to shake a groundhog out of his hole.

"Well, Joe Duvalle, you wasted the better part of my morning, you got me out here in the wilds without a morsel for breakfast, and I had to spend over two hours waiting here with a Canadian who only speaks hockey and waves Maple Leaves around. Just what have you got to say for yourself, my boy?"

Joe just laughed and waved at him.

Hollis continued with his stage voice disturbing the forest. "The sheriff's worried. Bosco Academy is worried. People are all upset about you in this freak of a storm straight from Beaupré's former backyard. I, for one, was not worried. I'm a doctor. I knew no storm was going to hurt a two-time Au Sable Adventure graduate. I told them they couldn't kill Duvalle with a double-bladed ax." Hollis halted briefly when Paul approached the jeep. He winked at Paul and continued, "In the middle of this once-in-a-century September storm, they asked, 'What could Duvalle be thinking canoeing in this storm?' Then I told them, 'Ah, hah, well, now there's the rub. Duvalle ain't known for thinking.'"

Laughing, the others trudged up to the empty jeep while Joe walked over to Doc Hollis and faced him directly. "I got this to say: I'm tired. I'm hungry. And I wanna go home."

Doc Hollis got out of the jeep, bear-hugged Joe, and said, "So do I! Let's go."

Joe threw his backpack in the rear and hopped in the back of Hollis' jeep. Jean Luc was in the front.

Kenny was directed to the back of Paul's jeep. Jean Luc reached in his bag and threw a Granny Smith to both boys. Hollis led the slow journey on the rutted two-track trail. They reached the Main Post well after one o'clock.

Getting out of the jeep after the long journey Kenny found his legs wooden and his back stiff. He noticed that Joe was quite stiff, too.

Hollis motioned both boys toward him and pulled Mark by the shoulder as he trudged by with both backpacks. "You two get upstairs and get a shower. Joe, you show him the place. We got hot water as of six o'clock this morning. Be happy! Mark, you get them the spare gym clothes from the adventure lockers and see that their clothes get in the laundry pronto. Now, Jean Luc—"

"I'm already on my way to the kitchen, doctor," Jean Luc interrupted. "Don't worry, there's more than one empty belly out here."

"Well, wonder of wonders, they can read minds up there in that frozen wasteland," Hollis loudly observed. "Beaupré, how about you—"

Paul cut him off with a wave of his hand. "Say no more. I'm hiking over to your cabin. I'll phone Father George myself."

"Well, now, that's enough work for me. It's exhausting doing the thinking for everyone around here," Hollis pronounced. "I'm going to stoke the fire and sip on some well-deserved coffee after I park these jeeps back where they belong. You guys are wearing this retiree out."

Three hours later, Jean Luc's breakfast had worked its magic and everyone was relaxing around the fireplace. Kenny had never appreciated a hot shower as much in his whole life. His warm-up suit was a Spartan green and white. Joe's was from Central Michigan University.

Superficial talk and the storm's impact on the area had accompanied the sumptuous pancakes and apple cobbler Jean Luc whipped up.

Beaupré brought news from the sheriff and the Bosco staff about the damage. "Hey, there are accidents, traffic jams, and

Scoutmaster Bailey's Discovery

many roads are still under repair," Paul said. "Those power crews are still working feverishly to get people back online. Father George said Bosco's only power is coming from an emergency generator. He powered off the dorm to conserve the gas. Only emergency lights are on in the halls."

Paul paused and looked over at his friend. "By the way, Doc Hollis, Father George said the repairs are going to take at least two days even with crews from Ohio. The dorm is without electricity. So, he asked if we can host these three rascals from Bosco for a few nights. Sheriff Jalonick was not optimistic about the bridge either. They got live wires down across some roads. The soldiers from the base at Grayling are guarding wires and providing security," Paul reported.

Smiling broadly, Hollis commented for all to hear. "Well now, whether your cabin or my cabin, the Main Post rule applies: Young, strong backs are for chopping wood. Seems like we may have an early rendition of the 'Woodchoppers' Ball', eh, Jean Luc? Besides, the first candidate is lying across the 'Partridge Path' between us, according to Mark. I'll bet there are others up River Road, too. So, are you boys up for some exercise in the morning? Say yes and we'll even feed you some dinner."

"Heck yes!" Mark bellowed. "I got schoolwork waiting for me at the dorm. None here!"

Joe and Kenny smiled and gave a thumb's up.

"I never chopped wood before, doctor. But I'm willing to learn," Kenny confessed.

Paul assured him, "We welcome eager learners here at the Main Post."

"Well, what exactly is a thimbleberry?" Kenny asked. "I've never had such tasty stuff on my waffles."

"Thimbleberry jam or not, I've never seen a kid eat that many waffles either, my boy. And I've been around this Bosco Bunch of pot lickers for years," Hollis retorted. "You kids keep eating like that and old Father George is going to get an invoice from me."

Paul volunteered the history lesson since Hollis much preferred razzing his company. "One of Doc Hollis' former patients is up in Copper Harbor in the Upper Peninsula. The berries grow in that region of the U.P. He always sends some jam down to the Main Post."

"Former patient? Heck, I still take care of that stump walloper all the way up in 'Yooper Land,'" Hollis contended.

Confused, Kenny questioned, "What's a stump wal—?"

Paul advised, "Don't listen to him. The jam man is retired and runs a fishing charter on Lake Superior in the summer. He charters for tarpon in Florida during the winter. Hollis never forgives a man for being a good patient."

"Good patient? He almost died. He came over here on a Sunday morning and said his stomach was upset," Hollis started to explain. "And, yes, Beaupré, I did go to church that Sunday."

"Wow, the ground must have been a shakin' throughout the township," Paul retorted.

Turning to look directly at Kenny, he continued, "He wanted antacids and I ordered him to go directly to the county hospital. When he would not go, I drove him myself. They transported him to U of M in Ann Arbor. They saved that hard head's life."

"Malabsorption syndrome or something like that wasn't it?" Paul sought to clarify.

"Heck if I remember. That's what they've got those egghead Wolverines for. I know a sick man when I see one. That's what they pay me for. Never took a dime from Jake, of course."

"Why not, doctor?" Kenny asked.

"He might just show up and disturb my Sunday morning again. That's why. You feed a stray, and they come sniffing back around," Hollis advised with all the sincerity and sagacity of Davy Crockett speaking to a pilgrim on the frontier. "They got that stump walloper back on the river in a month. His place was upriver about a mile from the Main Post. Been getting jam and

Scoutmaster Bailey's Discovery

Christmas treats ever since from his wife. Don't know why. He's still as ornery as a caged coon."

Hollis waved his hand as if to conclude the topic. He wanted to throw a change-up ball. "Enough with this, Kenny Boy. Mark tends to the pantry. He'll see that you get a jar to take home if you like. I got my own questions. Joe, exactly what did you do? Take this new kid through the woods and get a canoe from Quonset hut? If so, seems like we got a lotta work to do on this Kenny Boy. Following you around like a newborn puppy." He nodded directly at Kenny.

Mark got up and put a log on the fire. Jean Luc leaned back on the couch.

Joe, clearly agitated, stammered, "Well, I …"

Hollis continued, "A couple years back I'd expect that out of you. Not knowing enough to come in out of the rain. But we've been trying to cram some woods sense in that empty noggin of yours since you arrived. So? We got fanned at the plate again, Joe?"

Joe started to spin his tale. "Yeah, well, you remember where I caught that huge rainbow. I just wanted to get back there, that stretch upriver of Brown Trout Bend. Cowdrey was out of action so Kenny, my new suitemate, was good enough to—"

"You mean dumb enough," Hollis interjected.

Joe sheepishly nodded. In an apologetic tone, he threw his hands in the air. "I did not pay attention to the weather reports. Cripes, it's September, not November. I wanted to fish and I figured the rain would stop soon. I'm sure glad you had the Au Sable Adventure backpacks, ponchos and all, at the Quonset hut, doctor."

"Prior planning prevents …" Hollis enjoined. "Thank Beaupré over here, he sees to the equipment after every event. He makes them shipshape like a good sailor should. Now see men, how training from a good captain pays off." Hollis pointed his thumb to himself as the captain.

The Snipe Hunters' Deadly Catch at Muskrat Creek

Beaupré rolled his eyes and motioned with his hand for Joe to continue his story. "Well then, you hiked in the rain to the hut and then canoed upriver?"

Kenny looked over to Joe for help. "Uh, we …" and with his hand he gestured as if to lateral the ball to Joe.

Joe broke eye contact and got up, walked to the fireplace, and began to stoke the fire. He replied with his back to the men. "Yup. Took the Silver Beaver. Kenny here has a good stroke. We made decent time. But the storm caught us. We just got nailed. We had to get out of it eventually. The wind was just fierce."

"So just where is the canoe?" Paul demanded. "Are we going to have to launch the riverboat and go searching for it tomorrow?"

Kenny looked down and away toward the fireplace.

Groping about to thread together a story, Joe continued while turning only slightly toward the group. He much preferred pushing logs with the poker. "Dunno. When the storm let loose, we beached the canoe and sheltered inland about twenty yards. We came back during a lull in the storm and the Silver Beaver was gone."

"You know how to beach a canoe. How'd that happen?" Hollis demanded. "Did it grow legs and launch itself into the river?"

"Rope broke," Joe offered.

Beaupré countered, "We use nylon and you know your knots well enough—"

Joe quickly deflected responsibility. "I had Kenny tie it up. I was fussing with the backpacks. The storm was blowing us all around. I got scared. Remember, trees were falling."

Both Paul and Hollis looked at each other, and then over at Kenny for confirmation.

Kenny sailed forth into the unknown. "I'm from Catalpa Falls. Don't know a lot about this canoeing or forest stuff. I tried to…" He ran aground and stared at the floor for a moment.

Scoutmaster Bailey's Discovery

Recovering, he surfaced with a good excuse. "I ain't never been a scout either."

On the adult end of the room, there was a pause pregnant with nine months of full-term skepticism.

When Hollis and Paul chose not to question Kenny any further, Joe silently let out a sigh of relief in his heart.

Mark, sitting on the far right and eyeing Joe from the side, continued the probe. "So, just where did you beach the canoe?"

"We were upriver a piece from the high rollway area."

"So, presumably, it has to be downriver from there," Mark continued. "North or south side?"

"South."

"A bit brushy there, eh?" Beaupré interjected with a hint of incredulity in his voice.

Mark, picturing the area from his own solo days, asked, "So then you hiked through the bush during that storm to that railroad shed? That's a long hike."

"Well, yeah. And we skirted the river where possible," Joe explained.

"How did you even know about the shed? That's all a wilderness area by law. No buildings or cabins allowed. Plus, it's quite far from the high rollway." Beaupré observed.

Finally, the feeling of being tarred and feathered with lies left Joe. Now he could tell the truth. Joe nodded at Hollis. "You remember when I read you my diary from my first solo? I was posted near that wilderness tract about three miles from the logging road."

Hollis nodded. "Yup, I do."

"Well, I used my time to forage for those plants they said were edible. You know the morel mushroom, wood sorrel, ground cherries. I even found some blueberries. I tried some before deciding I wanted to know what it felt like to go three days and four nights without any food. I decided to practice some of the orienteering stuff you taught. I stumbled onto the logging road. I followed it across the river to that clearing with the railroad shed. The warehouse was long gone even then, but you could see the foundation for it."

Mark recalled his solo days, but not in that part of the forest. "So how about the shed? You tell me it was not locked? I've heard deer hunters have maintained it and use it. That's wilderness, but the U.S. Forest Service can't make them take it down because that piece of land still belongs to the railroad. But no building permits are allowed."

"Yup." Gesturing toward Mark with some amount of comfort, Joe continued, "Well, you know on solo we can't talk to anyone, only to ourselves, God, the deer, and a diary if we choose to have one. So, one day, I sat up on the hill to the west of the clearing watching a nuthatch pry apart a beech nut. Three guys came out of the forest and went to work on that shed. They worked all day and toward nightfall. When they left, I saw them lock the place up and hide the key. I was just lucky that the key was still kept there two years later."

"Well, okay, Sherlock, where do they keep the key?" Paul needled him in his best nagging voice. "I might get lost someday with a neophyte from Bosco Academy who thinks I know what I'm doing in the woods. I would not want to disappoint a true believer."

Joe laughed. "You know the most common tree in Michigan?" He decided to flip roles from his Au Sable Adventure training under Paul.

"The sugar maple?" Paul answered.

"Yup, but that's not the one." Joe smiled. The group laughed at Paul for being taken in so easily. "Adjacent to a ramshackle outhouse is a medium-sized pin cherry tree with a hole in its trunk about shoulder high. The key is hanging on a stick. It's right inside the hole. Can't be seen either. They got a regular brass cup hook screwed into the tree on the inside."

Kenny perked up and demanded, "You mean you did not

Scoutmaster Bailey's Discovery

know for sure if you could get us out of the storm and into that shed for the night?"

"Ah, the true believer begins to doubt." Paul Beaupré winked at Joe. "Apostle Joe, it's time to tend to your flock."

Hollis, eyes glinting, dove right in. "O ye of little faith."

"Kenny, plan B was the porch. Remember getting under the porch and out of the rain?" Joe sheepishly asked with a smile.

Kenny shot back, "Yeah, but it was still awfully cold in that frigid wind."

Joe shrugged his shoulders and continued, "So anyways, the next day on solo I tested the key out early in the morning before they came back," Joe reasoned. "I guess they had no cause to change spots in two years. It was pretty clean in there. There's just a little dust, cobwebs, spiders, ants. But, hey, with that porch protecting all that wood for the little stove, that's a nice hangout for a hunter come a snowy November day."

"Or perhaps a storm from Canada in late September," Hollis added with a wink.

Joe looked over at Hollis. "Hey, I'm sorry about the loss of the canoe. I don't think we'll ever see it again."

"Ah, worry not, Joe. Canoes can be replaced. Knuckleheads from Bosco Academy are harder to come by. Yet, by golly, they used to be more trainable, don't you think, Monsieur Beaupré?"

Paul stood up, smiled, and shook Joe's hand. "Hey, son, glad we got you out of the woods. We might run up the Au Sable with the riverboat someday. Check the backwaters and peek in some of the deep holes. Who knows? An honest livery man might collect it some weekend and call Doctor Hollis. The registration number is on it."

Paul smacked Kenny on the shoulder. "You, too, Bosco Boy to be. Welcome to the Main Post. We usually join in the initiation of the new Bosco students on our "Beans and Barbecue" weekend before school starts; then some sign up for the Au Sable River Adventure Program in the spring. But until then, I suggest you get an R.A. that knows how to keep track of you."

"Yes, sir," Kenny replied. "I'd like to learn all that. Learn what Joe knows and go on that adventure program. He told me to ask you about the snipe hunt when they are in season. I wanna get one."

Everyone laughed while Paul looked over and gazed into Joe's eyes. Joe, though known for practical jokes, usually forewarned Hollis and Beaupré about his next victim. "I see. He told you that already? Well, that's because Joe did so well on his first snipe hunt."

Hollis quipped, "Yup. That's a good tradition up here on the river."

"Are they big? Do you eat them?" Kenny inquired.

Hollis was quick to field this one. "No, son. Like a good brook trout fisherman, we practice catch and release. Sometimes we take photos though, you with your first snipe. It seems there are more snipes around the next year that way." Hollis, reporting like a professor at the podium, was very reassuring.

Jean Luc stifled the smirk on his face and headed for the kitchen.

"Hey, Mr. Chef. Yeah, you on the way to the kitchen; you got a good snipe recipe from Canada? You got a whole country full of snipe, other wild things, too." Hollis enjoyed roping Jean Luc into the fray.

Jean Luc deftly handled it. "Nope. We Canadians are ahead of you Yanks as usual. They are a protected species up our way." Then he exited. "I gotta visit the head now, boys."

Turning to Mark, Paul nudged his foot. "What do you think, Marko? A dog collar with a shiny metal bell on it might do the trick. You won't lose your new boy so easily," Paul opined.

Jean Luc returned adorned with a fancy chef's apron. It was the official chef uniform for the chief cook during deer season

Scoutmaster Bailey's Discovery

at the Main Post. "Hah! All this talk when the sun is starting to set. Who is up for some popcorn and ginger ale? The tea kettle is already on. This is a fair warning for you river rats. The galley at the Main Post is closing and it'll be a while before breakfast. So, sing out."

Minutes later popcorn was placed on the moose table next to a steaming pot of tea and ginger ale. A bowl of fruit was joined with a bowl of mixed nuts next to a stack of napkins. The well-lacquered knotty pine table sat low to the ground. With a wood-burning kit, a neighbor had etched an elk on one end facing a moose on the other end looking back. The hand-made Christmas gift was instantly popular. It was neatly positioned between the couch and the fireplace. Leather La -Z- Boy chairs on each side of the couch were angled toward the fireplace. Large floor-to-ceiling windows flanked the fieldstone fireplace and simultaneously allowed a view of the fire and the Au Sable River at the end of the lawn.

Kenny turned to watch a large blue heron feeding on the bank of the river. The conversation died down, and the focus was off the adventure he'd had with Joe. Watching the majestic wading bird allowed the problem of the missing canoe to float right out of his mind.

Peace descended upon the Main Post with its disparate collection of occupants gathered around the warming fire. Thoughts rose with each flickering flame.

Jean Luc retreated to a La-Z-Boy chair with his favorite book by Robert Service on the west end of the couch. Doc Hollis, on the east end of the couch, was reading "The Night They Burned the Mountain," by Doctor Thomas Dooley. An FM radio station was softly playing Hollis' favorite, Big Band jazz.

Paul Beaupré was playing cribbage with Mark, Joe, and Kenny. It was Kenny's first game ever. The only noise in this tranquil scene was their card chatter. Kenny's heart was at peace. He found he was comfortable with the Main Post and

Bosco guys. It was as if he had known them a long time. In truth, he had not had such peace since the week before his father's funeral.

Kenny interrupted the serenity with a question. "I love that tune. They have played that three times. What is the name of it?"

"'In the Mood,' played by the Glenn Miller Band," Hollis replied. "They don't make music or musicians like that anymore, my boy. That's classic stuff that'll never be beat in any generation. Mark my words, and tell your grandkids, sonny."

The evening's hours slipped away until Hollis put his book down on the table. "All right, you castaways from the 'Academy of John Bosco.' It's almost ten o'clock and I have to get my rest. Giving you advice and supervision tomorrow is going to take a lot of my energy. Mark, be sure to close up the fireplace before you hit the sack. Paul will show you two to your quarters for the night. I'm aiming for an early start tomorrow."

Mark looked up while holding his cards. "Thanks for today, doctor. I'll handle the fireplace."

Jean Luc closed his book and stood up as well. "I better turn in now, too. The galley has to be warmed up before you locusts descend upon my kitchen. Boys, I know you were cold out there in that forest, but read Service's 'Cremation of Sam McGee' some time. I promise you it'll make you cold in July. He writes like Jack London in 'To Build a Fire.'"

"Okay, Monsieur Jean Luc, but I'm all done with being cold for the time being. Thank you, though." Joe smiled and winked at Jean Luc as he was walking toward the stairs.

Hollis stopped halfway up the stairs with one last question, "Mark, I assume you'll be on the bench again tonight?"

"Yup," Mark affirmed.

Hollis continued on his way. "You can let the fire die out tonight; temperature's closer to normal now."

"C'mon guys. You get the 'Whitetail' room for the night."

Scoutmaster Bailey's Discovery

Paul waved for Kenny and Joe to follow him down the hall next to a large storage room. "During deer season, we have six men in here; four on the walls, two on cots in the center." The room had wooden bunk beds built into the walls on each side of the room. There was a nightstand with small lamps for each bed; the lamps for the upper bunks were built into the wall. By the entry door, there was a well-stocked built-in bookcase on one side and empty shelves on the other side. "The half bathroom is through here. I'll get you some soap and such. You caught us under-prepared. Even the bow hunters are not expected for a few days, eh?"

Paul returned after a short trip to the storage room, dropped two towels on the closest bed, and flipped them each a bag. "We keep overnight kits just for this type of occasion. Sleep well, guys, we got work to do. Get your clothes out of the dryer in the morning. Joe, you know Hollis never left the Navy, so be sure Kenny makes his bed."

"Aye, aye, sir," Joe said with a mocking salute. Paul closed the door upon his exit.

Paul prepared for bed in the upstairs bathroom and then walked down the hall to Hollis' room. Knocking, he stepped in and closed the door. Hollis looked up from his Dooley book.

Lowering his voice, he faced his friend. "I can't get my mind off that lost canoe; Joe letting the new kid handle it; not beaching it the way we teach kids. I keep replaying that story over and over in my mind. Can you picture that happening?"

"Nope. That dog won't hunt on my land." With that, Hollis nodded to him to close the door. Then he shut the lamp off.

Paul exited, closed the door, and retired for the night.

On the level below, Joe sprang up to the top bunk on the right. He flipped on the small reading lamp.

"You staying on top?" Kenny inquired.

"Sure. You afraid you'll fall without a rail, Kenny Boy?" Joe teased. He stretched and pulled his beads out.

The Snipe Hunters' Deadly Catch at Muskrat Creek

Kenny climbed up, inspected the setting, and gauged the drop to the floor. He did not turn his lamp on. He was not comfortable. "Naw, I'll try it, too. I got a question, Daniel Boone. How are we going to get that canoe back?"

"Dunno. I really don't know. Maybe we never do?" Joe's voice did not sound confident.

"Ah, Joe. I noticed you did not mention the tobacco bandits; Mr. Pistol Man and all? It was my rope tying that caused the canoe to float away?" The consternation was obvious in Kenny's voice.

"Right now, that's the only arrow in my quiver," Joe confessed.

The room fell silent for several minutes. And then it went dark when Joe shut his light off.

Kenny heard Joe murmuring. It continued for another ten minutes.

"Are you praying that rosary again? What for?" he demanded.

Joe exhaled into the darkened room, "Another arrow for my quiver."

With the last line of the Hail Holy Queen prayer, "... that we may be made worthy of the promises of Christ ...," Joe began to question lying about the canoe and the wisdom of his plan to sell cigarettes to the townies. Originally he reasoned that they'd get smokes from someone. Why not him? His own uncle had kept smoking after his heart doctor's warnings. But now? Now he was not so sure.

Sleep only came by retreating to Brother Edmund's favorite: The Prayer of St. Francis of Assisi. Murmuring, "Where there is doubt ..." Joe fell into a deep, if not restful, slumber.

Chapter Thirteen

A Grasshopper Strikes

Monday, October 1, 1979, 10:15 am, Paul Beaupré's Cabin

Mark, alone and seated on the ottoman, was gazing out the cabin window at the amber-colored waters of the Au Sable. The sun's rays were just touching the huge willow tree overlooking the water.

"So, how's this work again?"

Startled from his trance, Mark turned to his right to see Kenny fumbling with the bellows.

"Here, let me open the screen and add a couple skinny logs for you," Mark said. "I see you're an early bird, too."

He stuck a couple of logs on the glowing embers, gripped the bellows, and motioned for Kenny to kneel beside him. "Just aim at the underside of the log towards the red-hot embers." Gripping the handles, he demonstrated. "Open and close this a few times." Then he turned the bellows over to Kenny and stepped back.

"Yikes, this really works," Kenny chortled as the flames quickly licked up the sides of the split birch. "I like this fireplace. It is my first. The scent of that bark burning is neat." He knelt on one knee and leaned toward Mark. "Actually, I like this whole cabin and I'm glad to be here rather than starting up with classes."

Mark let out a chuckle. "So, you don't miss those art supplies back in Room 216?"

Kenny shot him a glance.

"Yeah, I heard Saltz talk about how you protect them," Mark teased. "Bernard described your entrance into Bosco Hall also."

Kenny's mind was catapulted back to his arrival at the dorm. His sneaky departure out the utility door with Joe flashed across his mind. He kept his back to Mark and faced the fire while pumping the bellows needlessly. The fire was advancing quite nicely already.

"Say, Mark, about my note and all the trouble we caused. I really didn't want it to work out this way. I like Bosco. I like you guys. The school part I don't know yet, but last night was the best I've felt in …" His voice trailed off, and his eyes returned to the welcoming fire with its pleasing scent. Entranced by the warmth of the flames, his tongue took flight of its shackles. "Three years," he continued. "This is so different from a hospital. My nightmare—" Catching his tongue floating like a mallard on a current of unusual comfort, he darted for a more secure shore. "I mean, I slept well last night."

"Hospital? You were sick or terribly injured?" Mark inquired.

"I was at Havenwood State Hospital," Kenny announced. Turning around to look up and directly at Mark while kneeling, he clarified, "It's a psychiatric hospital."

"Ah, I see." Mark was immediately uneasy.

"Well, you don't. And you won't. At least I don't want to talk about it. I'm just happy to be out. I did not think that I would be happy to be out. It was not my idea actually. My social worker convinced the administration to change the behavior plan or whatever they call it. They wanted me to be more social; go to a different setting. Spend more time with kids my own age. Heck, I never really trusted those … after the police came … no one could understand …"

Kenny was saying exactly what he did not want to with a tongue that was suddenly far too loose and comfortable.

A Grasshopper Strikes

Kneeling in front of the fireplace, he realized his chronic state of guardedness demanded a lot of mental energy. Were the flames melting an icy barrier protecting his painful past? That image of the bloody porch leaped up from the base of the fireplace and into his mind's eye. He jackbooted it underground and regained his focus. He stretched hard to grasp and hang onto the first sense of comfort he'd had in over three years.

"I'm on a trial basis. Probation they call it." Kenny exhaled some of his perpetual wariness of other people right into the Main Post's fireplace.

"I recall that from a chat I had with Father George," Mark said encouragingly. "We had another student, Clayton. He was on probation, too. He did well and graduated two years ago."

"I bet he didn't run off the first weekend," Kenny observed. "But honestly, I even liked the first meal in the cafeteria with the guys. Well, jeez, so the first thing I do is go off with Joe and cause all this hassle. I dunno what the Bosco people will do. Then there are hospital shrinks and state administrators. Whatever they do, I can't blame them though." He paused. "That was one barn-burner of a storm, eh?" He nodded to Mark for affirmation.

"Worst since I've been in Michigan. They did not even call it a tornado but look what it did to our town," Mark reported. "But, heck, we get three more days at the Main Post out of the deal."

"So, you like it here, too? Doctor Hollis, is he a psychiatrist?" Kenny asked.

Mark laughed. "No. But he'd have a lot of fun with that. Both Beaupré's would have even more fun razzing him; that's for sure. He retired as a family practitioner, internal medicine kind of doctor in Bay City for decades. He's had this cabin a long time. It was sometime after the Korean War or so. After a career in Bay City, he moved up here full time." Mark shifted in his chair. "Now he's on Bosco's board of directors, and does sports physicals for the schools, and volunteers at the county clinic once a week. He and Paul Beaupré run the Au Sable Adventure Program for us. It is modeled after some military survival schools. You learn how to handle yourself in the forest and on the river."

"Joe seems to know that forest and river stuff," Kenny said. "I call him Daniel Boone. He likes that fancy knife; that's for sure."

"Joe graduated from Au Sable Adventure twice. You know, four out of ten fail to finish the program. He got placed in two different solo sites. They have toyed with the idea of a short winter survival program over Christmas vacation. Actually, Hollis and Paul know some officers with the National Guard in Grayling who trained with the Army's Tenth Mountain Division. They'd volunteer and lead the program. The equipment alone would cost a lot. But do we ever have winter in the woods here!" Mark chuckled. "I don't think I'd try that winter program myself. But your buddy Joe would be the first to sign up."

They both heard the door on the bathroom close.

"Joe must be up," Kenny noted. Like a rabbit in an open meadow at high noon, Kenny's abrupt disclosures left him dangerously exposed. Yet, when in front of the fire, the melting of the icy barrier, three years in the making, actually felt good. "Hey, Mark, about this morning, can you keep our chat between us? Would that be okay, Mark?" Kenny pleaded.

"Of course," Mark said. "That's part of my job as your RA. But Kenny, you need to know, you are at the Main Post. We have rules here at the Main Post that govern how we conduct ourselves as men with one another. You may as well know that right now," Mark pronounced with emphasis.

"Wow, you're sounding like those lawyers I saw when I got arraigned," Kenny said. "Is this all legal-like here?"

"Well, I don't think anything is legal; it is more important than that. It is a code of honor. It's real simple, so it handles all

A Grasshopper Strikes

that's complex. Beaupré always says it is for men of character, discipline, and backbone; all others are welcome to pass on by. And some have been advised to pass on by, too," Mark instructed. "That's why they have so many friends come here. They come during the 'Woodchoppers' Ball,' deer season, the trout opener, sometimes during the snowmobiling season, too. A big group and yet they have respect and honor each other's differences. The older Bosco students always come to the 'Woodchoppers' Ball.' It's three days on an assembly line of men producing enough wood for three cabins all winter." Mark was revealing the magic of the Main Post.

"A code of honor …?" Kenny was confused.

"Yup. It's in a poem on the wall over there, just before you turn toward the storage room," said Mark. "There's the big head of a ten-point buck above it. He stares right at you almost. Have Hollis or Paul teach it to you."

Kenny silently considered how loose his tongue had been in front of the fire this morning. "Maybe there is a reason why. These men are different here."

A blur of color caught Kenny's eye as he stepped away from the fireplace. "Wow, what the heck is that right outside the window by that post?"

"Oh, that's our local hummingbird. Paul actually got a photo of him standing still in mid-air like that. It's the only bird that can fly backwards."

"Yikes, I've never seen that. It seems to just be hovering with its beak in that red liquid," Kenny announced.

"Yup. Paul put that feeder out to attract them, not the jays. They are a blur because some have been clocked at thirty-four miles per hour and they surely need energy. Some eat twelve times their own weight, but actually that's not much. Some weigh less than a nickel." Mark was recalling what he learned at the Main Post.

"You know a lot too, eh, Mark?" Kenny observed.

The Snipe Hunters' Deadly Catch at Muskrat Creek

"Huh, not me. Paul Beaupré. He can teach you all about the woods and animals. Heck, he's from French Canada. He grew up in Quebec and had a grandfather that was Ojibwa Indian. When you have the bonfire on Au Sable Adventure, you gotta get him to tell you guys the 'Windingo Story.' You might not sleep well that night though."

"Well, I already have that problem," Kenny commented to himself.

"You boys interested in some breakfast sometime soon?" Jean Luc stuck his head in the room. "I'm on my way to the kitchen."

"Absolutely," Mark called out.

"Yes, sir, Jean Luc," Kenny confirmed.

"Well, I got onions, peppers, and cucumbers that need to be chopped. Tomatoes, potatoes, and melons that need some cutting, and I'm looking at four idle hands over there by that fireplace. You guys coming my way or staying hungry?" Jean Luc challenged. "This Main Post is a do-it-yourself operation. You paddle your own canoe around here and you eat. You don't and you won't." Jean Luc winked and accentuated the warning tone in his best schoolmaster voice.

Joe Duvalle exited the bathroom and scurried up behind Jean Luc in the hallway. "Hey, I got a willing pair of hands to go along with an empty stomach if they don't."

Mark and Kenny sprang into action, lined up behind Joe, and followed Jean Luc into the kitchen.

Kenny witnessed the power and efficiency of teamwork all the way through the breakfast and lunch routine. In the ensuing hours, the Main Post men directed Mark, Kenny, and Joe in each phase of safely clearing Partridge Path of all the debris from the storm. Then the huge downfall was cut into sections, dragged over to the back yard between the cabin and the pole barn. A two-man team used a powered wood splitter to cut thick sections into fireplace-sized pieces. A third man used a

174

A Grasshopper Strikes

wheelbarrow and stacked the split wood in the shed. They took turns, rotated teams, and took breaks as needed to get the job done. Kenny enjoyed stacking the wood and marveled at how much work six men could get done with the equipment that was stored in the tall barn.

Jean Luc had just exited the kitchen with Mark when Hollis proposed a plan for the afternoon. "Let's load up the chain saws on the jeeps and take these young Bosco backs up River Road and be sure it is clear all the way to the highway. We need to check up on Widow Beleau up Woodcock Ridge, too."

Kenny asked Mark, "What's up with Woodcock Ridge?"

"Well, it's off River Road, but goes away from the river and into the forest," Mark explained. "No one goes up that half-mile road because there's only one lonely cabin in the forest. A widow lives alone and several of the neighbors here make it a point to check on her since all her family is out of state."

"The deacon from her church visits her a couple times a month. But I'll bet he's got his hands full in town now," Paul added.

During lunch, the local radio station had continued to describe all the damage from the storm. Bosco Academy and many others were still without power.

⋈

Dry, cool, sunny weather aided the men at the Main Post for the next two days in cleaning up after the storm and assisting the neighbors. Jean Luc and Joe drove into town for supplies and food. They returned with updates on the town's recovery from the storm. Kenny thoroughly enjoyed the evenings by the fire, playing cribbage, and learning from the men at the Main Post. The evenings were short though since everyone was bone tired from physical labor.

On the second evening, just before retiring early, Mark reported on the clean-up news he'd just learned from his Bosco buddies. "Father George assigned all the juniors and seniors at Bosco to a work detail under Sheriff Jalonick and city officials. Progress is slow because of the power problems. But today Sheriff Jalonick wanted to clear the logjams in the river. They found a lot of odd things, but no canoes. And, Joe, you can be sure I asked."

Mark walked over to the fireplace to put another log on before heading for his favorite bench-bed. "One odd discovery though. Three boxes, not cartons, but warehouse-sized boxes of tobacco stuff. I think he said Phillip Morris. Doctor Hollis, what's ATF? Brother Ed overheard him say he'd be calling them."

Joe, seated at the side of the fireplace, shot a sly glance at Kenny. Kenny furtively returned his glance and then continued to stare at his cribbage cards. But their ears were tuned to Doctor Hollis.

Doctor Hollis looked up from his Tom Dooley book just long enough to sound off, "Bureau of Alcohol, Tobacco, and Firearms, another federal bureaucracy designed to extract money from us taxpayers and make like they are doing something helpful in the process."

Mark turned back to the fire, knowing any topic concerning a government bureaucracy was a dead-end subject with Doc Hollis.

On the third day after the storm, Hollis announced plans for all those at the Main Post immediately after breakfast. "I'm going to take Mark and Kenny on the river for some fishing. We'll take the seventeen-foot Kevlar so I can sit in the middle and direct the strokes of this younger generation. Paul, I suggest you take Joe in the riverboat and go downstream of the high rollway and scout out the banks and deeper holes. See if the Silver Beaver shows up. Let's take radios so we can stay in touch. You take some extra ropes just in case."

Turning to face Joe directly, Hollis then inquired, "Joe, do you

A Grasshopper Strikes

figure you can get back to the actual site where you beached it?"

"Oh, sure, I'm pretty certain I can get within yards of it," Joe assured Doctor Hollis.

Kenny refused to look up from his knot-tying exercise. He had decided he wanted to learn some more woodsmanship. This was a perfect conversation to avoid. Yesterday he had mastered the square knot. Today was time for the sheepshank knot.

"Call us on the radios if you get lucky or need help," said Hollis. "Now that the storm and clean-up are mostly over, there will be more river traffic and some tourist might just declare himself the new owner of a canoe. It would be really easy to remove the registration number on it. I know all the livery guys would call me if they got it or had it turned in. I'm not so sure about a tourist or college kid."

Over two hours later, Hollis had landed two brown trout and declared it was time to paddle further downriver of Mio Dam. "You two paddle the way you have been, and we'll have time to get in a good fly-casting lesson for Kenny. Mark, steer this canoe toward McKinley Bridge. I found a nice spot there on the north shore. I'll tell you when to head ashore. There's a boat launching site and a campground there."

After an hour of steady paddling, the canoe nosed up to a wooden deck extending from the north shore. Mark walked along the shore and found the path to the bridge. Relaxing in the sun on McKinley Bridge, he tried to catch sight of a Kirtland's Warbler.

Kenny and Hollis beached the canoe and took their fishing equipment to a spot close to the wooden deck overlooking the river. "Here is a good place to practice casting a fly. There are no trees that'll hang up your fly or line."

Standing on the end of the deck, Doc Hollis demonstrated a downstream cast and then readied Kenny with his fly rod. "Now it's your turn. Don't horse it. The fly's not going to Fargo.

Just think: 'Mr. Rainbow' is waiting for his dinner right over there. Beaupré's gotten some big lunkers right out of these holes." Hollis clapped him on the back of his new Orvis fishing vest and then stepped back a little toward the shore side of the deck to observe.

For the next twenty minutes, Hollis coached Kenny on the intricacies of fly selection and placement. They were oblivious to the locals at the campsite located behind the picnic area.

Just as they spotted a trout rise toward the surface, three men left the picnic area advancing toward the deck. They were talking loudly. With crazed grins, they walked with an unsteady, lumbering gait. Their gestures were clumsy and exaggerated.

Leaving the company of his two companions, the largest man with a long and ungroomed beard came up behind Doc Hollis. He was wearing suspenders over an unbuttoned red plaid hunting shirt. The white T-shirt provided glaring contrast for the belly that protruded out in advance of him. He stopped short of the wooden deck. "You boys don't look like you belong here. Ain't seen you 'round here none."

Doc Hollis replied, "Well actually we're not too far away; upriver a piece, but still in Crawford County. I don't come too often anymore. But a neighbor buddy of mine float fishes this stretch of the river all the time. Sometimes he comes right here at night. How about you? Had any luck lately?" Hollis deliberately directed the conversation toward a more amicable topic.

"Can't have no luck when you outsiders come in here with your fancy Orvis gear. Ya take all the fish out, don't leave none for us." He said this while glaring at Doc Hollis and stepping onto the deck.

Behind him, one of his buddies chimed in on the talk. "Yeah, Lubbers, you tell 'em. We don't need no more Orvis types 'round these parts."

A Grasshopper Strikes

Observing Kenny's new fishing vest and Hollis' equipment Lubbers continued, "It was peaceful here till you showed up with your fancy Kevlar canoe and Orvis gear. Y'all fixin' to take all the trout right outta here. We was enjoying a cold drink till you showed up. Disturbing us." Raising his voice for emphasis, Lubbers yelled over his shoulder to the delight of his drinking buddies, "Ain't that right, boys?"

The taller man fueled the confrontation. "That's right, Lubbers. You tell 'em. We got a peaceful nature. Till you two showed up."

"These guys ain't local!" the shorter one chimed in. "Ain't got no Crawford county look on 'em! They's Orvis or L.L. Bean boys! They ain't local, now are they?"

The tall one bellowed, "Not in my book they ain't. Chicago, yes. Dee-troit, maybe. Local they ain't!"

"Oh, heck, no. They ain't Crawford county boys. They got that city smell to 'em," his companion sputtered while sipping from a beer can.

"Sure 'nuff. I can smell 'em over here," the short one said as he threw a cigarette butt on the ground. "How 'bout you, Lubbers? Got that city smell over there on that deck?"

Hollis shouldered his fishing rod and faced Lubbers. "Well, really guys. We just stopped for a short fishing lesson. The kid's new to fishing and I—"

Bellowing, Lubbers cut him off while walking closer to him on the wooden deck. He pressed forward to within inches of Hollis' face.

Kenny quickly pulled in his line and secured his fishing rod. He was standing behind Hollis, holding his rod up near his shoulder, just like Doc Hollis.

Lubbers, about four inches taller and much larger, looked down on Hollis. He angrily demanded: "Why don't you just get your sorry self outta' here? Now."

"Get 'em gone, Lubbers," hooted the tall one, egging him on.

"Off my landing!" Lubbers commanded. "You don't belong here! This here is for us locals"

"Well, sure, I ..." began Hollis.

Then Lubbers shoved Hollis backwards, almost off the wooden deck. Kenny grabbed his arm, stopping him from falling.

Lubbers then advanced toward both of them.

"Hey, boy, ya get outta here. This here is men's business. That is, if this here's a man!"

With that, the drunken Lubbers backhanded Kenny to the ground with one powerful swipe from his 250-pound frame. Hollis immediately stepped in between Kenny and Lubbers.

Kenny jumped to his feet close to the belligerent Lubbers. Kenny's nostrils flooded with the stench of alcohol. Facing Lubbers, who dwarfed the shaken boy, Kenny's face radiated hatred toward the large man. "Hey, that's Doctor Hollis, you don't push on him."

Doc Hollis immediately held up his hands, shielding Kenny with his body while trying to placate the drunken man.

Raising his voice and speaking with authority, Doc Hollis looked Lubbers in the eye. "Okay, settle down. There's no need for pushing here. We'll be glad to go." Turning to face Kenny, he said, "Kenny, look, son. Take the rods, go back to the canoe. Make ready to launch. I'm sure Mr. Lubbers and I can talk this thing through."

Lubbers looked back with a grin to his audience as Kenny left the deck and trudged back to the canoe with the equipment.

The shorter man cheered him on. "Yeah, you show 'em, Lubbers."

"Show 'em how to get that city smell off of them," The taller one teased.

"That city boy could use a bath from where I'm standing, Lubbers. Gotta be tough on your nose over there."

Lubbers shoved Doc Hollis back towards the water. Hollis

A Grasshopper Strikes

side-stepped Lubbers' powerful, but awkward blow. He kept his feet.

Standing on McKinley Bridge, the rushing water and the breeze in the trees distracted Mark from hearing the scene down below on the water's edge. He was chatting and sharing the binoculars with two campers. He had spotted a spiffy-looking kingfisher on the opposite side of the bridge looking away from the deck. He kept searching for a Kirkland's Warbler. Then he saw Kenny trudging off the deck toward the canoe.

What happened next froze Mark and the two campers in place. Their hands and feet seemed glued to the railing of the bridge. For Mark, it was as if the scene below was a troupe of movie actors instead of his friends.

Kenny placed the gear in the canoe. Then he looked off into space; a space now three years in his past. He exploded with a volcanic, "NO!" The scream seemed to erupt from the depth of middle earth and rocket forth from his very soul.

Mark's ears were pierced with the sound of that one word from Kenny.

Doc Hollis reflexively jerked around in the direction of the canoe.

Kenny was running with panther-like speed directly at the large man Lubbers.

"Kenny, no!" Hollis yelled.

Kenny's legs propelled him missile-like to within five feet of Lubbers. Then Kenny's body lifted into the air and his left leg arrowed into the blubbery chest of Lubbers with a thud. Lubbers kept his feet but staggered backward. With machine-like fury, Kenny resumed his attack as Lubbers raised his arms in a defensive posture. Running forward again, Kenny hurled his 170-pound body upwards into the air toward one side of Lubbers. With force born of buried anger, Kenny then thrust his body downward. His right foot speared into the outside of Lubbers' left knee with great velocity.

181

The Snipe Hunters' Deadly Catch at Muskrat Creek

A Grasshopper Strikes

Yelling in pain, Lubbers crumpled to the ground. Kenny landed on his butt, then immediately leaped up. Kenny advanced cat-like toward Lubbers.

Lubbers, unable to stand on his knee, pulled his large frame up to a sitting posture. "Just who do you think you—?"

Kenny executed a perfect front thrust kick directly into the immense belly of the downed Lubbers.

Red-faced and bug-eyed, Lubbers's face radiated a look of total shock. As if struck with a bolt of electricity from within, he jerked to one side and began to violently retch. A retch was heard way up on McKinley Bridge. A retch was heard across the river. A retch was heard in the campground. The contents of an entire six-pack spilled out onto the sand.

There was a pause in Kenny's machine-like fury and quickness. His eyes seemed to focus for the first time on the actual person of Lubbers, who clearly had no fight left in him. The large man was panting heavily between retches. He could not get up. Lubbers did not even look up at his aggressor.

"You don't never touch Doc Hollis." Kenny, still in his martial arts posture, screamed at the wretched figure before him, "NEVER!"

Lubbers' drinking buddies now came at a full trot right for Kenny. Kenny turned, faced them with a poised stance. His body gave no suggestion of retreat from the much larger, stronger adults.

Doc Hollis, standing transfixed at the scene before him, braced for the impending clash a mere six yards in front of him.

With a deliberate gaze right into the eyes of the men, Kenny remained poised. He was motionless as his aggressors gained speed. The distance between them quickly narrowed.

From the bridge above, the men seemed to overshadow Kenny.

Mark ran off the bridge and scrambled down the embankment. He took a paddle from the canoe. Brandishing

183

The Snipe Hunters' Deadly Catch at Muskrat Creek

the wooden paddle while panting heavily, he raced toward Kenny's side to face the oncoming aggressors, knowing he would never make it in time.

Collision was imminent. Mark and the locals watched as Kenny, seconds from impact, remained in his martial arts stance, arms and legs coiled for action.

The tall man skidded to a halt in front of Kenny. He raised his open hands up in a gesture of surrender. "It's all right, Sonny. We'll take it from here. We don't want no more trouble."

The shorter man had spun to his right and gone to Lubbers's side. He tried to get him to his feet. Whimpering in pain, Lubbers bleated to his friend, "My knee. My knee. Watch my knee." Lubbers used the man's shoulder to regain his feet and limped off the deck. He put weight only on his right knee. Grimacing, tears were flooding his eyes.

The campers from the bridge started to hoot and holler. "You go, Little Grasshopper. Teach the big boy some manners."

As Lubbers limped away, another local from the campground teased him, "Hey, Lubbers, you say something to upset that boy?"

The tall man, suddenly sober, turned around looking at both Kenny and Doc Hollis. "Hey, kid. Uh Mister, I'm sorry. My buddy … He ain't no bad guy. He don't mean to be no bad bully … He's a veteran. He's in the American Legion Post with me. Helps out on fish fries and river clean-ups … just now and then he gets to boozing."

The tall man now had a genuinely apologetic tone to his voice. "I guess we all got a little carried away, but, uh … You know boozing! Guys will do crazy things. Things they don't never think about else-wise. It's the beer talking."

As if poked in the side, Kenny relaxed his defensive posture toward the tall man and firmly pronounced, "Yeah, well, that … that even I know about."

Backing away toward the campground the tall man assured

A Grasshopper Strikes

them, "OK, then. We're sorry for your trouble. My buddy will sleep it off. Be fine tomorrow. You'll see. No meanness in him 'cept with the booze."

The almost mesmerized and very tense Hollis quickly grabbed Kenny's arm. "Look, son, it's over. We got to go now."

He guided him to the riverbank. The canoe was about twenty-five yards downriver from the fight scene. Mark followed along with the paddle in his hand.

"Mark, you take the bow and I'll stern this."

Placing both hands on Kenny's shoulders, Doc Hollis shook him gently but firmly. He introduced his medical procedure voice to the scene. "Kenny, you settle down now. Sit in the middle. You got to relax. We'll handle it from here. Mark, we need to get to the U.S. Forest Service campground called Buttercup. There's road access there. You know it? Do you remember it from your solo?"

Already aiming the canoe downstream and ready for Hollis to push off, Mark hollered back, "Yes, Doctor. I do. There's a sandbar on the north side, and then a big bend in the river just before it."

Hollis pushed off shore and jumped in the stern. "Let's go. Dig that paddle, my boy. We can get Beaupré to pick us up there." He brought the radio to life. Paul tuned in on his radio. "Paul, we're going further down river. Our take-out will be at Buttercup. We have no time for questions, just meet us there. I repeat, you need to meet us at the forest service site at Buttercup." After repeating the message loudly, Paul gave him a confirmation.

When they raced under the bridge, one of the spectators cupped his hands to his face and hollered down, "Hey, you, Little Grasshopper, you are welcome to come back and fish anytime."

Clapping from shore, two other men hooted, "Bravo to you. You taught the bully a lesson today."

The Snipe Hunters' Deadly Catch at Muskrat Creek

Kenny stared straight ahead. He said nothing. His mind swirled with past painful images. But when the merry-go-round got to today, he was glad he was able to stop this bully.

Apart from Mark warning them to duck a low-hanging branch as he negotiated a sharp bend, there was only the sound of paddles slapping the water for the next hour. Several startled blue herons squawked their displeasure at being disturbed. That was the only interruption from the river. This quiet peaceful scene of the three men racing downstream masked the storm raging inside Kenny as he sat quietly in the middle of the canoe.

"There it is, doctor. That's our take out," Mark called out as the canoe rounded the last bend before Buttercup.

"I'll beach it near that bent-over birch tree. Then let's get this canoe up to the access road for Beaupré's jeep," Hollis instructed.

In the comfort of a shade tree, Doc Hollis motioned both Kenny and Mark toward him. He spoke in a low voice, though the site was all but abandoned. "Look, guys, there'll be no chatter at the Main Post about this. Our extracurricular activities with Monsieur Lubbers are between us. You understand?" Hollis gestured toward the creel. "We got some trout and some exercise as far as they are concerned. I'll be in charge of this incident at McKinley Bridge from here on in."

Mark looked over at Kenny. Kenny simply looked up at Doc Hollis and nodded in agreement.

When Beaupré's jeep pulled up parallel to the canoe, Kenny walked to the stern and joined Mark in hoisting it up on the rack. He walked behind Doc Hollis as he stooped down to get some gear. He began in a low voice, "Doctor, I'm sorry for the trouble I caused back—"

Hollis interrupted with a wave of his hand. "No worries, Kenny," he assured him. "We'll have time for our 'Dutch Uncle talk' later at the Main Post." Handing him the creel of fish he continued, "You keep the fish on your lap and don't drop them."

A Grasshopper Strikes

Sliding into the passenger side of the jeep, Doc looked over at Paul in the driver's seat. "Thanks for being so quick. Now I say we get over to the put-in site, pick up Joe and the jeep and get back to the cabin. There's enough time to roast some corn, grill these trout and put an end to another great day on the Au Sable. What do you say, men?"

Kenny and Mark roared their approval from the back seat.

"Heck, I've been hungry for the last two hours," Paul said as he shifted the jeep into first gear. "Joe couldn't find the Silver Beaver but he got us two good-sized brown trout in the process. Let's go home."

… The Snipe Hunters' Deadly Catch at Muskrat Creek

Chapter Fourteen

Fireside Chat

Wednesday, October 3, 1979, 9:15 pm, Paul Beaupré's Cabin

"Mark, how about you bunk in with Joe tonight and let Kenny try out the bench by the fire for the first time," Doc Hollis suggested.

Doc Hollis encountered Kenny in the hallway putting the cribbage board away. "Kenny, when I had a person that needed a non-medical chat, I'd tell my secretary to schedule a 'thirteenth' patient of the day. That would be my last customer. Janie would close up the front office and go home. So, how about you become my thirteenth patient tonight?" Pointing to the fireplace, he continued, "Right over there is my office now. So, see you there after lights out for the other guys?"

"Yeah, sure," Kenny stammered out a reply before a thought entered his mind. "But can we visit the buck first?"

"The buck?" Hollis asked.

"You know, Mark told me about the poem by the buck." Kenny pointed down the hall.

Hollis laughed. "Yes, yes, of course. I forgot that this is your first time here." He strolled down the hall to the buck and slapped it on the side of its head. "I'll read it through slowly twice. You be thinking up your questions, Kenny."

Kenny heard the poem. "Those lines at the end are the best. 'The ears at the Post will honor it so. The ears of the world will never know." Is that the way it works here?"

"Here and at my cabin. The nickname Main Post applies to both cabins actually; and the poem applies to all who choose to so honor it and conduct themselves accordingly. It's a voluntary thing among the men here. It is one of our main attractions. During hunting season, some come here and never leave the cabin to hunt." Hollis gestured toward the fireplace. "You need a ginger ale? We can handle any more questions by the fire. Go ahead and take a seat, Kenny. It seems the lights are out for our cabin mates."

Hollis strolled in from the kitchen, handed Kenny a ginger ale, and took his place in the chair facing the fire at an angle. Kenny was on another angled chair opposite Doc Hollis with the roaring fire in between them.

"So, it's clear you know some martial arts. It seems you might know a little about alcohol, too. At least what it can do to men like Lubbers, eh?"

Kenny did not reply. His eyes were studying the flames licking the top of the fireplace.

Hollis calmly met the long moments of silence that followed by stoking the fire, adding new logs, and joining Kenny in inspecting each flame as it rose toward the chimney. It was a treasured pastime at the Main Post.

Minutes flew by. Kenny simply stared into the warming fire. Then he stared some more without so much as looking up at Hollis. The scene with the blood on the porch rose up with each flame. Inside the stone-silent exterior, his stoppers, all those frigid muscles holding back the dam of feelings were beginning to melt. The poem, the men of the Main Post, and the flames of the fireplace were melting the ice dam.

Tears began to stream down Kenny's face. He shook his head as if to say no to someone now three years in his past. His fists were curled up. He stood up, walked to the fireplace, and pushed the logs with the poker. The tears became more intense.

Fireside Chat

Words, formed in his mind, tried to escape his mouth. Emotions drowned those thoughts in their infancy. Kenny sat down and began to wring his hands. He thought about being courteous. He felt he should at least look up at Doc Hollis.

Tears were sins he swore he'd never commit. Through three years of group and individual sessions at Havenwood, he never talked. Now, he found an oasis for his wounds. Now he wanted to talk. The darn words would not come. He stood up. He looked at Hollis. He sat back down. Kenny averted his tearful face to the fire. The bloody porch was still there. It sought to be released. Its manacles were suffering from three years of rust and wear.

"Take your time, son. I'm not going anywhere. We got enough wood to last till Christmas," Hollis counseled with no hint of pressure in his voice. He did not move an inch in his chair.

Kenny slowly rose from his chair and faced the fireplace. He gulped in some air. His words, long drowned by emotions, had been muscled into silence for three years. It took more strength than putting down a 250-pound bully to retrieve them.

"It ain't right. It ain't right. It ain't right!" At the top of his lungs Kenny echoed into the fireplace. "I go to jail and he goes back to work. It ain't right! He killed Woody. And I go to jail. He shot him dead! He shot Woody dead right in front of me. It ain't right! He killed Woody. I go to jail and he goes on drinking and driving that freaking truck."

Kenny opened the screen on the fireplace and grabbed the poker. He stabbed at the burning wood. "He shot ..." Kenny stopped the sentence and stabbed at the wood. "He shot ..." Another stab at the burning wood. "Shot. He just shot ..." The stabbing sent embers and sparks into the air around and outside of the firebox.

Hollis moved not a muscle. Ash and sparks flew out of the fireplace. Hollis sat and stared into the firebox. Some sparks

Fireside Chat

landed on his pants. He brushed them off. He said nothing.

"He shot Woody. He shot Woody. Right in front of me. He shot Woody. It ain't right. It just ain't right. I go to jail and he shot Woody."

Kenny pushed the logs forcefully back and forth loudly, screaming at them: "He shot Woody. It ain't right!" Kenny knelt down by the fireplace and forcefully speared the logs while screaming, "It ain't right. Woody's dead and I go to jail."

Unseen by Hollis and Kenny, bedroom doors on both the upper and lower level of Paul Beaupré's cabin were slightly cracked open in response to the loud screams.

After several minutes, Kenny was bathed in sweat and tears. He gulped in more air. He finally looked up at Hollis while still clutching the poker.

"Don't you see, Doctor Hollis, it ain't right. He killed Woody, but I go to jail. Three years at Havenwood and he's still driving his truck."

Doc Hollis seized the moment and rose from his chair. "I'll get us some more wood. We wore those poor guys out, eh? How about you take a seat now?" Hollis slowly set about the task without ever expecting Kenny to comply. He placed his hands on the poker when he returned with the logs. He looked Kenny in the eye and addressed him in a low voice. "I'm going to need this now. How about you let it be my turn to play with the logs?"

Kenny paused, released his grip on the poker. Doc Hollis knelt down to tend to the fireplace. Kenny stood up over Doc Hollis. He put his hands on his hips.

Hollis lifted his eyes to meet Kenny's. "We often have to take turns. It seems everybody that comes here likes to play with the fireplace. Me too, though, so I understand. How about you take a seat now?"

Kenny studied his face. A full minute passed. Then Kenny erupted, "Jeez, Doctor Hollis. I have not talked about this in three years. Hospital doctors and social workers were prodding

The Snipe Hunters' Deadly Catch at Muskrat Creek

me all the time. And now you want equal time with the poker?"

"Well, it seems fair. You been playing with it forever and I haven't had a turn. Take a seat. You're all worn out. I've been listening like the poem says and, what the heck; you have not even told me who Woody is," Doc Hollis replied with his back to Kenny while he faced the fireplace.

Kenny slumped into his chair. He stared back into the flames. Now the distance was four years.

"Woody was my colt. Well, not actually, the neighbor's colt. The neighbor knew my dad from church. They were in the Knights of Columbus together and went fishing together. My dad died and Uncle Bobby, that's what we called him, would look after me and my mom. He took me fishing with his kids. At least until my mom started living with Henry, a trucker; no one got along with Henry. Henry drinks and beats people up."

Doc Hollis finished with the logs and took his seat. "So, Woody …?"

"Uncle Bobby offered me a proposition as he called it. If I got up and fed Woody every day before and after school, I could eventually own him and show him at the fair with the 4-H club. I got to ride him and go on outings with the other horsemen in the county. Uncle Bobby paid for all the food and vet bills. He had the barn for Woody. I cleaned the stalls. It was a way for me to own my own horse so to speak. At the end of the year Woody stayed in his barn right next to our property, but I was the owner. Uncle Bobby saw to it that we had papers that were legal. I earned that horse. Woody was mine."

Kenny got out of the chair. He loomed over Doc Hollis in his chair. He pointed his finger at Doc Hollis and asserted, "Woody was mine. I took care of that horse for over a year; I earned the right to own him. Uncle Bobby made it legal. I just knew my dad would be proud that I owned that horse."

"So, Henry just hated horses?" Doctor Hollis asked.

"One night I came home late. I fed Woody, cleaned up the

Fireside Chat

stall, and rode him because the weather was good. Henry was home from his long-distance trucking. He was drunk and hitting my mom when I came in the door. I ran at him and knocked him down. He beat me up, but I got up and hit him in the eye with my backpack full of books. It hurt him and he stopped. My mother ordered me to go to Uncle Bobby's for the night. Uncle Bobby and his family knew all about Henry. He went off on them, too. So, I took my books and left. Henry said he'd get me for hurting his eye."

"Did you stay the night with Uncle Bobby?" Hollis asked.

"Yes. I went to feed Woody before five o'clock in the morning and he was not there. I went home to ask my mom. Henry was usually gone trucking at that time. He was home. He told me to go on the porch. He brought Woody around from the back. He walked him onto the porch. Henry said, 'Look, punk, next time you think about hitting me, remember this.' Then he pulled a pistol out and shot Woody in the head three times. Woody fell down. Blood was all over the place and on me. There was a big pool of blood on one end of the porch. I see that pool of blood every day of my life."

Doc Hollis gasped, "Good grief, Kenny! What did you do?"

"I ran right through Henry's grasp and into the night. It was still dark. It was a little after five o'clock in the morning. I ran for miles. I ran toward the river. I was moving all day and into the night by the river and by some orchards. I could not go home to that pool of blood. I swore I never would go home. I swear I will kill that Henry someday. I ain't never been home since."

"What happened to Henry? Where did you go, back to Uncle Bobby's?" Doc Hollis asked.

"Police did nothing to Henry. Even Uncle Bobby tried to sue him. Nothing. They said I was a minor and could not own property. My parents did. Henry could do what he wanted with the horse. That jive drunk never even married my mom properly, like in a church. They went to a Justice of the Peace or something like that."

"So, no one helped you with this drunk, Henry?"

"Uncle Bobby saw to it that Henry had to move out. It seems his tires were always going flat. Uncle Bobby has four sons who are all crack-shot hunters. They got no stomach for drunken Henry. The sheriff showed up the third time when all four tires were flat. He advised Henry to buy some insurance. He said road hazards were legendary in Huron County. That was the end of the investigation. Uncle Bobby visited me in the hospital, and he told me he was standing right there with all four sons looking at that drunkard Henry when the sheriff told him. The tow truck driver had to drive Henry all the way to Lapeer. It seems Uncle Bobby made some calls. Every tire shop in town was suddenly out of his model of tire. Henry moved back to Kentucky. He eventually came back to a different city in Michigan though. When I get bigger, I'm going to find that drunk wherever he's hiding."

"How did you end up in Havenwood State Hospital?" Doc Hollis inquired.

"I stayed in a field the first night. I found a haymow and slept there. I ate apples from an orchard and tomatoes and cucumbers from gardens. On the third night, I slept in a barn. In the morning, I heard the radio news when the farmer came out to tend to the cows and chickens. The police were looking for me, but they made no mention of Henry or my dead horse, Woody. That made me mad. I was furious. All I could see was the pool of blood on the porch. Actually, that's all I see every night, even during the day. I wanted revenge. I roamed the cornfields and sugar beet fields until late in the day. I found a barn that was used to store equipment and hay. I made sure there was no animal in there. Then I set the place on fire. Turns out a cat, a mouser died, but I did not plan that."

"I see. Then what happened?" Doc Hollis was hypnotized by Kenny's story.

Fireside Chat

"The farmer and his neighbor came out to fight the fire. I was so tired I just watched them. They ignored me. When the fire department arrived, they came over to me and asked me a bunch of questions. They held me until the police came. The police recognized me and took me into custody. I lied and told them that Henry lit the place on fire. I reeked of the smell of gasoline. It was on my shoes and pants."

"You went to jail, then?"

"Yes, until Protective Services showed up. I was put in protective custody in a youth home because of my age, fifteen. I was convicted of arson and sent to Havenwood State Hospital. Not one thing was done to Henry, except by Uncle Bobby and his sons. That drunk would still be there otherwise. The sheriff knew the story though. He just couldn't do anything. The deputies wrote Henry tickets every chance they could. But he did not leave until he got tired of buying tires. Word spread through the police, the Knights of Columbus, and the veterans' hall. Henry could not buy a tire or get service on his truck in towns all around. He even complained to the insurance company and it went nowhere. To this day I wonder what Uncle Bobby told the priest in the confessional. He is a devout churchgoer. For that matter, I wonder about the sheriff too because Henry complained to the state police that his tires had bullet holes in them. Sheriff's investigation identified road hazards as a cause. Henry took it to court but the case was dismissed."

"How so?"

"Judge said there was insufficient evidence to proceed," Kenny said.

"Really, with bullet holes in a truck tire?"

"Yes. Uncle Bobby said his lawyer was there when the officials reported to the court that they were unable to locate the tires for their appearance before the judge."

"Long live the sheriff and the Uncle Bobbys of this world."

Doc Hollis joined Kenny in a good belly laugh. "So where is your mom?"

"She lost the house. Then she went to live with her sister, my Aunt Lou, in Bay City. She's just too dependent. Another Henry might come along. After my father died, she was never the same. Henry brought her money; allowed her to keep the home for a little while longer. I talk more with Uncle Bobby and his sons than I do my mom. Aunt Lou has to help her, guide her. My dad was everything to us. When he died, my mom was just, well, never the same. My dad would have a drink four times a year, Christmas, Easter, July Fourth, and November tenth. That's it. He had one drink four times a year. And she ends up with a drunk. That's how bad off she was."

"Could you tell me about Havenwood State Hospital, Kenny? How did that work out for you?" Hollis asked.

"I had group and individual sessions. I had psychological and recreational therapy with really nice and well-trained people. They meant well, I suppose. But I was mad at all of them. Not really them, I guess. Just all adults in authority; they all looked like friends of Henry for a long time. There ain't enough Uncle Bobby's in this world. One day I laughed so loud that the social worker asked to see Uncle Bobby and two of his sons as he left the visitation room."

"What was so funny?"

"Ray, Bobby's youngest son wants to be a sports photographer. He brought me before and after photos of Henry's truck with four flat tires. The first time, a local tow truck came and started to help. He got a radio dispatch call during his visit. Then he drove off, saying there was an accident on the expressway. After that, no towing service in a two-county area would respond to his calls. Then he showed me a photo of a tow truck from Lapeer, Michigan. That's sixty-seven miles away. It took two days for it to come."

Smiling, Hollis said, "Hey, I like that. No wonder you felt

Fireside Chat

better. That's friendship in the face of injustice."

"Yeah, it gets better, doctor. Bobby's oldest son visited me at the end of deer season. I did not know Art very well because he was a lot older than me. It was a short visit, but I remember what he told me after he showed me all the deer his family had at the end of opening day. There's a lot of well-fed deer in those cornfields, doctor. Art said, 'So, Kenny listen up now; I got a church story for you. At the end of Mass, a farmer chases me down in the parking lot and says he wants to help me during the upcoming hunting season.' I told him deer season was over. Then he says, 'That's not the season I'm talking about. I understand your family is the only one in the county licensed for rubber tire hunting.' I said, 'What?' He said, 'I'm Russell Noel. Let me know if you run out of ammunition. I got all you need.' That's what he said.'"

Doctor Hollis opened his hands with a quizzical look on his face. "So, did Art ever explain? What was he all about?"

"I burned Mr. Noel's barn down, doctor," Kenny said.

Doctor Hollis stared into the fireplace for a moment. The story and the images seeped into his bones along with the warmth from the flames. He smiled. "Wow, I think I'd like having those Huron County folks for patients. Did you share this information with your therapists?"

"Nope. I was stupid. I saw all the staff there as punishment. It was not until Ho Ho, my social worker, came along that I made use of the place. I have talked more to you now than I did in three years there. On visits, I talked to Uncle Bobby and his family, my youth pastor, and my coach. I refused to talk to my mom until Uncle Bobby told me that Henry was gone."

"What did you do with your time? You had school there?" Doctor Hollis asked.

"Yeah, well, sort of. I had tutoring and some independent study classes. But I did not tune in much. I liked art and used the gym. I worked out a lot in the weight room. After a year I got a therapist from the Philippines. He was a social worker with a black belt in two different martial arts. He forged a contract with me. He'd teach me the martial arts if I participated more in the social programming. Howard Hovsepian Ramos was his name, but Ho Ho was his nickname. Ho Ho is the reason I got to Bosco."

"It was this Ho Ho who taught you those flying kicks, then? The kicks Mr. Lubbers will remember for a long time?" Hollis asked.

"Yes, Ho Ho was the teacher. I made progress with his deal. I went on outings. I joined in group discussions and completed some classes. I started back with the chapel. I always liked church. I went with my father. I just tuned out after my dad died. My mom did not go and then along came Henry. Ho Ho convinced the board that I'd progress more if I was in a supervised setting still, but with kids my own age who were not adjudicated. You know, in trouble with the law, like I was."

Doctor Hollis interjected, "Bosco Academy will be a great place for you, Kenny, especially if you stop breaking the legs of drunks."

Kenny grinned. "Well, actually, I got one more drunk to go, doctor."

"Not tonight, but some other time we should talk about that, Kenny. You've done a good job blowing ballast tonight. That's enough work for one night," Hollis concluded.

"What's a ballast, doctor?"

"Sorry. It's a naval term. It's when a ship ditches the weight it has in its hold; makes the ship lighter. You unburdened your soul a bit tonight. There should be some weight off your shoulders now, Kenny," Hollis counseled.

"Yeah, well that's sure enough true. This Main Post fireplace has a way of getting my tongue to flow as quickly as the river," Kenny confessed. "I never talked to anyone like I did to you tonight, doctor. Thanks for listening, like the poem says."

Fireside Chat

Hollis pointed to the bench. "There's your bunk for the night. The blanket is in the drawer. Remember, Kenny, 'The ears at the Main Post will honor it so that the ears of the world will never know.' So, be at ease and sleep well. Now you close up the fireplace doors when you are done staring it into extinction, okay?"

"That might cost you some more logs."

Hollis turned as he headed up the stairs. He gave Kenny a salute. Kenny waved back. Then he turned toward the fire. The flames once again commanded the attention of his now-teary eyes.

The Snipe Hunters' Deadly Catch at Muskrat Creek

Chapter Fifteen

Back to Havenwood?

Thursday, October 5, 1979, 7:48 am, Paul Beaupré's Cabin

"Joe, you have any idea how we are going to explain our escape from Bosco Hall when we get back there?" Kenny asked as he exited Beaupré's cabin and traipsed along behind Joe and Mark.

"I dunno. I'm thinking on it," Joe whispered back to Kenny.

"Jean Luc surely knows how to make a 'Back-to-Bosco Breakfast', eh?" Mark asked as he led them down Partridge Path. The jeep was still in Hollis' driveway.

"He's the best this side of Marie. But Kenny here has got to know, Marie does not have any thimbleberry jam back at Bosco," Joe said in reply. "You want that, you'll have quite a hike to get back here to the Main Post. And, Kenny, I don't plan on any more adventures like this one."

Mark laughed. "Hah. Yeah. Kenny, you and Joe both have an appointment, a hearing actually, with Father George at one today, eh? When Hollis took the call, I did not hear Brother Ed mention my name. Maybe that means I won't lose my job because I let the new kid get lost after his first night on my floor."

"Hey, we'll stick up for you," Joe said. "You were not involved. We bamboozled you and snuck out. This is all on our heads."

"Joe, that weekend pass called for you and Cowdrey to be

picked up by Gino Pagnucco. How are you going to explain your cross-country jaunt to the Quonset hut?" Mark asked. "I saw your rosary lying by the bunk bed this morning. Does that mean you were up early praying for some inspiration? I could use some myself."

"Well actually, Mark, the truth is I aim to pray every night, not just when I'm in trouble," Joe replied in a quiet voice. "It's Brother Ed's idea from my first year here. I don't suppose I'll ever win a prize, but I know where to go for guidance along the way."

"Yeah, well, eventually I confessed the truth to Brother Ed. See, guys, I did not tell the Bosco staff about Kenny's note for a whole day. They started the search and called all the staff into a meeting. I cost them a lot of search time and trouble," Mark explained. "Doc Hollis and the Beaupré's helped me figure that out and do the right thing. You guys get enough sleep last night? You ready for the meeting?"

"What note?" Joe asked. Then he looked back at Kenny, who was last in line as they reached Hollis' lawn and headed for the driveway.

"Forget it, Joe. It's over," Kenny said. "I just have to find a way to stay at Bosco. I like it here. This was a dumb thing to do. I caused Bosco and the police a lot of trouble going AWOL. The Havenwood Hospital staff will probably be here. I'm on probation. I can be withdrawn from this placement at any time."

Mark explained, "Well, your community service in cleaning up for two days after the storm shows you know how to be a good citizen. I still have the note, too. That shows you want to stay at Bosco. Perhaps if I'd had the 'Pay to Play' talk with you after dinner, you would have avoided this. That was my call; that was actually my responsibility. I'll remind them of that. I already told Brother Ed, though."

Mark got in the Jeep Cherokee. "Okay, seat belts on. Now we get to see how the landscape between here and Bosco has

Back to Havenwood?

changed since the storm. I'm driving; you two can count the number of trees blown over."

✂

A group of six students including Saltz broke into spontaneous applause as the trio entered the dorm through the front entrance. A voice shouted, "Welcome back to Bosco!"

"Hey, you two, are you happy to be found?" another voice from the crowd asked.

Joe and Kenny walked through the front doors and paused to greet the six students. Bernard, the resident assistant behind the desk, whistled his approval while leaning on the counter. "Hey, Kenny, how does it feel to be a new guy around here? A stormy night in the woods is just part of our initiation. Bosco's got more coming your way. Count on it, new boy."

The excited voices were interrupted by clapping and some whistling. Saltz came out of the crowd. "Hey, let me get your bags."

Joe thanked the group and then turned and faced them as he headed up the stairs. "Let this be a lesson known to all those coming to Bosco in the future. Always start your stay with Mark's patented talk, 'Pay to Play!'"

The jeers and cheers grew a little louder and Bernard hollered, "I'll vote for that!"

Kenny learned his roommate was still in town with the foreign exchange student, but it was good to see Saltz. At lunch, the bombardment of questions began. Kenny's talk with Doc Hollis had allowed for a night without a nightmare. He was well-rested. He did not want to be burdened with any more secrets or lies. This Main Post sense of peace was new and welcome. After harboring his distrust and anger inside a fortress of silence for three years, Dr. Hollis had built a drawbridge over his glacial moat. Kenny suddenly realized a sense of relief that allowed him energy to embrace the day without a shield.

"Hey, I hear you guys lost a canoe in the storm," Bernard said as he sat at the end of the table. "Are you going back to look for it?"

Kenny, nodding, quickly deflected the question toward Joe seated across from him.

"We already did," Joe said. "No luck though. I guess it probably sank in one of the deeper holes. Maybe someone saw it beached after the storm and just claimed it."

"Hollis and Beaupré have all their Au Sable Adventure canoes registered with the state though." Saltz, seated next to Joe, joined in the chat. "Someone may turn it in."

Both Joe and Kenny had quick flashbacks of the tobacco bandit. The image of the pistol popped into Joe's head. "Ya never know. Who won the flag football game anyway?" Joe steered the chatter to more comfortable confines. In his mind, he was mulling over the one o'clock meeting.

><

Joe and Mark entered the board room adjacent to Father George's office. The room was large enough for staff meetings and community professionals servicing the students at the academy. There were four adults with Father George and Brother Ed at the large table.

Father George made the introductions. "Joe, these gentlemen are here from Havenwood Hospital on Kenny Dee's behalf: hospital administrator, Mr. Huddleston, and social worker, Mr. Howard Ramos."

"Hello, Joe. So good to see you again, Kenny," Ramos said.

"Hi, Ho Ho," said Kenny.

Father George continued, "And we'd like to introduce Kenny to Gino and Josephine Pagnucco, foster parents of David Cowdrey and Joe Duvalle. They are from nearby Grayling."

Thus began the most important meeting in Kenny's life since

Back to Havenwood?

he was adjudicated in a Huron County courtroom over three years ago. Joe and Kenny were seated at a smaller table facing the men at the conference table. Kenny wanted to speak from his new heart, the heart born at the Main Post. He learned to trust adults there. But this was just so new to him.

The tall man dressed in a business suit was the first adult to speak. "Well, boys, since I traveled the most to get here, I get to go first. I'm Mr. Huddleston from Kenny's former placement at Havenwood's Adolescent Unit in Tuscola County. Greetings to you Kenny. I'm ever so grateful to see you in good health. And, Joe, even under these circumstances I am glad to make your acquaintance. Only because I'm told your woodsmanship made a good outcome possible from the dire circumstances in which your foolish, ill-conceived escapade caused for all of us in this room."

He paused briefly as he looked at Father George. "Never have I or Father George been unable to account for a student placed in our care. You must know that Kenny is placed at Bosco but he is still a ward of the state. So, you need to understand I represent and am accountable to the state. We are here to decide if Kenny is to return to Havenwood, remain at Bosco, or be referred to the Department of Social Services for an alternative placement. All options are now on the table following your adventure in the woods."

Joe stood up. "Mr. Huddleston, Father George I'm the one at fault. I broke the rules. I know I should have stayed home. But I convinced Kenny to come so I could go fishing and canoeing. When Cowdrey got sick, I knew I had to convince Kenny to come. He is strong enough to canoe upriver. He believed what I said about the weekend pass. Now I know I was selfish; and unfair to a lot of people. I didn't even call Gino to save him a trip here during a storm."

At that, Father George deliberately cleared his throat and caught Joe's eye when he looked up. "Excuse me, I mean Mr.

Pagnucco and Mrs. Pagnucco." Joe nodded at them with a sheepish grin.

"It's alright, son. I was smart enough to stay home," Mr. Pagnucco replied. "I heard the news on the radio and just assumed the camping, canoeing trip was off. Then we lost phone service pretty early in the storm."

Joe continued, "But I did not think about anybody else. Honestly, I wanted to go so bad. I was so happy to be back in the woods. But if the storm didn't mess everything up, I probably still would not have thought about the trouble I made for so many people. I know it now though. It just wouldn't have been so bad without the storm. I planned to come back on time. And we actually had permission to use the canoe."

"But that permission was for you and David Cowdrey, not Kenny Dee," Father George interrupted. "And you two had just completed a trip up that stretch of river with Doctor Hollis the week before, right? Yet, you wanted to go back there."

"Yes, Father. But then Cowdrey got sick and stayed at the clinic. So, I know it was wrong, really wrong but that was why I got the new kid, Kenny to come. Like I said, he had to be strong because we were going upriver from the Quonset hut. Plus, we had some cross-country hiking to do. The truth is Kenny came along because of me. Leaving Bosco was wrong and it was all my idea. Really though, we were safe until that big storm hit us."

Father George agreed, "That's true. The storm was tough on us and the county. Losing communications and the use of the roads only made your foolish trip worse. Now you realize how selfish you have been. Our fear for your safety added to the stress of no power for over three days. Then we reported Kenny missing after one night in our care."

Father George looked over at Mr. Huddleston. "Mr. Huddleston here had to have faith. Faith that we knew what we were doing; knew where our students were at all times. The sheriff, your scoutmaster, several volunteers were all out

Back to Havenwood?

looking. But frankly, for too long a time, we didn't know where you were. No parent, educator, or social worker should ever be in that position, you have to know that." Father George paused. "I'm sorry for all the trouble. I just did not count on the storm being so bad. At first, I did plan on calling the Pagnuccos." Joe halted briefly, realizing that was a sentence he'd like to take back. Looking directly at Father George, he concluded his presentation. "At least, I thought we'd be back here by the eight o'clock curfew Sunday. I really did. The canoeing season is ending, so I thought I could get out just one more time. Nothing worked out the way I planned. I realize I failed to think about and be considerate of others in that plan, even without the storm."

Kenny was relieved that Joe was carrying the ball. Kenny knew he could not tell the story; he simply nodded at Joe and the adults. He had no interest in talking about his role in the adventure.

"Yes. Well, I understand you used your adventure challenge knowledge that Doctor Hollis and Paul Beaupré provide for our students. Called Au Sable Adventure, isn't it? You knew about that railroad shack from that program, right?" Father George's voice sounded understanding.

"Yes, sir. I've been through the program twice," Joe explained. "On solo I discovered the shack in the wilderness. We got there after dark. It was quite cold and raining cats and dogs then."

"Well, now, I'm grateful you provided young, trusting Kenny with appropriate guest accommodations on his second night with us, Joe. I can only hope the amenities were up to Havenwood Hospital standards." Father George glanced down the table at the Havenwood Hospital staff.

Everyone in the room had a good laugh.

Father George continued with an exaggerated Irish lilt in his voice, "Ah, and surely you'll be knowing that we insist on 'Good

Housekeeping Standards' for our Bosco Boys wherever they may choose to lay their head."

A smiling Howard Ramos countered, "Well, I'd have to inspect this shack. Perhaps sometime in the future, Kenny, you could escort us there? Give us a tour, eh?"

Kenny enjoyed Ho Ho's humor once again, but he did not like all the attention being placed on him.

Mr. Huddleston said, "Kenny, let's hear from you. You had one night at Bosco followed by an unplanned field trip into a stormy wilderness. Then you spent time in the custody of Doctor Hollis and his neighbor helping with debris removal and clean-up. So, what say you about Bosco at this point?"

"I like it here. I got some friends now. I wanna stay." Kenny paused while looking up at Mr. Huddleston. He shoved his hands in and out of his pockets. "I like the Main Post, the poem, and canoeing on the Au Sable River. I really want to stay and learn. Learn to be like Joe," Kenny blurted out.

Everyone laughed. Joe laughed the loudest.

"So, you want to be like Joe Duvalle, eh?" Mr. Huddleston asked. "Well, I actually don't think our staff had that in mind when we made this placement." Laughter pervaded the room once again. "What is a main post, Kenny? What do you mean by that?"

"That's where Doc Hollis and Paul Beaupré live on the river," Kenny replied. "It's a name they use for both cabins. Right, Joe?"

"Yes," Joe continued. "Sir, it is a nickname from when their cabins were built next to each other years ago; they shared them, still do. The name just stuck. They call that Quonset hut The Outpost. That's where all the canoes and other Au Sable Adventure equipment are stored."

Kenny explained, "Mr. Huddleston, that's what I mean about being like Joe, like on the adventure program. Joe knows about the river and forest. He knows canoes, compasses, knots, trees, fish, rules for survival, what plants to eat, the ones that are

Back to Havenwood?

poisonous, land navigation, the stars, rules for—"

"Staying in school?" Mr. Huddleston interjected.

The adults all chuckled.

Brother Ed leaned forward and winked down the table at Mr. Huddleston. "That's the adventure program run by Doctor Hollis and Paul Beaupré. They mentor our students here; those that are academically eligible can choose to participate. It has elements taken from military survival training; a number of students who start aren't able to complete it. Joe has been through the program twice. Looking back on this weekend, it was probably a good thing for Kenny that he had that knowledge, eh?"

Mr. Huddleston leaned toward Kenny. He spoke as if they were the only people in the room. "I am happy that you are safe and healthy. After all this, do you want to remain at Bosco Academy?"

"Yes, Mr. Huddleston, I do."

"If the Bosco staff maintains this placement, it will require strict supervision of any off-campus activities. So, Kenny, do you want to continue here under those conditions?"

"Yes, I do, sir. I want to be a success like Mark Dubay talks about. He says success is there for those who prepare. He has a poster on the second floor. They do help you prepare here, Mr. Huddleston."

"Who is Mr. Dubay, Father George?" Mr. Huddleston asked.

"He's the senior resident assistant in charge of Kenny's floor. He's a graduate of the adventure program, accepted into college, and earned some college credits this year. We sent him over to the Main Post just as the storm broke. He was stranded there and became part of the rescue team the next day."

Father George stood up. "Okay. Kenny, Joe, go to the library. We'll be calling you back shortly."

Joe and Kenny walked in silence to the library and strolled over to the window overlooking the garden. Kenny, looking at

Joe's back, asked in a bewildered voice, "Joe, what if … what am I going to do if …"

Joe stepped aside, motioned Kenny to be silent, and simply raised up his rosary. "I don't know, Kenny. Pray."

Twenty minutes later Bernard came to usher them back into the conference room.

Mr. Huddleston resumed the meeting as soon as they were seated. "Kenny, we are accountable to the State of Michigan for your welfare. We have to justify this placement. Now we have a police report showing you went missing, AWOL. So, do you understand that your placement here is," Mr. Huddleston paused, "well, a big concern for us, Kenny?"

Kenny simply nodded.

"Well, Bosco has an established reputation with the state; we've had one patient graduate from here. Both Doctor Hollis and Mr. Ramos spoke on your behalf. Mr. Ramos's support causes us to favor this placement. I did not think you were ready for Bosco from the beginning. Mr. Ramos did. That's why you are here. We are taking a chance once again. Don't make us regret it, okay, Kenny?"

"No, sir," Kenny stammered. "I mean, yes, sir, I don't want you to regret it."

"Father George, that's it from the Havenwood perspective unless, Mr. Ramos …" Mr. Huddleston turned to Ramos.

"I have nothing to add," Ho Ho said. "Only that I would like to visit with Kenny before I leave."

"Of course, Mr. Ramos," Father George said. Turning to his other side, "Mr. and Mrs. Pagnucco, what are your views?"

Mrs. Pagnucco replied, "Joe does not always make the right decisions. He's impulsive. We know he loves the outdoors. He loves algae in the river more than algebra in the classroom, but we enjoy having him as part of our family. Our boys always look forward to their adventures with him."

Mr. Pagnucco nodded at the priest. "He likes Angelo's

Back to Havenwood?

restaurant cooking, at least the pizzas. And Joe always helps out in the kitchen. He's a good worker, likes to earn money, and is not afraid to sweat. On one visit we chopped down a tree, stacked firewood, and then went for pizza. It was mostly work. But he was happy. Once we shoveled snow for two days. He never complains."

Father George nodded. "Thank you for your support of our boys and our program." He turned to address the boys. "Kenny, Joe, this meeting is over. Brother Ed will explain the new behavior plan, which will be part of your court records, Kenny. The eyes of Bosco shall be upon you. You earned the shadow of a chaperone with this adventure of yours. Understand?"

Kenny solemnly nodded.

Joe stood up and looked at Father George. "Yes, Father. Thank you." He guided Kenny by the shoulder to the door. They returned to Room 216 in somber silence.

Twenty minutes later Mark walked up behind Brother Ed and Father George as they returned to the office. Mark seized the opportunity. "Excuse me, Father George, I want to apologize for the note and all the trouble it caused."

Both men turned to face Mark.

"Good afternoon, Mark," said Father George. "I want you to know that it was so good to see you all got back here safely. But what note are you referring to, young man?"

Brother Ed, standing next to Father George, looked at Mark and winked.

Mark, recalling his tormented moral discussion with Dr. Hollis and Paul Beaupré's biblical quote, stood befuddled, searching Brother Edmund's countenance for meaning.

Brother Edmund cuffed Mark on the shoulder. "Hey, you just remember Wednesday I'm in Oscoda. So, who is running the first half-hour of volleyball practice?"

"Uh, yes Brother Ed, I remember. I mean, yes I'll do it."

Brother Ed then continued down the hall with Father George.

PART TWO

The Snipe Hunters' Deadly Catch at Muskrat Creek

Chapter Sixteen

A New Season

Sunday, March 30, 1980, 4:00 pm, Cadillac, MI

"Need another warm-up on your coffee?" The waitress at McGuire's Ski Lodge could not have been more pleasant as she poured another cup without waiting for a reply.

"Thank you, Carly; you've been great to us all weekend," Paul Beaupré replied and nodded at Kenny, Joe, and Mark. "Maybe the kids need some more hot chocolate."

When all three declined, Carly stepped away from their table. It was the last one occupied so late on a Sunday afternoon. Carly turned back to face them. "You boys have been out skiing all day, so I bet you have not heard about the snowstorm coming our way. They just revised the forecast. We're supposed to have a big one, a blizzard at that, hitting us any time tonight through all day Monday. It seems a Canadian cold air front is dropping a little too far south."

"Really, just think, Paul, this is the first time we've been allowed off campus in six months and Mom Nature is sending us another storm," Kenny said as he leaned back in his chair.

Carly rested the coffee decanter on an adjacent table and continued the conversation, "Are you headed back toward Grayling area tonight or sticking around to enjoy some more snow on those cross-country ski trails? We are certainly going to get some. Our manager expects one of our best weeks for this

The Snipe Hunters' Deadly Catch at Muskrat Creek

late in March."

"We plan to leave here tonight," Paul said. "We only have about seventy miles to get back home. But with thirty-two to thirty-six degrees today, we had some melting snow on the trails. It was pleasant, sunny, and ideal for skiing. It just does not seem like it will be cold enough for a blizzard."

Carly offered some advice as she nodded at her guests, "Well suit yourself; I suppose the guys have to get back to school. But you might want to get the driving done. Our forecasters have been right all winter for once."

"Yeah, well it is too warm now unless the temperature drops a lot after dark," Joe said to Carly. "Heck, we lost the sun to those monsters dressed in gray over an hour ago. Just look at those low-hanging gray skies; they could be hiding some of that white stuff for us,"

Paul gulped the last of his coffee and stood up. "Ok, guys let's get to the room and pack up. We'll shower and pack the jeep in shifts. We should get east on M-55 before any snow hits or we totally lose light. I want to be on northbound I-75 if we get hit with snow."

Thirty minutes later, Paul and Joe, the first to shower, were packing the Jeep Cherokee in the nearly empty parking lot.

"Actually, it has gotten warmer since we left the trails, don't you think, Paul?" Joe asked.

"Absolutely. It is thirty-six degrees on my thermometer. But the wind has kicked up. Look at that strange orange and bluish-gray glow off to the west."

Paul, standing on a metal milk crate, was strapping the ski equipment on the top rack. As if startled, he stopped, jumped off the crate, and moved to the rear of the jeep. He peered west through the haze that comes with the arrival of a wintry evening after a sunny afternoon in North Country. He cupped his hands over his eyes to block the orange and blue-gray sky to the west. "Joe, get me the binoculars from the dashboard. Be quick."

A New Season

Joe scooted around and entered the passenger side of the vehicle. He took two steps toward Paul and flipped him the binoculars in the black leather case.

"Joe, you remember when we were painting the Quonset hut, one of the guys accidentally leaned his roller on a canoe. Bernard wasn't it? It left a red line right underneath the registration number almost as if it was underlined on purpose. So, we just left it."

"Yup, no need to mess with the mineral spirits if we had 'Vincent Van Gogh' on the job, Hollis said," Joe reminded him. "And yes, it was Bernard."

"So, it was one of the aluminum canoes. Was it the Silver Beaver?"

"Yeah, why?" Joe, said as he edged closer to Paul. Paul handed him the binoculars.

"Look at that canoe on top of that station wagon. It's turning southbound on US 131. Quickly, traffic is starting to move."

Joe plastered the binoculars to his eyes. He scanned in the direction Paul pointed. He scrutinized the canoe from the back to the front. He quickly adjusted the lens when he reached the front where the registration number was located. "Oh my gosh. That's got to be our canoe. No one could copy a mark like that. We gotta get …" He looked over to Paul. "Can we catch them? It's going away now."

"Joe, it's moving out of sight now, southbound, and Mark and Kenny are still up in the room. I just don't know." Paul sensed his near panic.

"We gotta go. We gotta get it. It's our canoe!" Joe gasped. "We call the cops and have them verify the registration number on the canoe. That'll prove it is ours. We gotta get close enough to get their license plate number. That's all."

"Well, put the crate in. I'll let the guys know." Paul sprinted across the parking lot. Returning, he threw Joe his winter parka and jumped in the jeep. Joe, wearing a turtle neck sweater under a hooded sports sweatshirt, just put it at his feet. He was already belted in and had a map in his hands. "Whew, that's rain not snow on our windshield."

The Jeep Cherokee left McGuire's headed for US 131. Southbound traffic out of Michigan's North Country was always steady and sometimes thick on a Sunday night. It was worse when the weather had been cooperative with the season's activities all weekend. This had been a perfect weekend for late March. "Joe, I'm going to hurry, but I'm not going to speed, you understand, right?" Paul looked over at Joe. Within a minute, he switched lanes to pass a pick-up truck hauling a trailer of four snowmobiles. "You look around the traffic to see if you can spot the canoe. He's got a head start on us though."

"Yeah, sure, Paul, we gotta catch that station wagon. It's a good chance they just found it; don't you think? Maybe they aren't really thieves. But I just don't know."

Paul accelerated to catch up to the car in front of him. He waited for his chance and then passed it. Paul did this four times and, each time, Joe would peer down the highway, hoping to spot the canoe.

"I've been thinking about the canoe for six months," Joe said. "With our activities restricted and no off-campus privileges, I've had time to think it over."

Twenty minutes passed. The highway remained crowded, with no sight of the canoe. The rain continued as the sky lost all light to the monstrous gray clouds. Paul settled in behind a panel truck.

A few minutes later, Paul looked at his watch and let out a sigh. "Well, Joe, this runs straight south to the second-largest city in the state. And there are probably six major highways that intersect US 131 in the next 100 miles to Grand Rapids. Even if he has not exited, we might drive the whole way and not see him."

Paul switched lanes and continued, "Hey, we know the Silver

A New Season

Beaver is not on the bottom of the river. But we just can't head south anymore. We gotta get our guys and then it is seventy miles north just to get to Grayling."

"Darn it all. But okay I understand," Joe whispered. "It was a Ford station wagon. Seems it was not new, but not really old either. I don't know if it was blue or black at that distance. Do you recall?"

"We had the setting sun glinting in from one side. I know it was dark, that's all." Paul took the next exit and turned the vehicle north back towards Cadillac. "Looks like Carly's weatherman got his precipitation forecast right. But it's not going to be white stuff with this temperature. The good news is no one is going north at this time of night. We'll be picking up Kenny and Mark soon. They sure had enough time to get ready, eh?"

"Yeah. Paul, ya think we'll ever get the Silver Beaver back? Somehow?"

"Put your mind elsewhere now, Joe. We've done all we can tonight. It's dark and we have to get home. This rain is sure to slow us up tonight. So, how has it been for Kenny adjusting to the dorm, his studies, and his roommate? That's Fred, isn't it?"

Joe stretched his legs out and relaxed. He no longer had to lean sideways looking for a canoe on a rack. "Picture a teeter-totter on a playground. That's Kenny and Fred. That's what I see as their suitemate. When they get back from the cafeteria, Kenny will exercise and practice his katas and karate moves. Then he'll draw and sketch things, including cartoons of scenes around Bosco and school. We guess who he is lampooning. He makes fun of us and the teachers. Yet, we all laugh."

"Well, that makes for a lot of chatter with you guys. That's what Havenwood Hospital wanted out of Bosco Academy, eh," Paul observed.

"Fred is the complete opposite. Physically, if he has to break a sweat, he'll call his congressman. Fred enjoys relaxing on his bed with potato chips and a foreign language dictionary. He uses a tape recorder to record himself in Tagalog, the language of the Philippines. He grew up speaking Spanish and French. For a couple of weeks in September, he lived with the host family of a foreign exchange student from Manila and used his Spanish a lot. At this point, he's fast friends with the family and the Filipino student now."

Paul pulled into the right lane and slowed down below the speed limit. "Well, 'Mr. U-Haul' truck driver is not going allow us to pass and I'm not speeding up. No wonder we've never seen Fred on an Au Sable Adventure program, seems like a neat guy though. But I'm guessing that Kenny would have a tough time relating to the egghead type."

"I thought so too, but no dice. They are as loyal as newborn pups to one another. Back to the teeter-totter, what Kenny is up on, Fred is down on, vice versa. Kenny helps Fred with his math. Kenny hates to read, so literature, civics, and history are tough for him. Fred is a walking 'Cliff Notes' for all of us. One day, Bernard had a quiz on a book he had not read, 'To Kill a Mockingbird,'" by Harper Lee."

"I liked that book," Paul said.

"Yeah, my teacher calls Harper Lee the 'one-hit-wonder author'. So, egghead Fred coaches him up on the book as he walks him over for breakfast and then to the bus stop for the ride to Grayling High School. Bernard got a C+ on a short essay-type quiz where you gotta write out answers and interpret what you've read. Pretty good for a student who started the day thinking Harper Lee was writing about animal cruelty."

"Hah, I see what you mean," Paul chuckled.

"The guys on the floor marvel at them. Fred can't do one push-up. Kenny can now do five with Fred on his back. But everyone knows if you fuss with Fred, make fun of him or tease him like in P.E. class, you'll be answering to 'Mr. Karate' himself. Ain't no one hassling Fred. You can be sure of that."

A New Season

"Yeah, I guess so."

"And this Kenny is a kid who did not have one friend for three years at the hospital," Joe concluded.

"It seems you guys liked cross country skiing together, that's for sure," Paul observed. "For your first supervised off-campus visit in six months, I have good things to report as your official chaperone. It was awfully nice of Mark to volunteer to come along."

"Actually, Paul, I doubt if Father George would have approved of this venture without Mark's presence. Hey, maybe next year we can go to Hartwick Pines State Park. I'd like to cross country ski by lantern like that ranger told us about."

"That would be a delightful trip."

Paul pulled into McGuire's and found Mark and Kenny sitting in the lounge, checked out and ready to go. Paul quickly opened the back of the jeep. "Hop in, let's roll."

Kenny swung his bag into the vehicle. "Wow, it is a little colder now. Any luck chasing after the Silver Beaver?"

"Nope. We got a late start and traffic was thick. We needed a helicopter for that job. He could have exited on a side road. Anyway, there's just no time to go south when we're headed north." Joe slid into the back seat with a sullen look on his face.

Paul filled his coffee mug at the refreshment center and got in the driver's seat. "It's time to hit M-55 east and then north on I-75 to get home to Bosco. For now, we know the Silver Beaver lives on in the hands of others; wait until Doc Hollis hears that."

In the back seat, Joe and Kenny exchanged a quick, private glance drenched in guilt.

Paul fastened his seatbelt. "Well guys, for now we say goodbye to the town named for Monsieur Cadillac, founder of Detroit and one of the best canoeists in the history of North America."

"Really, was he the first explorer to come to Michigan, Paul?" Kenny asked.

The Snipe Hunters' Deadly Catch at Muskrat Creek

"Oh, no. Etienne Brulé and Grenolle were the first Europeans to see Michigan during the years 1611-15. And the priest who founded Sault Saint Marie in 1668, Father Jacques Marquette, beat him by decades. But Cadillac built Fort Pontchartrain in Detroit in 1701. Now that's a real canoe story. Like the missionaries and voyageurs, he also canoed all the way from Quebec. But a better story yet is his wife, Marie Therese. Now that's a canoeist with courage."

"Yeah, Paul, tell him," Joe said. "Kenny thinks women don't make good canoeists."

"Hah. Now that trip is a real gut check for any well-equipped man in this century, much less a woman in the fall of 1701. I don't know if it has ever been done, but I know I'd never try it," Paul said.

"You mean with all the canoeing you've done and all the survival training you've had, you wouldn't ..." Kenny asked with a sense of puzzlement in his voice.

"Well, imagine the scene there, Kenny Boy. It's a seven-hundred-and-fifty-mile trip through trackless wilderness within hostile Iroquois Indian territory. It is already September. Now, even you know what that can be like. Thus, Marie is up against the clock with the arrival of winter in North America always unpredictable. There's little time for errors, delays, backtracking, or getting lost. Monsieur Antoine, her own husband, took a different route, the northern route."

"Why?"

"Portage, Kenny Boy, remember that French word for carry?"

"Yeah."

"Well, there is a six-mile portage around Niagara Falls. While the northern route had thirty portages, it was shorter. Also, Antoine had a group of soldiers and settlers. To avoid provoking an attack, he took the most remote route. Seems a missionary priest, Father Vaillant, happened upon Madam

A New Season

Cadillac's party. He was shocked to see two European women and two of Cadillac's sons in the wilderness, much less in Iroquois territory."

"So, there were two ladies strong and brave enough to go canoeing through the forest? Wow, were they like half Indian themselves?" Kenny asked.

"Hah, hardly. Madam Cadillac's mother, Elizabeth Boucher, was connected to royalty through the Duc of Lauzon. The other woman was Anne Belestre, the wife of Alphonse de Tonty, Cadillac's second-in-command at the fort. But they both wanted to be with their husbands in that bustling city of Detroit-to-be, Fort Pontchartrain."

"Man, I remember being afraid of dumping the canoe on the Au Sable River, yet even I know the St. Lawrence is a much bigger river. But what's up with the Indians, the Iroquois? Why was the priest afraid of them?" Kenny asked.

"Hah, you ever hear the story of Madeleine of Fort Vercheres?" Paul asked.

"No, he hasn't, Paul. We don't get all these stories from French Canada in our history books," Mark replied for Kenny.

"Well, picture this. It is harvest season, October 1692 in Fort Vercheres, near what is now Montreal, Quebec. Fourteen-year-old Madeleine is outside of the fort doing laundry. A gun goes off. She looks up and sees fifty Iroquois Indians running at her. Other Iroquois are attacking the soldiers and settlers harvesting the crops outside. What would you do, Kenny?"

"Jeez, I dunno. Run like Speedy Gonzalez. Get some help?"

"Madeleine did that and more. She outran the attackers to the gate of the fort; shoved two recently made widows in ahead of her, and shut the gate just in time. Then it got really bad."

"How so? She's inside and there are soldiers there, right?" Kenny asked.

"Well, Madeleine found the only two soldiers inside. They were not up and doing their job protecting the fort. They were so fearful of getting captured by the Iroquois they refused to fight. They hid in the storehouse where the ammunition and gunpowder were stored."

"Yikes, what happened to Madeleine?" Kenny asked.

"The two soldiers hiding in the storeroom lit a match. They would rather blow themselves up than be captured. That's what it meant to them to be captured by the Iroquois. So, Madeleine knew she'd have to take control of the situation."

"Wow. So, if you get captured …?" Kenny asked.

Paul waved his hand. "I'll tell you that later. The, 'I'll kill myself first before I get captured', that approach was not as crazy as it sounds. Ask me about Father Jean Brebreuf sometime."

"Okay, back to Madeleine, Paul," Kenny insisted.

"Madeleine demanded that the women and children stop crying. She sent them into the blockhouse. The Iroquois had to believe there was a force in the fort, so she armed her brothers, age ten and twelve. They fired guns at the attackers through the loopholes. Later she fired a cannon and rescued a voyageur and his family who arrived by canoe during this attack. It was Madeleine, not the soldiers, who left the fort, went to the river, and escorted the man's family into the fort."

"She's younger than me and doing all of this?" Kenny remarked in disbelief.

"Yup. She duped the Iroquois. The military force in the fort for the night was Madeleine, her younger brothers, an old hired hand, and the rescued voyageur and his son. The six of them mimicked soldiers by calling out military terms and making a lot of noise. They were on watch for a whole week until a Lieutenant La Monnerie arrived. Yet when he arrived, he had his forces sneak up on the fort because they believed it had fallen into enemy hands."

"So, okay, I got it. That was one tough-minded girl there in Vercheres, Quebec, Paul," Kenny said.

"She lived until age sixty-nine and there's a monument to her

A New Season

in her hometown," Paul reported. "It was not the healthy choice to be captured. Most often you were tortured. Several priests and some settlers survived torture. But they were horribly disfigured. They thought the way of the tomahawk was clearly a preferable way to go."

"OK, Paul. I'll remember that if I get kidnapped by an Iroquois Indian." Stretching out in the back seat, Kenny sighed. "Right now, I just want to relax my skiing muscles."

Paul chuckled. "I understand, Kenny. Relax, now. But next time you get to the library, look up Etienne Brule' and find out how he died. That's another good Canadian story. I recommend you read that story on an empty stomach."

Passing Lake City, they found the traffic east on M-55 was steady, but not thick like the southbound artery US-131. The windshield wipers were at medium speed to cope with the rain. Visibility for a dark evening with rain was fair at best all the way toward US-127.

Turning north the road skirted along the west side of Houghton Lake. Looming tall trees defined the edge of the forest. They found the road deserted the minute the Jeep Cherokee pointed north. Joe and Kenny, legs stretched out and warm in the back seat, dozed off before they reached Lake City. Paul was cautious and reduced his speed. Mark, riding shotgun, cradled his head against the window. He was dozing off to the music of Copland's "Appalachian Spring" playing on the radio.

Then Mom Nature pulled the temperature down like a shade. The rain suddenly thickened. Within a hundred yards, fat, whitening droplets of rain turned to sleet. It hit the windshield with an accelerating speed. Paul turned the wipers up to maximum.

Lightning illuminated the entire horizon two minutes later. The dozing passengers were startled out of their slumber.

"Whoa, did you see that lightning up ahead there, straight down the road where we are heading? I can't believe how bright it is," Mark exclaimed as they all held their breath to listen for the ensuing thunder.

Joe leaned forward from the back seat and displayed his sports timer. "That last lightning bolt was exactly three miles in front of us. See, it was about sixteen seconds for the thunder on my timer."

"Yup, 'divide by five for the distance in miles,' says Mr. Garson. We are driving right into the teeth of this storm," Kenny said as he leaned forward to peer out into the dark night.

Upon touching the glass, the rain iced up the windshield. It was quickly encased in an opaque film. Paul began to brake, and exclaimed, "I can't see the road!" The frosty mix had Saran-Wrapped the windshield. Visibility was lost in an instant. Even on overdrive, the wipers were of minimal help. Refusing to release his grip on the wheel, he called out, "Mark, jack the heat up. Put the defroster on high."

The tone in Paul's voice jolted Mark upright out of his lethargic state and into action.

Paul decelerated to less than twenty-five miles per hour. He gripped the steering wheel ever tighter as the vehicle plunged toward the blanket of whiteness ahead.

Then the lonely jeep on this deserted highway entered a wintry whirlwind. The wind buffeted the car side to side, causing it to swerve onto the shoulder or adjacent lane, especially when the forest gave way to open land on both sides of the highway. "Thank God we are all alone out here," Paul said with a glance toward Mark.

Twenty minutes later, the ominous whiteness got thicker. Copland's music was drowned out by a drum beating on the vehicle's metal exterior. Coming in loud waves haul assaulted the sturdy Jeep Cherokee. Paul instinctively pulled his foot off the pedal. "Wow, I can't see twenty feet in front of me."

"What is happening? What's this noise?" Joe, totally agitated, demanded to know what was robbing him of a chance for some

A New Season

sweet slumber on the way home.

"Maybe Carly's weatherman was right, Mark. I can barely see now," Paul said. "It's awfully thick." Paul pointed over to the radio. "Mark, switch to a news station. See if there's an update on this. Hail means we got a serious storm system."

"You are doing less than twenty. The wiper's on overdrive. Still, I can't see much either, Paul," Mark reported as he fiddled with the radio dial.

Another thick blanket of whiteness lurched onto the road ahead. Paul braced for it by reducing his speed again. The hail pounded the roof. The noise was thunderous. The metal was no match for this fierce onslaught from above.

Startled out of his catnap, Kenny sat up and leaned forward. He was speechless as an avalanche of pounding thick, white hail beat the vehicle almost to a halt. "Can we drive if we can't see?"

Then the vehicle seemed to pass into another mini-climate zone. The hail lessened. The ice on the road caused the vehicle to swerve and fishtail. The sky filled with thick white snow. Snowflakes were overweight with moisture.

Paul reduced his speed to a crawl. His eyes studied the road. His foot was at the ready and almost resting on the brake. Still he had no news on the storm. The Grand Rapids radio station broadcast an interview with a professor from Aquinas College. He motioned toward the radio. "Mark, see if you can pick up WJR in Detroit or a Cadillac station. Someone's got to have a report on this."

"There's a report for you on the left up ahead," Joe announced.

On the southbound side of the highway, two cars about thirty yards apart were off on the far side of the road in a ditch. Their emergency blinkers were on. No one appeared injured. They seemed to have slid sideways off the highway. It was clear that only a tow truck could help them now.

Ten minutes later they encountered the blinking lights of a

sheriff's cruiser on the right side of the road as they passed just north of Higgins Lake, driving less than ten miles an hour. Three cars had not been as cautious or as lucky as Paul.

The jeep inched along on the glasslike, slippery pavement with its headlights knifing into the black night. Wind-driven hail alternated with bands of snow. Paul's arm muscles were as tense as his stomach, only he did not know it. Such was his focus on the road. Except for the radio, silence permeated the inside of the jeep as four sets of eyes peered out into the stormy night.

"I still can't see much. I have not seen another car driving out here forever, only those disabled ones. Have you guys seen any southbound cars? If I could pull off, guys, I would. This is crazy. One way or another, we might end up on the shoulder or, God forbid, in the ditch tonight."

"Nope, I haven't seen any moving cars, just those poor guys in the ditch," Joe reported. "Nothing has been moving north or south on this road except us for a long time."

"That is very odd. Southbound traffic on a Sunday night is always heavy. I have not seen one car. We haven't had any company behind us since we left M-55 either," Paul observed. "At eight miles per hour, this could be a long night, guys."

"When is the next exit, Paul?" Mark asked.

"I dunno. I have not been able to see the side of the road or any signs. I'm looking nowhere but straight ahead. Mark, you and Joe might be able to see exit signs or mile markers. I can't. Soon we should see a marker if it is not covered in white or iced up. I'm certain we merged onto it from US-127 already."

The radio program went silent. There was dead air for almost twenty seconds. Then the radio waves pierced the eerie silence in the car. A buzzing alarm was broadcast over the air. The wiper blades seemed deafening as all ears were tuned in for the ensuing broadcast.

"This is the emergency broadcast system for northern lower

A New Season

Michigan. Stay tuned for a notice from the National Weather Service." The buzzing alarm was then repeated, followed by a notice of the impending announcement.

"A travel advisory has been issued for all counties in the Lower Peninsula north of M-55. The Michigan State Police have closed major highways in this area due to extremely hazardous conditions. Roads are impassible due to the ice storm. All travelers are advised to take shelter immediately. We repeat, take shelter. Do not attempt to travel until further notice. Emergency personnel, including the National Guard, will provide further instruction as needed. The forecast calls for eight to ten inches of snow ..."

"Yikes, we are really stuck now. We are on a highway that's closed to traffic!" Mark interrupted the announcer.

"Settle down, Mark. We are still making about ... what, Paul, ten miles an hour?" Joe asked.

"Less than that, buddy boy. I like slow more than a ditch on the side of the road in this blizzard. I'd say eight miles an hour is about right. And I don't see any tire tracks in front of me. You guys wanna spend the rest of this night in this vehicle?"

"There's some kind of light up ahead. Way up there on the right," Kenny announced from the rear.

Mark looked back at Kenny, who had extended his arm into the front seat area. "You must have some eagle eyes or just wishing there, Kenny."

"I'm not dreaming. It comes and goes, like a flickering candle. But I saw it a couple of times before I told you. Look up and to the right of the road."

The cascading snow was blowing onto the windshield, further reducing their vision, but soon a red glow could be seen getting larger through the curtain of white.

The jeep crept forward until a line of roadside flares came into view. A semi-truck had overturned on an exit ramp. It was on its side as if placed by a toddler playing with a set of

Christmas toys. Police cruisers were on both the north and southbound ramps. Flares were illuminating the area around the police cars. Their light bars were blinking. More flares were across the highway. They preceded barriers blocking any further travel north. Other flares formed a pathway toward the ramp with the disabled semi-truck.

Paul eased forward at five miles per hour from the right lane onto the exit ramp. The state trooper's headlights were illuminating the sidelined truck. There was no sign of life around the truck. As Paul approached the trooper's car, the officer exited his car with a bullhorn.

"Halt your vehicle right here." The officer pointed to a spot next to the stop sign encased in ice. It was no longer red. He motioned for the window to be opened and stood with his back to the wind.

"Sir, this highway is closed to both north and southbound traffic. You need to seek shelter immediately. Do you have access to shelter in Grayling?"

"No, sir."

"Well, city hall and the high school are full. We were sending folks to some parochial schools but that was earlier. I'll go back and radio for instructions. You put the contact information for all occupants of this car on this sheet of paper here. Put the address of your destination at the bottom. Show me your license when I get back. You got any emergency gear in this car? Blankets, water, food, any camping gear?"

"No food. We have two canteens of water. We were skiing so we have winter clothing. We have a couple of wool blankets," Paul reported.

"Okay. How did you make it here? We got the National Guard going out in trucks to get stranded folks. Our vehicles just don't work on these roads. Even a salt truck ran off the road." The officer shined his flashlight in the back seat and nodded at Joe and Kenny.

A New Season

"I fishtailed doing eight miles an hour."

"I bet you did. You are lucky to be here. Okay, hang on. I'll radio in for you." The officer "penguin-walked" back to his car. The ice, hail, and snow crunching under the weight of his boots made a crackling sound.

"Hey, Paul, we still have two jars of peanut and raisin mix," Joe reported.

Mark turned back to face Joe. "I got five Granny Smith apples which I'll share. I got three Snickers bars which are not up for grabs, guys. Sorry. This might be a long night yet."

When the officer returned, he rapped on the window to signal his presence.

"They're using the American Legion Hall now. We had a lot of southbound folks take up all the commercial lodging as soon as the storm shut down traffic. There's not much to offer. We hope to get you shelter for the next two days though. You won't be moving in this stuff."

"You say two days, officer?" Paul asked as he returned the paper.

"At least. We are losing some power to these iced-up lines. Trees are coming down on transmission lines. This is a nasty one. This freezing rain came in a wave from the north. It trapped a lot of snowmobilers and skiers from downstate. I haven't had any travelers like you driving north tonight. You got any family still out there on the road?"

"No sir. I just gotta get these kids back to school, safe and sound."

"Did you see any stranded motorists on your way here?"

"Remember, Paul, we saw some on the other side." Kenny was leaning forward from the rear and listening to every word.

"Yes, on both sides of the highway," Paul reported. "But on the southbound side, about ten miles back. But it's hard to judge whether there were cars without any police assistance"

The officer nodded. "Okay, the National Guard is out with

233

their heavy trucks, they'll get to them eventually. Here's the address for the shelter. It is on James Street. Do you know Grayling well enough?"

"I can find it, sir," Mark replied for Paul.

"Okay, eight miles an hour might just do it." The officer handed his license back. "Do you have any flares, Mr. Beaupré?"

"Nope, I just have two flashlights," Paul reported.

The officer handed him three flares. "Use if stranded. You need to get to shelter immediately if you run off the road. Do not get caught outside in this storm. Weather service says this'll get worse tonight."

"Okay, officer," Paul replied.

The officer backed away and tipped his hood at Paul. "Be the steady turtle tonight, sir. We can't play rescue, even some of the National Guard soldiers could not report for duty."

Chapter Seventeen

A Season of Second Chances

Sunday, March 30, 1980, 10:45 pm, Grayling, MI

The Jeep Cherokee crawled forward to enter the city as the wind howled outside. Inside, few words were spoken. Eight ears reverberated with the sound of the rhythmic whine of the wipers paired with the fan blowing its warm air on the windshield. The Cherokee slowly lumbered forward. Evidence of a besieged city loomed into view. Two gas stations, each with banners proclaiming "Open 24 Hours," were closed. Abandoned vehicles cluttered their service lanes and the side streets.

Joe pointed down a side street. "Do you see that?"

"What?" asked Paul. "My eyes are on the road dead ahead. Mark, we keep straight here, right?"

"Yup. We got a left turn in a few blocks. I've never been here without seeing another car moving on the streets."

"There's a plow truck with a huge blade lying on its side!" Joe exclaimed, looking out from behind Paul. "Looks like it couldn't make the turn. It knocked down a tree and bashed in the side of a parked car."

The pavement was snow-encrusted. Underneath the snow, hail rested on a thick sheet of sheer ice. Movement at almost any speed was treacherous.

"My side of the street has lights, but your side looks dark,"

Kenny said to Joe.

"It's been that way for a couple of blocks, actually," Joe agreed.

"Here's our turn coming up, Paul," Mark advised. "At the end of this block, turn left. We have two blocks to go."

Paul applied several soft touches to the brake. The jeep entered the deserted intersection for a left turn. There was no need to honor the blinking stoplight.

The vehicle lost traction. "Oh. Oh. Look out, guys!" Paul shouted. The Cherokee began to slide, sidewise at first, then spinning in circles across the width of the intersection.

"Yikes, Paul!" Kenny screamed. A telephone pole came flying at him as if on a carousel. Instinctively, he embraced the seat in front of him.

"God help us!" Mark cried aloud in response to the amusement park sensation of being hurled through the air. He gripped the dashboard with both hands.

The vehicle crashed into the side of the curb. It came to rest pointing southbound on the northbound side of the road.

There was a hush of no sound for seconds after the crash. Everyone expected something else to happen. Nothing did. A collective exhale could be heard in the cabin of the jeep.

"Yikes!" Paul exclaimed. "Mark, you okay? How about you guys back there?"

"We're fine," Joe bellowed back.

Mark gave a thumb's up. "Imagine if we actually had any speed going into that turn."

Paul looked around at the boys. "I'm finished driving on this ice. I'm all done sweating it out behind this wheel. Next time I drive, I want tires on pavement, not ice. From here on, guys, we're walking. Mark, how far we got to go?"

"Not far," Mark said. "Two blocks, this is one of them."

"Okay, guys. Gear up. Let's put the parkas on. The blankets are in that canoe dry bag back there, Joe. Mark, put those

A Season of Second Chances

canteens and food into your backpack. It is time for a personal meet and greet with 'Frosty the Snowman', guys. Driving is over for tonight. We're lucky we didn't hit anything." Paul exited the vehicle and opened the rear door for his bag.

Kenny followed Joe out of the rear. As Kenny got out, he stooped down to pick up something that cascaded out the door and into the snow. "You been praying on your beads again, Joe?"

"Ever since the storm hit, but I forgot to pocket them after we got off the expressway. Talking to the police got me off task."

"Do you figure it helps, Joe?"

"Well now, all four of us are in one piece so far. And the Jeep Cherokee's still working." Joe patted his pocket and nodded at Kenny. "What do you think?"

"Well, you did hit something, Paul. But it seems minor." Mark was on the curb side of the car. He pointed to a 'No Parking' sign resting in the snow and ice. "The jeep broadsided it. But we just got a little crease here."

Mark pulled his hood up against the knife-like wind. He waited for Paul to look over and then pointed down to the crease in the metal as he pulled his glove on. Joe and Kenny ignored the damage and busily grabbed their gear. The wind blasted at them. They zipped up their parkas.

Paul hunched over against the wind and inspected the damage. He said nothing. He motioned for the guys to huddle up around him. "Okay, Mark knows the way. Fall in behind Mark. We'll walk single file on this ice just like mountain climbers. Put your feet in the footprints already made. Mark, there's no rush now. Steady does it. We don't need any slips, slides, or falls. Just keep moving. This wind wants to turn us into icicles."

Mark led off with Joe last in line. Mark chose his path carefully. He firmly thrust his foot into the mounting snow. It crunched with each step. The wind filled his ears. The

The Snipe Hunters' Deadly Catch at Muskrat Creek

A Season of Second Chances

snowflakes still bit into his face, though well protected by the snorkel-like hood. He looked up only to maintain progress. He avoided the sidewalk.

The last intersection loomed into view. Mark trudged into it. There were no footprints or tire tracks in the snow. His three companions were hunched over. They thrust their feet into his steps with machine-like precision. Joe's head jerked up propelled by his nose. Wood was certainly burning somewhere. A frosty blast of snow bit into his face.

Mark counted the buildings on his right and looked skyward. There was no sign of electricity on the street, but then a light appeared in front of a building and on the right. Mark slogged carefully over the sidewalk in two steps and aimed for the flickering beacon in the frosty night.

Two glowing kerosene lanterns inside the American Legion Hall slowly emerged into view. The aroma of smoke invaded his nostrils. Mark's mind echoed the words off the sides of his skull: lanterns and smoke, warmth and life. Smoke meant there's some sign of life! Yet the scent was faint as the chimney's smoke was stolen and vaporized by the frosty wind.

Paul filed in behind Mark in front of the door and halted.

Mark knocked twice and waited.

Holding his hood against the tempest, Mark looked back at Paul. The wind whirled around them. It ripped at any exposed flesh. Snow pierced their eyes as they studied the door awaiting a response.

Paul gently pushed Mark to one side. He tried the door. It opened. Mark and Paul filled the doorway. Warmth and a faint light greeted them. Their frozen eyes squinted. Mark, magnetically drawn to light from the large hearth, stood still. The warmth enveloping his body immobilized him.

A voice came from behind the door. "Well, alright, now. You are welcome. But you are not welcome to heat the whole block. Come on in here guys. Let's get this door closed."

The Snipe Hunters' Deadly Catch at Muskrat Creek

A square, solidly built figure wearing bib overalls and a canvas Carhartt work jacket loomed into view from behind the door. He gently pushed Mark forward into the room and then stepped into the doorway. "Oh, we got more walking icicles do we, happy days are here again."

He pulled Joe in by the collar of his snorkel hood. Kenny quickly followed. "Well, you got the right gear for the night young man. I'm Gene. You better get in here before I get any colder and shut the door on you. I'm tired of being cold today."

He shut the door and surveyed the four snowy figures in front of him. Paul stepped forward and removed his hood and glove. He extended his hand. "I'm Paul Beaupré. We are from Bosco Academy. We were sent here by the State Police. This is an emergency shelter, right, sir?"

"It is now. I'm Gene Hartwig, Assistant Post Commander here." Gene shook Paul's hand and stepped to one side. "The police pressed us into service when the town filled up with all these stranded folks. I got here by skiing across town. I'm not silly enough to drive in this. The National Guard delivered one family to our door. Then we lost power. How'd you get here? Where's your car, anyway? I didn't see it."

"We have a four-wheel-drive Jeep Cherokee. It slid into a snow embankment two blocks back at the blinker. We walked from there." Pointing to Mark, "This young man, Mark, knows Grayling. He led us here pretty much like penguins for two blocks."

"Ah, it is a good night for penguins, to be sure." Stepping toward the center of the room, Gene pointed to one side. "Well, Bosco Boys, get on in here. You might want to put your penguin gear over there on those benches. Then come join us at the hearth. We just got a good fire going. We got no furnace. The power's been out for hours."

Mark stepped toward the bench. He touched Gene on his shoulder. "Sir, we are so happy to be off the road and out of this storm. Thanks for making your facility a shelter for us. You had to leave your home and ski here in this mess, eh?"

"Well, now smart people don't run in my clan, boys. Ain't got no Bosco Academy folks in my family tree ... yet, anyways." Laughing, Gene looked at Mark and Joe. "The guard boys know me. When the state police and governor called them out, several of my heavy equipment buddies made it in to play rescue. When they ran out of room, they called me on my CB radio."

Looking over at Paul, Gene winked. "Hey, with a storm like this, I might just ignore a regular call. But that one I gotta take, eh? Now I'm stuck here with you 'penguin boys'. So be nice or I'll throw you out, lock up, and ski back home for some dinner. I didn't even get a chance to eat before I left home." Turning to look at the Bosco boys with a serious face, "People around these parts have been known to get ornery when they miss supper."

"Sir, we got apples and some peanuts we can share," Joe declared as he placed his parka on a bench.

"I got a candy bar, Mr. Gene," Mark offered.

Chuckling, Gene declined Mark's offer with a wave. "You boys are the right kind. Actually, we have one other post member that made it in tonight. He's in back scouting out our pantry. We got propane stoves back there. Hot water is boiling for tea and chocolate. But food we don't know about yet. We do have a Michigan State University professor though. The professor thought it would be a good time to visit a colleague up at Michigan Tech. That school is almost a five-hundred-mile trip one way."

Paul nodded, "Yup. I've been there."

"So that's a thousand miles during a Michigan winter," Gene said. "He should be happy he had clear sailing until now. But he says they got snow back in Korea where he's from, so he's not intimidated."

Gene walked across the room to five figures huddled around

The Snipe Hunters' Deadly Catch at Muskrat Creek

the huge fireplace. Paul followed behind Gene. "Professor Han, we have some 'penguins' that dropped in on us for the night. They're from a local school, Bosco Academy. Introduce yourself, boys."

Professor Han stood and explained that his family was new to the country and did not speak English. Kenny addressed him in Korean and bowed. Professor Han's face exploded with elation. His oldest son stepped forward to listen in. They exchanged several sentences in Korean.

"You Bosco Boys are always good for a surprise," Gene said.

"Well, it's a surprise for me, too, Gene," Paul nodded at Gene with a smile.

Kenny finished with a respectful bow. Professor Han returned to English and politely greeted everyone. Then they all gathered around the huge fireplace to soak up some heat. Joe walked back to retrieve something from his parka pocket. He motioned for the guys to gather around him.

Sitting on the raised fieldstone that flanked the fireplace, Joe pulled out his knife and deposited a handful of hail. "Well, guys let's see if Mr. Garson's story is true."

"Oh, yeah I remember. You can tell something about the thunderstorm from the hail," Mark said. "You have to cut it in half, right?"

"Yeah," Joe grasped the largest one of the bunch, still well frozen, and cut it in half. "Okay, Mark let's count the rings. This one is about one inch. That's large."

Using his pocket flashlight to beam light on the specimen, Mark announced, "I count six, Joe."

"What's that mean?" Kenny asked.

"Yeah, that's odd. It has rings like a tree. What does that mean, Joe?" Paul asked.

"Hail starts life as a drop of water in a cloud with an updraft forcing it up to a colder region, where it freezes. Each trip up to the cold region forms a ring and makes it heavier. When it weighs too much for the next trip up, voila, as Mr. Garson would say, you get a hail storm. It comes down; the larger the hail, the more intense the thunderstorm."

"I am going to guess that six rings on a one-inch piece of hail means a very respectable storm," Paul observed. "When we shovel out the Jeep Cherokee, I bet we have some pockmarks on the metal."

Joe nodded at Paul. "I do, too. That darn storm disturbed my nap. I was tired from all that skiing."

"So, when the weather service warns us that Joe's nappy time is going to be disrupted, we'll know to take cover, eh?" Mark quipped.

"You Bosco boys sure know a lot of science. I've lived through a lot of storms and never heard that about hail," Gene said as he placed a metal pitcher of steaming hot water on a fold-out table. "I'll be back with tea bags and packets of hot chocolate."

Paul explained his journey and the professor related how the storm had hit them earlier in the day. He had spent long hours unable to move.

"After hours of waiting, the police directed us to abandon the car at a rest stop," Professor Han said. "Then a National Guard truck brought us here. Other places were closed or filled to capacity. Thank God for radios."

The toasty glow from the fireplace conspired with the warm tea and chocolate to make all the weary travelers sleepy. The peanuts and raisins had already been shared, along with Mark's apples, when Gene announced that there would be no food tonight.

He was working on a plan for the morning, however. "The guard dropped off twelve cots, wool blankets, and some jugs of water. Also, we have four couches at this post and one that folds out into a bed."

Gene gestured to one side of the room beyond the kitchen

and winked. "Seems the one in my office is spoken for, and the sergeant's going to claim one. But that leaves two for you adults. I'll let you guys squabble over them democratic-like. Young folks get the cots though, that's my rule as the commander here."

Paul stood up to face Gene. "Thank you, Gene. The professor and his wife will get the couches, and that'll be my rule, commander, with your permission. My 'penguins' will do just fine on the cots for the night."

A metallic creaking noise came from the back of the room. A door adjacent to the kitchen opened. A tall, clean-shaven man wearing a ski cap entered the room from the rear pushing a metal cart loaded with wood. His large athletic frame was covered with a Carhartt canvas coat. He did not look up at the crowd around the fireplace.

Gene pointed towards the large man. "The sergeant here will explain how you turn the heat up tonight when you get cold. I recommend you saddle up close to the fire because that's all the heat we've got until the power comes back on."

Smirking, the sergeant stacked the wood on the side of the ornate fieldstone fireplace and looked over at the group and said, "Well, folks, welcome to radiant heat, colonial style. Just keep some of these going in there regularly. You'll stay warm. You young bucks wanna help me load this up one more time? That way we'll have enough heat for another ten, twelve hours past midnight."

Mark, Joe, and Kenny scrambled to their feet and followed the sergeant out to the back porch. A large deposit of stacked firewood was sheltered on a well-made porch protecting the wood on three sides. Stepping onto the porch the wind hit the Bosco boys hard from the open side.

Grinning, while still wearing his jacket, the sergeant boomed loudly over the howling wind. "Work quickly or freeze, young men. I'll hold the door for you."

A Season of Second Chances

The metal cart had three levels. Without a word they worked as a team and stacked the split hardwood quickly. The Arctic wind searing into them compelled them to hurry. At last, the cart was lined up at the entranceway.

"I got it, boys." The sergeant smoothly lifted his end of the heavy cart over the threshold. Mark and Joe then lifted and guided their end of the cart over and along the short hall and into the great room with the fireplace.

"All right, young men, I'll take over from here."

Mark raised his hand up toward the sergeant when the cart came to rest. "We will stack the wood, sir. It is the least we can do."

Joe and Kenny, ignoring the sergeant, immediately began to unpack the cart.

"Sir, we'll handle this," Mark insisted. "You have given us shelter from this blizzard and warmth for the night. Let us unload." He looked the sergeant in the eye and paused. "So how about you just relax and allow us to say thanks for what we could not do without tonight. Imagine what it would be like for us out there, on the side of the road."

Joe looked up, with his arms full of wood. "I'm chilled to the bone from just a short time on that porch, Mr. Sergeant."

"We saw some folks stranded without police help on the way up here, Mr. Sergeant," Kenny reported as he stacked the wood neatly. "I can only hope they got rescued by folks like you."

"Okay, but 'sergeant' will do, boys." The sergeant then paused. He took his hand off the cart and stepped back. "Well, now, you boys been trained up, that I can see. Are you from a scout troop or something?"

Paul walked over. "Not a scout troop, sergeant. We're on a field trip from Bosco Academy. We were returning from a cross-country ski outing in the Pere Marquette Forest near Cadillac. I think if we'd left one or two hours earlier, we could have beaten the darn storm home."

"Maybe, but I doubt it. It was light-switch quick. The rain came as I ended my therapy session. When I went to a nearby restaurant, as I always do afterwards, things were stormy, but I expected to get home after dinner. Then the drop in temperature and freezing rain made the expressway a skating rink. Gene called me at the restaurant. Here I am, thirty miles from home, bunking up at my own legion post."

"Hey, that's good for us," Paul observed.

"Hey, your Bosco kids got it right. The weather boys got it right. And so do the emergency folks on the radio. There's no way it makes any sense to travel tonight. Even huge National Guard trucks have to go slow."

The sergeant reclaimed the empty cart and nodded at the Bosco boys. "Commander Gene was smart to ski over here. If the ice gets you, then you don't have a trip to the body shop or worse. Just a sore rump, eh, Gene?"

Gene waved at the sergeant and winked at Mark. "I don't fall like I did when I first took up cross country, boys. And this is not the first time I've found it useful for travel."

"Well, now, you boys promise this tired sergeant who can't ski you'll never tell the cook how we used his favorite cart, okay? I got a couch and a down sleeping bag in the back there. I wish you all a good and toasty warm night, young men."

"Goodnight, sir." Mark and Joe waved at the big man as he ambled down the hall with a slight limp in his left leg.

The professor dragged the spare couch across the room and folded it out to face the fireplace. Their two youngest children snuggled on the smaller couch close by. His oldest claimed a cot.

"I know how to stack logs now, Joe. I can handle this." Kenny smiled as he arranged the wood on the expansive hearth. "The fireplace at the Main Post was good training for me."

Twenty minutes later, the men from Bosco were bedded down on U.S. Army cots facing the fireplace feet first.

A Season of Second Chances

"I got another wool blanket if you need one, Kenny. Notice the Main Post blankets are the same as the blankets from the National Guard?" Mark asked from the cot next to Kenny. "Army Surplus Store comes through again."

"Thanks, I don't think my feet ever get warm except when I'm sitting on the hearth there."

Mark flipped the blanket over to Kenny. "Man, you hear that wind out there howling away? Sure glad we happened onto this place. Thanks to the Michigan State Police and National Guard, we have a warm berth for the night."

"Hey, Mark," Kenny said. "Look at Paul. He fell asleep the minute he pulled that wool blanket over his shoulder. That sergeant and Gene are awfully nice to make this our home for the night. You know we might be luckier than the folks who went to a hotel. This place has a fireplace. Once the power is out, I wonder what happens in a hotel or motel. Not all of them have wood-burning fireplaces."

"You're right, I never thought about that. Let's get some rest. I gotta believe we are going to be shoveling some snow tomorrow. Just imagine ten inches of snow getting plowed off streets. That wind will have all night to build up snowdrifts. Plus, it will be just great for walking with that sheet of ice underneath. Do you remember where our Jeep Cherokee is located?"

"Sure. It's exactly where a plow deposits snow," Kenny replied. "Okay, I got your point, Mr. RA. My feet just got warm by the way. I suppose I'll be putting wood on about three o'clock so … hey, you were right, my parka works well as a pillow. Goodnight."

><

"Commander Gene, are you going to answer the back door or not?" The sergeant asked from his couch at the far side of Gene's office. "You are closest to the door."

Rolling out from under his nest of wool blankets, Gene grumped back at his friend. "It's six o'clock, sergeant. Didn't you take the first watch?"

The knock on the wooden door now sheathed in snow was muffled but incessant. Loud enough to rouse the men, it could not be ignored. Gene stepped onto the floor and reached for his sturdy Carhartt coat.

"Man, that floor is cold. This room is downright chilly. Sergeant, check that thermometer on your wall." Gene slid into his Red Wing boots, stepped to the door, and pulled it open. Two men behind the storm door were wiping the storm window clean and peering in from the dark. Dawn had yet to arrive. Ice had riveted the storm door to the frame.

Gene had to thrust his shoulder into the door twice before it would open. "Sorry, fellas, you get on in here now." Gene opened the door and stepped back. The two visitors entered to one side of Gene's office.

"Hey, Gene, get those guys in and shut that door. That puny propane heater got us up to a balmy forty-six degrees." The sergeant pulled his suspenders up over his woolen mackinaw and stepped into his rugged Red Wing boots as well.

"Howdy, guys, we are from the Lutheran church two blocks south of here. We heard you had some hungry visitors to your post. We got breakfast fixings for about forty people on the sled out there. You interested?"

"Hah, ever seen a duck hesitate in front of a June bug?" Gene welcomed the first man with a bear hug. The second man immediately turned and retrieved four large cardboard boxes with handles.

Depositing the boxes on the kitchen counter where Gene was pointing, the first man announced, "I'm George and this is Fred. There are eggs, pancake mix, dozens of sausages, potatoes, onions, some canned peaches, fresh pears, and a large jar of peanut butter, and several loaves of bread. But the best is yet to come and I'm not just talking condiments and ketchup."

"Oh, yeah? You guys are batting a thousand right now from my end of the icicle," the sergeant said while patting George on the shoulder.

Brandishing an old stovetop percolator, George swung it up high in the air. "I know you have no electricity, so those large pots are useless. But this post has some propane stoves, right?"

"Yes, thanks. And several unopened cans of coffee." Gene smiled and took the pot from him.

"We figured there might be some coffee drinkers waylaid here. There always are in our deer camp," Fred said.

"Well, hang on; I'll fix us a pot." Gene turned on the stove. "Take your coats off. Dawn's not even here yet."

"Thanks, but we can't stay. We got a couple trips to make. The National Guard has asked us to help out. But we only have breakfast fixings. You'll get a visit later from the Knights of Columbus. They are donating all of the food they have for their Lenten dinners. Seems you'll be eating some fish tonight, guys. We have Scout troops from four churches ready to slog through the snow if necessary."

"Well, thanks so much. Got any news on the electricity?" the sergeant asked as the flames were glowing under the coffee pot. "Some have it, and some of us don't."

"Not much. The radio is your best bet. You got a CB radio, so check around. The guard is escorting the power crews as needed. At four o'clock this morning they found some frostbitten motorists stranded, so they are still playing rescue. I fear some folks might have frozen to death out there last night. If you go off-road, in a ditch in this blizzard your car could be invisible in no time."

"Well, guys, I sure appreciate your help," Gene said.

The sergeant slapped both men on the back while holding the door open.

Twenty minutes later, Paul bolted upright on his cot. His

The Snipe Hunters' Deadly Catch at Muskrat Creek

nostrils told him coffee was brewing somewhere. On his way to the bathroom, he passed Kenny and Mark building up the fire with the ample stores of split wood.

He stuck his head in the kitchen on his way back. "You guys hiding any coffee back here?"

Smirking, the sergeant extended Paul a blue ceramic mug with an Air Force insignia on it. "Actually, we were hoping you wouldn't thaw out until we had a chance to drink it all."

Three hours later, everyone was well fed and relaxing around the fireplace. Gene reported that the authorities would open the roads for travel only to emergency vehicles and then only in the afternoon. Power crews were making steady progress. Gene got a radio message that dinner from the Knights of Columbus would arrive before dark.

"Hey, want to practice some Tae Kwon Do with me?" Kenny asked Hong, the thirteen-year-old son of the professor.

With a broad smile he replied, "Yes. I want." He looked up at his father. "Okay?"

Hong's father nodded his approval, and they moved away from the fireplace to the open area by the front door.

Those not warming themselves gathered in a semi-circle to watch Kenny and Hong perform their katas. The sergeant walked in from the kitchen and noticed the martial art display. Then he walked to the far side of the room near the door.

The sergeant watched intently for several moments. Then Kenny backed toward the sergeant as part of his routine, in tandem with Hong.

The powerful sergeant sprung forward, grasped Kenny by the back of his neck with one hand and the seat of his pants with the other. With a swift and powerful move, he expertly pressed him above his head.

"Whoa! What the ..." Kenny laughed as he went aloft with his four limbs outstretched.

Holding him aloft he turned to the crowd, "Okay, guys, I got a kata of my own. How many 'overhead Kennys' to qualify for dinner today?"

Paul and the Bosco boys began laughing and counted as the sergeant pressed Kenny's whole body twelve times above his head. The professor started a clap that was paired with each overhead press. Hong followed his family in the fun.

Laughing, but feeling slightly embarrassed, Kenny was happy to be put back down for number thirteen.

"Thanks for the exercise today, young man. It feels good." The sergeant said. He extended his hand to Kenny.

Kenny shook his hand and looked at the sergeant, who was panting. He had some sweat on his brow.

"Wow, sergeant, that's a lot of exercise." Commander Gene had joined in the clapping as well.

Kenny released his hand after the handshake. But then the sergeant re-grasped his whole forearm in a vice-like grip. His hand wrapped around Kenny's forearm in a python-like squeeze, he pulled Kenny closer. The sergeant looked at Kenny with a probing glare. "Son, you don't recognize me, do you?"

"No way!" Mark sprang up from his chair across the room. "That can't be the guy from …"

"No, sir, Mr. Sergeant," Kenny gasped as he looked up at the tall man.

"Well now, son, take a good look." The sergeant laughed and patted his stomach. "Picture a beer belly, a beard, some booze, and bad manners. Now subtract six months from the calendar and add seventy-five pounds on me."

Kenny had a flash of recognition.

"I'm Sergeant David Lubbers! We first met on the Au Sable River. You had to fly through the air with some of your karate moves just to teach a drunken bully some manners one afternoon. You remember, now?" Sergeant Lubbers modeled his walk with a slight limp in his left knee.

Kenny froze in place and looked up at the powerful man who

had just pressed his whole body above his head. "Sorry, I really did not mean to ..." He groped about, awash with feelings, fright at first followed by sorrow. "Jeez, I'm sad about the leg, sir," Kenny stammered.

"Don't be, Kenny. That's not the first time I took the hard road to learn a good lesson."

Paul leaned over to Mark. "What's going on here? You two know the sergeant?"

"Shhh ... quiet, Paul. Please, not now," Mark said.

"Actually, I want to thank you, young man." Sergeant Lubbers put his left hand on Kenny's shoulder and shook his hand with his right.

"Me, sir? Why me? You got hurt. I mean, I hurt you," Kenny stammered.

"Well, let's go over there and have a chat, just you and me." Sergeant Lubbers pointed to the fireplace. Sergeant Lubbers looked over at Hong, "Can you take a break from your karate lesson, young man?"

The professor spoke for him, "He sure can, Sergeant Lubbers." Professor Han then spoke to his son in Korean. Hong bowed to the sergeant.

The sergeant and Kenny walked past the three men from Bosco Academy.

Mark stepped up to halt the sergeant's progress. "Ah, Mr. Lubbers, I'm Mark. I was on the river that day. I did not recognize you either, sir. I'm really sorry that ..."

Sergeant Lubbers interrupted him. "Don't be sorry, young man. I'm actually glad I met you guys, really." With a sincere look at Mark, he clapped him on the shoulder and spoke with military authority. "At ease, young man." He continued past him toward the fireplace.

It was as if an unspoken command had been given, everyone withdrew toward the kitchen, allowing Kenny and Sergeant Lubbers the privacy and warmth of the fireplace.

A Season of Second Chances

"You didn't completely shatter my leg. You came close. But you did shatter the hold booze had on me. Not right away either. Time in the hospital and more time in therapy got me to thinking. Doctors and drugs for pain made me booze-free for the first time since I was a recruit at Camp Lejeune. I had me some clear thoughts for the first time in decades."

"Sergeant, you pushed Doctor Hollis," Kenny explained. "He meant a lot, ah, well, he still does mean a lot to me."

"Well, you got me convinced of that in a hurry, Kenny. To fly through the air and attack a drunken bully my size, you had to have some reason."

Kenny scoffed, "Well, I did not really even see you or your size, sergeant, I ..."

"No matter. Your aim was good enough. My therapist can testify to that."

Kenny realized he'd injured a veteran. Engulfed in regret, he wanted to apologize.

"No, no, none of that. That's bad water under a good bridge. Let me tell you why. I am an alcoholic, a hard-headed one at that. I've learned so much in the last six months. Sure, I got therapy for my knee, but also for my ..." The sergeant pointed to his head.

He continued, "You see, it wasn't until I used a crutch for my leg that I learned I was using booze as a crutch for my life. I learned how to take control of my life. I learned that some of my friends are really not my friends. Drinking buddies sometimes really only want me around for a joint ride from reality, a reality they are escaping, just like me. I learned in the service that courage is not being unafraid. Everyone is afraid in combat. Courage is taking the next step while 'Captain Fear' himself is riding tall right on your shoulders, digging his stirrups clean through to your innards. That's courage. Taking the next step, and not knowing what is going to happen. That's courage."

"You saw combat, sergeant?" Kenny asked.

The Snipe Hunters' Deadly Catch at Muskrat Creek

"Yup. But we ain't talking about that. I've been booze-free since the day you flattened me out on the Au Sable. I'm still in physical therapy for my knee, Kenny, but the therapist says I can lose my limp. I bet I can because I already lost seventy-five pounds. I'm five pounds away from my Camp Lejeune days."

"I bet you can, too, sir," Kenny said.

"Now I take a half a shot of booze one day a year. That's my tradition on the tenth of November. That's all it's ever going to be."

"Why on November tenth, sergeant? I know another man that used to do that, too."

"Well now, Kenny from Bosco Academy, listen up the next time you are in your American History class." Sergeant Lubbers winked at Kenny. "Do you good to learn some of that 1775 history."

Kenny and Sergeant Lubbers were both seated on the raised fieldstone hearth with their backs to the fire. They were turned slightly sidewise toward one another and visible to all from the kitchen.

"Seems like Kenny and Sergeant Lubbers have a lot to talk about, eh, Mark?" Paul observed as he paused from playing cards.

"I'll let them chat all they want. If we get the green light to dig out the jeep, we'll let Kenny chat. Gene said there will be a bulletin after two o'clock."

Kenny began to feel comfortable. "So, Sergeant Lubbers, maybe you could help me. You see, I ..."

Apart from tending to the fire, Kenny and Sergeant Lubbers were then lost in a thoughtful chat. It had a somber, almost advisory tone at times, but there was some raucous laughter, too.

The radio reported the travel advisory was lifted only for a couple of hours. The roads would re-freeze at dark. Paul borrowed shovels and the janitor's broom. The three of them

A Season of Second Chances

"penguin walked" to the Jeep Cherokee and excavated the vehicle from the mounded snow. It was almost dark as the post came into view. Standing outside, Gene was thanking the men from the K of C for the timely delivery.

A little after six o'clock, the lights came on in the building. Two hours later, baked scrod, baked potatoes, and baked green beans were served, along with coleslaw and squares of brownies for dessert. The furnace was pumping heat.

"You gentlemen eat well up here during Lent. I may come back next season." Professor Han addressed Commander Gene and Sergeant Lubbers. Both were decked out in the chef's aprons.

"If you come this way, let me know. I'm leaving. You are bad luck, Mr. Professor. We have not had this combination of bad weather since I was a kid," Commander Gene joshed.

"Speaking for Bosco Academy, gentlemen, we appreciate your hospitality and this is certainly good eating for us as well," Paul said. "Our guys will take over kitchen patrol. You two relax now."

"Thanks, Paul, we could use a rest," Gene said as he exited the kitchen.

Sergeant Lubbers addressed the group, "The police have lifted the travel ban as of dawn tomorrow." Everyone applauded the news. "The radio reports a warm front arriving, that ice will be slush by mid-morning. And, hey, don't you guys just love a working furnace?"

PART THREE

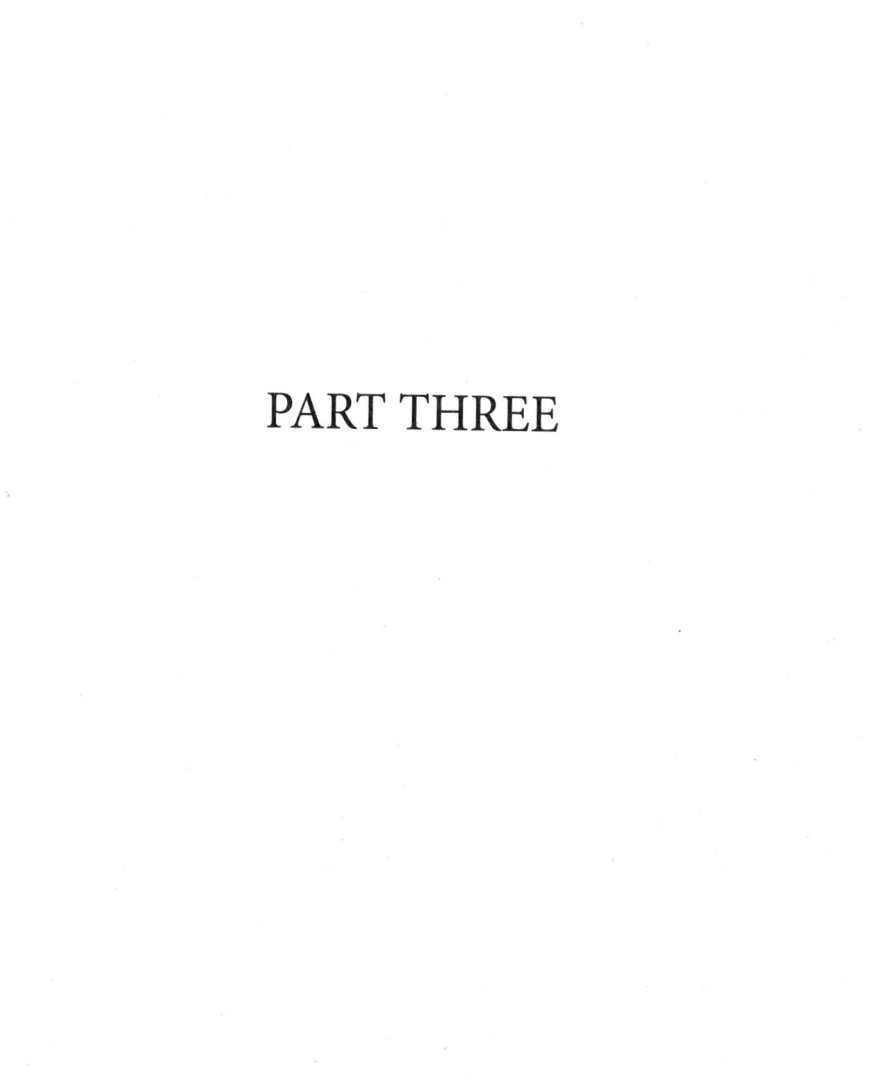

The Snipe Hunters' Deadly Catch at Muskrat Creek

Chapter Eighteen

To the Shores of Muskrat Creek

Saturday, April 12, 1980, 3:49 pm, John Bosco Hall

"Hey, Kenny, the pear tree blossoms have been out for a week and the sun is shining!" Joe, reclining on his bunk bed, continued, "We ought to schedule a canoe trip with Doctor Hollis and Beaupré next weekend. This is prime snipe hunting season. Remember, during our first canoe trip you admitted that you never caught a snipe. We gotta correct that."

Fred, who was sprawled across his bed in the same dorm room, jerked his headphones off and looked over at Kenny. "Kenny, you really don't need to … I mean there's no …"

A pillow crashed into the side of his face. It ended the sentence right there. "Hey, what are you doing? Those are my new glasses," Fred exclaimed as he retrieved them from the floor.

"You get your certified intellect and those glasses down the hall pronto. Vincent is tearing his hair out in frustration over his French quiz," Saltz said in a loud, booming voice. He stepped into the room from the bathroom that connected the suites. He placed his body between Fred and Kenny on the other side of the room.

Saltz then grabbed Fred by the elbow and brusquely guided him toward the door. "I promised him a savior and that savior is you, Monsieur Frederico."

The Snipe Hunters' Deadly Catch at Muskrat Creek

Fred turned back as he got to the door; he glanced at Joe then at Kenny. "Kenny, you should talk to me before you go hunting the—" Fred called out as Saltz half-dragged; half-escorted him out of the room.

Saltz discreetly put an elbow into Fred's side, ending another sentence.

Fred was gasping for breath as they turned into the hall. Saltz closed the door and quick-stepped Fred about twenty feet down the hall. "Hey, why are you pushing me?" Fred complained as he looked up at the muscular Saltz.

"Fred, for a smart boy you don't take a hint very well. Have a quiet voice about Kenny's snipe hunt, will you?"

"You mean I'm just supposed to let him think—" Fred protested.

"I'll tell you what you are supposed to do," Saltz persisted. "Get lost in the library for about an hour. That's easy for you. You got five hundred of your closest friends waiting to hang out with you. Lord knows some don't even speak English. When you get back to the room, you mind your own business. There will be no chatter from you about the snipe hunt. That's the story, Monsieur Frederico. Got it?"

Fred replied, "What about the French quiz, Saltz? Vincent's not in the library!"

Saltz put his arm around Fred knowing his question was genuine. "Fred, Fred, Fred. You're my favorite Monsieur Frederico, but what am I to do with you?" Saltz loudly moaned. He escorted Fred to the library and finished his consultation with him there.

Back in the room, Kenny, anxious to get out on the river again, wanted to pursue Joe's idea. "What about Spring break? That's about ten days away. Could we visit Doctor Hollis and Paul at that time? Do you think Father George would approve us to go if we got the green light from the guys at the Main Post?"

Joe put his book down and looked out the window. He grabbed his baseball glove and put his windbreaker on. "I dunno. But let's go throw some. The sun is shining and warming the place up a little."

Kenny moved his art easel to one side and laced up his shoes. "Baseball is my favorite. You don't need to ask me twice. Suppose we ask Mark to check it out with Doctor Hollis? Maybe Brother Ed would go to bat for us. Maybe even recommend an extended weekend pass for us," Kenny looked over at Joe as he headed toward the door.

"Well, how are your academics?" Joe asked. "As I recall, you had a research paper overdue last week. You'll never get a green light from Brother Ed with poor academics. People send their kids here for Brother Ed, the patron saint of discipline." Joe turned out into the hall and flipped a baseball to Kenny.

"Well, okay. You're right," agreed Kenny. "I got an extension on it. I suppose I better ask Fred for some help. I gotta compare and contrast the character traits and flaws of Cicero and Cataline. Then I have to apply those lessons to modern life."

"Ah, yes. Lucius Sergius Catilina engaged in behavior contrary to the laws of both God and man, at least in the eyes of his nemesis, Cicero," Joe said in an exaggerated voice. "Or, as Mr. Garson would have it, Marcus Tullius Cicero, whose writing was of such importance as to be the second book after the Bible to be printed when Johann Gutenberg invented the printing press."

Impressed, Kenny said, "Wow, you know all that stuff, like Fred? When I came here, I didn't know anything about Greece or Rome. Now I have to write a paper about a guy who chopped the head off his own brother-in-law. Maybe you can help me."

As they approached the stairs at the end of the hallway Joe raised his voice, "'Teach me goodness, discipline, and knowledge,' says Brother Ed. Now when you write your paper, Kenny Boy, don't list the head-chopping as an example of goodness. That's the extent of my advice. You want more help?" Joe descended the stairs and used his back to open the door and exit outside.

"Yes!" Kenny begged.

Joe flipped him the baseball. "Then ask Fred."

After several minutes, a few guys from first floor joined Joe and Kenny. They went to the fields and had some batting practice before it was time for dinner in the cafeteria.

After dessert, Kenny found Mark, his favorite resident assistant, and asked for some advice about the camping trip.

"You can ask Brother Ed about camping, of course," Mark suggested. "But I would not ask until your paper is turned in. It better be on time as well. How did you ever get an extension from Mr. Garson anyway? That guy never really left the US Navy either. I'm surprised he didn't have you walk the gangplank."

"Well, I am the lucky new guy, I guess. I have a week to complete it. I know Fred will help me on the writing part. But do you suppose you could ask Doctor Hollis and Beaupré about spring break?" Kenny asked. "Just so we know if there's room for us."

"Sure, I can. We are coming up on the trout opener. There's always a lot of activity at the Main Post then; actually, at the Outpost too. Still, there are enough canoes to go around." Winking at Kenny, Mark concluded, "Even if the Silver Beaver is still missing in action, I think they can get everybody on the river."

Kenny flinched a little. "Well, Mark, I hope so. I still feel bad about that."

"Ah, don't, Kenny. It is just that it is such a mystery. We all know that it is still out there somewhere. It seems from your ski trip, it ended up on the west side of the state, eh?" Mark observed.

"Tell Paul I want to go on my first snipe hunt. Joe says this is

To the Shores of Muskrat Creek

the best time of the year," Kenny insisted.

Mark looked at Kenny in surprise and then laughed. "Oh, yeah, I forgot about that adventure. He's right. Springtime is best. Beaupré will help you guys out on that score."

Thirty minutes later, Kenny returned to his room. Fred was at his desk typing a paper.

"Say, Fred, could you help me on this Cicero project?" He described his plight in more detail. Fred listened intently. Then Fred rose and put his sweatshirt on.

"We're off to the library. It's always cold in there at night. Bring your notebook. You got your notes, I presume." Fred handed Kenny a fresh batch of sharpened pencils.

"Really, we're going already? Why not go in the morning, after breakfast maybe?" Kenny balked.

"Well begun is half done," Fred announced as he grabbed his book bag and headed for the door.

"Joe calls the library 'your' room. He says it's 'The Land of Fred's 500 Friends.'"

"There are more volumes than that," Fred asserted with authority.

"Well, get the point. There's more there than I will ever read. But he probably knows you've read 400 of them."

"You should be happy we have a library here in the dorm. We don't have to go in town to Grayling High School. It saves you time." Fred closed the door behind them. "Besides, it is quiet in there for study."

"Yes, of course. You would like that!" Kenny said as he trudged along behind Fred.

><

Mark was up early the next morning. He went to the dorm director's office to make the phone call. Paul answered Doctor Hollis' phone. "Hey, just the man I wanted to speak with. Mr. Beaupré do you suppose …?"

The Snipe Hunters' Deadly Catch at Muskrat Creek

Later that night, back in the dorm, Mark found Kenny typing at his desk.

He came up behind him and announced the news. "Doctor Hollis and Paul were happy to hear about your interest in getting back on the river. They have some 'Trout Unlimited' guys coming up for the week. The trout season is upon us. Still, they said not to worry about room. If there's not enough room at the Main Post, you could go to the Outpost. You'd have access to all the Au Sable Adventure camping equipment there also. Actually, Joe may want to go camping anyway. The farther you are away from people, the better chance you'll have to see a snipe."

Kenny stopped typing and turned to face Mark. "Hey, thanks. That's good to hear."

"Now, don't stop your work. Get back to it. I'll tell Joe. You aren't going anywhere until you've mastered some Cicero and made Mr. Garson a happy man. Look at it this way, Mr. Artist, you paint a smile on Mr. Garson's face and you'll get a green light from Brother Ed for the trip."

Three days later, Joe ascended the stairs to the second floor after another late evening on the ball field without Kenny. He spotted a light in the library and slowly opened the door. Fred was seated at a table. Kenny was standing behind an old wooden podium usually stored in a closet.

"What's up, Kenny? Are you giving a speech to Frederico here?" Joe asked.

Kenny shrugged his shoulders.

Annoyed, Fred responded without turning around to face Joe. "Leave us be, Joe. He's got to be prepared to defend his paper and justify his views to Mr. Garson. We have to concentrate."

"So, I suppose you are Mr. Garson for the evening?" Joe taunted.

"Who could be better?" Kenny shot back. Then he pointed

To the Shores of Muskrat Creek

his finger to the door and beckoned Joe to leave. "Vamanos!"

Nodding, Joe closed the door and entered his own room a minute later.

"Hey, Saltz, I think Kenny's going to do well with that Cicero project. Fred is down in the library grilling Kenny like he's Mr. Garson himself."

"Hah! Joe, you know that Fred is a professor in the making. Heck, I'd bet on anyone who gets coached up by Fred," Saltz said.

Three days later, Kenny and Joe were called into Brother Ed's office. "When I received your application for the field trip, I of course confirmed the arrangements with Mr. Beaupré and Doctor Hollis. It seems you two stand tall in their book, even in light of a missing canoe from your fall adventure."

"Well, sir, we only made the field trip application after Mark called them. There's no use troubling you if they did not approve of it or were not available," Joe replied.

"But since the grades are not posted yet, I called Mr. Garson. Kenny, it seems you've made considerable progress in Western Civilization since last semester. An A-minus is some distance from a C minus, especially in his class." Brother Ed smiled. "Well done."

"Thank you, Brother," Kenny said.

"So, this field trip will involve your roommate and suitemates, Joe?"

"Gosh, no, Brother Ed, it will only be the three of us. Fred's idea of a trip to a forest would be watering the coleus plants at the far end of the library," Joe explained.

Everyone laughed.

"I was wondering about that," Brother Ed smiled.

"Well, I'm going to submit this request to Father George with my approval, providing you have your resident assistant join you. He'll need to get a substitute as well. That puts Saltz and Mark Dubay in the second canoe. That should balance out a two-man canoe a little better, don't you think?"

"Yes, that's true, sir," Joe said.

"Thank you, Brother Ed," Kenny said.

Brother Ed stood up from his desk. "Please tell Mark to stop by my office after his rounds tonight. Okay, men, keep those grades up."

Sitting on his porch Doctor Hollis was finishing his morning coffee. The Jeep Cherokee lurched into view and settled down at the end of the driveway. Mark slammed the door and quick-stepped across the lawn.

Hollis surveyed the equipment inside and on top of the vehicle. "Do you have everything you need?" Hollis smirked, stood up, and folded his arms across his chest. "It looks like you have equipment for a whole squad of men."

The cabin door slammed shut as Paul stepped out onto the porch behind Hollis.

"Well, Doctor, for fishing, camping, and also Joe has some ideas about ropes training for Kenny. Look, by now Kenny's halfway down Partridge Path to Beaupré's cabin. He wants to start his first snipe hunt off with another evening around your fireplace. Just so you know, Paul." Mark winked as he nodded at Paul.

"Of course, he can have a fire," Hollis said. "The temperature is dropping into the forties tonight. A roaring fire would be in order. I suppose you'll want some popcorn to go along with that fire, eh?"

Paul held the door open for Mark as he entered Hollis' cabin. He dumped some gear on the porch. "Hey, could we have some popcorn? That would be great."

Paul was smiling as he replied, "We can, and in style. At Christmas Jean Luc got me a thick asbestos glove for that long-handled popper we use over the fireplace. Ours had a certain

To the Shores of Muskrat Creek

American character about it since it was scorched black and had a hole in it. But J.L. says no more roasted fingers to go along with the popcorn now."

Exiting Hollis' cabin, they headed down Partridge Path toward Paul's cabin.

"Also, Kenny will need one of your Canadian woods stories to send him off on his snipe adventure. We all had to work hard to keep Fred from telling him the reality about his first snipe hunting trip. We don't want to spoil it for Kenny."

"That'll be great fun for you guys. Have you decided where you want to camp?" Paul asked. "I suggest you start at Lake Huron, in the Oscoda area, and come 22 miles westward; that's the route the logger's used. Last year Jean Luc and his boys were spellbound by the majesty of the river, the towering forests; and they loved the Lumberman's Monument in the state park."

Mark replied, "I think Joe is going to choose the camping site. He seemed to have a place in mind when we planned this back at the dorm. Thanks for hosting us and getting Father George to approve this trip."

Paul opened the door to the cabin. He held it for Mark to enter first.

Paul stepped into his cabin and found three Bosco Boys stacking wood in his wood box. "When we need help eating roasted popcorn, we know who to call. Hello, Kenny. Welcome once again, Joe and Saltz. This is my answer to Henry David Thoreau. He had Walden Pond. I've got the Au Sable River. I know he had a fireplace, but I bet mine is bigger. I bet my popcorn tastes better, too. You wanna experiment, test out my theory tonight?"

"Heck, yes, Mr. Beaupré," Kenny bellowed out. He pulled off his leather gloves and shook hands with Paul.

Joe and Saltz followed suit and slapped his shoulder as well.

"Winter treated you well, Mr. Beaupré. You're looking good," Joe observed.

"Hey, remember it is 'Paul' on the Au Sable. Let's hear about your put-in with the canoes?"

"The place I went to two years ago on the Fourth of July," Joe asserted.

"You'll have to remind me." Paul slumped into the easy chair and pulled an enlargement of the county map into his lap.

Joe sat at the edge of the fireplace. "You remember the camping spot we went to with the guys from Bay City? We all met at the 'I Forgot Store' and followed them there. They had a secret fishing spot. We camped at a federal campground, but they had their own spot. No one but the Bay City Boys ever went there."

"Oh, yeah, we've never been since. It's secluded, well forested, and just upriver from a big wide stretch of the Au Sable. That can be tough canoeing with the water open to the winds. There's a large impoundment downriver, near Five Channels Dam as I recall." Paul was fingering his map.

"You're right. The shoreline is pretty much all forest," Joe said. "There's not much available for campsites either. It seems there are one-hundred-foot banks in the area, a tad tough for camping. But the Bay City Boys found a little feeder creek and followed it. They discovered a great spot to camp. They showed it to me once. That's where I'm going. They called it 'Muskrat Creek.'"

"So, what's up with the ropes? We know Kenny likes to practice his knot tying, but it seems you got something else in mind?" Doctor Hollis asked.

"Well, when I got trained in rappelling last summer, we went to the high places in the Upper Peninsula, like around Munising and at the Cut River Bridge. Now Kenny wants to learn some mountain climbing skills," Joe explained. "We'll have some time for rope training after our snipe hunt."

"So, Monsieur Voyageur, you want me to believe you found a mountain in the Au Sable River Valley?" Doctor Hollis quipped.

To the Shores of Muskrat Creek

"Ha! That would be historic. But there are steep river banks, some over a hundred feet straight up. Part of that area is within the Huron National Forest with tremendous wooded hills. They come right down to the shores of the river. Once we are there, we can do some rope work after Kenny catches his first snipe," Joe winked. "He might even be ready for the U.P., if we get the chance this July."

"Mark, Saltz, have you guys been to this Muskrat Creek? You tell me it's off the Au Sable and has a secluded clearing for camping, but I don't see it on the forest service map," Paul asked.

"Nope. And I don't think you'll find 'Muskrat Creek' on the county map either," Saltz said while sprawled on the couch.

"But again, that's the name of the place, Muskrat Creek, nothing else in the name?" Paul looked over at Joe and then back to the map.

"Nope," Saltz replied. "It got its name from the Bay City Boys. The story is they followed a family of muskrats on the main river to a little creek. When they explored inland, the forest opened up into a small, flat plain that was great for camping. It was like it had been cleared by loggers. The site is invisible from the main branch of the Au Sable."

Mark was seated in a La-Z-Boy chair. "Paul, I have not been there. But I must have floated by there. I've put in downriver of Loud Dam and float-fished my way to Oscoda more than once."

Joe looked up at Mark. "Loud Dam, that'll probably be our put-in spot. Camping permits aren't required upriver until May fifteenth, but no one knows about Muskrat Creek, except the Bay City Boys. So, we don't need to see the rangers."

Doctor Hollis, wearing a tan Gokey shirt with an Orvis fishing vest over it, walked into the room and joined the conversation. "The Bay City Boys I know only come up on the Au Sable for the month of July."

"That's the guys I'm talking about, doctor," Joe said.

The Snipe Hunters' Deadly Catch at Muskrat Creek

Paul dropped his map on the table and clapped his hands as if concluding a peace treaty on the frontier. "Nothing is named after a muskrat on my map."

Paul paused and then said, "Well, why don't you take one of the jeeps? They have four-wheel drive. You've got the Jeep Cherokee full of your equipment. Put the canoes on the vehicle. That will enable you to handle your own put-in and take-out. Saltz, you and Mark both have your license to drive with you, right?"

"Sure, Paul," Saltz replied.

Mark signaled with his thumb up.

Paul fist-bumped Kenny on the shoulder. "Sounds like you have a plan for a great snipe hunt, Kenny."

"Actually, when we were gearing up at the Outpost, Joe insisted we take all the stuff in the backpacks just in case. He said it will be like we are ready for the Au Sable Adventure Program. That way I'll get to learn more for this July. I'm anxious to go." Kenny proudly reached under his shirt, pulled out the lanyard, and tooted his whistle. "We're ready."

The evening shadows found the men of the Main Post gathered in a semi-circle around a roaring fire on Beaupré's hearth. Kenny and Joe fed the fire. Paul readied the popcorn.

"Get it going so the bed of coals will mature and put out a lot of radiant heat. That's best for a quick pop," Paul called out to Kenny and Joe, who were facing the fire.

"I like watching the fire. I like putting the birch logs on the fire. I like it when the pine logs give off all that aroma," Kenny replied. "Besides look outside; you can just about see that forty-degree air rolling in from the north. There's fog out on that river. Be glad you are in here. I'm keeping us warm, too."

Paul stretched out on his La-Z-Boy and smiled at Kenny.

"Uh-huh. We know you like the fireplace, Prometheus. Just keep it inside the grate this time, okay?" Hollis teased.

Kenny put the tongs down, closed the screen on the

fireplace, and returned to his chair. "Okay, doctor, tell me about hunting snipe. You've done it, so how do I go about this?" Kenny asked.

"Well, you've got a good guide in Joe there. He's one of the best snipe hunters I've ever seen," Doctor Hollis advised. All eyes in the room turned to Joe.

Joe, startled out of his trance-like reverie with the fire, took the lateral. "Yeah, well I guess we'll see about that. But I'm taking you to one of the best spots I know. And trout season is a great time. The opening of Muskrat Creek onto the Au Sable River is at an angle and easy to miss. The forest is dense there. Plus, it's very marshy going up the creek, so perfect habitat for snipe."

"Yeah, the snipe is a marsh bird, and they don't like being around people, that's for sure," Paul confirmed.

"It is very remote along that stretch of the Au Sable River from what I recall," Mark added.

"So, who can tell me about the snipe? I don't even know what they look like," Kenny confessed.

"They remind me of a woodcock in flight, but they act a lot like a sandpiper in marshlands with the way they use their beak to eat," Joe said. "Their coloring reminds me of a ruffed grouse, just a little lighter. They blend in with the woods, too."

"Well, in Canada I think we only have the pin-tailed snipe. It is protected. Native Canadians typically catch, photo, and release. Releasing is the law," Paul continued in his role as the wise, experienced hunter. "We use a burlap sack. Just like your potato sacks. Hollis has some in the garage. Need some, Joe?"

"Ah, jeez, yeah. That would be great," Joe said.

"Are we taking photos, Joe?" Kenny asked. "I could show Uncle Bobby."

"You can borrow my Polaroid if you like. I got some film for trout season," Doctor Hollis volunteered.

"Just be sure you sit still and study those bushes. Snipe have

The Snipe Hunters' Deadly Catch at Muskrat Creek

great camouflage," Mark added his part to the story. "You can stand next to them and not know it until they fly off. But you sure are lucky to be going this early. There won't be many mosquitoes."

"So, Saltz, have you been lucky enough to get one?" Kenny asked.

"Yup. We were up on Saginaw Bay by Quanicassee. My uncle and cousins go duck hunting there. But I was not smart enough to get a photo. I had to get a snipe to prove to my cousins that I was a man of the woods. It was a long night for me. Are you guys going early or late, Joe?" Saltz asked.

"I think we'll put Kenny on the riverbank long before daybreak, maybe four-thirty in the morning." Joe gave Kenny an owl-wise nod. "You get in place. Be real quiet. You can let them walk right into you. You gotta sit still, Kenny."

"You mean I'm alone? I'll be by myself?" Kenny said with an air of panic in his voice.

"It's the only way to hunt snipe, young man," Hollis said.

"It's gotta be done solo, Kenny," Paul nodded at Kenny. "It's the only way to be a man of the woods."

Joe, Mark, and Saltz nodded and stared at him with sober, serious eyes.

Then Saltz walked over to Kenny and put his hand on his shoulder. "Hey, right now you are nice and warm by the fire with your popcorn. Your own fan club here is rooting for you. It's not like that on the snipe trail. You are alone with nature for hours. That's the challenge. You gotta face it like a man. It's you, the woods, and the wily snipe. It takes some amount of discipline. No one can help you. You come home with a snipe or you don't. It took me three tries." Saltz stood over Kenny and looked at the others in the room as everybody tried to keep from laughing.

Mark counseled in his best resident assistant voice, "You remember what Mr. Garson said about the message those

Spartan soldiers got. 'Come home with your shield or on it.' Same kind of thing here, Kenny. You go get your snipe. Now is the time."

Kenny was stammering. "Oh, I guess I didn't know. It is just that … Well, I've never been alone in the woods. I just don't know about the woods like you guys. And snipes I don't know at all."

Hollis stood up to offer his advice. "Hey, you'll do fine. Quit worrying. Joe's got a great place picked out for you. The bugs won't bother you. Be still enough and you might have one walk right up and sit in your lap."

Paul stood up and walked to the kitchen. "It's time for one more batch of popcorn. Are you staring at the fire or popping corn, Kenny? If one could find a snipe in the flames, you'd be our snipe hunter of the year."

><

By noon the next day, two canoes with the four Bosco Boys were slowly plying their way up the very reedy and skinny Muskrat Creek. They launched, paddled, and found the creek just as Joe had predicted. The weather was perfect with a light breeze. It was a sunny sixty-five degrees at high noon and the high for the day was going to be sixty-eight.

Joe guided the canoe up on shore. He stepped out and surveyed the area. "This clearing is still perfect for camping. What would you guess, Mark? You think it's about two hundred, maybe two hundred and fifty yards off the Au Sable?"

"Longer as the stream snakes its way along, yes. I'd say it's less if you pushed through the bush straight to the Au Sable," Mark replied.

Saltz pulled his canoe up the steep bank. He and Mark unloaded it and scouted out a flat site for their two-man tent.

"Gee, Joe, it looks like this little clearing was carved out of the forest by Paul Bunyan himself. Were the Bay City Boys

The Snipe Hunters' Deadly Catch at Muskrat Creek

scouting out a place for a cabin or hunting shack?" Saltz asked.

"Well, if so, they must have a problem reading a map. This is either state or federal land all along here. I don't know how far inland it goes. We never go inland. But most of the land is under government ownership. You'll see cabins when it turns private," Joe said. "Kenny, Mr. Prometheus, you take the hatchet and hunt up some firewood for our bonfire. I'll get our tent going. It's going to be great sleeping weather tonight. The low will be fifty. It'll be great for snipe hunting in the morning, Kenny."

Kenny returned several times from the perimeter of the clearing, dumped the wood in between the two tents, and then gathered up some rocks to border the campfire. He used an entrenching tool to dig out a fire pit, and then he shaped dry sticks in the form of a teepee. The bigger pieces were stacked at the ready nearby.

When the tents were finished, Kenny stood proudly over his creation and announced, "Well, guys, I'm ready. Also, over there to the north, it seems like there's a path going inland at the far end, leading away from this clearing."

"That would be a deer trail, my voyageur-to-be, Kenny," said Joe. "The deer come out of the forest to the creek and get a drink. Glad you are so observant though. The snipe are pretty elusive so you gotta keep studying those woods."

Then Joe called out to Mark, "You can leave the ropes in the canoe. Just be sure the bags are tightly tied."

Even though the bonfire was blazing bright three hours after sunset, Joe decided to declare an early end to their first night on Muskrat Creek. "Mark, you and Saltz can sleep in. I'll canoe down to the Au Sable with Kenny and drop him off at the mouth of the creek. That should be the perfect spot for snipe to be running at dawn. We'll all have breakfast back here after Kenny gets his snipe."

Joe stood up and tapped Kenny on the shoulder. "Okay, let's move along now. You can still see the flames from the tent if you like, Kenny. We aim to have you at the ready with your burlap bag long before daybreak. I'll start the breakfast fire by seven and then come back down the creek for you. You'll have a snipe all wrapped up in your sack by then."

Mark remained seated at the fire but waved at them. "Goodnight, snipe guys. We don't have to keep such early hours even if we decide to have a go at some trout."

Kenny's eyes grew heavy while watching the flames of the bonfire through the mosquito netting. The last sounds of the night for the worried snipe hunter were hoot owls. Then sleep overtook him.

An hour later, Saltz and Mark banked the fire and retired to the melody of the owls. Muskrat Creek would never again be so tranquil.

The Snipe Hunters' Deadly Catch at Muskrat Creek

Chapter Nineteen

A Snipe Hunt Like No Other

Saturday April 26, 1980, 4:15 am, Muskrat Creek campsite

Joe's travel alarm went off at four-fifteen. It was completely black inside the tent. Joe retrieved his flashlight, got dressed, and exited. He inspected the campsite, the fire pit, and examined Mark's tent. All was well.

Kenny remained motionless until Joe grabbed his foot and shook him awake. "Okay, Kenny, the snipe are coming down the trail and you aren't going to catch one in your sleeping bag. Let's go."

Kenny slowly rose up on his elbows. "Okay, Joe. Jeez, I was just getting comfortable in that sleeping bag."

"It is chilly, probably fifty degrees. Grab your sweatshirt, jacket, and hat. I'm going to ready the canoe. We want to be in place at the mouth of Muskrat Creek before five-thirty. They get active at daybreak. So, I want you sitting still in the bushes waiting for 'em, Kenny Boy. Bring your flashlight."

Minutes later Kenny trudged down to the creek and found Joe at the stern of the canoe eating a peanut butter sandwich.

"I got our gear," Joe said. "Everything you need including a canteen of water is in your daypack here. We'll leave the ropes and climbing gear in the canoe for now. I don't want to fuss with that stuff in the dark. Now ya gotta eat because you are going to be sitting still for hours. You want a sandwich, an apple, or some

The Snipe Hunters' Deadly Catch at Muskrat Creek

peanuts?" He shined his light on a brown bag stuffed with Marie's goodies.

"Where's Beaupré's leftover popcorn?" Kenny asked while leaning on a tree adjacent to the canoe. "We waiting until dawn or canoeing down in the dark?"

Joe, handing Kenny a brown paper bag, said, "You and roasted popcorn, I should have known. Here, I'll put Marie's lunch in your day pack. We eat here, but we'll canoe there before dawn. It's a pretty skinny creek. It should be easy. Eat up. 'Mr. Snipe' is waiting for you on the snipe trail."

Kenny munched his popcorn while looking up and downstream with his flashlight. "Joe, you notice how the branches and vines hang over the water up the creek from this campsite? But downstream from here, all the way back to the Au Sable, it is cleaner. It's almost like someone cleared the way. You know, cleaned it up for us. But Hollis said the Bay City Boys vacation in July."

Joe turned his flashlight upstream and then downstream. He inspected the trees and the banks of Muskrat Creek from his perch in the canoe. He finished the peanut butter sandwich and stuffed the rest of his lunch bag into his day pack. "Well, you are getting to be a good observer of Mom Nature. Yes, I see what you mean. But I dunno. When I saw the Bay City Boys, it was summer that's for sure. Okay, got your burlap bag there, Mr. Snipe Hunter? You ready?" He pulled a paddle into one hand and steadied the canoe with his other. "Hop in."

Kenny sat in the bow with his flashlight in his lap. He turned back to Joe before pushing off from the bank. "Joe, when we get back after the snipe hunt, I'd like to explore that path I found. You know, when I got wood for the fire? You called it a deer path."

"Sure, Kenny, we can get to it after breakfast if you like."

Joe shoved off, and the canoe slowly edged its way down Muskrat Creek to the mouth where it opened out and dumped

A Snipe Hunt Like No Other

into the Au Sable River. Kenny only paddled occasionally. He used his paddle to keep the canoe in the middle of the narrow creek. Reaching the end of the creek, Joe silently nosed the canoe through the weeds. He used his ears at first to note where the main stream was. Joe chose to go to the upstream side of Muskrat Creek.

Kenny strapped his day pack on, stepped through the weeds, and pulled the canoe half-way up the bank. With skillful steps, Joe walked to the front of the canoe and stood next to Kenny with the paddle and flashlight still in his hand.

"Jeez, Joe, you see that lightning over there? I thought we had no rain in the forecast for a week." Kenny pointed upstream after the flash of light played across some treetops.

"Yup, it's true. We got good weather all week. Forecast comes from the guys the trout fishermen rely on. Where do you mean? I didn't see anything." Joe turned and faced upriver.

A flash of light, piercing the still-dark skies, slowly came into view. It was an erratic, but focused beam of flight. It was not coming from the sky above. "Kenny, that's not lightning. I don't know what it is. I can't figure what could be causing …"

Then, in the distance, the drone of a motor could be heard. The light was more visible and now shining from the river onto their side of the shore.

"Kenny, something is not right. This is not the fourth of July. Trout fishermen don't use lights like that on a river."

"The light is coming from the middle of the river and shining on our side of the shore, Joe."

Joe stood motionless for another minute. He studied the light. The flashing light edged downstream. It was getting closer.

"Joe, will this mess up my snipe hunt? You know, scare the animals away? You guys told me I had to sit very still. I bet lights shining in the woods would spook a lot of animals."

"Yeah, that would include me right now. Kenny, I don't know

The Snipe Hunters' Deadly Catch at Muskrat Creek

about this. It's strange."

With his eyes upstream on the canoe, Joe unconsciously put both hands in his pocket and then fingered his favorite knife-compass in a leather holster strapped to his belt. Joe's head turned owl-like from his gaze upstream. He rapped Kenny on the shoulder. "Let's go, Kenny. Grab your end of the canoe."

Joe darted to the rear of the canoe and picked it up out of Muskrat Creek. "Let's get this outta sight and get in the bushes, Kenny."

"Are you sure about this, Joe?"

"What I'm sure about is this: they ain't fishing for trout."

Kenny moved inland away from the shore, using his flashlight for guidance. Joe guided him in silence at the rear of the canoe. The forest started to thicken up and Kenny halted.

"See that downfall to your right, Kenny? Let's put it on the forest side. No one will see it. Douse your flashlight now."

They maneuvered the canoe through the bush using the faint glimmer of light emanating from the nascent dawn creeping into the sky above. Joe pocketed his flashlight. Kenny hauled his end of the canoe up and balanced it on the dead tree. He pulled his body up, sat on the tree, and swung his feet over the tree. Joe steadied the canoe from the rear.

Kenny's feet hit the ground with an explosion. A flurry of noise, a blast of movement detonated beneath his feet; Kenny recoiled to one side. He fell with his heart in his throat to the ground. The noise continued upward and away from him.

Stunned, Kenny froze in place out of sight of Joe. Panting like a runner with his heart pounding, every muscle tensed up. He sensed an attack was imminent and instinctively grabbed for his knife. He stared into the dark.

"Are you alright there, Davy Crockett? I can't see ya but I hear you breathing," Joe said with an unseen smirk on his face.

Seconds, feeling like minutes, passed. "Just what was that? Was that a snipe?"

"That would be a partridge, Kenny," Joe said. "Without the benefit of the pear tree. Up north hunters call them ruffed grouse. I think you stepped on a pair of them or a whole family. It's too dark for me to tell."

Kenny stood up, sheathed his knife, and then pulled the canoe to his side of the tree. Joe lifted his end over and guided it to the ground.

"Joe, I have never been that afraid, honest."

"You know the sign on the path between the cabins, 'Partridge Path' with a date on it? Do you how it got there? That's when Mark dumped everybody's lunch all over the floor of the forest. Now you know why."

"Well, I can understand, Joe."

"It happens to everyone if you traipse around the woods long enough. It's their home, not ours. Okay, Kenny, let's get our backpacks on and get back toward the shore. We have to see what's up with those lights. Bring your flashlight but keep it off. Follow my steps."

Joe threaded his way through the woods like a voyageur. He found a spot that allowed for a view of the river as it received water from Muskrat Creek. The brush and a poplar tree growing at an angle provided cover for Joe and Kenny. They took their packs off and settled on the ground.

"I got my burlap bag. Is this place good for snipe, Joe?"

Joe exhaled loudly and stared out on the river. "Ah ..., well, I suppose it would be ... if you were alone. You see ... you never snipe hunt in pairs." He turned and looked at Kenny. "It would be best if ... you can put the snipe bag away for now. We gotta figure out what those guys with the lights are up to. I don't have a good feeling about this, Kenny."

The low drone of the motor revealed that the canoe was coming their way, but slowly. Periodically, a glimmer of light flashed through the trees. The direction of the lights confirmed its route. The vessel with the lights was definitely coming

The Snipe Hunters' Deadly Catch at Muskrat Creek

A Snipe Hunt Like No Other

toward them. Kenny rested up against a stump. He had a perfect view of the opening of Muskrat Creek. Joe could see a little of the Au Sable upriver of the creek's opening. The canoe was coming downriver. Joe discreetly pulled out his beads, as he crouched on the floor of the forest.

"Jeez, Joe, at a time like this you start praying again? So, why don't you teach me this deal? You teach me about knots, canoeing, hiking in the woods, and snipe hunting. Why don't you teach me about praying? Must be important … I gotta believe you think it is."

"Sss-eesh, will you? You'll scare all the snipe clear down to Saginaw County. I don't want those people to know about us, till I know about them."

"But why do you pray, Joe? Why now? What's the deal?" Kenny insisted.

"That's for you and Brother Ed or Father George to discuss sometime, not me."

Exasperated, Kenny said, "Well, we're here now. And we ain't going nowhere and that boat won't be here for awhile. And you just said the snipe aren't coming, remember? We are together, not alone, and the snipe like singles, I guess. Brother Ed is not here to do the teaching thing. So, why not you? Why not here? And why not right now?"

Joe looked through the shadows to see his friend's insistent face. Kenny peered right back at him.

"Joe, you got me up at some uncivilized time to paddle here, and now we ain't hunting snipe. You said so yourself. So, talk. Like you said we gotta wait for these lights. So start talking," Kenny demanded.

"Well, it is kind of private, a person's prayer life, you know," Joe said in a low voice.

"It's just me and the snipe listening."

Joe chuckled aloud as he regarded his insistent friend. "Well, jeez, Kenny, you … see, it's not just for priests and nuns or holy people." And he turned away and looked back upriver. He hoped that would be enough.

The steady drone of the motor broadcast its continued approach. Glimmers of light pierced through the canopy of the forest, but still at a distance.

"Well, that might be enough for your snipe friends, but remember you hauled me out of a warm sleeping bag at—"

Joe interrupted, "My uncle parachuted with the 101st Airborne on D-Day in World War II. He lost the full use of one leg but survived the war. He wore the rosary on his neck the whole time; still does. And that ain't all."

"So, I heard that 'Hail Mary' part. Does that mean you pray to Mary, but not to Jesus?" Kenny asked.

"No, of course I pray to Jesus. It's called intercessory prayer when you invoke the aid of a saint or Mary, Jesus' mother. I pray to Jesus, through Mary. Know why, Kenny?"

"Well, no Joe I'm new to …"

"Well, okay, I'll quiz you like Fred, Kenny Boy. What was the first miracle Jesus ever performed?"

"I'm guessing the loaves and fishes story that Brother Ed talks about."

"It was the wedding feast at Cana. When informed that there was no more wine, Jesus told his mother, 'My hour has not yet come.' The Virgin Mary simply said to the servants, 'Do whatever He tells you.' Voila, as Mark would say, some pretty good wine came forth from ordinary water. Hey, I bet growing up even you learned to listen to your mom. Am I wrong?"

"Well, yeah, I used to," Kenny reflected. "What's intercessory again?"

"Listen up this time, Kenny," Joe commanded. "I was on deck waiting to come up to bat in our league championship game. The score was close. The coach whistled me out of there. Our heavy hitter went to the plate. So, like a coach, I have to ask: "Who do I want going to the plate for my cause, Joe Duvalle or

A Snipe Hunt Like No Other

the Virgin Mary? That's intercessory. I talk to Mary. She talks to Jesus. It works. Just ask the wine drinkers of Galilee."

Joe paused, looked back at the Au Sable, and then returned to Kenny. He exhaled loudly and looked back at his insistent friend. The bushes moved by the creek less than fifteen yards away. Kenny tensed up. He grabbed the burlap bag. Joe peeked up over the tree. A doe had led two fawns down the bank. They were drinking out of Muskrat Creek. Kenny put his bag down.

Joe continued, "Kenny, the Lord knows I've never won any awards as a student, but one thing I've learned is that when Brother Ed starts talking, you better listen up. You know Brother Ed follows a Basilian approach to education."

"What's that mean?" Kenny asked.

"Brother Ed is a monk from the order started by Saint Basil. Among other things, they got this motto. It's up in the library next to the painting about the naval battle by Juan Luna. 'Lord, teach me goodness, discipline, and knowledge.'"

"What's that painting all about anyway?" Kenny asked.

"It's another good reason to pray the rosary among other things."

"Joe, you are telling me that you pray the rosary because of some ancient sea battle?"

"Think this through, Kenny Boy. It was the Battle of Lepanto in 1571. The Christian forces were outnumbered about two to one; they were down about 80 ships to the Turks. The Turkish leader had many victories to his credit. The Holy League was led by one inexperienced and young commander, Don Juan of Austria. They actually had a twenty-four-year-old in charge of the whole fleet. Pope Pius V decided to have everyone pray the rosary. Christians were praying throughout Europe." Joe held up his wooden beads. "Soldiers actually went into battle with these beads in their hands."

"Really? Then they actually faced death with your favorite prayers?"

The Snipe Hunters' Deadly Catch at Muskrat Creek

Joe waved his finger at him like Mr. Garson. "All prayers are efficacious, if I got that word right, according to Father George. But I like to stack the odds in my favor. Just like someone you know from that battle."

"You are saying I know someone from 1571?"

"Absolutely."

"You are nuts. That's over four hundred years ago," Kenny exclaimed.

Joe paused again to inspect the river. The sky above was lightening up with dawn's steady approach. Yet, the ground below clung to darkness and the forest its shadows. The hum of the motor droned on toward them.

"Remember the entire class went to Central Michigan University for that musical?" Joe asked.

"Heck, yeah, I sure do. Our whole bus stopped for a pizza dinner. It was about some crazy Portuguese guy charging windmills. The teachers really liked the songs. I wasn't so keen on them."

"Yes. The guy was Spanish. That play, Man of La Mancha, comes from the book Don Quixote. The author fought in that battle and was shot three times," Joe asserted.

"Jeez, did he live?"

"Yup. Miguel de Cervantes not only lived through that battle, but also survived five years in captivity as a slave. Cervantes became one of the most famous authors in the world. Even though he lost the use of his left arm, he said fighting in that battle was the proudest moment in his life. They repelled the invasion. That victory prevented the Turks from occupying Western Europe." Joe paused and looked at Kenny, "Like Brother Ed says: 'You want power? You want guidance to do the right thing? Pray!'"

"Hmm ... I see. So maybe you can teach me about those beads, eh?"

Joe looked over at Kenny with a solemn gaze. "Ya never teach

A Snipe Hunt Like No Other

the beads on a snipe hunting day."

"Ha! So how's your uncle, the guy that parachuted into France?" Kenny asked.

"He is the manager of a real estate office and has rentals—" Joe froze in mid-sentence. "Get lower. The light is getting closer."

Kenny copied Joe and scrunched lower while peeking through the leaves of the poplar tree.

The motorized canoe loomed into view. The dawning sky silhouetted three figures in the long riverboat. The man in the stern was operating a trolling motor. A man in the bow of the boat was aiming a spot light along the shore looking for something. Even though they were close to shore now, the motor and distance muffled the sound of their voices. But the shape of the object held by the man in the middle was unmistakable.

"Joe, he's got a rifle," Kenny exclaimed. "What's in season now?"

"Nothing I can think of. And I ain't going to ask them. That's for sure," Joe whispered.

The boat approached the opening of Muskrat Creek. The bowman held up his hand. The motorman cut the engine. There were gestures exchanged between the two men. They paddled out into the mainstream in an arc. Then the bow was aimed directly at the angled mouth of Muskrat Creek. The motor lurched back to life.

"Look! They're coming our way. They are headed up Muskrat Creek, Joe. What about Saltz and Mark, Joe?" Kenny whispered urgently to his friend.

Joe held up his hand and pointed.

"Look at the motorman, Kenny."

The skies were brightening though the sun's full illumination was denied by a bank of clouds. Yet, the uniform was visible.

"Is that ranger state or federal, Joe?"

287

The Snipe Hunters' Deadly Catch at Muskrat Creek

"Green is federal, Kenny. He's got a pistol, too."

Crouching in the brush and behind the poplar, Kenny and Joe watched them glide by. They were not more than twenty yards away on the opening of Muskrat Creek. The man in the middle rested his rifle and brandished a paddle in response to the narrow passageway. The motor was almost at idle and providing minimal thrust.

Joe and Kenny remained frozen in place until the riverboat canoe disappeared up Muskrat Creek. Kenny broke the silence after a few minutes.

"What do we do now, Joe? Did we break the law camping without a permit? Are they going after Mark and Saltz? How did they know about us?"

"This creek is not on the county map. It is too small and I think too new. Only the Bay City Boys ever used it. They are the only ones to even refer to it. It is easy to float by Muskrat Creek and not see the opening. It is at an angle and well-concealed by these willows and poplars."

Joe stood up and sat on a stump behind a poplar. He looked down at Kenny. "I think they were looking for the opening all along. Remember all that gesturing between the motorman and the guy in the bow with the light? They had to be looking for this, what we call Muskrat Creek, but why? Better yet, why was the guy in the middle carrying a rifle?"

"What about Saltz and Mark back at the campsite? That motorized canoe will be there shortly. It's just getting to be daylight and those guys wanted to sleep in." Kenny stood up and looked at Joe.

Joe looked up at Kenny. "Well, at least one of them is a ranger or conservation officer of some sort. And we haven't broken any …"

Joe, looking beyond Kenny out onto the Au Sable, stopped. He said nothing. He reached up and grabbed Kenny by both arms. He pulled Kenny down into the bushes.

"Freeze. Don't move. Don't talk," He whispered.

A Snipe Hunt Like No Other

The motorized canoe came into sight of the campground. The ranger in the rear cut the power. The craft beached without making a noise. The men left the canoe. They surveyed the campsite from three separate locations in the bush. Muskrat Creek's campsite was still and quiet. The three men, guns at the ready, quickly approached the two tents. Rabbits skirted out of view, mourning doves cooed, and back on the creek a chickadee was lustily announcing the arrival of a new day.

Mark heard the zipper on the tent flap. A blast of daylight burst into the tent. Someone gripped his foot and Mark sat up.

"Get up and out, men. Keep your hands in view."

Mark and Saltz blinked awake. The brightness of the dawn's first light ended a good night's sleep. They sat up. A uniformed man was pointing a gun at them. Another armed man was holding the tent flap open. Speechless and startled, Mark and Saltz moved slowly. They followed directions and exited the tent.

Once outside, one man inspected their tent. The other man put a wristband on Mark and then tied Saltz's wrist to Mark's. He did the same thing to their ankles. Any future movement would now be together and have to be coordinated.

"Sit down now," the man with the gun ordered.

It was then that they noticed a U.S. Forest Service Ranger walking toward them from the far perimeter of the campsite with a compass in his hands. He joined the two armed men with Saltz and Mark. "The path's there just like I was told. What are we going to do first?"

The tall officer was examining their wallets while the shorter one was rummaging through their backpacks. "So, you must be Mark. It says here you are a student at Bosco Academy. What are you doing camping here?"

The short man spoke before Mark could reply.

The Snipe Hunters' Deadly Catch at Muskrat Creek

"Both tents are clean. There's nothing in the bags. No weapons. Their gear so far: a filet knife, an ax, some fishing and camping knives, and a collapsible saw. Their canoe has ropes and some gear for fishing. That's all."

Mark stammered out his reply. "Well, sir, we just came ... we just came here to camp, fish, and have some fun with a couple of other guys." Nodding at his backpack, he continued, "We got fishing licenses if you want to see them."

The chill of the morning air was getting to Mark. The shock of seeing a pistol had sent a wave of numbness from tongue to toe. He relaxed a little when he saw the ranger walk up. The ranger nodded and the other men filled their holsters.

The tall officer turned to the short officer. "The other kid is a Bosco student, too. So where are your buddies and how many are there?"

"We got two other buddies," Mark reported. "They got up early to go on a snipe hunt."

All three men broke out in laughter. The ranger muttered under his breath, "Really, we busted up a snipe hunt?" He put his arms on his hips and looked over at the officers.

"Just what are you saying?" the tall man demanded with a frown on his face. "You guys came here for a snipe hunt. Is that what you want us to believe?"

"Sir, I gotta pee," Saltz interrupted. "I'm cold. Can I put my clothes on now?" Sitting on the cold ground in his boxer shorts and T-shirt was very uncomfortable. A slight breeze was adding to the chill.

"Okay, go over there in the bushes. You get to practice some teamwork on the way." The tall officer directed them to the border of the clearing. He cut the bands on their wrists but left the leg bands intact.

Saltz and Mark trudged in tandem to the bushes. They kept their backs to the police. When out of earshot, Saltz asked Mark, "What did we do wrong? Why do we have police pawing

A Snipe Hunt Like No Other

through our tent looking for weapons and tying us up?"

"Dunno, Saltz. It's got to be Muskrat Creek. Maybe Joe's Bay City Boys are in trouble with the law. That forest ranger is not checking licenses. Those cops, well they aren't county sheriffs."

The ranger whistled for them to get back to the campsite. They trudged back in bare feet. The damp morning dew made them colder. The ranger was alone. They saw the two cops following the deer path that Kenny had talked about after gathering wood.

"How long you boys been here and what have you done since you arrived?" The ranger demanded.

Shivering, Saltz ignored his question. He interrupted Mark as he began a polite reply. "Sir, will you free up our legs and let us get dressed? I'm cold and I ain't done nothing but camp overnight at this darn Muskrat Creek."

The ranger did not move. He regarded Saltz's face and looked over at Mark. "Muskrat Creek, eh? I been here twenty-five years and that's a new one on me." He raised his hand and beckoned for Mark to reply.

"Well, sir, Saltz is right. We canoed here from the dam and set up camp before dark. We ate, had a campfire, and then you woke us up."

"What about the other two snipe hunters? Are they students with Bosco Academy, too?"

"Yes, sir. Joe Duvalle is a senior and Kenny Dee is a transfer student new to Bosco this year."

"Sir, snipe hunting and trout fishing ain't against the law. Can we get dressed?" Saltz demanded.

The ranger smiled as if he had forgotten something. He pulled a leather pouch from the pile of belongings the police had dumped near the campfire. He dumped the contents on the ground. Next to the bandana, a Swiss pocket knife, a compass, and a waterproof container of matches was a small black leather coin purse along with a pack of Clove gum. He turned the purse

The Snipe Hunters' Deadly Catch at Muskrat Creek

upside down. A black beaded rosary fell out.

"Who owns that?" The ranger demanded.

"That would be Joe. He's off on the snipe hunt, sir," Mark replied.

The ranger stepped forward, bent down, and with one swift motion withdrew a switchblade from his boot and slit the bands from their feet. He gazed down at Mark from his athletic-looking six-foot-four lanky frame. "So, we have a snipe hunting Christian, eh? You boys gotta be alright. I ain't religious unless you count throwing Hail Mary passes. I got a number of those to my credit. And, hey, some even got caught." He winked at Mark and stepped over to Saltz and extended his hand. "I'm Officer Becker, U.S. Forest Service. My guess is that the new boy Kenny is on his first snipe hunt?"

"Yeah, yes, sir, that's right. Joe was going up toward the mouth of Muskrat Creek. But he was supposed to be back a while ago. We were all going to have pancakes together," Saltz replied.

"You boys get dressed now. Then you can make your breakfast if you like."

Kenny was now down on his hands and knees. Joe inched up next to him and lowered one of the branches of the poplar tree. It provided a clear view through the bushes out across the bank on Muskrat Creek and onto the sparkling waters of the Au Sable. A motorized riverboat was on the river.

"You see what I see? Anybody look familiar?" Joe whispered.

Kenny peered through the bushes. "Jeez O Pete! That's them. There's Mr. Bad Breath himself. That's the Tobacco Bandits. They stole our Silver Beaver canoe. This Muskrat Creek is getting popular just when I wanna catch a snipe," Kenny whispered back. "What are they doing here?"

"You watch that riverboat. I bet they arc around and head up

A Snipe Hunt Like No Other

Muskrat Creek," Joe whispered back.

As if on cue, the riverboat swung around, found the angle for the entrance up Muskrat Creek, and aimed for it with very low throttle on the trolling motor.

"What are we going to do, Joe?" Kenny whispered and stared over at his mentor.

Joe put his hand on the back of Kenny's neck and gently nudged him down into a prone position. "Right now, we blend into this bush just like a snipe, Kenny Boy."

The riverboat with the two men edged toward the opening. They began to ascend Muskrat Creek. The Bosco Boys watched their adversaries pass within yards of them. They remained motionless in the forest looking through the bracken fern on the floor of the forest out onto the skinny creek.

When the bandits had ascended the creek and were out of sight, Kenny sat up, faced Joe, and whispered with force, "How are we going to help Saltz and Mark?"

"Nothing good can come of this, Kenny. The Tobacco Bandits are headed to the campsite with our guys and that crew with the Forest Service Ranger. I can't think of anything good happening." Joe stood up and scouted out the Au Sable for any more traffic. He paced back and forth while conjuring up a plan.

"C'mon, let's go."

Joe guided Kenny back to the canoe. When he got there, he stopped and put his hand on Kenny's shoulder. Thinking aloud as he looked over Kenny's shoulder he declared, "Shucks, no way. We can't get caught on that creek with that riverboat. We'd have no chance."

Joe found himself staring into the canoe and fingering his backpack. He paced about while Kenny stood nearby. The forest was quiet except for some chickadees singing. Joe was muttering to himself. Kenny could hear one refrain, "That won't work. They got guns."

Abruptly, Joe stopped and looked at Kenny as if he'd received inspiration from above. "Got your hiking shoes on, Kenny? We got to bushwhack our way back to camp. We can't get caught on that skinny creek. Plus, there's no place to hide. Remember, they got guns and we got …" He gestured toward his belt where he had his hunting knife in a leather sheath. "Put your backpack on. We'll think of something. They didn't see us. Neither of them knows we are here. That's good."

Kenny grabbed his backpack and cinched it tight against his shoulders. Joe did the same. He glanced down again at the bottom of the canoe. He scanned the environment for his resources. His mind was ablaze with the mantra from his past training: "Adapt, cope, innovate."

"Ok, Kenny. That's it. We have about four hundred and fifty, maybe four hundred and seventy-five yards cross country to get to the campsite. We bushwhack quietly, at least when we get close. They don't know we exist. We'll figure something out when we get there."

Joe led off through the brush and trees of the forest. Kenny followed. Twenty yards into his journey, Joe put the brakes on and stopped. He turned back. He looked at, but really through, Kenny. "That's it! Plan B. We got some things they don't."

He marched back to the hidden canoe and took his backpack off. He grabbed some of the neatly packed gear still stored in the canoe. "Now, Kenny, you get to use some of the skills you been learning all winter. Ditch your backpack for now. Grab that hatchet. Follow me. We got some work to do." Joe unsheathed his knife and headed toward Muskrat Creek.

Thirty-five minutes later, Joe and Kenny began to bushwhack their way through the forest to the campsite. Guided by the gurgling of Muskrat Creek on their left, they plodded along. Joe was repeating the mandates from his survival training, "adapt, cope, and innovate," commanding his mind to overcome obstacles, use resources, and out-think his adversary.

A Snipe Hunt Like No Other

"Is that your favorite breakfast, Mark? Peanut butter and strawberry jam wrapped inside a tortilla-sized pancake?" Saltz asked as he wolfed down number three while sitting by the blazing fire.

"Well, out here it is because it's easy and tasty." Mark, sitting next to Officer Becker with his back to the creek, finished up and grabbed his canteen. Officer Becker was sipping a hot cup of tea.

Saltz, facing the creek, looked up to see two men approaching them at a fast pace. "Officer Becker, are you expecting some ...company? There's ..."

Officer Becker shot up and turned toward the creek.

A tall, bearded man with a worn-out hat was pointing a rifle at them. Off to one side was another shorter man who had a pistol pointed at them. "Best to be calm now, yes?" the tall man said with a thick accent. "No quick moves are good, eh? Accidents can happen. Not good for accidents in these woods, eh boys?"

The tall man advanced quickly on them and went directly to Officer Becker. He pulled Officer Becker's gun from his holster. "No need for this anymore, eh? Deer season is over, yes, officer of the forest? All done hunting today."

The shorter man reeked of poor hygiene. He was unshaven and unkempt. He waved for Mark and Saltz to stand up. He frisked them both and then shoved them away from Officer Becker and toward a tent.

He pushed them forward and then into the tent. "You two, get inside there," the shorter man said. "Now you sitting and quiet, yes?"

Mark and Saltz were enveloped in darkness when he zipped the flap shut.

The bearded leader emptied Officer Becker's pockets, while

The Snipe Hunters' Deadly Catch at Muskrat Creek

the shorter man held his gun on him. Then he took his holster belt and hat and rudely shoved the ranger into the other tent. He zipped it shut and tied the flaps down.

The leader stood in between the tents and raised his voice. "Now, you boys inside tent, you safe. You coming outside is not so safe. Maybe you get shot. My friend here no liking you outside of tents. So best to relax and stay in tent, Okay, boys? You understanding my agreements? You say 'okay', now."

"Yes, okay," Mark bellowed loudly.

Officer Becker yelled, "Okay."

"This is good for you. Okay is good for you, trust me, boys. Okay mean no shooting today. This is best, yes?" The leader spoke again in a loud voice.

Silence fell upon the campsite at Muskrat Creek for over thirty minutes.

><

Joe stopped and raised his hand as the light penetrating from the forest canopy revealed an opening ahead. He motioned for Kenny to halt in place. He dropped down on all fours and crawled the last twenty yards on his hands and knees. His place of concealment was a small ridge Mr. Garson had taught him was a drumlin. Joe flattened his belly to the ground to study the campsite about forty yards down the tapered end of the drumlin. There was no movement. The campfire was smoldering.

"What do you think, Joe?" Kenny whispered.

"No sign of life now. There's been a fire though."

"Wanna go down there and check it out now, Joe?"

"Heck, no. We have to be right. They don't know we exist or at least where we are. That advantage we can't give up. Remember they got guns."

Ten minutes went by with no sign of life and no sounds apart from the birds. Kenny and Joe remained motionless. Then Joe

A Snipe Hunt Like No Other

turned to Kenny. "So, are you up for a mission, my Daniel Boone to-be buddy? We can't risk both of us getting caught. You gotta go solo on this one."

"Sure, Joe, sitting here is driving me nuts. You think they already took our guys away or killed them?"

"Well, dunno," said Joe. "But we ain't heard any shots or seen any bodies. The strange thing is that all the camping gear is in a pile near the campfire, except the sleeping bags. The tent flaps are shut so they aren't airing them out. Let's find out about the canoes."

"What do you want me to do?"

"Take your pack off. You got your knife on your belt. Take the hatchet with you. Stay low on your hands and knees. I figure we are about fifty to sixty yards inland from the creek, straight left. Find out how many canoes are there and get back here. If things go wrong, run back to our canoe, hide there out of sight. If you see me wearing my red bandana, you know there's trouble. Stay hidden. Fight only if you have to. Today, running is the best option, even for Daniel Boone."

"Okay, Joe. But what if I run, hide, and later you come wearing that bandana?" Kenny paused. "What do I do then?"

Joe winked. "That's when you get to adapt, cope, and innovate there, Kenny, just like Daniel Boone. Remember, he did so well after his capture the Shawnee adopted him."

Kenny pulled the hatchet from his pack and turned left. "Jeez, Joe, you always got answers."

Joe flattened out amidst the fern and scrub pine. He studied the still landscape downslope of the drumlin.

Twenty minutes later, Kenny crawled into sight and gave Joe a thumb's up. Joe was smiling as he neared him.

"How many we got there, Mr. Boone?"

"All of them, Joe. There are the two riverboats. Mark's canoe is up on shore. There is no evidence that anyone has gone downriver."

The Snipe Hunters' Deadly Catch at Muskrat Creek

"So, the Shawnee let you go this time, Daniel?"

Kenny was still huffing and puffing from exertion. "Huh?"

"Never mind, welcome back and nice job, Kenny." Joe nodded at him when he took up a spot next to him on the ridge.

"Joe, you remember that deer path I discovered gathering wood. It's over on the far end of the clearing. You can see where the tall grass is parted and beaten down. The brush over there is parted, too. Keep your eye on it. I think that's not just for deer."

Joe began to study the area. A hat came into view. "Lookey there, Kenny Boy. You are right. It's also a path for our Tobacco Bandit. He's still toting his rifle."

"Yeah, and that looks like his number two man behind him," Kenny added.

"You ushered him into the side of a riverbank at a high rate of speed as I recall, Kenny Boy."

"I'll bet he hasn't brushed his teeth since then, either. What are we going to do, Joe?"

"Lay low and watch every move they make. For this to end our way, we gotta separate them from their guns, Kenny. And we want to do that before they get used."

Kenny and Joe could see but not hear the Tobacco Bandits. They unzipped the flap of the nearest tent and stood back. Officer Becker crawled out. He remained seated on the ground. They tied his hands up in front of him. The same happened to Saltz and Mark, but they were put back into the tent. Officer Becker was pushed to his feet in the direction of the canoe landing.

Joe rose up on his knees, slapped Kenny on the back, and then backed away on all fours. Kenny followed suit. They stopped after twenty yards. "Okay, Kenny, we hit the woods at track speed now. Close up your backpack and just keep running steady. We got to get back to the mouth of Muskrat Creek before they do."

Joe stood up once he was clear of the ridge. "Let's go, Kenny, it's downhill off this ridge."

Kenny was once again following Joe through the woods. He made it a point to keep up and place his feet exactly where Joe did. He did not want to fail. His thoughts turned to the first day he followed Joe out of Bosco Hall. He admired Joe's fitness then and he admired it once again.

Joe tripped forward, and immediately pulled his arms in and rolled with the descent to the bottom of a knoll. He was up when Kenny reached him. He remained a step ahead of him. They kept a great pace aided by their earlier bushwhack through the woods to find the campsite.

Joe found their canoe and stopped. His chest was heaving. He was gasping for air as he tore off his backpack. He motioned for Kenny to do likewise. "OK, Kenny. You get out of sight where I showed you this morning. Take the hatchet. Now show me your whistle."

Kenny ditched his backpack in time to whirl around and pull his whistle into sight. "Yeah, it's right here."

"You know our plan." Joe smacked Kenny on the shoulder and then held him by his shoulders. He forced him to look at him directly. "Kenny, focus on me now. The whistle blows, you fly like an arrow. You must disarm and disable your man. Remember our guys are counting on us, and the bad guys are not expecting us. You already know from last time how to bash a bully. They got guns, so bash 'em good."

Kenny nodded in silence. Joe ran out of sight toward the mouth of Muskrat Creek.

Kenny slithered into his place by a willow tree with a small crop of reeds and bulrushes leading to the water. He was well hidden.

Five minutes later, the riverboat came around the last bend before the creek opened out into the river. It was traveling at a higher rate of speed than expected. Joe saw that Officer Becker was seated in the middle of the canoe between the two bandits.

The Snipe Hunters' Deadly Catch at Muskrat Creek

A Snipe Hunt Like No Other

His hands were tied in his lap but he appeared unhurt. The leader with the worn-out hat was operating the motor. Joe began his countdown to the preplanned spot in the creek.

Joe gripped his whistle and blew hard.

Kenny responded to the signal and pulled a length of rope.

The men in the canoe reflexively looked to the far side of the creek in the direction of Joe's whistle.

The rope sprung up out of the creek neck high. It smashed into the bowman's throat while he was still looking toward Joe. He was raked over the side of the canoe and into the creek. Officer Becker bent backward and went overboard. The leader in the stern screamed. But there was no escape. The rope raked him up and over the back end of the motorized riverboat. The riverboat, minus its occupants, careened at an angle into the far shore.

Kenny charged into the water after the leader. The bearded man was gripping his neck with one hand. He was looking at the far side of the creek in the direction of Joe's whistle. He started to grope for his pistol in knee-high water. He did not see Kenny coming from the near side of the creek.

Kenny smashed the blunt end of the hatchet into the collarbone on the leader's pistol arm. The bearded man yelped in pain. His arm went limp while still holding the pistol. Kenny swung around and aimed for the hand with the pistol. The sharp end of the hatchet hit on target. The gun, now out of the holster, went to the bottom of the creek. The water turned red with blood. The bearded 'Tobacco Man' cried out in pain. Kenny advanced closer. He rose up on one leg. He delivered a front thrust kick to his belly. 'Tobacco Man' fell backward, holding his arm and screaming in pain.

Joe splashed into the water behind the bowman who was gasping for air while kneeling close to the far shore. Joe was frantically trying to locate the pistol and disable him. Joe clubbed him once on the back of the head; then twice on his pistol arm with a thick branch. Incredibly, the bowman got back up. He turned toward Joe while reaching for his pistol. Joe stepped back to swing with more force. He lost his footing and fell backward into the knee-high water of the creek. The bowman seemed unfazed by the blow to his head. He splashed toward Joe while coughing and gasping. Blood was coming from the back of his head and out of his mouth. His pistol arm dangled at his side. He reached for his pistol with his left arm and pulled it from the holster.

Joe lost his club in the water. He saw the bowman advancing on him. When he saw him reach for his pistol with his left arm, Joe instinctively reached for his hunting knife. It was on his belt but now under the water. Joe was frantic as he saw the pistol clumsily removed from the holster.

A piercing scream came from the bowman. The pistol fell from his hand into the creek. The bowman fell face forward toward Joe. Joe stood up, with the man writhing at his feet. Blood was coming from his back. The bowman could not keep afloat with his wounds. It was then that Joe noticed Officer Becker standing behind the bowman with his switchblade in his hand.

They teamed up and dragged the drowning bowman by his belt through the creek to the near shore. Officer Becker searched the moaning man who continued to gag for air due to his neck wound.

They looked up the creek for Kenny. He was kneeling on the back of the motorman, his hatchet at the ready.

"Damn you and your pistol," Kenny screamed over and over in a frenzied state. Kenny had pinned both arms of the motorman to his back, holding them there with his knees.

The motorman, with a smashed collarbone, moaned in pain. Crying out in a foreign language, he seemed to be seeking mercy. Kenny had none to give.

"Kenny," Joe said quietly. "Don't."

A Snipe Hunt Like No Other

Officer Becker approached Kenny and Joe, who were still breathing heavily. "I'll get the boat, guys."

"Hey, Kenny, you forgot to blow your whistle," Joe jibed him.

"Darn you, Joe. I got pistol man, didn't I?" Kenny blurted back.

"Yup, you sure did. Today I'd say it's even better than getting a snipe," Joe teased.

Officer Becker retrieved the long riverboat canoe from the far shore, turned the motor off, and waded back across the creek. He positioned the boat to go back up Muskrat Creek and then stepped on shore. "You must be the snipe hunters from Bosco Academy, eh?" Officer Becker declared. "I'm Officer Becker, U.S. Forest Service." He took three deep breaths and continued, "You guys are simply outstanding. They got me. They tied up two ATF agents. But some snipe hunters from Bosco Academy put them on the bottom of Muskrat Creek. That's what your buddies call it, eh, Muskrat Creek? Well, you can name it what you want, snipe hunters. You beat these criminals on your own. You've got my salute."

"Officer, thanks for your help. That guy was going to shoot me left-handed. How did you do it?" Joe asked. "They had you tied up. I saw them do it. I was hiding in the woods."

"I got a special holster in my boot for my knife. My hands were hidden from their view so when I went over into the creek they were already free. I'm happy to help out you snipe guys. I had no idea where they were taking me. But the Bureau of Alcohol, Tobacco, and Firearms figures their base is in Canada. They cache their bootleg tobacco here in the forest for distribution into the states."

"I see," Joe said. "He's whining in some other language. Where are they from?"

Officer Becker smirked. "The ATF boys say the Middle East, probably Iran. Be a while before they get to go home now."

Joe motioned the officer's attention toward Kenny who had

not moved from his position kneeling on his adversary's back.

"Well, snipe men of Bosco Academy, we have to get back to the campsite and free up our friends. Then we better get these clowns some help. You two want to watch these guys or go up the creek to the campsite?"

"I'm done with these guys. I'm going to the campsite," Kenny announced. "But I'm not leaving until these guys are tied up."

Officer Becker chuckled. "I was just kidding, guys. I'm the law enforcement officer here after all. But you snipe hunters could probably do it all anyway. Don't forget to follow that path about a hundred yards into the woods. My men are tied up next to a huge cache of tobacco camouflaged to blend in with the forest."

"How did you find out about this place?" Joe asked.

"One of my regular customers, so to speak, told me about it. He runs traps along this stretch of the river. He tipped me off."

Officer Becker tied up the moaning tobacco men.

Joe and Kenny manned the riverboat and headed up the creek.

As they passed Officer Becker, he touched his hand to his head in a slight salute. "You snipe hunters are 'A-okay'. Bon voyage."

Chapter Twenty

The Silver Beaver

Friday, June 20, 1980, 11:46 am, Doc Hollis' Cabin

Doctor Hollis was perched in his favorite patio chair overlooking the amber waters of the Au Sable sparkling in the mid-June sunshine when Kenny, Joe, Mark, and Saltz walked up. The table was set. Paul Beaupré was manning the grill.

"Hey, now, today is my day. I have the pleasure of dining with the Heroes of Muskrat Creek." Hollis stood to shake hands and welcome all four of them individually.

"C'mon now, doctor, that's not what we call ourselves," Mark protested.

"Hey, I got it on good authority. Paul here saved the article in The Bay City Times with the police and the ranger commending your skills and bravery. If I had only known what quality of character I had staying in my humble abode." Hollis snatched the paper from under his chair and displayed the well-worn article.

A smiling Paul walked over from the grill to warmly greet the Bosco Boys. "Easy now, Hollis, I'm doing the roasting here today," Paul said, brandishing his spatula.

Hollis, using a sports broadcaster's voice, quoted the paper. "'Snipe hunters from Bosco bash bandits to the bottom of Muskrat Creek.' It doesn't say why it took over a month for the story to get out, so I'm guessing you had a hand in writing it."

The Snipe Hunters' Deadly Catch at Muskrat Creek

Mark rose in their defense. "Ha! You would."

"Well, I'm sure it gave you time to meet with your English teacher and dress up your story. After all, there aren't that many people out hunting snipe these days, especially after all the excitement you boys had. You probably gave snipe hunting a bad name around these woods," Hollis winked at Kenny.

Kenny, now enjoying the verbal parry and thrust of Main Post conversations, shot back, "Bad names, eh? Before you sent me on a snipe hunt, I believed doctors could be trusted!"

Dr. Hollis chuckled in response.

Joe replied, "Actually, keeping quiet allowed the ATF to set a trap. They knew their accomplices would come looking for the tobacco once they realized their buddies were missing and not coming back. The law was waiting for them."

Undeterred, Hollis continued, "See, you guys never think about the taxpayers in all your heroics. You should have set those boys adrift back across Lake Huron. Let crooks take care of crooks. You capture them and all those wounds you inflicted get treated at public expense. I'm a doctor, I know about those costs. I say you boys worked a hardship on the taxpaying public. Me!"

"Well, write your congressman and the ATF. But can I get a burger now or do I have to wait for a governmental response there, doctor?" Joe jibed right back.

"It's coming right up, Joe, with your favorite, pickles, and onions," Paul interrupted. "Ginger ale and Coke are in the cooler behind you. You boys help yourselves."

"Kenny, that bandit you bashed up won't be throwing any footballs for years," Hollis nodded at him with his wise old owl look.

"Where he comes from, they don't play football. And I got an idea he's not going to get any team opportunities of any sort where he's going either." Kenny grabbed a burger and tipped it at Hollis.

The Silver Beaver

Paul filled up their bowls with his famous baked beans and they all sat around the patio table. At the end of the yard they could see fishermen and tourists floating by mostly in canoes, but also on inflatable rafts and fishing tubes.

"Speaking of going, where are you going for your summer break, Kenny? Isn't your mother staying with an aunt in Bay City?" Hollis asked.

"Yup. I got travel arrangements approved and permission to leave from Brother Ed last week," Kenny said.

Dr. Hollis stretched, and leaned back with his hands behind his head, and inquired, "Say, Kenny, that drunken stepdad of yours, Henry, is it? I hope they get the Bay City Times wherever he's hiding out. I'd love to see his face reading about your heroics as a snipe hunter."

Kenny smirked, "Dunno if the paper gets to Dearborn, doctor. That's pretty far to the south. But, yeah, when sober, he can read."

"Father George released me and the Jeep Cherokee for a week to take him to Bay City," Mark added.

"This sounds suspicious," Hollis teased. "It does not take a week to get to Bay City."

"I'm visiting my neighbor back in Catalpa Falls and seeing my therapist over at Havenwood State Hospital also," Kenny said. "My mother doesn't have a car. My aunt and uncle can't take time off. So, Father George is doing us a big favor. He gave Mark the use of the jeep for ten days actually." He dove into Paul's baked beans.

"Ah, the hero returns to his hometown, and without a brass band or a key to the city?" Hollis teased.

Mark interjected, "Well, actually we're going to a dinner in Kenny's honor at his dad's VFW post."

Saltz looked up from his bowl of beans. "I thought you were on the outs with your dad. You hated him or something like that?"

The Snipe Hunters' Deadly Catch at Muskrat Creek

Paul and Hollis looked up in unison. They both riveted their eyes on Kenny at the end of the table.

Kenny replied coolly with a pained expression, "That's my stepdad you are thinking of, Saltz. He's a trucker in Dearborn. I don't have anything to do with him and neither does my mother anymore. My real dad is deceased. He was a veteran and active with the Huron County VFW in Catalpa Falls."

"Oh, I'm sorry," Saltz said. "I guess I got that mixed up."

"Yeah, the sheriff's association and the VFW are hosting Kenny for their Independence Day party. I get to go as his escort and driver," Mark announced with pride. "Besides, they consider me a snipe hunting hero, too, just because I was there at Muskrat Creek."

"Aren't you applying to college, Mark?" Hollis taunted. "That ought to look good on your resume, 'accomplished snipe hunter.'"

"Well, you gotta admit that no one's got snipe quite like Muskrat Creek," Mark retorted.

Kenny and Joe laughed aloud. They both jeered Hollis and gave a thumbs up to Mark.

"Well, alright boys. You got me there. I can't argue with that." Hollis tipped his glass at Mark. "Touché."

After lunch, Paul asked Joe, Kenny, and Mark to carry some chairs from his cabin to Hollis'. He abruptly stopped halfway down Partridge Path. He waved his hand, called them forward and pointed toward a Mountain Ash tree flanked by some cedars. "Look at that. There's another lesson from Mom Nature, guys."

"I don't see anything but a bunch of birds. They are pretty but I don't see ..." Kenny said.

"What kind of bird are we looking at, Mark?"

"I see mostly cedar waxwings, Paul."

"That's correct. They are known for a special type of behavior."

"What behavior is that, Paul?" Kenny asked.

The Silver Beaver

"Look up at the top. Ignore the ones flying about or on the ground. See that branch with about six birds on it?"

They all found it with the help of first Paul and then Mark.

"Yes. We can see them now."

"Study the one on the end. Watch what he does."

"That bird ate one of the berries from the bunch," Kenny replied. "I can see that."

"Watch what else the one on the end does with the others."

"Well, okay," Mark said. "He reaches out on the end of the skinny branch to get the berries and then … is he passing them back?"

"Well, golly, that's right," Joe agreed. "That's what I see. He seems to pass the berry along to the bird behind him and then each one passes it along like a team. So, they all get something to eat. Teamwork!"

"Correct," Paul said. "There's care and concern for the other in the animal kingdom. Isn't that amazing?" He turned to Kenny. "Kenny, you have been doing your studies, right? Name the saint that is famous for observing spirituality in nature and animals?"

"Jeez, I don't know."

"Well, now, I'll give you a hint. There's a certain statue in Bosco's garden."

"I still don't know." Kenny was glancing around hoping for a tip from Mark or Joe.

"Hey, I know you are Bosco Academy's new guy so I'll give you one last hint," Paul said. "He was the very first person to set up a Nativity scene and it was in Italy."

"Jeez, I'm not sure. I didn't go to church after my father died so … I mean, Joe talks about St. Dominic and the rosary? Is that right?" Kenny guessed.

Paul turned to Mark and teased, "Okay, Mark, the reputation of Bosco Academy is on the line."

"Yes, sir, I'll take Italian History for forty dollars. That would be St. Francis of Assisi, Mr. Paul."

"So," Kenny joshed. "Cedar waxwing birds study the Bible and know about the Beatitudes, eh, Paul?"

"Ha! Well, some of us humans can learn a lot from Mom Nature, boys. Now, let's get these chairs to the cabin."

They entered Hollis' cabin to a ringing phone.

Paul took the call as the boys arranged the chairs. Paul mostly listened after identifying himself.

"OK, we'll be there."

Paul hung up the phone. "Kenny, sprint back and get Hollis over here. The sheriff has taken the Silver Beaver into custody. It's in Grayling."

The Silver Beaver was on top of a jeep in the parking lot of the county sheriff's office. Paul parked right next to it. Hollis was the only one who entered the building. The rest of the group surrounded the canoe.

"It's in good shape," Joe said. "I don't see any dents or scrapes. The bottom looks the same as we left it. It's worn but river-worthy, that's for sure."

Hollis produced the paperwork and his identification and got the story from the deputy on duty. "Based on your report, we don't think we can charge them with being in possession of stolen property. You lost it in the storm. A fisherman and his three sons report they pulled it out of a deep hole. They got snagged up on it while retrieving a steelhead lure. They claim they didn't know about the license number on it. I tend to believe them."

"So, you are the one who found it, officer?" Hollis asked.

"I just happened to park at the restaurant right next to it. The owner of the restaurant is on Bosco's Board of Directors. He recognized the model of canoe from your Au Sable Adventure program."

The Silver Beaver

"That must be Brian Sovelle then?" Hollis asked.

"Yes, sir, and he asked me to run the license number," The deputy said. "I'm sure glad you were home when I called."

"What about the family, the man with the canoe?" Hollis asked.

"They gave me no resistance at all. He's been very respectful, doctor. I explained that it was registered in your name. The man was real apologetic. He said he never thought about the sticker. He was just glad that his kids got a chance to fish and canoe with their new find. He said it's the first craft they've ever had as a family." The deputy paused. "I believe them. The kids tell me they have only fished from shore until now."

"Where are they from? Hollis asked.

"He lives in a small town a little north of Grand Rapids. He works at Sparta Foundry. They come here to fish and hike in the forest. They are camping at Hartwick Pines Campground. We checked them out with the rangers; they are regulars, camping there for years."

The deputy walked out to the parking lot with Hollis following behind. "Have you inspected it, guys?" the deputy asked.

"It is fine," Paul said.

"It looks great, doctor. I can't even tell it was in the storm," Joe said. "Where did they find it, officer?"

"I don't know." The deputy turned to Hollis. "They are still at the restaurant, doctor. He wanted to apologize to you in person, but I suggested he stay put until I met with you. Legally, there is no need for you to meet. You are free to take the canoe and go home, sir."

"That's just great," Kenny said.

Joe stepped toward the bow of the canoe, beginning to feel relief that the canoe debacle was coming to a close, but nervous that their part in it may be revealed. Mark stepped closer to the jeep and loosened the bungee cords on the rack.

"I'd like to meet the man, deputy, if he is still in the restaurant," Hollis said.

Joe and Kenny look at each other.

"Well, I have to be present, sir," the deputy replied. "I'm sure he is there. He seems like a man of his word. You want to load up the canoe and follow me over there?"

Hollis looked at this watch. "Yes, I want to go to the restaurant. We'll worry about loading up the canoe later. I don't want to hold up the man and his family any longer than I have to. Let's just go."

They all followed the deputy's jeep to the restaurant in downtown Grayling and parked in the adjacent lot.

Hollis and Paul walked over to Mark as he exited his vehicle. "Mark, Paul and I will handle this. I don't want to overwhelm him. You guys stay put."

Joe and Kenny watched Hollis and Paul walk into the diner, with a sinking feeling that their carefully kept secret would finally be revealed here at the very end of the school year.

The family of four was seated in the front of the diner in an alcove very popular during busy times. Since it was two hours before the dinner crowd would arrive, they had the section to themselves. The man stood up and stepped forward when the deputy turned toward him. Hollis and Paul stood behind the deputy.

"Mr. Van Horn, these are the owners, Hollis and Paul. They wanted to meet you."

Mr. Van Horn, a tall man wearing blue jean coveralls with suspenders, stepped away from the table and extended his weather-worn hand. He looked Hollis in the eye. "Sir, I thank you for coming. I'm sorry I had your canoe. I just want ... I want you to know I really did not mean to—"

Paul and then Hollis quickly shook his hand. Hollis immediately waved his hand in front of him to interrupt Mr. Van Horn. "There is no need to apologize, Mr. Van Horn. The

The Silver Beaver

deputy explained how you found it and didn't know the significance of the sticker with the number. I understand that. It's okay."

"Really, sir? You understand? I told my boys that I didn't rightly know about that registered thing. And my boys, they been raised up to follow rules, sir. What we got ain't much, but we came by it in the right way, sir. I aim to teach my boys right. Your canoe is your canoe."

Mr. Van Horn's three sons turned their chairs toward the men. The deputy stood off to one side and between the two parties.

"Mr. Van Horn, why don't you introduce me to your boys, I understand they are fishermen like me," Hollis said. He stepped toward the table.

"Boys, I want ..." began Mr. Van Horn. But his sons stood up, sprang forward, and each politely extended a hand in friendship.

Hollis jumped in, "Well did you boys catch some fish and have some fun canoeing in our Silver Beaver?"

Justin, Clement, and Calvin excitedly described their exploits on the Au Sable to Hollis and Paul.

"So, Calvin here, the youngest, caught the steelhead, but you netted it, Justin?" Paul asked after listening to the excited and confusing chatter about their exploits.

Mr. Van Horn answered, "Well, Mr. Paul, the canoe is seventeen feet long so we can all fit in, but trying to land a steelhead without breaking a line is very hard. We had to paddle toward shore to tire him out. Calvin was standing in knee-high water when we came up behind it and got our net under him."

Chuckling, both Hollis and Paul were thrilled to hear the adventures of the Van Horn family. Hollis changed his tone and turned to Mr. Van Horn. "Was that pie you had any good?"

"Why, yes sir, it was."

Hollis turned to Paul. "Paul, will you please excuse me for a moment? You carry on with the boys."

Paul simply nodded in his direction.

"Well, Mr. Van Horn, I'm going to see if I can get some of that raspberry pie to go. Will you come to the counter and help me pick it out, Mr. Van Horn? I wanna get the right one."

"Sure. You can't go wrong with pie in this place, doctor."

Hollis turned and motioned for the deputy to accompany him to the counter. Once there, Hollis beckoned the waitress forward. "Could you wrap up those three pies for me and leave us by ourselves for a moment, young lady?" He handed her a fifty-dollar bill. "Please keep the change."

Mr. Van Horn had a look of puzzlement on his face. The deputy leaned forward and scrutinized Hollis's face.

"Mr. Van Horn, I appreciate how you have kept my canoe safe and sound all these months and put it to such good use with your boys. I want you to finish your vacation with the canoe. In fact, I want you to keep the canoe for future use with your boys."

Mr. Van Horn's face registered bewilderment. "You wanted pie … and now you want to …"

Hollis looked at the deputy. He tugged at his elbow and drew him to the counter.

"Deputy, here is my registration and the original invoice on the canoe. I'm signing it over to Mr. Van Horn effective today for the price of one dollar. This will serve as a bill of sale. Could you duplicate it at your office and see that I get a copy of it?" Hollis signed the form.

The deputy studied Hollis's face. Stunned and disoriented, he groped for words. "Well … yes, we have a copy machine. I'd be glad to help. We do have your address. But do you really … Have you thought this through?"

"Thank you, officer. Mr. Van Horn, could you sign here please?"

Mr. Van Horn stepped to the counter, examined the invoice

The Silver Beaver

and registration papers, signed, and looked at Hollis wide-eyed, searching for understanding. "Sir, there's no way I could afford this. That paper says I'm going to be the owner now? I just don't know how … but I really want to … thanks so much, sir. My boys will have so much fun."

"Well, you must promise me to get it registered in your name. You must promise me that you'll give the canoe to one of your sons when you are done with it. Can you do that for me, Mr. Van Horn?"

"Yeah, yes, sure, sure I'll do right by your words and that paper, sir. I promise," Mr. Van Horn said.

Hollis pressed a hundred-dollar bill into Mr. Van Horn's hand. "Bring your boys back for dinner tomorrow, my treat. You celebrate your purchase of the canoe and welcome the Silver Beaver into your family in fine style."

Hollis waved the waitress over. He scooped the pies off the countertop from her. He shook hands with the stunned Mr. Van Horn and the wide-eyed deputy.

"Well, gentlemen, I've got some hungry kids out in that parking lot. You know they can't sit for too much longer. Thanks, officer. Mr. Van Horn, you and your boys keep those paddles wet for me, eh?"

Paul caught up with Hollis as he exited the restaurant and walked up to the two vehicles. Hollis slapped Mark on the shoulder. "Okay, Mark, follow me back to the Main Post for some homemade pie. We have some celebrating to do."

When Hollis drove past the sheriff's office parking lot and back toward the cabin, Kenny and and Joe were anxious and puzzled but guessed that they'd be coming back the next day for the canoe. Neither could have guessed what Hollis would announce around the dinner table later.

"I want you all to help me celebrate," said Doc Hollis. "The Silver Beaver has found a good home where young men and families get to enjoy fishing and canoeing on the Au Sable, which is what Paul and I want to see. So have a slice of raspberry pie. Let's all plan for some more great times on the river this summer while knowing we made it possible for others to join in our type of fun also."

Joe leaned in close to Kenny, both starting to feel relief and amazement as Doc Hollis' generosity began to sink in. "I guess we ain't going back for that canoe, Kenny."

Kenny grabbed some pie and sat, ruminating. "Hmm, Joe, this is what I'm thinking. Our buddies the Tobacco Bandits are nursing their wounds and bound for the federal prison in Milan. They don't want to add canoe stealing to their legal troubles. And the Silver Beaver can't talk. So that leaves me and you who know the real story. And I ain't telling."

Joe winked at his friend in relief. "Have some more pie, Kenny."

EPILOGUE

Monday, June 23, 1980, 8:53 am, John Bosco Hall

Kenny followed Mark out to the dorm's parking lot. He plopped his luggage in the rear and jumped in the passenger's seat.

Mark was studying the map. "We are early. If we leave now, we'll be in Bay City before noon."

"We leave now. I have one visit before we head south. Take me to the Main Post one last time, Marko."

Mark started the engine. "Are you sure about this?"

"I'm only a hundred percent sure, Marko."

"Well, okay, Kenny Boy. We got time. There is no question about that."

><

Doctor Hollis' cabin was empty. They found Hollis and Paul in Paul's shed, varnishing a knotty pine Adirondack chair.

"I got a gift for you guys." Kenny handed them a poster-sized square package in brown wrapping paper.

Hollis rose from his seat and graciously accepted the gift. "I see you favor Currier and Ives décor when you wrap gifts, Kenny boy."

Paul stepped next to Hollis and cuffed him on the shoulder. "You can't afford to talk like that to people who give you gifts, doctor."

"It's a painting for the Main Post," said Kenny when the

The Snipe Hunters' Deadly Catch at Muskrat Creek

brown paper fell away.

They began to study Kenny's work, a collage of key scenes from the adventures earlier in the year on the Au Sable.

"So, I see two guys canoeing toward two men on shore," Hollis said, "Huh, I bet I know the name of that little creek coming in behind them."

"The hatchet on the bank has a nice effect for sure," Paul observed.

"I know why the canoe is silver and I see the image of the beaver on the bow. You have a colorful bird out in front of it. What kind is it?" Hollis asked.

"That would be a cedar waxwing, doctor," Kenny replied. "They show us that 'there is actually care and concern for the other in the animal kingdom.'"

Paul winked at Kenny.

Hollis shook Kenny's hand. "For years to come, this will make it easy to tell your story at the Main Post, Kenny Boy. Thanks."

"My story is not done, doctor, but can you put the painting up by the poem?"

"I surely will. Now, aren't you off on vacation today? You've got a mom and aunt waiting for the hero of Muskrat Creek as I recall."

Mark stepped forward for a farewell handshake. "Yes, you're right. We're off and onto the highway. It's my job to be the chauffeur today, guys. Let's go, Kenny."

><

As Mark drove to town to gas up, Kenny started to chat. "Say Mark, I do wanna thank you for volunteering to be my chaperone again. Especially since Huddleston and the state say Bosco can't let this snipe hunter loose without a chaperone." Laughing, Kenny continued, "You can be sure they don't wanna see me and Joe head out the door together again. So, thanks."

Epilogue

Mark nodded, "Yeah, well, it's been an adventure."

After leaving the gas station, Mark drove 20 minutes through the backcountry roads until he reached the entrance to southbound I-75 in Grayling.

"Here we are, Kenny. Ninety-six miles to go."

"Yup."

After a few minutes of driving Kenny said, "Say Mark, have you ever seen the musical 'The Song of Bernadette?'"

"Whoa now, Kenny, where did you hear about this?"

Kenny thrust his hands up in frustration. "Heck, Joe's all private about praying his beads, so I went to Brother Ed to learn about the rosary. Brother Ed said just wait till you see this movie. It is going to be shown soon to the whole school, probably when we get back. It is by some priest with a foreign name."

Mark laughed. "Foreign he was. But Franz Werfel was a long way from being a priest. He was not even a Christian."

"So, how did he write about the Virgin Mary appearing in France?" Kenny inquired. "And how come you know about this anyway?"

Mark exhaled deeply, "My mom visited the Shrine of Our Lady of Lourdes." Mark paused and shifted in his seat. "You see, Kenny, I've never told any of the guys this, but my mom died of cancer."

"Jeez, Mark, I'm sorry. I did not know. I just wanna understand about—"

"That's okay, Kenny. Fr. George and Brother Ed know and now you. Let's keep it that way."

"Sure, Mark, I know how to be quiet, remember? Did you say your mom went all the way to France?"

"Yup. Thousands go every year for physical and spiritual healing. It's the second most visited city in France."

"I see. Mark, back to this Franz guy who was not even Christian, did he get cured or something?"

The Snipe Hunters' Deadly Catch at Muskrat Creek

"Kenny, remember when you were hungry and being chased on the Au Sable by that nasty Canadian storm? In 1940 Franz Werfel was a hungry and tired Czechoslovakian Jew on the run from the Nazis. Of the thousands on the road, he got directed to Lourdes where the clergy and people took care of him. Before he escaped through the Pyrenees Mountains to Spain, he learned about Bernadette Soubirous seeing the Virgin Mary and the miracles."

"Then Franz did not see Our Lady at Lourdes?"

"No, no, Kenny. Bernadette's apparitions and the miraculous spring of water was in 1858. The brave generosity he found in Lourdes inspired him. He vowed to tell the story if he survived. Keep in mind that if the Nazis caught him, they would have executed him and the folks helping him."

"Huh, I see. What happened to him, Mark?"

"Eventually, he ended up in America."

Kenny grunted and looked pensive. "I see. So after he got free and was safe in America, he kept his promise to those folks back in France."

Mark concluded, "Yup, that's true. His book was a best seller and they made that movie you're going to see. But it's not really a musical. I hope that does not disappoint you."

When there was no reply, Mark continued. "Brother Ed said Franz Werfel was a voice for victims of man's inhumanity to man. You see, he also wrote 'The Forty Days of Musa Dagh.' It's about how the Christian Armenians fought back against the Ottoman Turks during the century's first genocide during WWI. Then he survived the second genocide of the century conducted by the Nazis during WWII."

While continuing to stare out onto the woods, Kenny replied in a vacant voice, "I see. Werfel was a brave man who kept his word."

Kenny was thoughtful for a few more miles as Mark continued driving down the highway. "By the way, Mark, how

Epilogue

did Father George approve you for this trip anyway, after your handling of my note when I went AWOL during the storm? Because Brother Ed, the dorm director, is your boss, right? What did he say? What did he think of you for hiding the note?"

"Dunno actually," Mark said, with a sidelong glance.

"What?" Kenny asked in surprise.

"You remember that meeting when they put you and Joe on probation? After it was over, I went to apologize to Father George and Brother Ed as they were walking down the hall. I mentioned the note. Father George turned and said, 'What note?' I looked at Brother Ed. He just winked. Then they walked on to the office."

Mark shook his head. "Man, I've thought about this a lot. All the trust Bosco placed in me. Then I don't even disclose the note. And facing my dad and brothers with shameful stuff like that … And, jeez, if I lost my R.A. job, my dad would … But gosh, if Brother Ed wants to bury it, I say, 'Rest in Peace.'"

"Seems like he forgave you without you even asking for forgiveness, like in confession," Kenny reasoned aloud.

"That he did. On Sunday I learned even more about forgiving. I overslept but made it to Mass in time for Father George's homily. Kinda glad I did, Kenny. The whole talk was on forgiveness. What he said was puzzling. He said it helps the forgiver more than the forgiven."

Kenny leaned forward. "You mean like in the Lord's Prayer? Forgive us our trespasses as we forgive—"

"He told gut-wrenching stories from the Capuchin Monks' Ministry in downtown Detroit, Kenny. One guy became Catholic in prison. Embraced the truth of Jesus' Gospel. Dig his message, Kenny: 'Hating someone is like drinking poison every day and expecting it to harm your enemy.'"

"I guess I can see that," Kenny replied.

"Twenty-six miles to go, Kenny. Get ready for Bay City."

"Uh-huh."

The Snipe Hunters' Deadly Catch at Muskrat Creek

Kenny, staring out onto the landscape, was silent for the next twenty minutes. His mind had once again mounted upon some dandelion fluff and drifted far off the scene. He considered a porch, a pool of blood, and a promise of revenge to a trucker in Dearborn. He weighed these dark thoughts against recent lessons of forgiveness and helping others.

After driving another long stretch of the highway, Mark decided to break the awkward silence. "Hey, 'snipe hunter extraordinaire', are you ready for Bay City?" Mark reached over and gently cuffed him on the shoulder.

Startled from the land of reverie, Kenny replied without looking at his friend. "Nope. Mark, take me to Dearborn."

Epilogue